NOT What I EXPECTED
Special Edition

Jewel E. Ann

NOT WHAT I EXPECTED
SPECIAL EDITION

JEWEL E. ANN

Copyright © 2020 by Jewel E. Ann

Special Edition Paperback

ISBN 978-1-955520-42-3

All rights reserved.

This book is a work of fiction and is created without use of AI technology. Any resemblances to actual persons, living or dead, events, or locales are purely coincidental.

Without in any way limiting the author's exclusive rights under copyright, any use of this publication to "train" generative artificial intelligence (AI) technologies to generate text is expressly prohibited. The author reserves all rights to license uses of this work for generative AI training and development of machine learning language models.

Cover Designer: Jenn Beach

Formatting: Jenn Beach

NOT What I EXPECTED

AUTHOR'S note

This story began with a request to my readers: Tell me what drives you crazy about your significant other.

Your responses turned this into a women's fiction novel. It has all the elements of a love story, but it morphed into a life story about women, relationships, children, and friendship. It could have just as easily been written from a male's point of view. But it wasn't. Not this time. So ... here we go, ladies.

DEDICATION

To my readers and every woman who has ever asked herself—Can the next chapter be about me?

"What the caterpillar calls the end of the world, the master calls a butterfly." - Richard Bach

CHAPTER one

I miss him, but I don't miss the pick, roll, and flick.

Everything in moderation.

Those were my husband's words, not mine.

"Don't give me that look, Elle. It's low-fat turkey bacon."

My absentminded gaze remained affixed to his plate—toaster waffles smothered in butter, drowned in syrup, topped with three blueberries (so he could say he had fruit), and four pieces of bacon on the side.

Orange juice from concentrate.

Coffee with creamer and sugar.

The stench of bacon hung in the air since he refused to turn on the exhaust fan over the stove when he cooked it. The noise made it hard for him to hear the news on the TV in the corner of the kitchen.

"Elsie," I murmured, blinking at his plate as I lifted my quart Mason jar filled with warm lemon water to my lips.

"What?" he mumbled over a mouthful of fat, salt, and sugar.

"My name is Elsie, not Elle."

"I've called you Elle for twenty-some years." He concentrated on his phone next to his plate.

Every inch of me melted into a paralyzed state. I'd succumbed to the depths of my fate, unable to peel my back from the stainless steel fridge door. After twenty-two years, three months, and six days of marriage ... I couldn't do it anymore. So there I stood—an idle statue deciding whether or not I had enough life to stand up. *Really* stand up. "I know, Craig. And I've gone from tolerating it to hating it."

He lifted his head along with one curious eyebrow while licking his grease covered chops and burping.

Did he burp like that when we first met?

Did I say "I do" to that drawn out belch?

If he was that way when we met, I must have been wearing the rosiest colored glasses.

He pounded his fist against his chest to ... I had no clue. Work out a few more disgusting sounds like aftershocks of an earthquake? Then he picked his nose right in front of me.

Pick.

Roll.

Flick.

"You *hate* when I call you Elle?" He dismissed me with a *pfft* and an eye roll. "Whatcha got on under that robe? The kids won't be up for another hour or so. Feeling like some Saturday shaboink?"

I hadn't always been repulsed by him. The seventeen-year-old version of me chased him. Craig Smith—

starting point guard for our Midwestern small-town high school—endured *all* the girls chasing him. He chose me, little Elsie Stapleton, to be his prom date two years in a row.

Craig said it was my thick, light brown hair and ornery green eyes that caught his attention. I always knew it was my perky breasts on a tiny five-three cheerleader's body.

Narrowing my eyes, I drank the rest of my lemon water and set the jar on the counter—slowly, with a deep breath, and tension so tight I felt my last straw a blink away from snapping. "No shaboink. No bump and grind. No log ride."

"Did you start your period?"

"NO!" I jumped at my own outburst, hands balled at my sides.

Craig jerked his head back.

Meadow, our five-year-old golden retriever, scurried into the kitchen, paws dancing in place like she did only when she was nervous.

Winter howled in strong gusts, revealing all the tiny cracks and spaces in the house and in our marriage. I gazed out the window at yet another round of snow whirling in the wind. Our rural town of Epperly had already been pummeled with over three feet of snow in less than two weeks.

Emotional meltdowns never came at the right moment. And just days before Christmas seemed like the worst time to let my mind spiral out of control, exploding with all the things I could no longer endure.

Not one ... more ... day.

"I deserve more," I said with wavering control to my words, a dam ready to burst.

"Here we go again. You deserve more. I work my ass off to provide for this family. I've worked my ass off for years so you could stay home with the kids. So you can have coffee every Friday morning with the other women in the neighborhood, who also don't have to lift a goddamn finger beyond raising kids. Three of our kids are in college. Bella is a junior. What do you do all damn day? Walk with Amie? Sew shit?"

"I do the books for your business! I grocery shop for *your* parents. I make them meals. I mow their lawn and shovel their snow. I pay our bills—"

"I pay our bills!" He glared at me. "You don't have a job. You don't pay for anything."

That!

That betrayal—that complete lack of acknowledging my worth—drove a knife deeper into my heart than any affair ever could have done. An affair said, "My gaze wandered." But *that* said, "I don't see you at all."

"I just don't get paid for my work!" I panted, my hands on my hips as my heart thundered with rage, agony, and grief.

"Oh, so all these years, spending time with our kids, helping out family ... that's been a *job*? Wow ... that will make the kids feel really wanted."

I shook my head. "That's not fair. And that's not what I meant."

He shoved his chair backward and stood. "Yes. That's what you meant, and it's such a double standard. Isn't it? For years, when you needed to do stuff after I got home from a long day, and I acted the least bit tired when you asked me to watch the kids, you got so pissed off. And always delivered that stupid lecture every time I used the word babysitting. Parents don't babysit … it's called *parenting*. That's what you said. So don't give me this crap about raising our kids being your job."

"*Job* was your fucking word, not mine."

His eyebrows shot up his forehead. Swear words never fell from my lips. Not around him. Not around the kids. It was the first time he heard me drop the f-bomb.

"I said *work,* not job." I ignored his shock at my language. "A lot of things in life are work. Planning a vacation. Decorating the house for the holidays. Cooking meals. Exercising. Pretending that my husband referring to sex as 'Saturday shaboink' doesn't utterly repulse me. It's *all* so much *work*, Craig."

"Elle—"

"MY FUCKING NAME IS ELSIE!"

His jaw unhinged like a stiff door. "Do … you need a minute?"

My heart thudded against my chest, a racehorse coming into the final turn. It *hurt* so much I thought it would just stop beating—*because* I loved him.

Because I had loved him for as long as I could remember.

Because we'd made a life together—a beautiful life.

But that life went to college. That life moved on to start new lives. And I didn't like my new life.

"I don't need a minute. I need out." Holding on was painful. Letting go—it ripped me to shreds. It felt selfish but necessary for my own self-preservation.

His unkempt eyebrows knitted together. "A few hours away?" He rolled his eyes to the ceiling and blew out a slow breath. "Whatever, *El-seee*. I wish I could take the day off every time I woke up on the wrong side of the bed."

I glanced around the house we'd have to sell, but before I let all the memories it held thwart my moment, I returned my gaze to him. "I want out of this marriage." Tears instantly burned my eyes. I wanted out, but saying the actual words cut deeper than I imagined—like something died. Like *we* died. The shock on Craig's face hurt more than I imagined too.

"Be..." he shook his head as if it would unscramble the words I said, and they would not mean I wanted a divorce "...because we had a little fight? Because I call you Elle? Because I joked about sex?"

The tears escaped down my face, but I made no effort to wipe them. "Because I'm miserable." Why did finally valuing myself feel so ... incredibly ... selfish?

He coughed a sarcastic laugh. "Miserable? Our house is paid for. We have four amazing kids. I've invested so much money we could retire tomorrow. You have a brand-new car. I don't cheat on you. We don't fight about money. Every year we take a vacation. You have the life most women would kill to have. What in the hell could possibly be making you miserable?"

He was right on all accounts.

"Money doesn't buy happiness."

"So it's me?"

I nodded.

"Well, what do you want me to do?"

"Nothing."

"Jesus! You want to end our marriage because of *me*,

so there must be something I can do. I don't get one chance to make things right?"

"It's not ..." My head eased side to side. "It's not that simple."

Because I've fallen out of love with you. You will always own a piece of my heart, but you are not the reason it beats.

"You're not perfect either."

My focus shifted to my feet, the purple polish chipping off my toenails. "Believe me ... I know."

When we were younger, before we got married, we'd break up and get back together. This happened several times before I got pregnant with the twins. Breaking up was okay then. Not feeling the same way about someone was okay. A simple "I can't explain it. I just don't feel the same," was enough. There were usually hard feelings for a while, but it wasn't the end of the world. Giving up after four kids and twenty-two years of marriage felt like the end of the world.

Why was I okay with letting the world end?

"What? Just tell me what I did to make you feel this way."

"It's not ..." I blew out a slow breath and forced my tear-blurred gaze to meet his again. "It's not one thing, Craig. Like it wasn't one thing that made me fall in love with you. It's a whole bunch of little things."

"Like what? Elle and Shaboink?"

"Yes." I glanced out the window, grieving with more tears. It all made sense in my head. Everything put together made sense. It was enough. I just didn't want to tell him everything because I knew it would be heartless and self-centered. It would sound petty. And saying it was unnecessary because it wouldn't have changed anything.

"And?" he prodded.

"Let's not do this."

"No." His tone held a sharp edge. "If it's over, then we're sure as hell going to do this."

I shook my head and batted away the tears. "No," I whispered.

"Fine." He stepped closer to me. "I'll go first."

"Craig ..." I continued to shake my head. I didn't want to do it.

"You're a fucking nag all the damn time. Always nagging me about leaving the cap off the toothpaste. I don't make the bed right or load the dishwasher right. You've been riding my ass about fixing the shower drain, but the reason it doesn't drain right is because of all your hair clogging it. When I don't use perfect English, you just can't help yourself. You *always* have to correct me like anyone else gives a shit if I say 'ain't' or 'gonna.' And why the hell should I make some grand effort to woo you when half the time you shoot me down? Are a dozen roses really going to get you to spread your legs for me? Shouldn't you do it because you're my wife and I work my ass off to be a good provider?"

"No! I don't *spread* my legs for roses or a paycheck. I'm not a whore, Craig." I fisted my hands and gritted my anger through clenched teeth. "If you want me to spread my legs, maybe you shouldn't pick your nose, roll it up, and flick boogers all over the house! Maybe you shouldn't overeat like a garbage disposal and burp in my face two seconds before kissing me! Maybe you shouldn't wink at every woman you see and play it off as you being friendly and me being a snob!"

"You *are* a snob!" He pointed a stiff finger at me. "A

food snob. A book snob. A cleaning product snob. If someone smokes, you look down on them. If someone drinks more than two drinks, you look down on them. Gordon uses chemicals on his lawn, but you just *know* his kids and dog are going to die from cancer, yet they haven't. We're the last to arrive at parties and the first to leave. Snob ... snob ... such a nose in the air *snob*."

I opened my mouth to spew a second round of insults. Then I closed it, cupping my hand over my mouth, and pinching my eyes shut as I silently sobbed.

Twenty-two years.

Four kids.

Memories I would cherish forever.

Why did it have to end like that? Slinging insults.

Because it's real ... and truly heartbreaking.

"W-what's going on?"

I choked on my emotions, swallowing them back down my throat as my eyes flew open, landing on our daughter, Bella.

Craig grabbed his truck keys from the counter and brushed past our daughter in her long, red nightshirt, black hair like his—but long and ratted like mine in the morning—eyes like a raccoon's from not removing her makeup before bed. "Ask your mom. She's the one who's trying to break up our family."

Two seconds later, the door slammed behind him, and a confused Bella redirected her attention to me—eyes unblinking with confusion as Meadow sat at her feet. "Mom?"

CHAPTER two

I love him, but I don't love the fifty pairs of stinky socks in his trunk.

FINN MADE his way downstairs shortly after Craig stormed out. He was home for the holidays, and the twins were arriving the following day. I sat Bella and Finn down for some real talk, knowing I owed them an explanation, but also knowing that I would have to repeat everything with the twins—but with Craig's point of view too. No other option existed. I had to trust my two youngest with feelings I couldn't fully explain because some of them weren't well-defined by words.

Bella cried. Finn showed no emotion.

"Now what?" Bella asked, wiping her eyes.

"Well, I don't know for sure. We might have to sell the house, but we won't do it until you've moved to college."

"So ... you'll what? Live together—divorced—until Bella graduates?" Finn asked, eyes squinted.

"No. One of us will move out. Maybe rent something

close until she graduates." I shook my head slowly. "Or maybe we'll both stay in the house. I ... I don't know yet."

Because the straw broke, and I didn't have time to plan cleanup of the collateral damage.

"Well, it should probably be you who moves out since Dad paid for the house."

I blinked at Finn several times. "Wow. I thought I taught you better than that."

"Jeez, Finn. Don't be such a sexist pig. Mom works. She just doesn't get paid. But she contributes, and that means she should get half of everything."

Finn's head jerked back. "Whoa ... half? For staying home?"

"*Dude* ... you are such an idiot!" Bella barked at him.

"Bella ... Finn ..." I rubbed my temples. "Don't. Please. Just ... don't. We will make sure your lives are disrupted as little as possible. But you'll feel it, the tension. For that, I want to apologize. Bella, I'm incredibly sorry you had to hear us arguing earlier. Twenty-two years of marriage doesn't end without hurt feelings and anger. We'll work through this, and we'll make sure you don't feel like you have to take sides or worry about who lives where or who gets what. Okay?"

They nodded.

Everything would be okay. The hardest part was over. We'd tell the twins later. We'd work through the anger and make the divorce amicable for the kids. Craig and I would be bound for life by our four children. Eternity was a long time to hold a grudge. I refused to do it.

Later that day, the kids headed off to be with friends. I considered calling the twins, Chase and Linc (Lincoln), but I thought it would be best to let Craig in on the conversation after he cooled off.

However, he didn't come home that night. Only one other time in our marriage did he leave and not come home until the next day. It was when we had a fight over him losing his temper with Bella when he caught her vaping late at night in the front yard with friends. She'd just turned fifteen, and I wasn't happy either. We simply disagreed on the appropriateness of making a huge scene in the front yard, embarrassing her in front of her friends, and waking up the neighbors and all dogs in a mile radius.

"Stop telling me how to parent my child! I don't tell you how to discipline the kids!"

I replied with, *"Take a breath, Craig."*

He sped off in his truck, spent the night with Leroy, his buddy from college, and came back the next morning with his head hanging and a much calmer demeanor.

So I wasn't surprised when the "ending our marriage" announcement didn't bring him back home the same night.

"Are you worried?" my friend, Amie, asked as we chatted on the phone around one in the morning. We'd been best friends since fourth grade and still lived in the same town of Epperly. She was a chiropractor and my most trusted sounding board. Asking Craig for a divorce wasn't a surprise to her, just the timing—on the cusp of Christmas.

"He'll come home. He's impulsive and his ego gets bruised easily, but he loves his kids. I know he'll want to plead his case or make his feelings known to them. I just hope it doesn't involve throwing me under the bus. We really need to be civil about this. I refuse to let this turn into a taking sides situation."

"That's very mature of you. I think a lot of couples try to be mature at first, but when it's time to discuss splitting assets and sharing kids, things get messy. You remember how it was with Travis and me. And we only had a dog and some furniture to fight over."

I sighed, leaning back on my bed and picking at the frayed hem of my long-sleeved tee. "I'm going to move out and let him stay here in the house *he* paid for ..."

Amie laughed.

"And when Bella goes to college, we'll sell the house and spilt everything fifty-fifty. I won't ask for a dime from his business, even though I helped keep it going all these years. He can keep his investments. I don't want any of it."

"Well, it's an outdated food specialty store with *nothing* special, Elsie. You can do better. But he made some really smart investments when you first got married. I wouldn't let that go so easily, especially since some of that money was inheritance from your grandparents. You have half a degree. Go finish it. I agree. Let Craig keep the soft cheddar cheese, rolls of turkey sausage, and tins of caramel corn. Sorry, but it's all outdated—even for Epperly's low standards."

"Right?" I rolled onto my side, burying my nose in Craig's pillow.

What happened to pheromones? I was crazy for his scent when we met. Clean, sweaty ... it didn't matter. My nose always went straight to his neck. I stole his sweatshirts just to wear his scent.

My nose scrunched as I rolled the other way onto my pillow. What happened? I was no longer attracted to anything about him. It wasn't that I hated him ... even if I hated some of the things he did or said. The passion was gone. The attraction died too.

"Amie, he didn't see it coming. Not even a tiny glimpse or subtle vibe. The look on his face was that of complete shock. Like ... how could he not sense it?"

"Because you married him. You took the for-better-or-for-worse vows. You've been together *forever*. You have four kids. It's called insurance. You're more relaxed when you know you have insurance on something. It doesn't guarantee nothing will go wrong, but you're covered. You know? Or really more like a contract. The reason you get married is so it's not so easy to just walk away. Right?"

"No. I got married because I was raised to think you needed to get married or you'd go to Hell."

"*And* you wanted all the women who used to chase your husband to back off."

I rubbed my hand over my face. "True. Where did those days go? The days of being insanely jealous. The days of wanting to jump him the moment he walked into the house. I used to wrap my arm around him and slide my hand into his back pocket when we were in public just so other women would know he was mine. Now ..." My heart constricted.

I *wanted* to still feel that way about him. It just wasn't something I felt anymore, no matter how hard I tried. And I couldn't fake it.

"Now you secretly hope other women notice him. You secretly hope he notices them. You've been secretly hoping—"

"He'd end it first." I finished her sentence.

"Being faithful isn't a flaw."

Grunting a laugh, I stared at the ceiling fan slowly turning. Craig was always excessively warm, so I had to live in a house with the thermostat set at sixty-five degrees year-round and the bedroom ceiling fan always on.

Not that night.

I climbed out of bed and shut it off.

"I know being faithful is not a flaw, but it would have been so much easier if we would have fallen out of love together the way we fell in love together. Selfish? Yes. But it's my truth."

"Falling out of love is not a flaw either, Elsie. So don't beat yourself up over your feelings that you can't control."

Turning on the bathroom light, I put my phone on speaker and set it on the vanity while I shed my clothes and slipped on a nightshirt. "I'll beat myself up because I don't have control over my guilt either. After all, it is a feeling. And it's just how incredibly petty it sounds when I list all the things about him that drive me crazy. Like ... not a single one by itself would warrant a divorce, but all of them put together are just too much."

"You're preaching to the choir. Travis had a million little things that drove me crazy. Squeezing the toothpaste in the middle. Using my kitchen towel to clean messes on the floor then putting it back on the counter as if I wanted to use a dirty towel to dry my clean dishes. But let's be honest ... it was the trunk that pushed me over the edge."

"The socks?" I tore off a piece of floss.

"YES! Gah ... it was ridiculous. Fine, I get it. You don't want to wear your dirty work boots home and get the floor mats of your car muddy but toss your socks in the passenger's seat before you put on your flip-flops so you remember to take them inside. Right? I mean ... I was just blown away when I opened his trunk and found *literally* over fifty pairs of smelly socks in there. And the odor was horrendous. I swear to god I *tasted* it."

"Exactly! Some things are just gross. And I'm not implying women aren't gross sometimes too. I just think we're more likely to be self-conscious about things like that or at least receptive if someone brings our attention to it. I'll never forget the time we had a bad storm and the garbage got delayed almost a week, which meant we didn't empty the trash container in the bathroom, and I'd had my period. A week's worth of tampons ... Craig mentioned the 'special odor' from under the sink, and I was mortified. Since then, I've taken out the bathroom trash every single day during my period week."

The doorbell rang.

"I have to go. Someone's at the door. Probably Finn. Bella forgets over holiday breaks that she's not always the last one home, and she locks the door. I'll call you later."

"Okay. Chin up, Elsie. You've got this. I'm proud of you for finally telling him you want out of the marriage—even if your pre-holiday timing is shitty."

I frowned, slipping on my robe. "I know. It just ... happened."

"Night."

"Night." I disconnected our call and headed downstairs as Meadow waited patiently at the door for me to answer it. "Did your bro get locked out?" I leaned down to ruffle her fur as my other hand opened the door. "Oh ..." I stood straight and tightened the sash to my robe as my stomach coiled into a nauseating knot.

I didn't expect two police officers.

Finn had been arrested six months earlier during a protest that got out of hand. I wanted to give him the benefit of the doubt, but my thoughts immediately went to wondering "what he did this time" to get into trouble. He wasn't a bad kid. He just had a knack for being in the wrong place at the wrong time.

But ... it wasn't Finn.

"Elsie Smith?" The female officer questioned.

I nodded, narrowing my eyes.

They identified themselves and asked if they could come inside.

Again, I nodded slowly.

"Is this about Finn?" I asked, shutting the door behind them.

"No, ma'am. Is your husband Craig Smith?" The male officer asked.

"Yes ..." My voice cracked on that one syllable.

I knew.

I knew it before they said the words.

My heart fractured before they had a chance to do it with their news.

Blurred vision.

Ringing in my ears, making it hard to hear the words.

The room spun as bile worked its way up my throat.

"Is there anyone else home with you?"

"M-my daughter," I whispered as the tears leaked from my eyes and all the air left my lungs.

I. Just. Knew.

"Your husband was involved in a serious collision about an hour ago. As a result of the injuries he sustained, he died. We are very sorry for your loss."

CHAPTER three

I miss him, but I don't miss pictures of his turds.

Ten months later ...

"Elsie, do you have anything to share today?" Rhonda asked. She waited all of two seconds before moving on. "How about you, Beth—"

"I do," I said, my voice monotone, my gaze lifting to meet Rhonda's face. A rare first.

After Craig's accident, I spent a solid month grieving and wallowing in the fact that I was responsible for his death. Granted, I didn't kill him with my bare hands, but he wouldn't have been on that road at that time in that weather had I not announced my need to end our marriage.

Days before Christmas.

After the first month, I let myself slip into the anger phase. That lasted another month or so until I finally found home in the warm cocoon of denial. My grieving

NOT WHAT I EXPECTED

didn't take the normal psychological pattern. To appease my family and friends, I joined our church's grief group for women only. They had one for men too. Christians were fair like that. Apparently women opened up better around other women.

Not me.

I didn't open up to anyone until ... ten months later.

Months of attending the group.

Months of keeping my dead gaze to the paisley carpet.

Months of listening to other women, who had lost their spouses, talk about their regrets and pray for God to do something magical in their lives to show them the way. They thanked God for His comfort and assured Him that they understood it was all part of His plan.

"I trust His plans for my life."

"I know my husband is with Him in Heaven."

"I'm grateful for all of the other ways He blesses my life daily."

"I feel my husband's presence like a guardian angel sent from God."

"It's His will, not mine."

They felt guilty for their anger and prayed for peace and acceptance. They apologized for their anger and asked for grace and forgiveness. They spent hours and hours sharing stories about their husbands.

Their amazing husbands.

Great fathers.

Spiritual leaders.

Missionaries in their own communities.

They all lost perfect men. Or so it seemed.

"Oh, Elsie, please ... go ahead." Rhonda couldn't hide

her enthusiasm, and I didn't miss the perked ears, wide eyes, and straight spines of the other women in the group, salivating at the thought of me *finally* speaking.

After ten months, I emerged from my grief coma. Praise the Lord!

Secrets ... I had this huge secret. Some days, keeping it felt vital to my existence. Other days, well, I wanted the truth to come out, even if it meant leaving Epperly to escape the gossip.

Four living people knew.

Only four.

After the news of Craig's accident, Finn suggested I—*we*—not tell Chase and Linc about the fight, about me wanting a divorce. He didn't see what the point would be when it no longer mattered. I thought it was a terrible idea. After all, I felt guilty and needed to confess my part in his death. Then Bella spoke up, also thinking I shouldn't tell Chase and Linc or anyone else for that matter.

Maybe they didn't want the truth on top of the already horrific reality. Maybe they knew how painful and unbearable the *real* truth was, and they wanted to save their brothers and everyone else from that pain. So I agreed not to tell anyone. The truth stayed among us—me, Bella, Finn, and Amie.

The roads were bad that night. Craig hit an icy patch on a bridge, and he lost control. Praise the Lord he didn't kill anyone else.

Still, it didn't settle right with me. I killed him.

My not-so-perfect husband.

"Craig left dishes sitting around everywhere. I had to presoak everything before it could go into the dishwasher. He never understood why it bothered me. He dismissed my irritation with, 'You could have it worse. At least I'm not a drunk and I don't cheat on you.' And he was right. I could have had it worse. I just hated that I couldn't take issue with anything he did and not be labeled a complainer."

After a few blinks, I scanned the room. The faces studying me held odd expressions.

Shock?

Pity?

"I know." I chuckled shaking my head. "I don't speak for months, and the first thing that comes out of my mouth is something negative about my dead husband. I'm going to Hell, aren't I?"

Rhonda cleared her throat and slid the pendant on her necklace back and forth. A forced smile bent her matte red lips. "Maybe we could pray for you."

"That I don't go to Hell?" I quirked an eyebrow at her.

"No. Just asking our Lord to—"

"Grant used to trim his beard and leave the whiskers in the sink. If I dropped my contact lens, I'd have to throw it away."

Everyone shifted their attention to Jennifer. Her husband, Grant, died of a heart attack five months earlier.

"And..." she continued "...he'd trim other parts of his body and sweep the hair under the bathroom scale. The first time I found it, I swear I thought someone had shaved their entire head in my house. I blamed the kids."

"Jennifer, dear ... I'm not sure this is productive—" Rhonda made an attempt to intervene, but Kathy cut her off.

"Rick used to dribble urine down the front of the

toilet, but he always said it wasn't him. I knew it was because he also had pee spots on the front of his pants. Like ... would it have killed him to stand there a few extra seconds to give it a little shake?"

A few women snickered, but not Rhonda. I stayed silent, not anticipating my ill manners instigating such confessions.

"Eddie used to order fries from McDonalds, tear off the corner of the ketchup packet, and alternate between squeezing the ketchup into his mouth and shoving fries into it like he mastered the perfect ratio of fries to ketchup. When I asked him why he couldn't just dip them like a normal person, he said he wasn't that boring."

A few more people laughed.

"Jared used to sing along to every song on the radio, and he didn't know any of the words. He'd just mumble random stuff and ruin the song for me."

"When I was at work, Eric texted me a photo of his turd in the toilet. He couldn't believe it came out of his ... uh ... backside. And he compared it to me giving birth. As if ..." Kelly rolled her eyes.

That made everyone laugh, even sour-faced Rhonda cracked a smile before ending the meeting. "Time's up. Let's pray."

So ... we prayed.

And afterward, several women cornered me in the church foyer.

"Thank you. Thank you. Thank you." Bethanne hugged me.

I stiffened in her embrace. You'd have thought I saved her child's life or something heroic like that.

"For?" I returned an awkward pat on her back.

"Saying what no one else has had the courage to say." She released me and sighed with a huge smile. And tears ... yep, those were tears in her eyes.

"That my husband left dishes everywhere?"

"No, silly." Pam grabbed my hand and squeezed it. "You told the truth."

I didn't tell the truth. Four people knew the truth.

Pam continued, "You weren't afraid to share the imperfect parts of your marriage. We've all been so afraid to be completely honest. Of course, we miss our beloved husbands, but if we were to be honest like you, not every day was a walk in the park." She looked right then left and lowered her voice. "Not every night ended in an orgasm. And no matter what anyone says ... size matters."

Bethanne nodded.

Craig never had size issues, but I understood where they were going.

"Speaking of size ... did you happen to get a glimpse of the new guy in town?" Bethanne fanned herself with her hand in spite of the cool forty-degree day.

"New guy?" I squinted.

"The store across the street. Kaylee messaged me right before our meeting and said they just put up the sign. It's called *What Did You Expect?*"

"The store is called *What Did You Expect?*"

"Crazy right? But ... not going to lie, I'd go into it in a heartbeat just because I'd have to see if it's what I expected."

Fiddling with my earring, I returned an easy nod. "So what kind of store is it?"

Bethanne shrugged. "No idea. All of the windows are still covered in black paper. You'd think they'd want people to know what they plan to sell, especially with the holidays upon us. Anyway, Kaylee saw the owner coming out the front door and she took a picture." She held out her phone and the photo of the man with a gray, slouched beanie, trimmed dark beard, and huge smile. "Kael Hendricks. That's all I know until I get home and talk to her. Clearly, she asked his name. She's a little nosey."

"I hope it's a yoga studio or maybe a cycle gym. I could use some structured exercise again." I wrinkled my nose at my lack of exercise.

"Did you give up your membership to the *All Hours Fitness*?" Pam asked.

"Yeah." I shrugged. "I've resorted to taking the dog on longer walks instead of enduring the poor-Elsie look that everyone gives me. Amie usually walks with me too. *All Hours* is just treadmills and a few elliptical machines and free weights. Nothing like yoga or cycling classes."

"I hate that widowed sympathy look. I swear it doesn't go away until you find someone new and everyone is convinced that you're officially okay."

Did I want someone new?

No.

Asking Craig for a divorce and the dull pain of my chronic unhappiness with my marriage had nothing to do with another man. It was me. I hit a point where to save "us" I would have had to let part of my soul die. Was anyone worth that? I didn't know that answer. Maybe no one did. Maybe there was no distinguishable line between selfless and selfish—each required a sacrifice. We existed somewhere in the middle, but that middle was incredibly hard to find. Happiness wasn't given; it was self-possessed. It had to come from within to be real.

I needed something real again.

CHAPTER four

I love my husband, except when he gropes me at two in the morning.

CRAIG'S PARENTS started *Smith's Specialties* nearly fifty years earlier. It flourished as the go-to place for gifts and a few home decor items. However, in November and December, they made more money than the other ten months combined. Everyone went to *Smith's* for gifts and specialty foods for their holiday parties. After my husband took over the business, he added things like monthly box subscriptions and free twenty-mile delivery on all gift baskets.

In a small Midwest town like Epperly, friendship and loyalty meant everything. And no one was friendlier than Ron and Mary Smith. In return, they had the most loyal customers. Craig carried on that great family tradition and nourished those relationships. When he died, I felt obligated to keep the business going—for him, for the children, for his parents, and maybe even for the loyal customers who I knew would be disappointed to see their favorite specialty store go out of business if I didn't step up and take over.

"*What Did You Expect?* is having a soft opening today." Amie floated into the store like an angel carrying lunch—chicken noodle soup and fresh sourdough from *Spoons,* a soup cafe and bakery three shops down from *Smith's* in the quaint Epperly town square. A line of maple trees and a small sculpture park filled the center of the square. Photographers fought for space in the fall when the leaves turned brilliant shades of red and gold. In December, they constructed a skating rink, our own version of Rockefeller Center.

"I love you." I opened the brown bag when she set it on the checkout counter as a few customers milled around, browsing the new holiday inventory.

"Hot soup. Warm bread. Of course you love me." She grinned, eyeing the new display of holiday caramel corn tins. On Fridays, she closed her clinic at noon and brought me lunch. It was a tradition that started after Craig died. I felt certain it was her way of making sure I was emotionally still hanging in there. After all, she was one of the four who knew the truth and therefore knew my true level of grief and guilt.

So much guilt.

"So what is it? Is it what you expected?" I stirred the soup and blew at the steam.

"Haven't gone in yet. As I was leaving *Spoons* with lunch, they were taking down the black paper. The lights weren't on yet, but as Penelope was getting my order ready, she said Kael—the owner—stopped into her cafe yesterday and gave her some twenty-percent-off coupons to distribute to her customers if she wanted to help spread the word." Amie tore off a piece of bread and dipped it into her soup.

I nodded for her to sit on the stool as I leaned my butt against the edge of the counter. "But she didn't say what he's selling?"

"He just said it was a mix of awesomeness and that he would be offering some classes as well." She chuckled. "Not going to lie, I'm dying to know what he defines as *awesomeness*."

"Classes." I perked up a bit. "It has to be an exercise studio of some sort. That's my hope. Did you get a coupon for twenty percent off? We should think about joining. We could do early mornings since you don't open until nine and I don't open until ten. As it gets colder, we're not going to want to walk outside every morning."

"I don't know. Penelope said he's pretty hot. I'm not sure I want to slide into tight, synthetic fiber and sweat a ton in front of some hot guy."

I rolled my eyes. "If he's running a fitness studio, he's probably young and out of our age range."

"Speak for yourself. I'm expanding my acceptable age range. Since I'm forty-two, I think I can go fifteen years in either direction."

I sipped my soup. "Fifteen? So you'd date a guy in his twenties?"

"Funny how you go in that direction. As a matter of fact, I would absolutely prefer a guy in his twenties to a guy in his late fifties. Why go gray-balling before you absolutely have to?"

I choked on my soup and reached for a napkin. "I can't believe you just said that."

"I agree with Dr. Amie." Susan, a fifty-something,

longtime customer, set a few things on the checkout counter. "Go younger. Bill—my gray-balled husband—overeats at dinner then falls asleep on the sofa. He wakes up at two in the morning and starts groping me for sex because he's had six good hours of sleep, and his prostate wakes him up with an urgent need to urinate. So he figures since he's up, I might as well wake up and let him do his thing with me. But I'm up late reading, and my body has no desire to be invaded at that insane hour of the morning."

Amie gave me a wide-eyed look before laughing. "Susan, you have made my day."

I sat my soup aside and rang up her items while chuckling and lifting my gaze to see if the two other women in the store could hear our conversation. Since I didn't recognize them, I thought we should keep the conversation G-non-groping-related.

"Pauline told me about your confession at your meeting," Susan whispered as if that needed to be said in privacy, yet gray balls and two-in-the-morning groping required no level of privacy or discretion.

Such a small town. Zero room for secrets. Gossip was the only form of entertainment that didn't involve a screen and a Hulu subscription in Epperly.

"It was probably inappropriate given the audience and the fact that it was at church. Sixty-two eighty." I totaled her products and put them in a bag.

"Pauline said you were a breath of fresh air. Saying all the things everyone else in the group had been dying to say."

Amie raised an eyebrow at me. "Clearly, you didn't tell me everything."

I shrugged, nodding for Susan to go ahead and swipe her credit card. "I had a weak moment, and in turn, a few other women decided to have a weak moment too."

"Not weak." Susan shook her head. "Honest. A breakthrough for some of those women. Acknowledging your truth is not weak; it's strong. It makes you feel vulnerable to let people in like that. So the fact that you did that makes it not only brave, but it allowed the other women in the group to speak their truths too."

I chuckled, handing her the receipt. "And what truth is that? That our loved ones are dead, but we can't let go of the irritating things they did?"

Susan tapped her finger on the tip of her nose. "Exactly. Saying *I loved him* is only half the truth. I loved him, but he drove me crazy ... now that's being honest."

I loved him, then I despised things about him, then I fell out of love, then I asked for a divorce, then he died.

My honesty was embarrassing, regretful, and tragic.

"Thanks, Susan." I went with the less-is-more route.

"Anytime. I'm going to pop into the new place across the street. You know ... to see if it's what I'm expecting."

"Well, report back if it's something amazing." Amie smiled, and Susan nodded while heading to the door.

That afternoon, the traffic in my store came to a screeching halt. The holidays were upon us. Late October to November always ... *always* brought a steady stream of traffic. Standing at the door, I squinted to see through the windows of *What Did You Expect?* But the reflection of the sun obscured everything—except the line all the way down the sidewalk.

Were people really waiting to go inside? For what? Fitness classes? Was he running a flash sale on memberships? Right at the door, taking a step inside the mysterious new business, I recognized Valerie Middleton's pink hat that I knitted for her two years earlier when she was going through chemotherapy for breast cancer. I texted her to get the scoop on the situation.

> Elsie: What's in the store. I have to know!

She quickly replied with a wide-eyed emoji.

> Valerie: Um ... it's a specialty store. Sort of.

> Elsie: What products do they sell?

She replied with a hand-covering-the-mouth emoji and a cringing emoji.

> Valerie: Food and other stuff.

My store was considered a specialty store.
I sold food and other stuff.
Shit ...

I had competition? Going into the holidays, I had some new guy selling his own tins of popcorn, tubs of cheese, and rolls of turkey sausage? That wasn't what I needed—not with my first holiday season without Craig, not with the store officially belonging to me.

Switching screens, I messaged Amie.

> Elsie: I did NOT expect the new store to be my competition!

> **Amie:** Yeah, I was going to call you later. After lunch I slipped inside to take a quick peek.

> **Elsie:** And?

> **Amie:** It's different than your store.

> **Elsie:** Different good or different bad?

> **Amie:** Not sure. Probably a matter of personal taste or opinion.

> **Elsie:** And what's yours?

> **Amie:** Just call me when you get home. Too hard to describe via text

.

I didn't message her back. Instead, I remained planted by the window, watching the steady line of people congest that entire side of the square, waiting to gain access to see if it's what they expected.

Kandi, one of my employees, arrived at four for her shift. "Wow! The line still hasn't gone down."

Twisting my lips, gaze fixed to said line, I nodded slowly. "Did you go in?"

"Yeah. I checked it out before my hair appointment."

"And?"

She tucked her purse under the register and shrugged off her coat. "And I think you should go see for yourself. It's hard to explain. But it's definitely not what I expected."

Glancing over my shoulder, I kept my expression neutral. "What did you expect?"

Kandi sipped her grande coffee in a white to-go cup and lifted a shoulder. "I wasn't sure. Frame shop. Bath and body store. New restaurant. But I can say with absolute certainty the biggest attraction right now is the owner, Kael. He's *hot*. And incredibly nice. Nice like Craig."

Everyone loved Craig.

But they didn't live with him for twenty-two years.

Yes, in a romantic sense, I fell out of love. In another sense, my love for him grew deeper because my appreciation for his work ethic and the way he loved our children never faded. It aged into something admirable and unforgettable.

"I'm going over." I snagged my coat from the hook behind the counter and meandered across the square to get in line. Never had I waited in line *outside* in Epperly. Even at the grocery store, it was rare for the checkout lines to be more than two customers deep. It took twenty minutes to get to the door.

"What the heck?" I whispered to myself.

Two registers.

At least a hundred customers.

Fire code violation?

I sure thought so.

As I wormed my way through the store, familiar faces glanced at me for two seconds before turning away to avert their attention.

Shame.

They were ashamed for having their arms and shopping baskets filled with things from my competitor's store instead of mine.

Flavored vinegars and olive oils in stainless steel vats lined two full walls. Eager customers snatched tiny cups of free samples before grabbling bottles of all the flavors. The middle aisles contained everything from special syrups and spices to unique kitchen items, gourmet *organic* hot chocolates and coffees, and loads of gift sets.

I had never seen any of the brands or items. So no ... not what I expected.

Worse.

So much worse.

"Welcome! Can I tell you about any of our items or get you signed up at twenty percent off for any of our cooking classes?"

My gaze drifted to his crisp white apron with words embroidered in green stitching.

I'm Kael—Like Kale.
Just as healthy.
Twice as sexy.

"I have four kids. I can cook." I narrowed my eyes a smidge. He looked familiar. Celebrity familiar.

As his welcoming grin swelled, I made the connection. Captain America. He bore a resemblance to the superhero.

Chris Evans, with a beard. I happened to like Chris Evans.

A lot.

Too much.

"I believe you *can* cook, but I don't believe you have four kids."

"I do," I deadpanned. "Four kids. A dog. And a business on the opposite side of the square." I jabbed my thumb over my shoulder toward the front windows.

"Oh! You must be Elsie Smith." He held out his hand. "It's a pleasure to meet you. I've heard so many good things about you and your family's store. I need to make it over, but we've been slammed trying to get everything ready to open."

My teeth dug into my lower lip as I internally bristled at his enthusiasm over stealing my customers going into the holiday season and the anniversary of Craig's death.

Not cool, Cap. Not cool.

I might have been a little chapped that he looked too hot for Epperly. Too hot for a retail store owner. And too hot for me to think about all the ways he looked too hot.

"Oh yeah? What sort of good things have you heard about me and my store?"

He chuckled as if he didn't expect me to ask him that—like when people asked how you are, but only to be nice. They didn't really want to know about your dishwasher on the fritz or the shoulder pain that you recently noticed after no apparent injury.

"Well ... I've heard your husband was loved by everyone. Sorry for your loss. And I've heard your store is a staple for the classics."

"The classics?" I tilted my head to the side.

"Yeah, the things that make us feel comfort during the holidays. Things we feel guilty splurging on during other times of the year unless it's a gift from someone."

Tipping my chin up for an extended pause, I returned to my squinty eyes and dropped my head in a sharp nod.

"Yo, Kael!" one of his aproned employees called him.

"Listen..." he started to turn, but he kept his eyes on

me as his hand slid into his pocket and pulled out a small card "...the cooking classes are more like a social hour with wine where I force everyone to make their own food. Come for free next Friday and bring a friend. Seven o'clock. Right when your store closes." He winked, pretty proud of himself for knowing that. Then he handed me the card (a voucher for a free class) and turned, zigzagging his way to the checkout. Kael smiled and thanked everyone in his path for visiting his store.

At *Smith's,* we thanked them when they walked out the door or made a purchase. Based on the way his customers added five new items to their baskets after he showed his appreciation, accompanied with that Captain America smile, I needed to up my greeting game. Brilliant marketing: make them feel appreciated and they'll carry a spark of indebtedness to buy something just because you showed a smile and gratitude for them walking through your door—before they'd made up their mind on the purchase.

Well, I wasn't going to buy anything, but Elsie seems so appreciative that I'm here, I'll go ahead and buy this candle in a jar. As if I need one more ugly candle in a jar.

The classics. Smith's sold the classics. I'm pretty sure that was code for outdated shit no one wanted anymore. Kael didn't open a fitness studio, but he might as well have opened one. Everything in his store gave off a trendy, healthy vibe.

Organic, cold-pressed oils.

Posh flavored vinegars.

Natural this.

Fair-trade that.

My large tins—filled with GMO popcorn covered in

high-fructose corn syrup, salt, and artificial flavorings and colorings—felt anything but trendy and healthy.

Kale Kael.

Artificial Elsie.

Just ... great.

CHAPTER five

It's hard to love a man who puts your bank account into the negative, buying foot porn on the internet.

"It's a specialty food store!" I ran my hands through my hair before pouring a generous glass of wine for myself on Amie's deck. It overlooked a pond filled with geese and ducks, lending a sense of privacy.

She hugged one leg to her chest and swirled her wine with her other hand as the wind caught her blond hair, which made me slightly jealous. It was a few shades lighter than my hot mess of brown and random grays I fought to hide. "It's apples and oranges. Not that many crossover items. Maybe the hot chocolate. And you're still going to be the top pick for gifts. Hello! Popcorn. Sausage. Cheese. Do you really think people are going to forego their favorites for a bottle of vinegar?"

"Yes." I nodded a half dozen times. "If I gave a tin of popcorn to my friends and family every year but had the chance to give them a bottle of white balsamic vinegar infused with quince and pomegranate, I totally would do it. I don't even know what quince is! But that's what would make it such a cool gift. And cooking classes that people will love. They'll do girls' nights and birthday parties. It's a brilliant marketing idea. I'm sure he'll use all the fabulous products from his store, and he'll make money on the classes and all of the products people buy after the class. I can't compete with that. I can't compete with *him*. I mean, did you see his apron? Come on!" My hand jerked with my frustration, splashing wine onto the deck.

Amie chuckled and sipped her wine. "You mean ... did I see *him*? And hell yes. I can't stop seeing him. He should come with a warning. But ... you always said running that store wasn't going to be your destiny. If he runs you out of business, maybe that's a sign, the opportunity to do something for you."

Her words packed a punch. I had said that—so many times—but that was before Craig died and the fate of the store landed in my hands. As long as his parents were still alive, I didn't have the heart to close the store, move out of Epperly, and follow new dreams.

Guilt was a wide, all-encompassing storm that I couldn't escape, so I'd weather it every single day.

"I think helping them stay in their home is enough. At this point, it's probably too much. But I know why you do it," Amie said with reverence in her voice.

I sipped more wine and focused on the birds congregating on the water. "If I say they won't live forever, that sounds horrible, like I'm waiting for them to die. If I say I don't mind and my dreams don't matter, then I'm lying. The truth feels really selfish, so I just ignore it. Leaving Craig wasn't going to be easy. Divorcing him would have felt like divorcing his family. And I knew he wouldn't let them stay in their house for long after I stopped taking care of things for them. But I was okay with that. I knew it would be on his shoulders—his conscience dealing with that. Not now. It's all me now. Can I really be responsible for Craig's death *and* his parents losing the last of their independence?"

"When is it okay?" Amie rested her glass on the arm of her chair.

"When is what okay?"

"When is it okay to be happy without anyone's permission, without judgment? And I mean *anyone*. Your parents, Craig's parents, your children, your friends, the people who go to your church, *me*? Were we really put on this earth to please other people? Are kindness and love defined as doing whatever it takes to make someone else happy?" Amie finished with a slow exhale followed by silence.

Truth?

She didn't know the answers. I was her sounding board, and she was mine. We drank wine and contemplated life's greatest mysteries. That was our thing.

"I don't know," I murmured. "I don't know where that balance exists—the one between loving yourself and loving others. Maybe it doesn't exist. It feels like balance is this brief moment ... a breath ... a second in the middle while we teeter between the two. And sometimes it's just so ..."

"Exhausting."

I nodded slowly.

"Angel Brayhill flagged me down at the grocery store

after work. She said she heard you were so inspiring at that last meeting."

I rolled my eyes. "It was a slip of the tongue. Ten months of silence fermenting in my conscience."

"Well, clearly a lot of widowed and divorced women in this town feel imprisoned ... *silenced* too."

"Angel's on her third marriage. I'm not sure she's been silenced."

Amie laughed. "Well, today's revelation was news to me."

My nose wrinkled. "Do I want to know?"

"No. But I'm not keeping this image to myself."

"Don't." I shook my head. Angel always managed to find the worst men. A magnet for the worst of the worst. "Please don't tell—"

"And I quote ..."

"No!" I grimaced, shaking my head.

"I simply asked how she and Merlin were doing, and her response was, 'It's hard to love a man who puts your bank account into the negative, buying foot porn on the internet.' And then she threw your name in there with an 'Elsie would understand.'"

I coughed on a laugh. "What? That's so wrong. No. I don't understand. Saturday shaboink is not the same as spending your last dime on foot porn."

We laughed.

And laughed some more.

"I needed that." I finished giggling and took another sip of my wine.

"Me too. You know what else we need?"

"Chocolate?"

Amie grinned. "Well, duh ... always that. But I'm

thinking more along the lines of a cooking class this Friday."

"You want me to support my competition?"

"No. I want *us* to spy on the enemy."

My lips corkscrewed for a few seconds. "It's not a terrible idea."

THAT FRIDAY, Amie helped me close up shop so we wouldn't be more than a few seconds late to the class.

"Good evening. Welcome. Are you here for the class?" A young, black woman with cute, curly hair greeted us.

"Hi. Yes. We are." I returned a warm smile.

"Did you purchase the class here or online?"

"Oh … uh … Kael invited me and a friend." I jerked my head toward Amie.

"You have a free voucher. Cool." She tapped the screen of her phone. "What's the name on the reservation?"

"The reservation?" I cringed.

"Yes. The coupons for the free classes have a number or online website to book your class. No reservation?"

Maintaining my cringe-worthy level of embarrassment, I shook my head. "I didn't even read the card. I'm sorry. We'll come back another night when we have reservations." I glanced past her to the glass wall between the store and the room on the other side, a test kitchen type area. Ten or so people (all women) were seated around the island, all wearing aprons. Kael animatedly talked and busied his hands with holding up different bottles.

"I'm sorry. Do you want to go ahead and schedule while you're here? We just don't have any more space for tonight's class."

Kael peered in my direction, and I whipped my body around, putting my back to him and my front to Amie. "I'm sorry. I really should learn how to read." I facepalmed my forehead.

She chuckled. "It's fine. Let's go ahead and try next week."

The young woman pressed her lips together. "Mmm ... sorry, we are actually booked out for the next four weeks. I can put you on the waiting list, but I'll also go ahead and get you reserved for early December."

"Sure. Thanks." I felt stupid, especially since my competitor (the enemy) saw me ... on the wrong night ... no reservations.

Classic Elsie.

I was the classic middle-aged woman, making the classic mistake of not reading the fine print, probably because I was too busy defending the classic (outdated) food at my store.

"Hey, did we mess up and overbook?" Kael asked, poking his head out the glass sliding door.

I plastered a mature grin on my face and turned.

"Got it handled, boss," his employee murmured as she glanced up at me. "What's the name you want on the reservation? I'll need a number to either call or text confirmation and to let you know if we get a cancellation."

"Elsie Smith," I said to her before shifting my attention to him.

Hot.

Captain America.

Way too young for my fantasies ... Kael.

And enemy number one.

"Not your mistake. Mine. I didn't read the card close enough to see that I needed a reservation. Which clearly I would need one since you're obviously busy."

Wooing my customers!

"Nope, my mistake for inviting you this week and not going ahead and reserving two spots. Come ... we'll make room."

"No. Really ..." I shook my head as a nervous grin clung to my face since everyone in the other room had their attention fixed on me. Why would Elsie Smith—new reigning queen of the Classic Holiday Guilt Food—come to a class offered by her competitor?

Such a good question.

"We'll come back in December or after the holidays if you're still doing the classes."

His thick eyebrow lifted a fraction. "You mean if I'm still in business?"

"Yes. No." I shook my head, biting my lips together.

"Trendy stuff can be a tough sell in the Midwest." Amie shrugged.

Kael eyed her with amusement before shifting his ornery gaze back to me. I allowed myself two seconds, maybe three, to relish the way his gaze made me feel.

Twenty. He made me feel like a young girl with nothing better to do than flirt with cute guys.

Only ... I wasn't young. And Kael wasn't flirting with me no matter how badly my body misread his cues.

"So true." He nodded several times. "But ... when I first scoped out Epperly for my business, I instantly got this trendy vibe. Like the residents here are hungry for something new."

He did not just say that!

As if he read my mind, his confidence fell a few degrees. "What I mean is that Epperly has a good mix of people—those who like the traditional stuff and those who are a little more adventurous. Plenty of people and different tastes to support all kinds of businesses."

"Well, I hope so for your sake, young man."

That was when it happened. The moment I aged myself two full decades. Forty-two to sixty-two.

Young man.

Maybe I needed to verbally put it out there for myself and the whole universe to remember that Kael was a young man. Not as experienced in life or business as I was. Not as experienced in marketing. Not as experienced with sex.

Scratch that last part. I didn't actually think that. Okay, I *did* think it, but it was a fleeting thought at most. Maybe not even my thought. What if Amie was thinking it, and my brain hijacked it? I had to consider all possibilities.

My young-man comment brought a supercharged grin to his face. "Well, *Mrs. Smith*, either way ... tonight I have a class going on, and you and your friend are invited to join us." He stepped back to make room for us to enter the kitchen.

"There's no room." My head resumed its shaking.

"Holy. Sexual. Tension. *Mrs. Smith,*" Amie whispered under her breath. I prayed to God that no one else heard her.

"Come on. We're all friends tonight." He jerked his

head toward the group of people and raised his voice. "Everyone refill your wine glasses and get cozy with your neighbors. We have two more ladies joining us this evening. For those of you who might not know, this is the lovely Elsie Smith, owner of *Smith's Specialties* across the street. I hear the sharp cheddar is to die for. And her friend ..." Kael smiled at Amie, waiting for her to fill in the blank.

"Amie." Her lips pulled into a tight smile.

Everyone at the table knew us, but they all managed to avert their gazes while crowding closer to accommodate us. Kael filled two more glasses with wine and jumped right back into his high-energy speech on vinegars and olive oils.

I spent the next hour avoiding eye contact with him as well as Amie's glances at me. It felt like we were in high school again, and she wanted to make sure I knew some guy was checking me out.

Kael was not checking me out.

At least, that was what I told myself, but I had no way of knowing because I refused to look at him.

"More wine, Mrs. Smith?" He pressed his chest to my back as he leaned over me to grab my glass while everyone ate the fruits of their labor.

Amie kept her head down toward her plate, but I didn't miss her wide-eyed expression as our teacher invaded my space.

"Th-thanks," I croaked, catching a whiff of his culinary scent. Herbaceous and spicy.

"Are you ladies enjoying yourselves? Would you like me to demonstrate anything else for you tonight?"

"Elsie hoped you were opening a fitness club. Do you happen to have a six-pack under that apron and shirt?"

"Amie!" I coughed, choking on the food that lodged in my throat when I gasped at her comment. "Cut her off, please. She can't handle her alcohol."

Everyone ... *everyone* heard her, and the room broke out into laughter. The whole room was high on food, buzzed from a long week, and drunk on wine.

I was ten shades of red, pitting out, and unable to breathe as Kael stayed right behind me where I couldn't gauge his reaction.

"If Mrs. Smith needs a private trainer, I can check my schedule."

More laughter. A few really embarrassing whistles. And *Mrs. Smith* dying. Seriously ... I was dying.

I used to be the Queen of Snappy Comebacks, but I had nothing except fire in my cheeks, sweat pooling between my cleavage, and a dry mouth.

"Kidding." He rested a hand on my shoulder for several seconds before his presence behind me vanished and I could breathe again—but just barely.

My hand gripped Amie's arm. "You are dead to me."

She snorted, wiping her mouth before reaching for *my* wine since he did, in fact, cut her off. "Our teacher likes you. Oh my god ... does he ever."

Way too much wine for her. And I thought chiropractors were a little more health oriented than four glasses of wine on a Friday. I stood, grabbing my purse and hers, slinging both over my shoulder. "It's past our bedtime. Thank you, everyone, for accommodating us tonight."

"Our bedtime? Are we sleeping together now?" Amie

stood on weak legs and looped her arm around mine. "I knew we would be lovers someday."

Giggles ensued as I dragged her toward the door.

"Thanks for coming, ladies. Kira is out there if you want to make any purchases before you leave. Everything purchased tonight is twenty-five percent off." Kael had the nerve to make a last-minute sales pitch as I struggled to get my drunk BFF out the door.

Classic ...

CHAPTER SIX

I hated the way he couldn't make one freaking decision by himself. I'm not saying his mama failed him, but ... yeah, she failed him.

EPPERLY GOT its first snow of the season in early November, and it was a big one.

Ten inches.

Like everyone else, I anticipated a dusting but woke to plows on the streets and my driveway covered. After Craig died, Finn made sure he was up and running the snowblower early in the morning. His natural instinct to step up and be the man of the house brought me to tears. He took off a semester of school to grieve and be with me and Bella. But he was no longer at home for the man-of-the-house call of duty.

"I'll never get out." I frowned, peering out the window as I sipped my lemon water.

Bella slid her eggs onto her plate. "You have four-wheel drive. You'll get out. But I'll help shovel the driveway."

I shook my head. "No. I'll do it. I need to figure out the snowblower since Finn is not here this winter."

"Have you used the snowblower before?"

"No. Hence the *figure it out*. Your dad didn't like—" I stopped myself. It wasn't that I was getting ready to say anything that I wouldn't have said in front of her when Craig was alive, but it suddenly felt disrespectful to say anything negative about him in front of our children—especially since she and Finn knew the truth.

"Say it."

I shook my head.

"Jeez, Mom ... just say it. I didn't think Dad was perfect. I hated the way he always rolled his eyes when I wore something sexy or too much makeup. I hated the way he acted like I was going to be this irresponsible teenager getting pregnant and ruining my life. I hated the way he couldn't make one freaking decision by himself. I'm not saying his mama failed him, but ... yeah, she failed him." She sighed. "Too soon?"

I snorted, shaking my head slowly. She had no idea I initiated major venting in my grief group. "His mama? That's your grandma."

Her serious face cracked, revealing a smile. "I know. But it's the truth."

My eyes narrowed as I sat opposite of her at the kitchen table. "Did you hear me say that?" I couldn't remember saying it, at least not in front of her. But I thought it. Oh boy, did I ever think it.

"No, Mom. I have my own superpower of observation. Everything was 'ask your mom.' And he asked you what he should have for a late-night snack. He'd ask you if he should shave his mustache or grow out his beard. He'd buy three pairs of shoes and wear each pair around the house for a week before making a final decision and taking the other two back. And even then, he'd ask all of us, a million times, which pair we liked best."

I laughed. She was right. Very observant.

Craig liked to be the man of the house—in theory. Basically, he liked to have the appearance of being the man of the house. Consequently, I never used the lawn mower or snowblower. Except I did mow his parents' yard, and sometimes I shoveled their driveway if his dad was having knee issues. But at our house, appearance meant everything. Craig hated the idea of the neighbors seeing me instead of him doing the "manly" chores around the house.

Had the neighbors heard his commentary during sex, they would have questioned his manliness.

"You like that?"

"Uh-huh ..." I replied as he moved over me.

"You sure?"

"Yes." I breathed heavily.

"Harder?"

"Um ... sure."

That was fine. How kind of him to make sure I was enjoying it. Right? But as the years progressed, it felt like he lost his confidence, and I had no idea why. After all, I was the one with a little extra around the waist from having four children. I was the one with stretch marks. I was the one with boobs that looked and felt like two punctured balloons sagging to the sides when I was on my back.

"Do you want me to touch your clit?"

"Okay."

I can't tell you how many times he rubbed just to the right or left of it, missing it altogether. And he *knew* ... when we first started having sex, he knew where it was. It hadn't relocated.

"How's that?"

"Fine."

I never had the nerve to tell him he wasn't rubbing my clit.

"You like that?"

"Sure."

"Do you want to come?"

~~*"That would be nice, but it's not looking likely."*~~ *"Uh-huh."*

He'd pick up his pace, which was good, and the sexiest thing he could have done at that point would have been to shut up.

Nope.

He needed more validation.

"How am I doing?"

"Good."

Fine. Sure. Good.

Not exactly the best sex life. Over and over again, I tried to pinpoint the time in our marriage when he went from the man I wanted to jump the second he walked through the door to the man I avoided until I felt guilty for making up reasons to not have sex. I'd get myself psyched up to just "get it done," knowing it would buy me a good week of him not propositioning me.

What kind of life was that?

I didn't confirm anything Bella said about Craig nor did I deny it. She'd heard too much that morning we fought for the last time. "I'm going to clear the driveway."

"You sure you don't want me to help shovel?"

Rinsing out my cup, I shook my head. "I've got it. It's a snowblower. Not an army tank. How hard could it be?"

Come to find out ...

Pretty fucking hard.

It wasn't an electric start snowblower; it was a pull start. The worst thing imaginable for someone with no upper body strength.

I adjusted the choke and pulled the cord. It caught on me. I never understood how men made pull starts look so smooth and easy.

The second time I pulled it, it caught again.

"Come on!" In that moment, I started thinking the lack of finding my clit didn't matter. Craig could pull start anything.

"Ouch!" I grabbed my shoulder after the third attempt, feeling certain I'd torn a ligament or dislocated it. In that moment, I made a mental note to encourage Bella to be strong.

Not emotionally strong—that was fine too. But emotional strength wasn't going to pull start anything. She needed upper body strength to pull start snowblowers and open stubborn jar lids.

"We're shoveling. Aren't we?"

I glanced up at Bella in her long coat, hat, and gloves.

"It's looking that way." I frowned, rubbing my shoulder.

Shoveling put me fifteen minutes late to the store, but no one was waiting at the door, so I was fine. At first I assumed the lack of a Saturday morning crowd during the holiday season was a symptom of the big snow.

But ... *What Did You Expect?* had people piling into their store.

There were actually two people shivering by my front door, Kandi and Tiffany. I asked them both to work since weekends during the holiday season were insanely busy.

Were being the keyword.

"Hey, girls! Sorry I'm late." I unlocked the door. "I didn't know so much snow was forecasted."

Tiffany laughed as the three of us skittered into the store to get out of the cold. "You should get a snowblower."

"Yes. Great idea. Can I give you two young girls some advice?"

"What's that?" Kandi asked, turning on the display lights while I unlocked the register.

"Focus on strengthening your upper body. Pull-ups, pushups, curls … whatever. Just don't become so obsessed with your legs, butt, and thighs that you set yourself up to be completely helpless someday if you're ever widowed."

"O-kay …" Tiffany lifted her eyebrows while turning on the *Open* sign.

"Where's this from?" I picked up a hot drink cup; both girls had carried one into the shop when I unlocked it. I sniffed the steam coming from the opening in the lid.

"Oh, it's from *What Did You Expect?*" Kandi took a sip of hers as I returned Tiffany's cup to the counter. "Free organic hot chocolate until noon today in celebration of the first snow. So when you weren't on time, Tiff ran over and got us hot chocolates."

"I also picked up several bottles of vinegar. I'm so addicted to it. I use it for a fat free salad dressing."

"How nice of him," I murmured as I gazed at the lineup outside of his shop.

By noon, less than ten people had walked through my door, and less than five made purchases.

"I'm going to grab soup. You girls want anything?"

"Brought my lunch," Tiffany said as she rearranged the ornaments on the tree by the display window.

"Me too," Kandi hollered from the back room, unpacking a new shipment of popcorn tins.

"Okay. I'll be back." I slipped on my white, down North Face jacket and donned my wool mittens before heading out the door. The line for *Spoons* was nearly as long as the line had been that morning at *What Did You Expect?*

"Hey, Elsie. Did you have any trouble getting out of your driveway this morning?" Jan, my neighbor, asked as she sidled up to me. We'd made it to the lucky part of the line—the part that was inside instead of the ten-people-deep part still outside.

"It was touch and go at first. I didn't think I was ever going to get the snowblower started. And I didn't." I laughed. "But Bella helped me shovel it."

"We have Anderson's plow ours. Takes them three swipes and they're done. Twenty bucks."

"Twenty bucks?" I tugged off my mittens and shoved them into my pockets. "Pfft ... this morning I was so frustrated I would have exchanged sexual favors for someone to plow my drive in three swipes."

She chuckled as did I. Jan didn't attend my church, or any church, so I could get away with remarks like that.

"Hmm ..."

I made a one-eighty-degree turn to see where the deep *hmm* came from.

Kael stood behind me, grinning from ear to ear. "You

know, Elsie, I have a blade on my pickup truck. I'd be happy to make a few swipes for you."

I loosened my scarf and unzipped my coat several inches. "Oh ... for twenty bucks?"

With his hands buried in his front pockets, he lifted his shoulders. "Sure. Or we can barter ... per your earlier suggestion."

"My earlier sug—" It hit me. The turd had been eavesdropping.

Jan laughed as I searched for words, but they were nowhere to be found.

He shot Jan a tiny wink, a reward for her engaging in his inappropriate humor. "Or I can do it for free, a courtesy for my fellow small business owner. We have to stick together, you know?"

Eyes wide, words clogged in my throat, I slowly faced forward again.

Jan leaned over and whispered in my ear, "I can think of worse things than getting stuck to that hunk."

A few minutes later, we'd crept to third and fourth in line as my stomach churned out hungry noises. "I know they're really busy around lunch time, but this is crazy even for them."

Jan nodded. "Right?"

"It's the coupons. Cross-promotion."

Again, I eased my head around to Kael and his relentless eavesdropping.

He grinned. "When I opened, they handed out coupons for my business, and in return, I handed out ones for theirs today. Free sourdough roll with the purchase of a large bowl of soup. We could do some cross promoting too if you'd like."

I rubbed my slightly dry lips together for several seconds before rewarding his offer with more than an eye roll. "We own specialty shops. Competitors of sorts. How and why would we cross promote?"

"The why is simple—because small business owners should support each other. We should never think of the other as competition. And the how ... well ... I'll give it some thought. I'm not open on Sundays, but I see that you are, so maybe I'll check out your store tomorrow and something will spark an idea or two."

"You're closed on Sundays?" I couldn't imagine how a specialty store could be closed on a Sunday, especially during the holiday season. Not that I was disappointed ... Sunday shoppers would come to my store.

"Yep. I need a day of rest. Like God. I think I heard He took a day off, right?"

"Oh ... you're closed for church? We used to do that too, but during the holidays, it was hard to close one day a week when so many people in Epperly work Monday through Friday and only have the weekends to shop." I shrugged.

"Church? No. Just rest. I don't attend church."

"Are you an atheist?" Jan asked.

"Shh ..." I elbowed her. "You can't ask people that."

She narrowed her eyes. "What? I've never actually met one before. I have so many questions."

Kael laughed. "I was raised Catholic. I just don't go to church, and my beliefs are based on experience and observation more than translated scripture."

"So you *are* atheist?" Jan's eyes remained unblinking as she nodded several times.

"Jan, you don't attend church." I eyed her.

"True. But it's not because I don't believe. I just don't like the expectations. The accountability. You miss one Sunday, and the following week, everyone gives you the third degree. You know, inadvertently butting their noses into your business. 'Hi, Jan. We missed you last week. Hope everything's okay?' And you can't just say that you didn't want to get your ass out of bed and come. Nope, that's frowned upon like you were too lazy for God, so you have to lie. Isn't that fantastic? Christians lying because they don't want to be judged, which happens to be a rule they are the *very* best at breaking. And don't even get me started on the snoopiness and shame that comes with passing on the offering plate." She rolled her eyes.

I tried to hide my grin, but Kael barked a laugh and tipped his head back.

Luckily, I was next to place my order, so I didn't have to think of any response. As I waited off to the side for my soup, Jan grabbed a seat when a table opened up just as her friend Paula arrived.

"Come here often?" Kael asked with a smirk as he tucked himself next to me in the corner of the crowded cafe to wait for his to-go order as well.

Pursing my lips, I tried to hide my grin, keeping my eyes focused on the busy employees prepping orders. "That sounds like a cheesy pick-up line, but I know you mean it very literally. So, yes. I come here a lot."

"Nope. I totally meant it as a cheesy pick-up line."

"Stop." I shook my head and let my grin have its way, but I still didn't let my gaze get anywhere near his face. "I'm a little too old for you."

"You mean you think I'm a little too young for you."

"Same thing."

"No. It's only for me to say if *I* think you're too old for me. Which I don't. So for you to say it, it's just your backward way of saying I'm too young for you."

"How can you say you don't think I'm too old for you when you don't even know my age?"

"I didn't say it. *You* said it."

On a sidelong glance, I murmured, "How old are you?"

"I'm legal."

I coughed a laugh. "Legal. Wow ... that's not as comforting as I think you meant it to be. It sounds like a defense for a statutory rape claim."

"I'm not too worried about you raping me, Mrs. Smith."

"Stop ..." I giggled as they called my name for my order. "You're obnoxious." Before he could say anything else, I hustled to the counter to snag my bag of food. Then I took the long way around the line to the exit—anything to avoid Kael.

CHAPTER seven

I miss him, but only because there are fifty unfinished projects around our house.

SEX DREAMS.

Forty-two years without having sex dreams—at least that I recalled.

Then Kael Hendricks made a few borderline inappropriate comments, threw out the cheesiest pick-up line ever, and I woke up in a hot sweat with my hand down the front of my panties and my legs scissoring back and forth.

What if Bella would have peeked into my room? I never fully closed my door. Was I making noises? In my dream, I made all kinds of moaning sounds. So there I was, still panting, eyes wide and focus stuck to the ceiling while I contemplated finishing what I apparently started in my dream.

"Mom?"

Whoosh!

Bella's voice drifting closer to my room ended that

thought in a heartbeat as I yanked my hand out of my panties and jumped out of bed. I ran into the bathroom before she saw me in my hot-mess state.

"In the bathroom, sweetie." Turning on the cold water, I scrubbed my hands and splashed water on my face.

"I have a headache. If it goes away, I'll go to the late service."

After blotting the water from my face, I opened the door.

"Sorry, babe. Did you take something for it?"

Bella nodded, yawning then grimacing as she pressed her fingers to her temple.

"Well, you know I can't go to late service. So if you don't feel better soon, just stay home and rest."

"Okay." She turned and dragged herself back to her bedroom.

I showered and dressed for early church service in record time. The idea of skipping crossed my mind, but Jan was right—church family had a special gift for guilting absentee members upon their return. And ... I needed a little prayer time to seek forgiveness for my naughty dreams.

Wearing my red, cowl neck sweater dress and black boots, I hurried off to church in my dirty Tahoe. We sang hymns, prayed for our wellbeing, guidance, and dreamless sleep. Okay, *one* of us prayed for dreamless sleep. Then I had to sneak out a few minutes early (as usual) to get to the store in time. To my knowledge, no one ever judged my need to leave early because I *did* tithe well every week.

A real live customer waited at the door to my store as I

walked down the sidewalk. "Good morning! Let's get inside where it's warm."

Then ... *he* turned around. Kael really needed to stick to one jacket and one beanie to make himself more recognizable.

"I like the sound of that." Mischief spread along his face.

My smile faltering, I brushed past him to unlock the door. The sex dream made it really hard to keep eye contact. "Both of my employees for the day called in sick, so I might not have time to chitchat with you today. Feel free to look around and brainstorm while I get things opened up."

"Chitchat ... do people say that anymore?"

"Yes, Kael. I'm a person, and I just said it." I liked saying his name as I would one of my own children. It felt imperative to think of him as not only young but inexperienced and in need of role modeling.

However, he demonstrated lots of experience in my dream the previous night.

Dear God, please make it stop! Take a magnet and wipe my brain.

"Can I help you with anything?"

"Nope." I turned on the *Open* sign and shrugged off my long, wool coat.

"Wow ... you look great in red."

I ignored his compliment as I turned on the other lights, unlocked the cash register, and hooked up my phone to play holiday music over the speakers.

"So tell me about your kids." He picked up a jar of sweet honey mustard and read the back of it. When he shifted his attention to me, I averted my gaze and busied myself behind the counter, tidying up a few things.

"I have three boys in college, and my daughter, Bella, is a senior in high school."

Kael's head bounced in a slow, impassive nod as he returned the jar to its shelf before resuming his inspection of my store.

I cleared my throat. "Do you have kids? A wife? A dog?"

He chuckled, his twinkling eyes finding mine, ensnaring my gaze far too long. When my cheeks permeated with heat, I tore my attention away from him and tidied up the candy display on the counter.

"No kids. No wife. No dog."

"Well, you're young."

"So you keep reminding me."

"I just mean, a lot of people are waiting longer to get married and have kids. Not everyone gets pregnant in college like I did."

"I'm sure you regret nothing."

I narrowed my eyes and glanced over my shoulder at him while he perused the products in my store. "That's an interesting assumption."

"Is it?" His gaze lifted to meet mine.

"Yeah, I mean ... I think wonderful things happen to people by accident, but that's not to say that given the chance again—not knowing the future or outcome—that we'd always make the same decisions."

"So if you had it to do again, you would have had him wrap it up?"

I blushed again and turned my back to him. "I'm saying, I hope my daughter plans her pregnancies."

"So you don't believe God has predetermined your life?"

"I ... I don't know."

"It wouldn't make sense. Him taking your husband from you. Right?"

No. That part made total sense. She's not in the Bible, but her name is Karma. "Not sure."

"Well ..." Kael straightened the tins of popcorn by the windows. "I don't believe in marriage."

"That's just your way of saying you don't want to be monogamous."

"No. It's my way of saying I'm not a fan of marriage. Beyond shared insurance and hospital visits, I just don't get it. Besides ... I'm not entirely sure humans are meant to mate for life. I think sometimes it works out that way for different reasons, but if you look at the rate of divorce and cheating, it speaks a different truth."

"Love."

He shook his head. "You don't have to be married to love someone."

"No, but maybe you want to be married *because* you love them."

"Why?"

"I just told you."

"Live with them. Sleep in the same bed. Have lots of sex. Hold hands. Make meals together. Whatever ... but why the need to be legally bound to them like property?"

"Well, for one ... religion."

"A lot of religious marriages end in divorce. So what do those vows really mean if you're not truly staying together forever? Is it just a certificate to have sex? Is it just the marriage-before-sex thing? Seems like a lot of time and effort just to rub genitals."

I snorted a laugh. "*Now* I know why you're not married."

"Don't you worry about it. I have a romantic side."

"Not worried. Don't care."

He disappeared around a display. "I'm thirty."

I cringed. Thirty ... I had sex dreams about a thirty-year-old.

Kael's head poked around the corner, and he grinned. "I know you've been dying to know my age."

"Dying is a strong word. But don't think it means I'm going to tell you my age."

"I don't care about your age. But ... you have three kids in college, and you said you got pregnant pretty young, so you have to be in your early forties."

"So ... does no marriage mean no kids for you?"

He removed his beanie, revealing his messy dark hair, and he tried on an Epperly baseball cap. "Humans suck at conserving. We like to overconsume and pop out kids. It's not sustainable. So ... no kids."

"Maybe you should have been a priest."

Kael smirked, still wearing the Epperly hat. "I like sex too much."

Squinting, I pointed a finger at him. "I knew it wasn't really marriage that bothers you the most. It's monogamy."

"It's mating for life, and they're often one and the same. But they don't have to be. There are open marriages. There are also people who never get married but choose to be with the same person for life. Freedom of choice. That's why I'm a little anti-marriage. If I'm going to be with someone, I want it to be a conscious choice every day. 'Til death do us part is a little crazy in my mind."

"So if one day you don't want to be with them ... that's it? All over? A small fight means you're done?"

"I don't think people get divorced because of a fight. They get divorced because of all the little stuff that adds up over time. And why wouldn't it add up over time? You agreed to forever to be with this person. No rush to call them out on their shit or vice versa."

He had no idea how hard those words hit me. Four people ... only four people knew.

Kael edged his way closer to the checkout. "My friend Meg from high school left her husband after five years of marriage. The first two were good, the last three were miserable *because* they were married, and that little legal document made them feel *accountable*. Her word. Mine would be guilty. He died six months ago from a stroke. The last time I saw her she said, 'I miss him, but only because there are fifty unfinished projects around our house.'"

The corners of my mouth quirked. Another woman being brutally honest about her feelings.

Kael started piling stuff onto my counter.

"What are you doing?"

"Buying some things. Isn't this a store?"

Yes. It was a store that had been open for thirty minutes on a Sunday during the holidays and no customers—even with the competition closed.

"Thought you didn't eat this stuff?"

He held up a roll of beef sausage. "This good?"

"Not sure. I haven't tried it."

His right eyebrow lifted a fraction. "How about that cheese?" He nodded toward the tub of cheddar he'd set on the counter.

"Do you want Elsie's answer or Mrs. Smith's, owner of the store, answer?"

"You don't eat the stuff you sell?" His hazel eyes widened.

"Again, do you want Elsie's answer or Mrs. Smith's, owner of the store, answer?"

Pinning me with his unblinking gaze, he held out his hand. "Scissors."

"What are you doing?"

"Just give me some scissors."

I retrieved scissors from the top drawer and handed them to him. He snipped the closure to the beef stick and peeled back the wrapping before holding it to my face. "Take a bite and tell me if I should buy it for my dad."

My nose wrinkled and I stepped back. "It's one of our best sellers."

"Thank you, Mrs. Smith. But right now, I want Elsie to taste this and tell me what she thinks of it."

I drank lemon water every morning. I ate mostly whole foods that didn't need a label. My meat consumption was borderline vegan. That roll of meat had enough sodium in it to give half the town of Epperly a stroke.

"You will pay for that since you opened it."

"You should take a bite, have a food orgasm, and cut up the rest as samples for your customers, so they can have a food orgasm too."

My comeback readied itself as I glared at him—a racehorse eager at the gate, but the bell never sounded. Customers? What customers?

"I think it's alarming that we've had four encounters and you've used the word orgasm twice."

Amusement played along his lips. "I think it's notable that you're keeping a record of our encounters. If you would have asked me to put a number to it in less than a second, I wouldn't have been able to do it. I'm flattered, Mrs. Smith."

My formal name coming from him sounded dirty and forbidden, like a student hot for their teacher. It made my whole face wrinkle in disgust. Kael was twelve years my junior. I could have been his teacher.

I snatched the partially opened beef stick from his hand and scanned it along with the other items on the counter before shoving them into a bag. "Eighty-two dollars and ninety-five cents."

Kael held a cocky expression on his face that leaned toward complete amusement. "It's like a chef who won't eat her own food. A baker not tasting the batter." He tapped his credit card on the reader.

My eyes wanted to roll, but I remained visually unaffected as I handed him the receipt. "Have a nice day."

Kael plucked the receipt from my hand and dropped it into the bag. "We haven't discussed cross-promotion yet."

"I think we stick with fad food and *classics* since you like that word."

"Fad food? You mean healthier food?"

"I mean overpriced trendy food."

His lips parted as if to speak, but nothing came out for several seconds. "Why do I sense anger in your words? Have I done something wrong?"

The nerve ...

"Epperly is a small town, in case you haven't noticed, so someone opening a specialty food store across the street from mine doesn't exactly make me happy."

He chuckled and scratched his scruffy neck. "In case *you* haven't noticed, we don't exactly sell the same products. You don't see decorative tins of popcorn and tubs of cheese piled on my shelves, do you?"

"That's not the point." I crossed my arms over my chest. "You sell specialty food items that people buy for gifts. So if Joe Blow wants to buy his wife a gift for Christmas, he's going to either buy something from your store or something from my store, but it's unlikely he makes purchases at both places."

After a few unreadable blinks, he smiled. "Joe Blow lives in Epperly? The famous Joe Blow?"

My scowl intensified.

"Do Jane and John Doe live here too? What about the Joneses? Mr. and Mrs. X? I bet Mr. and Mrs. Buttinski live here for sure or at least have a vacation home here."

"I'm going to take you down." Yeah, those words fell from my lips. When I heard them, I didn't recognize my own voice. Who was that woman boiling over with anger?

"Take me down?" He laughed. "Okay. Just be careful. Women your age can easily break their hips."

Women your age?!

"You are nothing but a wolf in sheep's clothing, and I'm going to expose you to the whole town until they run you out!"

For real. Who was that woman saying such crazy things? Adrenaline hijacked my brain until the craziest nonsense shot from my mouth. But I couldn't take it back. I had to own it.

His expression morphed from playful to the way one looked at a lunatic. "Um ... okay." He shrugged. "I mean ... I do like a good wool sweater and warm socks."

"Get out." I tipped my chin up as my eyes narrowed into pinpoints.

His smirky lips rubbed together before he zipped up his coat, grabbed his bag, and sauntered out the door. The bell dinged and a gust of cool air swept through the store, diluting the potent cinnamon scent from the potpourri.

It didn't help my insane case when he made a point to smile and greet every person he encountered in the square like he'd never met a stranger. They loved him, falling hard for his superhero charm. That was it. I needed to be more charming.

And I needed to bone up on my marketing skills to outsmart him. Sometimes products sold themselves, but more often, genius marketing was what made people open their wallets during the holidays.

And for the love of my future mental health, I needed to stop with the sex dreams.

CHAPTER eight

I married a slurper, and now I want to murder him every morning.

"It's sexual tension."

I rammed my elbow into Amie's arm on our brisk walk at seven in the morning—coats, boots, yoga pants, warm headbands, and Meadow pulling the hell out of my non-ramming arm. "There is nothing sexual about us. I'm twelve years older than him. He's trying to run me out of business. And ..."

"And? That's it? Age and free enterprise?"

"Free enterprise? Don't say it like that. In a big city, it's free enterprise. In Epperly, it's ruthless thievery. He's stealing my customers! There are not enough people in this town to keep both of us in business."

"And that's a bad thing?"

My head whipped to the side, and I pumped my arms harder as Meadow propelled forward. The smell of exhaust gagged me when a diesel truck barreled down the road past us, tires kicking up moisture and sand left from our first snow of the season. "Is what a bad thing? Going out of business?"

"You want out, and you know it. This could be your chance. No one would blame you. It's life. Out with the old, in with the new. Established businesses go under all the time because someone with a better idea, a better product, comes along."

"Craig kept it going. Maybe I need to offer free shipping on all orders—expand our delivery. *Not* that anyone is buying anything to be shipped or delivered. We've had less than ten monthly box subscriptions this whole year. The. Whole. Year!"

"That's your ego, Elsie. The signs are everywhere. You're not Craig. You don't live and breathe that store, and people know that."

"Craig's parents don't know that."

"His mom has cholesterol off the charts, and his dad has lost most of his hearing *and* struggles with dementia. The truth? They need to be in assisted living. You think they're sitting around all day thinking about the store they had years ago, but they're not. They're focused on taking their pills every day and remembering where they put the TV remote."

"Now you sound like Craig." I frowned.

"He wasn't wrong. You have this innate need and capacity to take care of people and nurture them. But sometimes you forget to nurture yourself."

"That's what I was trying to do and look how that turned out."

"So you stumbled. Get up and try again."

I laughed. "Stumbled? I vented all my anger to my

husband, he stormed out and died in a car accident, and you call that a stumble?"

Amie grabbed my arm and pulled me to a halt, facing her while Meadow tried to keep going by ripping off my other arm. "Everybody dies, Elsie. And few die at the perfect time ... if there is such a thing. You want to talk about thievery? Let me introduce you to a little monster called regret. The last thing it wants is for you to be happy. If you let it, it will ravage your soul. There's always more to be said, one last kiss, one last hug. Don't go to bed angry. Don't walk out the door with anything unsettled. Don't fucking blink. Don't be *human*. If you live your life in fear, it's not a real life. Fear will rob your joy. Regret will cripple your happiness. Let. It. Go."

It had been a while since I cried over Craig, but Amie pulled a few tears out of me. "Maybe I don't deserve joy and happiness."

She released my arm and took a step back, slowly shaking her head. "Then drive your car off a bridge. Slit your writs. Put a bullet in your head. Find yourself worthy, or stop taking up space and stealing precious oxygen."

Swallowing hard, my emotions doubled. Hot tears raced down my cold cheeks. Watery snot slid over my lips.

"You are loved, Elsie. And the people who love you want nothing more than for you to love yourself." She pressed her mittens to my cheeks as redness filled her eyes. "Live, Elsie. Truly *live*."

"K," I managed past the lump in my throat just as she hugged me.

"And have sex. Lots of middle-aged, carefree, sex."

My laugh came out as a partial sob.

"The cafe has hot cider today. I'm going to get one. Can I get you one too?" I asked Kandi as she stared aimlessly around the empty store.

We'd been open three hours and only one customer had come in ... to return something.

"I'm good, but thanks."

"I won't be gone long."

"Take your time." She winced the second the words left her mouth.

The elephant in the room.

She could do the math. The shop was losing money ... paying her to babysit an idle door.

I grabbed a hot cider and made a casual stroll around the square.

"Spying on your competition?"

"Jeez!" I jumped and some of my hot cider spit out from the lid.

Bella cringed at the cider on my gloved hand. "Sorry. Figured you heard me coming up behind you."

"Well, I didn't." I wiped off my glove and licked the pooled cider on the lid. "Why aren't you in school?"

"It was an early out day. Thought I'd help out at the shop, but you weren't there. Kandi said you went for cider. And where are all the customers?"

"Here." I scowled through the window of *What Did You Expect?* as we inched our way along the sidewalk.

"Jaden said the owner is hot. Let's have a look."

My arm dove for hers, but it was too late. She pulled open the door, drawing attention to us.

"Whoa ..." she whispered as the enemy eyed us for a brief moment before returning his attention to the mile-long line of customers. "This place is so cool."

"So cool. Sure, Bella. Because you know so much about spices, vinegars, and olive oils. It's overpriced and impractical. Who wants vinegar in their Christmas stocking?"

Truth? I *loved* everything at his store. That was why I hated him so much. It was complicated.

"Well, they have chocolate." She glanced over her shoulder and winked at me before plucking a sample square from the dish. "Mmm ... better than sex."

I pinched the skin on the back of her arm through her jacket.

"Ouch! What?"

"Could you lower your voice a few notches. And how would you know what sex is like?" I murmured close to her ear.

"Um ... how do you think?" Bella scuffed her Ugg boots along the wood parquet floor.

"You've had sex?"

"Shh ..." Bella hissed while continuing to peruse the aisles. "Now who needs to lower her voice?"

"Can I help you ladies with anything?"

I kept my back to Kael, but my sexually active teenager spun around and batted her eyelashes at him like I used to do to her dad.

"You must be Bella." How awesome of him to remember her name.

"Yes." She unzipped her jacket, pulled back her shoulders, thus shoving out her chest, and offered her hand.

My jaw dropped at her brazen little move. Did I raise a hussy? Of course, I loved her more than life, but the thought did enter my mind.

"I'm Kael. It's nice to meet you." He shook her hand.

Bella giggled.

Whoa!

Why was she giggling?

And why was he holding her hand for so long? And *looking* at her like he'd looked at me?

"Nice to meet you too." She tipped her chin to her chest and cocked her head to the side. Things were not good. Not good at all.

I cleared my throat and eyed their joined hands. "It's the start of flu season. I'm not sure handshaking is advised by the CDC."

The human mom had no boundaries when it came to protecting her young. And Bella was young and in need of protection from the vegetable-named gawker giving her *way* too much attention. We needed to get out of there and go straight to the doctor for pregnancy and STD testing. I knew it would happen. I knew Craig's overprotectiveness and shaming at church would drive her in the direction of promiscuity. He refused to let her be on birth control, and religion taught abstinence.

"Sorry, Mrs. Smith." He released her hand.

I glared at him through narrowed eyes for a few seconds when Bella wasn't looking at me.

"I love your store. It's so modern and … clean."

Clean? Was my daughter implying my store was dirty?

"Thanks. We basically gutted the inside, left the exposed ceilings and duct work to give it a modern feel, and added more windows. I laid the flooring myself." He tapped it with his foot.

"It's beautiful." Bella dropped her gaze to admire it.

"The carpet we removed was the most disgusting thing I'd ever seen. Talk about bad vibes from the moment you walk into a store."

Bella laughed. "See, Mom ... maybe if you'd get rid of the carpet, more people would come to the store."

After her pregnancy and STD tests, we were going to talk about her lack of respect for the business that fed her for eighteen years.

"Oh, sorry, Mrs. Smith ... I forgot you have carpet over there. My apologies. I didn't mean for my observations to sound so harsh."

He did. And I could see it in his barely restrained smirk and twinkle of asshole in his eyes.

"It's fine. Your generation has no filter. I wouldn't expect anything less. When you grow up, you'll learn to think before you speak."

"Mom ..." Bella's eyes widened. "That's rude."

It was rude, but necessary.

"Crap ..." Bella glanced at her phone. "I forgot I told Nila we could hang out. She's waiting for me. I gotta run. Bye, Mom." Bella kissed me on the cheek. It was one respectful and loving thing she still retained. "Nice meeting you, Kael. I'll be back later to buy some stuff."

The girl had no money. Was she really going to muster the nerve to ask me for money to buy goods from my competitor?

"It was nice to meet you too, Bella."

Kael and I watched her exit his store.

"Stay away from my daughter." I snapped my attention back to him.

"Uh ..." he chuckled. "Okay. That will be hard if she stops by again."

"You know what I mean. I saw the way you looked at her. She's a young girl."

"I thought you said she's eighteen."

"Listen, perv ..." I glared at him, stabbing my finger into his chest. "She's a senior in *high school.*"

He glanced down at my finger pressed to his white apron, a smile on his lips mocking me. "You think I'm interested in your daughter?"

A customer passing us stole our attention, and we smiled at her on cue as I withdrew my finger.

Lowering my voice, I made a quick glance around to see if anyone else was in earshot. "I think you sell products because you flirt with anything that moves."

His lips pursed to the side as if I wasn't speaking English. "You know what I think? I think you're upset that I'm nice to people. I think marriage and years of fearing God has made you paranoid that if you smile too big or shake someone's hand too long, people will think you're flirting and therefore cheating. Maybe if you smiled like you were offering your customers more than stale popcorn, even if you're not, then you'd see long lines at your shop again. I bet your husband knew how to smile at customers. Now ... I have work to do. Thanks for stopping by." He winked. *Winked* at me like he was selling more than vinegar and oil.

That wasn't part of Marketing 101. There was another word for his level of ruthlessness. I needed a few minutes to unpack all the nonsense from his little speech, so I headed back to my store, mumbling to myself the whole way. "Craig did not flirt to get customers and sell products."

Did he?

"Oh, Elsie ... wait up!"

I stopped ten feet from the door to my shop and spun around. "Rach, what's up?" I opened my arms and hugged one of my good friends from high school whom I hadn't seen in years. "Did you move back here? Or are you just visiting?"

"I lost my job, so I had to move back home. How embarrassing, right? I have one child in college and another who got married last year, and I'm living with my parents ... at forty-two!"

I jerked my head toward my shop. "I'm running the Smith family business that has *no* business and apparently terrible carpet. No husband. Kids are basically grown. Bella just informed me that she's not a virgin. And my parents now have a place in Arizona, so I see them during the summer and on Christmas. When Bella goes to college next year, I might quit my job and go live with them, so really ... it's life."

Rachel laughed. "Who knew the forties would be such a shit show. And who knew you would be the talk of the town." She rolled her lips together and eyed me with wide blue eyes.

"What do you mean?"

"My mom said you're in a support group at church, and you brought out the evil side in some of the widows."

I coughed a laugh. "Um ..."

"It's fine." She waved off my stuttered response. "It

stirred up some good conversation between us. I can't believe all the stuff my dad has done over the years that drives her crazy, and I never knew. Like his slurping. She said that first cup of coffee in the morning touches her soul, and she likes to enjoy it in a quiet kitchen, slowly bringing her senses to life for a new day. But then my dad wakes up, pours himself a cup, and slurps it over and over again. She said she's seriously considered diving across the table and strangling him. Slurp. Slurp. Sluuurrrppp. And I totally relate because Trace used to slurp his smoothie every morning. And he chewed with his mouth open, whole body hunched over his plate like a caveman, constantly smacking and slurping. God ... he was so loud. Then he'd lift his plate and lick it, kid you not ... lick it clean. *Even* in restaurants. And I just sat there with this grimace of disgust stuck to my face, and he'd have the nerve to say, 'What?' Then one day ... I answered his what. The next day we decided to end our marriage."

She was my person. I could tell her my truth, and she wouldn't judge me. But just as I started to say something, the shop door opened behind me.

"Elsie, I'm not feeling so well."

I turned toward Kandi and her pale, almost green, complexion. "You can go home. Need a ride?"

She shook her head. "I think I can make it home."

"No. Call your mom." I turned back to Rachel. "I have to go, but we should get together soon and talk more."

"Absolutely. I've got to get to work, but maybe I'll stop by your shop later and get your number."

I noticed she pointed over her shoulder when she said *get to work*.

"Where are you working?"

"The new place. *What Did You Expect?* It's amazing! Have you had a chance to check it out yet? And don't *even* get me started on Kael, the owner. He's so freaking hot. Young-ish, but so hot. And nice. Gah! The guy will do anything for anyone. Izzy Stanton said he removed dead limbs from her tree and fixed her broken front porch steps. And she didn't ask him to do it. He just noticed she needed some help around the place."

"Does he know she's married?"

"Why?" Rachel laughed. "You think he did it to get into her pants? I'm pretty sure he knows Lane is in the service and hasn't been home in over a year. Epperly has grown since I moved away fifteen years ago, but it's still a small town. I think he's just genuinely a nice guy. He changed Violet Ryan's flat tire two days ago. He fixed Arnie's and Mable's bent windmill and raked their huge yard before the snow. And Tess Jacob needed a ride to Fullerton last week, and Kael drove her two hours there, waited another two hours while she visited her daughter in the hospital, and drove her back home. He's a saint. And single." She waggled her eyebrows.

I had no comeback for his saintly actions. "He's single because he doesn't believe in monogamy."

"What?" Rachel drew her head back.

"It's a long story. I'll share it later."

"You better. Bye, Elsie."

CHAPTER nine

I take care of three young kids, cook, and clean. I shouldn't have to dominate him in the bedroom too. Grow a pair, buddy!

THE UPSIDE to having grown kids—they were rarely home. The downside to having grown kids—they were rarely home. I liked my space—a quiet house—but I missed my people. I missed stories about their day, even if it was a bad day. I missed watching a rerun on TV while we cleaned up after dinner before taking Meadow for her evening walk. I missed the home that used to be my house.

And I wasn't alone, as was evidenced by the full room of widows at our weekly support meeting.

"Tonight, I want to talk about moving forward with the grace of God leading us," Rhonda opened the meeting. "I know it's too soon for some of you, but others have approached me privately about this. So I think it's something worth discussing. Our husbands would have wanted us to be happy. And everyone has a different definition of happiness. But if yours involves finding love again, then you shouldn't feel ashamed or hindered by guilt. It's possible to move on and love again if you pray for it to happen, and you let God help open your heart to someone special. A lot of women in our congregation have gone on to find love and marry again. One person in the group (who shall remain anonymous) called me last week with something heavy on her heart—intimacy. And I think this is a need that doesn't go away just because we lose our spouse. So I want all of you to know ... it's okay. It's okay to remarry. Some of you are so young, it would be heartbreaking to think of you giving up on love and a family. So ... who wants to go first on this topic tonight?"

Everyone sat in silence for several awkward minutes.

"What if ..." Kelly bit her thumbnail and wrinkled her nose.

"Yes, Kelly?" Rhonda prompted her. "There is no judgment, honey. This is a safe place."

It wasn't a safe place. It was the opposite of a safe place. It was a prayer room, a room to judge and be judged. We all knew it.

"What if I want intimacy, but I don't want the uh ... other stuff?"

"Sorry, I'm not following," Rhonda said. "What do you mean other stuff?"

"Well, like ... marriage. I'm not sure I want to be married again."

"Why not?"

She shrugged, squirming in her seat. "It was exhausting. And I like my space. I like my time alone. I didn't need it so much when I was younger, but now I do. But sometimes I just want ... intimacy."

Rhonda nodded slowly and folded her hands on her

crossed leg. "Maybe you could find an online pen pal or join a club. The church has a coed volleyball team for singles that you could join and find someone who might enjoy occasional stimulating conversation. Before my husband and I got married, we used to meet at a park and watch the birds and squirrels for hours while discussing the second coming of Christ. I would walk home feeling so intellectually satisfied." Rhonda let out a slow sigh of contentment.

Bethanne raised her hand slowly. We didn't have to raise hands.

"Yes, Bethanne?"

Bethanne cleared her throat and shifted her attention to me. Why me? I had no idea, but it drew everyone else's attention to me as well. And I started to sweat.

"I think ... I think what Kelly means ..." Bethanne cleared her throat again, wringing her hands together. "Well, I think since Elsie took the first step in really opening up our group to *honest* discussion by being brave in the face of the unknown, I want to do the same. So I'm just going to say it."

I had no idea where she was going with any of her nonsense. My intentions were never to open the group up to some greater level of honesty. I wasn't a hero or role model. I made a mistake. Period.

"Sex. Kelly wants sex. That's what she means by intimacy. Not marriage. Not commitment. Not stimulating conversation while watching wildlife. She wants to feel a man inside of her again."

Well done, Bethanne. My *honesty* garnered a few wide eyes. But Bethanne's honesty drew a collective gasp from nearly everyone in the room, but none louder than Rhonda.

"Oh stop!" Bethanne went from nervous Nellie to an errant child not happy about being told she has to go to bed early. "I know we are in a church, but this group isn't a sermon. And we've all had sex. Why can't we call it that? Why can't we be honest about our feelings regarding it? Either our hidden gratitude that we never have to have it again or our secret desire to have it with every guy we lay eyes on."

And there it was ... the Elsie moment. The moment when you just vomited your unfiltered emotions onto the group and prayed someone threw you a lifeline by admitting they, too, have had similar feelings.

Right.

Wrong.

Or just incredibly needy and *human.*

Validation meant everything when you felt completely cut off from the world.

"Kelly, maybe you should—" Rhonda began to make her mandatory intervention, but I threw poor Kelly a lifeline first.

"I miss sex. I miss the warm fullness that just can't be duplicated with something from Amazon. I miss the way my nipples get really hard and sensitive from a single touch. I miss the heavy feeling slowly growing between my legs, all warm and tingly. I miss falling off that cliff as my eyes roll back in my head, my jaw goes slack, and my toes curl. I miss the moan of pleasure from another human finding me so sexy."

"I miss having someone take charge." Pauline sighed. "Toby and I were going through a rough patch a few years before he died. We saw a counselor, and she walked us through some exercises to help open up our lines of communication. Come to find out ... I just wanted a night to myself to take a hot bath without hearing my kids screaming and to enjoy a good book. Toby ... well, he wanted to be dominated in bed. I took care of three young kids, cooked, and cleaned. I shouldn't have had to dominate him in the bedroom too. My whole day involved being in charge, in control, on alert. I just wanted someone else to take charge once we got into bed. I wanted him to grow a pair."

A few of the women sniggered.

"Ladies, this is highly inapprop—" Rhonda made another attempt to diffuse the conversation.

"Well, I just want everyone to remember, most of us have children. This is a small town. And God is *always* watching. So maybe instead of ordering things from Amazon and missing things that are purely selfish and physical, you should spend more time in prayer, giving thanks for what really matters. What would Jesus do?" Aurora was basically a slightly younger version of Rhonda. I had a hard time imagining either one of them actually letting go of their inhibitions, spreading their legs, and allowing a penis to enter their bodies.

"And ..." Rhonda jumped in on the wake of Aurora's big speech. "Please take some time and spend it in the word of God to cleanse your minds from all the impurity of sexual immorality. The marriage bed is sacred. We need to pray for each other, that the Lord will deliver to you a God-fearing man if that's what your heart desires. But we cannot and should not encourage sexual intercourse or any other kind of sexual immorality outside of marriage. Just because you are no longer virgins, doesn't mean that it's okay to commit sexual sins—in real life or in your mind."

Great. I had to magically control my mind while sleeping. It wasn't like I hadn't prayed for G-rated dreams and pure thoughts. I had. A lot. God was clearly busy with bigger things than my hate-lust relationship with Kael. Besides, after Craig died (thanks to my perfect meltdown timing), I'd been questioning the status of my salvation.

My non-virgin daughter wasn't home when I walked into the nearly empty house. Meadow greeted me for five seconds, and then she disappeared, returning silence to my new existence. After perusing the lackluster contents of my fridge, I ordered takeout and stopped by the store on my way so I had some fresh fruit for the next morning.

"Great minds ..." Kael pushed open the door to the Mexican restaurant just as I grabbed the handle to open it. Spices and the aroma of charred meat and chilies wafted past me along with the heat from the crowded building. "After you, Mrs. Smith." He stepped back and held it open for me.

My hackles were up, but my tongue remained idle because of all the things Rachel said about his Good Samaritan work in Epperly for people who really needed it.

Dang it! I was a sucker for that sort of kindness, hence the reason I was still working at a store I didn't love for in-laws that I *did* love. It was the reason they were still in their house, and the reason I took care of their chores and did their grocery shopping.

But ... I wasn't a sucker for *him*, so I forced a tight smile and brief eye contact as I stepped inside the restaurant. A soft "thank you" squeaked past my throat, showing my own unavoidable kindness.

Before he could say anything, I hustled to the takeout counter and breathed a sigh of relief. My body did weird things around him—things I didn't consciously welcome. It was all the sex talk at the church meeting earlier. Sex talk and church in the same sentence—never saw that coming.

After paying for my half-order of veggie fajitas and guacamole, I snagged my to-go bag and headed outside to my vehicle just as a new round of snow fell from the night sky. Epperly wasn't immune to early lake-effect snow. After scorching heat and drought all summer, most everyone welcomed the moisture and cooler temperatures.

"Heard we're supposed to get another foot or so."

That voice. How did God expect me to keep my dreams clean and thoughts pure with Satan, disguised as Captain America, and constantly breathing down my neck?

I ignored him as I opened the door to my SUV.

"Want me to plow your driveway in the morning?"

"No. No. No. No," I whispered only to myself as my impure mind let other plowing images come to life. Keeping my head in the vehicle, I set the bag on the passenger's seat and took several deep breaths.

Sexual immorality. Sexual immorality. Sexual immorality.

As I stood straight again, he shut his truck door and

sauntered toward me, looking entirely too hot and *young* in his cargo pants, tan boots, pullover jacket, and beanie. Without the beard, I felt certain he would have looked fifteen.

"I have a snowblower, but thanks." I tugged at my scarf, cringing at the itchiness against my sweaty skin.

"It's no big deal. Three swipes." He wet his lips.

Why? Why wet your lips and say three swipes?

"I'll be in and out in no time."

Please, God ... make it stop!

With a nervous laugh, I averted my gaze. "I can do it myself." Biting my lips together, I closed my eyes for a few seconds. I had to hope he wasn't interpreting my words with the maturity of a teenager like I'd been doing.

Kael innocently referenced snow removal while I imagined sex the whole time.

He took two steps closer, resting his hand on the top of my open door. "I'm sure you can, but why go to all that work when I'm right here ... offering to do it for you?"

On a nervous laugh, I yanked my scarf completely off. Steam rose from my body like a hot tub at a ski resort. "I'm sure you can." My gaze avoided his like repelling magnets.

"What's that look about?"

I shook my head.

"Are you..." he pressed his finger under my chin and lifted my head "...blushing?"

"No." My gulp did nothing to make my response believable.

His gaze danced along my face as he left his finger under my chin. A smile captured his mouth the way my lips wanted to capture it.

No. No. No. No!

"Come over to my house."

"W-why?" My numb tongue stumbled over the shock of his invitation.

"Because it's eight o'clock and we have nothing better to do." The bend of his lips intensified into pure sin.

My nervous laugh made an encore performance. "Sorry. I'm not following. You're inviting me over to your house to eat my dinner?"

"Sure. That too."

"No." I shook my head, breaking our physical connection. "Sorry, you don't get to say 'that too' without further explanation. Call me dense, but you're going to have to spell it out."

"S.E.X."

"With me?" The words flew out on their own.

Kael chuckled. "No. I've invited someone else over for sex. I just thought you'd like to watch."

My eyes narrowed. "Not funny."

"I think if you said yes to watching me have sex with someone else, some people would find it quite hilarious. Not a lot." His lips twisted. "But a few people in this town have a solid sense of humor."

"You're my nemesis. Twelve years younger than me. And my side of guacamole is going to go brown if I don't get home soon and eat it."

"Brown guacamole would be a serious shame."

My head dipped into a weary nod—my reluctant gaze glued to his, measuring his reaction, gauging his sincerity. It wasn't that I thought his offer wasn't real—even if being the recipient of Saturday shaboink for so many years had chipped away at my sense of self-esteem. His angle interested me the most.

Why me?

Epperly wasn't a huge town, but it was home to a fair number of single women in his age group.

Why the widow with four kids?

"Maybe I can be your nemesis during the day, but at night ..."

That stupid grin. No wonder all the women in town were buying up his inventory. Snake charmer.

"I'm out of your league." I mentally high-fived myself so hard my head spun. I didn't say the *why me*. I thought it, but I didn't let him see anything but my artificial confidence—as satisfying as a diet soda.

Not older.

Not wrinkled.

Not flabby.

Out of his league.

Brilliant!

His laugh. That smile. The visceral energy he exuded. I wasn't immune to any of it.

"I'll give you that. So what does one have to do to get into the major league with you?"

"Look ..." I drew in a confident breath and found words to match my age and expected level of maturity. "I don't know how things work in your world, but in mine ... I have kids, and a dog, and responsibilities that involve making smart decisions. And I'm fairly certain that what you're suggesting isn't smart or mature or really even sane. So I'm going to have to pass on your offer or invitation or whatever it is that you just suggested."

"I suggested you come to my house for sex. But I can take a raincheck if you're busy tonight."

A weird feeling settled in my chest and tickled my tummy. Giddiness ... maybe. It was hard to say. I couldn't remember the last time someone made me feel that way. Craig did when we met. He had this confidence that rode the arrogant line without completely crossing over into the asshole category.

Confidence.

I missed a confident man. Maybe I became Craig's safe place in life. Owning a business and doing things like starting equipment with pull cords probably zapped all his alpha energy, leaving me with the leftovers—insecure sex commentary and painful indecisiveness.

Kael exuded confidence, and that by itself made it unlikely that I wouldn't repeat my immoral dreams. Adding in the Captain America resemblance and the recent discovery that he had a thing for Good Samaritan work ... it pretty much left me doomed to do something stupid.

"A part of me wants your business to go under. Do you still want to have sex with me?"

His eyes, along with his white teeth, illuminated the night sky. My words seemed to have the opposite of their intended effect. "Elsie, I nearly fucked you in your shop the day you said you were going to take me down. I would be epically disappointed if you surrendered your obsessive desire to destroy me."

Over twenty years of marriage, not once did Craig use the f-word in reference to sex with me. I think it would have seemed a little crass. That wasn't us. We had sex and made love. Sometimes we'd "do it." However, I would have preferred "fuck" to "shaboink" any day of the week.

Clearing my throat, my shaky hand curled my hair behind my ear. "I uh ... was there that day in my shop. And I can say for certain that you were nowhere close to doing ... *that* to me ... with me." I shook my head as I tripped over my words. "Whatever."

His head canted to the side. "Really? Huh. I'm usually not wrong about those vibes. Like now. It's in the thirties and snowing, but you're burning up, ripping off your scarf and unzipping your jacket. If I were to take a guess, I'd say you're thinking about me in ways that make you feel irresponsible and rather hot."

I wasn't hot. I was an inferno. "I need to go. My fajitas are getting cold."

Kael's tongue grazed his lower lip. "Follow me to my house. I can warm up your fajita."

My age crept up on me like I knew it would if I spent too much time in his company. A big part of me knew he wasn't referring to anything in my to-go bag, but I wasn't aware of slang meanings for fajita. Possibly vagina—just based on the shape—but that wasn't enough to give me the confidence I needed to land a solid accusation.

"I'm going home to eat it. I mean ..." I cringed. "The fajitas in the bag. The ones I just picked up inside."

Kael laughed a little, and it elicited actual sweat between my cleavage. "Do you have another fajita? Is that why you're having issues forming complete sentences?"

I narrowed my eyes. "I don't know. Do I have another fajita?"

When the skin at the bridge of his nose wrinkled, I

realized he was only referring to the actual food I ordered.

Kill. Me. Now!

"I have to go." I leapt into my SUV and sped out of the parking lot, fishtailing a bit from the accumulating snow. In a year's time, I'd gone from feeling stuck and suffocated in a lifeless marriage to unimaginable grief and guilt to ... Kael. He knocked me off-kilter, barged into my passive dreams, and turned them into pure sin.

His smile.

His laugh.

The mischief in those eyes.

The *offer!*

Since when did people start throwing out offers for sex as casually as suggesting a cup of coffee?

CHAPTER ten

I loved him in all his forms as he had always loved me in my many forms. It was the blatant letting go of everything and the gross stuff that came with it that he didn't try to hide— even a little.

As soon as I stepped through the back door and greeted Meadow, I headed straight to the office and plunked down into the chair, setting my bag of food on the desk two seconds before my fingers glided across the keyboard, doing an internet search for slang meanings of fajita. With the urban dictionary on the screen in front of me, I read over the possibilities as I ate my dinner.

My sexual dinner.

Just as I'd thought, fajita could be interpreted in a distasteful way.

While I finished my dinner, I called Amie and put her on speaker phone.

"I know. It's snowing, so we won't be walking in the morning," she answered her phone as if my call were all too predictable.

"Kael Hendricks offered me sex."

Silence.

More silence.

"Amie?"

"Yeah, I uh ... wow ... so how was it?"

"I didn't have sex with him! Geesh ... do you really see me like that?"

"Like what?" She laughed. "Single. Available. Able. Willing. Yes. I see you as all of those things. Why are you talking to me when you could be In. His. Bed?"

"Seriously? Wow ... where to begin answering your ridiculous question. Let's start with the age gap. Hello! Twelve years. He's my competition. The enemy. He's cocky. I have four children. He doesn't believe in marriage or monogamy."

"You said ... and I quote, 'I'm not ever getting married again, Amie. Don't ever let me even consider it.' And I agreed with you. No need to anchor yourself again after finally seeing a glimpse of freedom. By this time next year, you could be living by yourself. Hell, you practically are now. Do you really sit around at night missing a man?"

"I miss ..." I cut myself off before I spewed out my knee-jerk response that would have landed me in her trap, making her point for her.

"You miss the sex. Just say it. Then I can say WHAT ARE YOU DOING TALKING TO ME?"

"I have kids. Are you not listening to me? What would happen if ... and this is one hundred percent hypothetical ... *if* I had sex with him and my kids, specifically Bella, found out. Not to mention other people in this small, gossip-fueled town? My church family would disown me."

"You don't have to tell anyone. And I highly doubt Kael would run around town flaunting the fact that he nailed you."

I winced. "Nice language. What are you? Fifteen? And why wouldn't he tell people? Do you think he'd be too embarrassed because I'm so much older?"

"For real, Elsie? Are you seriously offended by the notion that he wouldn't tell anyone?"

"This conversation is ridiculous. I'm not sure why I even called you."

Amie chuckled. "Because you wanted me to tell you to have sex with him."

"No."

"Yes. You're just pretending to be offended that I actually think you should do it, but deep down, you're looking for me to validate your feelings."

"Pfft ... and what are my feelings?"

"You tell me. Do you want to have sex with Kael Hendricks?"

Silence.

"You just answered my question."

I sat up straight in the desk chair. "I didn't say anything."

"Exactly. And that breath of silence said everything. Now ... go shave your legs and maybe buzz the muff a bit. Lotion. Perfume. And wear something sexy—which is code for borrow something from Bella."

"What? No. No to shaving and buzzing. No to lotion ... okay, I like lotion, but there will be no perfume because

I'm staying in tonight. And I'm a little taken aback that you think Bella owns sexy things."

"She's eighteen, Elsie. Trust me. She owns things you have never seen. She just doesn't put them on until she's out of the house."

"That's not true." I shook my head, internally dying because I also didn't expect my daughter to lose her virginity in high school and casually mention it to me in a retail store.

The doorbell rang.

Every muscle in my body tensed, and my heart thundered. Since Craig's death, every time the doorbell rang, I replayed the night the police came to my house to give me the devastating news.

"I have to go. Someone's at my door. I hope it's not …" I couldn't even say it.

"Don't go there. I'm sure it's just Bella forgetting her key. Bye, Elsie."

I didn't tell Amie that the back door was unlocked, so I knew it wasn't Bella forgetting her key. And my three boys no longer lived at home. My heart remained lodged in my throat as I made my way to the front door. The knot in my gut told me it wasn't good.

Opening the door, my fears were confirmed. It wasn't good.

"You dropped your scarf on the ground in the parking lot. Figured you might need it to clear your drive in the morning since you rejected my offer."

I snatched the scarf from his hand and started to shut the door with a mumbled "Thank you. Do I want to know how you found my house?"

"Small town. How were your fajitas?"

Stopping with the door opened only about two inches, I peeked one eye out. "Fine. Night."

"You could invite me inside and offer me something warm since I came all this way to return your scarf."

"Cute." I squinted my one peeping eye through the crack in the door. "And by something warm, you mean sex?"

He rubbed his mouth to hide his grin. "You're a ballbuster, and you don't even mean to be. I was thinking tea, coffee, hot chocolate, cider ... but sex would definitely warm me up if that's all you have to offer."

I drank hot lemon water every morning. We hadn't had coffee in the house since Craig died. Bella occasionally grabbed a sugary coffee drink on her way to school. I had no tea. No hot chocolate. No cider.

And as all of that realization hit me, I started to shake with laughter.

Kael glanced around and drew his shoulders close to his ears as the gusting wind intensified, swirling snow in all directions. "I'll take that as a no. See ya around, Elsie." He pivoted and headed toward his truck parked in my driveway.

My phone vibrated in my pocket as I closed the door.

> Bella: Staying the night with Erin. Be home by noon tomorrow.

I frowned at the screen. Why did I suddenly not trust that she was staying with her friend? Oh, that was right. She was sexually active, and I wasn't ready to deal with that.

"It's just the two of us, Meadow." I sighed as I heard the rumble of Kael's truck starting. His huge tailpipes made way more noise than was necessary on my quiet street. Meadow trotted over to the bench under the mirror. She put her front paws on the bench and bit her fleece blanket, pulling it partially off the bench to ... hump it.

"Not cool, Meadow. Not cool at all."

Not only was it not cool that Meadow had a blanket to hump, my daughter was most likely in bed with a guy instead of eating popcorn and watching a chick-flick with Erin.

"Here goes everything ..." I rolled my eyes at myself and opened the front door. Waving my arm above my head, I grimaced against the cold wind as Kael backed out of my driveway.

He stopped, shifted into drive, and pulled back up my drive. He killed the engine and shut off his headlights as he opened the door and hopped out.

"Shit ..." I whispered to myself, my pulse racing. "Shit ... shit ... shit." The reality of what I was about to do made my knees weak and my breaths embarrassingly erratic.

Kael insisted on making his trek back to my door the slowest one ever. "Need something?"

Need? That was a good question. Probably not, but I sure wanted it in the most self-serving way imaginable.

"I don't have anything warm to drink." I hugged my arms to my chest.

His grin swelled as his boots gripped my porch steps. "Where's your daughter?"

"Friend's house." I allowed a matching grin to steal my lips, knowing that once I let it takeover my face, there would be no going back, no erasing it, no acting cool.

His boots kept moving, forcing me back a few steps as he crossed the threshold of my front door.

On a hard swallow, I took three more steps in reverse while he popped off his hat and deposited it on the top of my coat-tree followed by his jacket.

What am I doing? What am I doing?

I feigned confidence as he hunched down to untie his leather hiking boots. I hadn't had sex for nearly a year. And I hadn't had sex for the first time with a guy since I was eighteen. *And* ... I had only had sex with one man my whole life.

Did the younger crowd have sex differently? Were certain positions and particular foreplay moves outdated? Yes. Those thoughts went through my head. My kids loved reminding me how ancient I was from the clothes I wore to the words I spoke. And everything they said went over my head. I didn't speak young person. It took me years to stop calling flip-flops thongs, and apparently videotaping was no longer a thing because there was no longer a tape involved.

No gagging with a spoon.

No barfing out the door.

No more having cows.

And the word grody coming out of my mouth ensured my kids rarely invited their friends over to our house.

"Where are you?"

My gaze snapped up from my mental *videotape* of forty-something insecurities to find Kael in front of me, towering over my short five-three stature by close to a foot. "Just thinking about the twelve years between us."

"Why?" His hand snaked around my neck.

I stiffened, releasing a shaky breath. "Because I'm not sure I will ..." I covered my face with my hands. "*What* am I doing?"

He peeled my hands away from my face. "Finish what you were going to say."

My gaze didn't quite make it to his face. The pressure of looking in his eyes while saying the embarrassing words was too heavy. "I'm not sure I do *things* the way you're used to doing them." Biting my lips together, I closed my eyes. That sounded ridiculous. Utterly ridiculous.

Meadow squeezed between us, and we looked at her between our socked feet. Kael wore a pair of red and gray striped wool socks that made me grin. My socks were wool as well, but light pink and white and super fuzzy.

"This is Meadow."

"Hey, Meadow. I'm going to fuck your mom. Are you good with that?"

There was that word again. I felt it in a physical way—a quivering feverishness, the palpations and jolt of electricity. It felt wrong and forbidden. Yet coming from Kael's mouth, I felt those things in the best possible way. The Saturday shaboink girl craved to be fucked by a Good Samaritan with an uncensored mouth.

Kael's arousal-inducing gaze inched up my body, painting my skin shades of deep pink in its wake.

"You're shaking." He leered at me as my gaze bounced off his several times before sticking for more than three seconds.

"I'm being a bad hostess. Can I get you something?"

"You."

My nerves got the best of me. "Maybe you should

make yourself at home while I go upstairs and change my clothes."

His ear-splitting grin made me feel lightheaded, like a dream. "I don't think clothes are required."

"I need to shave ... some things."

"You don't."

"I didn't brush my teeth after dinner." I cleared my throat as what little confidence I had completely shriveled.

"Turn your brain off." His fingers deftly unbuttoned my jeans and inched down my zipper, causing massive arrhythmia. "I don't want you clean and smooth." His hand made its way down the front of my pants, arresting my breath. "I want you dirty with all your rough, unkept edges. I want a few of the buttons on your shirt to pop off when I'm too impatient to use any sort of dexterity to remove it properly. I want to hear you moan profanities that would make your church friends clutch their pearls."

I wanted the floor beneath me to open and swallow me whole when he touched me where no other man aside from Craig had touched me. Two of his fingers found their way inside of me, and for a few seconds, I felt horrified, completely wrecked by my emotions and my inability to turn off my brain.

"Shut. It. Off." Kael dipped his head and stole my lips and my breath. He didn't ask me how I liked his touch. He didn't ask me a string of questions that didn't matter, that only served to magnify his own insecurities.

This is happening. What am I doing? Should I stop?

My stupid brain ran through the laundry list of insecurities that never revealed themselves with Craig. Not once did I wonder if he thought my vagina was overly stretched from pushing four humans through it. Laxity of my labia also never came to mind until that moment.

Pubic hair.

Stretch marks.

Wrinkles.

Vaginal wall strength.

Thank God I had my own teeth and didn't have to worry about my dentures displacing as his tongue probed my mouth. The fast pace of casual sex left me feeling a little off-kilter, three steps behind.

I knew how to date.

I knew how to have a boyfriend.

A husband.

I knew there was an order—flirting, a first date, hand-holding, kissing, bases to be explored multiple times before going all the way. And "all the way" meant something. It meant you were a couple if that hadn't already been agreed upon.

Sex. Only sex. Casual sex. Get-right-to-it sex. It was all new to me. Having fingers inside of me before a first kiss. What was that? Who did that?

Kael Hendricks and apparently me too.

As each second passed, I lost all ability to judge Bella for doing God only knew what with God only knew who.

"You're overthinking this," Kael murmured as he worked his way down my neck, a faint hint of a smile teasing my skin between kisses.

"How do you know that?" I closed my eyes.

"Because your hands are balled at your sides instead of unzipping my pants." He nibbled along my collarbone.

I relaxed my fists and fumbled, searching for the button and zipper of his cargo pants. "Should we go to my bedroom?" My voice trembled, sounding just as erratic as my fingers felt fumbling with his pants.

"No need." He made tiny steps toward me as I moved backward. We did this dance until the back of my legs hit the sofa. That triumphant grin held strong as he removed his hand from my pants the second I unzipped his, and he hunched down, peeling my jeans, panties, and socks off slowly.

My hands covered my privates.

Kael's eyes shifted upward to meet mine, his mouth a breath away from my hands. "What are you doing?"

"We really should shut off the lights."

"Then I can't see you."

I frowned. "Sex is meant to be felt, not seen."

"I disagree." He tried to tear my hands away, but I locked them into place.

I needed to shave, but that would have made my situation down below more obvious. My laxity issue. The hair hid it, but I didn't want his mouth near me with all that hair. I needed to at least give it a minor trim or run Meadow's defurring brush through it. I shaved it during the summer for swimsuit season, but it was November.

Such a dilemma.

The overgrown bush or the turkey. Yes, turkey. A beakless turkey. The labia was the wattle and the clitoris was the snood. And who wanted to tongue a beakless turkey with all the lights on?

I might have been getting ahead of myself. He hadn't confirmed his intentions. But his face was level with my bearded turkey, so of course my mind went there. The mind was a playground with drug dealers, child molesters, and psychopaths. Anyone who said they never had insane thoughts and crazy images once in a while was a liar. I refused to believe it was just my brain.

However, since I wasn't a lunatic, those thoughts never left my brain. Kael would never *ever* know that my brain detoured in the direction of the similarities between my lady bits and turkeys while he seduced me. At that point, fajita didn't seem so crazy or crude after all.

Kael pushed himself to standing again and rested his hands on his hips with a slow sigh. "This isn't happening, is it?" He eyed me with expectancy. It wasn't a rhetorical question; he expected me to answer. Amusement twitched along his lips, assuring me he wasn't mad.

Just amused.

Had he been able to read my mind, that amusement would have been the snow kicking up behind the back tires of his truck as he sped away from the crazy woman as quickly as possible.

I eased my naked butt onto the sofa and snatched a pillow to cover my exposed bits. "Gah ... I swore if I ever had this kind of chance, I would not talk about my dead husband. But ..."

"But you feel like you're cheating on him."

I shook my head. "No. Not that. You see ... we met in high school. Back then, I was confident and rightly so. I was this petite cheerleader—strong, toned, thick hair, perky boobs. When the star basketball player gave me a second look, I wasn't surprised. I felt worthy. And over the years, we sort of..." I chuckled "...aged and fell apart together. So the thought of you getting a close look at all of me just spooked me for a moment."

After he didn't respond, I risked a glance up at him and his contented smirk. "I mean ... don't get me wrong.

I've worked hard to eat well, exercise, moisturize, do all the age-defying things. It's not that I think I'm grotesque or that I don't have any sex appeal. I'm just not ... thirty."

"Okay." Kael shrugged off his fitted, thermal shirt. "Good talk, Elsie. Are you done?"

My wide-eyed gaze affixed to his midsection. *Hello, man abs. Longtime no see.*

Craig used to have all the abs, a lean, athletic build with perfect muscle definition. By his mid-thirties, he surrendered to beer, regular fried foods with the guys, and he got a little lax on his exercise routine. It wasn't an image or number on a scale. I loved him in all his forms as he had always loved me in my many forms. It was the blatant letting go of *everything* and the gross stuff that came with it that he didn't try to hide even a little.

More flatulence.

More burping.

More body odor—onion breath from his takeout burgers being my not-so-favorite.

"We can just sit naked on the sofa for a while until you feel comfortable." He inched his cargo pants over his hips, and they dropped like a Broadway curtain to his ankles, leaving him in nothing but black briefs and an impressive erection.

As soon as he hooked his thumbs inside the waistband of his briefs to remove them, I snapped out of my ab coma. "Whoa ... wait."

"Don't worry; I've got a condom." He leaned down and retrieved a condom from the back pocket of his cargo pants. "Pregnancy isn't an issue. I've had a vasectomy, but I have to be responsible. I have no idea where you've been."

My mouth fell open and a gasp released. "Me? How dare you—"

He cupped the back of my head and kissed me, pushing me back on the sofa. It took me a few seconds to surrender to the invasion of my mouth, his hips planted between my legs, and the erection behind his briefs stabbing me *right there.*

Poof!

There went my insecurities, crowded out of my head by an urgency to remove the cotton barrier between us. Foreplay used to be a big deal. I needed it. Not at that moment with Kael. I needed him inside of me so badly it ached.

Sex.

I needed sex.

Not love.

Not commitment.

Just. Sex.

And I needed it to be okay—but that need took a backseat to the other needs. I knew I'd work out the details of my sins later.

He tugged off my shirt, popping off a button as promised, and I unhooked my bra in the front, not giving the sad state of my breasts a second thought. Kael didn't seem bothered by them, or the lack of them, as evident by his pleasurable moan when his mouth covered one. My hands explored his backside, slipping into his briefs and claiming as much firm muscle as I could hold.

Maybe he was a midlife crisis.

Maybe he was perspective.

Maybe he was simply a stupid mistake.

I just knew that, in the moment, I didn't only let go of

my incessant worry—I abandoned forty-two years of hard-earned common sense.

His arm shot down to the floor, pressing his hand flat to keep us from rolling off the sofa, but I pushed him in that direction until he somewhat gracefully landed on the floor with me on top of him.

Kissing his mouth.

Kissing his chest and enviable abs.

Kissing along the waistband of his briefs.

Then I pulled them down just far enough to release him before kissing my way back up his chest.

"Condom," he muttered.

"In a sec ..." He felt warm and hard between my legs. I wanted that feeling just for a few seconds as I rubbed myself up and down him. There was nothing special about latex, so I let myself indulge in skin to skin just for a few seconds.

We kissed.

He rocked his hips sliding against me.

Just on the outside.

I rationalized every move.

My hands pressed to the carpet beside his head, and his hands rested on my hips, guiding our movements ... or maybe he was taming mine. I drew back from his lips and tipped my chin to watch us sliding together.

"Condom ..." he whispered through heavy breaths.

I returned a slight nod. "In a sec ... this feels too good."

And I don't know if it was him lifting a little higher with his hips or if it was me sinking a fraction lower with mine, but he sort of ... slipped inside of me. The head of his erection snagged, stopping our motions.

We stared at each other and then down at what was a textbook visual of "just the tip."

"Condom," Kael said with a little strain to his voice, but he didn't move. Not one inch.

"No" was my knee-jerk reply. Followed with a hasty, "I mean, yes. But just ..." I panted like a woman in labor who wasn't supposed to push.

If we didn't move, nothing bad would happen.

If we didn't move, we could just enjoy the most erotic view and *feeling* ever.

If we didn't move ... we wouldn't have needed a condom.

Right?

"Just a sec ..." I was on top. I held the most power.

It. Just. Felt. So. Good.

His left hand fell from my hip and moved to the side. "It's right here." He held the condom in front of my face. "But if you don't want me to use it, I won't."

That grin. *That* was what made me come to my senses. In that moment, he was no longer just some hot, young guy rubbing his naked body against mine. That grin was my nemesis. The bane of my existence as a retail store owner in Epperly. He wanted to see me completely lose myself in the moment—in him.

"The hell you won't." I couldn't even look at him when I said it. Instead, I lifted onto my knees, plucked the packet from his hand, and rolled the condom onto his cock.

Really, that grin had to go. Sure, it was charming and sexy. But I didn't like how it made me feel like a flighty young woman enamored by him. I would stroke his dick for our mutual pleasure, but not his ego.

"Lose the grin and kiss me, you sexy idiot."

Kael doubled down on his grin, keeping it firmly locked in place as he sat up with me straddling him. When I leaned in to kiss him, he moved just enough to deny me.

I narrowed my eyes.

"God ... you're feisty as hell."

Feisty? I could live with that. "You have no idea."

He grabbed my ass harder than anyone had ever grabbed my ass before. And I liked it. Too much, really.

"Let's see whatcha got, Elsie."

My breath caught in my throat when his hands jerked my hips downward onto every inch of him with unmeasurable confidence. Mesmerizing eyes greedily drank up the view of my reaction—heavy eyes, lips parted, and a long moan vibrating from my chest.

Yeah, yeah ... you're a fucking stud, Kael Hendricks.

CHAPTER eleven

I loved my husband despite his inability to undress correctly. And yes ... there was a correct order.

"Well, that was ..." I hooked my bra with my back to Kael as he searched for his clothes scattered around the sofa along with pillows, blankets, and two condom wrappers.

Two.

I hadn't had sex twice in a twenty-four-hour span since Craig and I were in Mexico for our ten-year anniversary.

"Don't leave me hanging. That was what?"

Unforgettable.

Mind-blowing.

Hot as hell.

Sexier than anything I could recall.

"Not what I expected."

His easy laughter filled the otherwise quiet room as I pulled on my jeans. "What did you expect?"

I walked right into that one. A reminder that we were competitors.

"I think I expected to be a little rusty. But I clearly wasn't. I was quite good." All lies. Well, the first part was true. I turned toward him as I fished my arms into my shirt. My mouth remained firm, giving nothing away as I kept my chin up. It was all about appearance.

After he finished pulling on his socks, he stepped toward me, hooking two fingers into the waistband of my jeans to tug me into his chest. My hands splayed over his shirt, head angled toward his face. Still, I held every ounce of confidence as if I really felt it.

"I'm not backing down. It's just sex. It's my family's business. I'll do whatever it takes to get back my customers you've tried to steal."

He rolled his lips together, no doubt hiding a grin. But the playful sparkle in his eyes hid nothing. "Elsie," he adjusted himself. "You're giving me a hard-on again. I'd be disappointed if you rolled over and surrendered. I like you on top ... *taking me down*."

My smart mouth had a comeback. I think the sex boosted my confidence. However, before I could spew more than a tiny sound, his hands held my head between them, and his mouth covered mine. That tongue did wicked things to mine. Even our intimacy felt competitive.

"Stop trying to jump me *again*, Mrs. Smith." He abruptly pulled away and straightened his shirt like a better-dressed man would straighten his tie.

"Stop calling me Mrs. Smith. It makes me sound like your teacher or your best friend's mom. Like a dirty old lady."

"No comment." He smirked and pivoted, taking his cockiness and swagger to the front door where he donned his jacket and boots. "Tell Bella I said hi."

"I will do no such thing. And you will not tell *anyone* about this. It's a one and done."

"We did it twice, *Mrs. Smith*. And I let you lick my cock a few times because you wouldn't stop gawking at it."

No matter how hard I tried to subdue my reaction, my cheeks flushed with heat, crawling up to the tips of my ears. That heat evaporated all moisture in my throat along with my next words.

Kael opened the door and glanced back at me. "Don't fret. I fully intend on plowing your driveway in the morning, and I'll owe you a second one as well." He winked and closed the door.

THE NEXT MORNING, I dragged my ass out of bed with less than an hour to get showered, eat breakfast, and get to work. As promised, my driveway had been plowed. Sex until one in the morning didn't stop Kael from getting up early to remove snow.

When I arrived at the store, there were three customers waiting at the door. "Good morning. Sorry, I'm usually here thirty minutes before opening." I cringed. "Not three."

"It's fine, Elsie." One of the women smiled.

My gaze shifted to her hand and the *Smith's* bag in it. I held open the door for her. "Do you have an exchange or return?"

"Yes. A return." She stomped the snow off her boots and stepped inside.

The other two customers had *Smith's* bags in their hands too. All three ladies lined up at the register as I flipped on the lights, the *Open* sign, and the jolly holiday music.

As I turned on the register, I caught a glimpse of the long line outside of *What Did You Expect?*

"Have you met the owner?" Lilly asked me as she set her bag on the counter with her unopened gift set in it.

"Who's that?" I pretended not to know.

"Mr. Hendricks. He's the nicest guy."

"Yeah, I've heard okay things about him. Is there an issue with the gift set?" I pulled it out of the bag and inspected it.

"I found something else. It's for my in-laws. But I get them the same kind of stuff every year. I just thought I'd mix it up and try something a little different."

"Well, do you want to look around first? Or I can give you back a gift card with credit if you don't have time to browse today?"

Lilly's face wrinkled with discomfort. "Like I said ... I already picked up something else. Can I just get you to refund my credit card?"

"Let me guess. Vinegar and oil?"

Lilly kept her scrunched expression in place as she nodded.

"It's fine. It's new. A fad. A novelty which will quickly wear off."

"How *is* business since ... well ... Craig passed?"

I issued her refund. "It's fine. Why do you ask?"

Lilly pressed her lips together and glanced around the store. Yeah, it was dead.

"Just ... curious."

I handed her the receipt. "Thanks. Happy holidays, Lilly." The fake smile on my face nearly cracked it.

"You too, Elsie." She shoved her wallet into her handbag and started toward the door. "Oh!" Pivoting back around, she smiled. "I've heard you've been quite the inspiration to your church group. Tillie Cunningham is making dinner tomorrow night for Mr. Hendricks. It's the first date she's had since Al died three years ago. She said you gave her the courage to let go and move on."

"*Kael* Hendricks?"

Lilly nodded. "Uh-huh. Can you really imagine two nicer people finding each other?"

I. Really. Couldn't.

As soon as it was time to close up shop later that day, I grabbed my purse, shut off the lights, and locked the door behind me. It didn't matter that I'd had only two hundred dollars in sales that day. Nor did it matter that I had to formulate the most brilliant marketing plan ever to get back my business.

All that mattered in that moment was avoiding any chance of running into Epperly's most popular gigolo.

"Elsie!"

I made it ten feet and mere inches away from turning the corner to the parking lot at the end of the street. So *so* close ... I should have used the back door.

"Elsie!" Rachel yelled my name again.

After squeezing my eyes shut for a few seconds, I turned and painted a neutral mask on my face as I waved back at her.

"Come here!" She motioned again for me to go *there*.

"I need to get home. Let's meet up later!"

"Just a few quick minutes!"

Five people knew about the fight I had with Craig before he died—me, Amie, Bella, Finn, and God. How could I keep thinking four? I forgot God!

God wasn't happy with me. I felt it like a heavy cloud. I let petty things ruin my marriage and kill my husband. I disrupted a peaceful grief group at church. And I talked about sex just feet from the sanctuary.

Oh ... I forgot. There was also the sex out of wedlock the previous night that involved questionable STD prevention and the Lord's name used in vain a few too many times.

God wanted me to suffer, starting with Rachel blowing my cover as I attempted to escape seeing Kael until I had a better plan. I grumbled all the way across the center of the town square and ended with a plastic smile. "What's up?"

"Come in. It's cold. We're closed. But you have to try this."

"Try what?" I surveyed the store, internally paralyzed by the possibility of seeing Kael.

Rachel led me to the kitchen where I'd been for the cooking class. "Kael made his first batch of peppermint bark. It's to *die* for." She snagged an irregular piece from a stainless steel tray and handed it to me. It smelled like Christmas.

I frowned at it. Seriously? He made candy?

I hated him—in the most Christian way possible, of course.

Chewing it slowly, my complicated feelings toward him continued to twist into knots.

Amazing—*AMAZING* sex.

But just sex.

My competitor.

Chocolatier.

Tillie Cunningham's upcoming date.

"Better than sex, right?" Rachel smirked.

I had mixed feelings about that too.

"Oh!" She glanced over my shoulder. "I never did catch for sure ... have you met Kael?" As she nodded toward the door behind me, I finished chewing the peppermint bark and swallowed hard before pivoting like a stripped nut on a rusty bolt—my finger wiping chocolate from the corner of my mouth.

He wore a red, long-sleeved shirt under his white untied apron hanging loosely around his neck. Dark jeans hung almost as loosely around his hips. And those boots ... they were the same ones that had waited by my door as we did *things* the previous night.

"We've met." One corner of Kael's mouth curled into a conspiratorial grin.

"Hope you don't mind. I had to let Elsie try your peppermint bark." Rachel covered the tray of holiday goodness.

"Not at all. Mrs. Smith can taste anything she'd like to taste." He lived to embarrass me. "Rachel, your windshield is cleared, and your car is warm."

She nudged my arm with hers. "Told you he's the best. He does it for all of his employees. Ready?"

I remained unmoved by his generosity. My glare said it all, and he knew it.

"I'll walk Elsie out after I have a word with her. We've been trying to finalize some ideas for cross-promotion."

"That's an awesome idea. Well, maybe dinner this Friday, Elsie?"

I gave her a single nod and a quick glance with a stiff smile. "Sounds good. Night."

Kael walked her to the front door and locked it behind her. Then he shut off the shop lights, leaving on some LED accent lights around his holiday decorations.

"Nice boots." He leaned his shoulder against the doorway into the kitchen.

My chin dropped to the red ankle boots I wore with my light gray leggings, cream velvet tunic dress, and charcoal wool coat. "So ... you start your employees' cars and clear the snow from their windshields, huh? That's very nice of you."

It *was* very nice of him, but I didn't make it sound that way.

"Your windshield is cleared too. But I couldn't find you to get your keys to start it."

"I can start my own vehicle. Thanks." I glanced up, feeling the undeniable spark between us, so I turned and meandered around his kitchen, looking at anything but him while increasing the distance between us.

"Can I get you something to eat? I have some leftovers from the lunch I made my team today."

"Your team?" I leaned in and sniffed fresh herbs in the trays under the grow lamp—rosemary, thyme, basil, and sage.

"My employees. But I call them my team. We're in it together."

"How nice of you."

"It really is."

So damn cocky.

"Want more peppermint bark? It was just a fun experiment, but everyone loved it, so I'm going to package it and sell it."

"No. I don't want more chocolate." I continued to navigate my way around the big island.

"Well, if you don't want dinner or chocolate, can I offer you anything else like ... me?"

Grunting a laugh, I shifted my attention to him. "We're not having sex again."

"No?" He canted his head to the side, hands partially planted into his front pockets.

"No. It wouldn't be fair to Tillie Cunningham." I clasped my hands behind my back, gaze unblinking at him.

"Why? Are you having sex with her too?"

"Yes. I'm bisexual." I rolled my eyes. "I know you're having dinner with her. And that's fine. I really don't care. But she's in my grief recovery support group, and I'm not going to get in the way of your budding relationship."

He chuckled. "Budding relationship? It's dinner. I did some stuff for her, and she invited me to dinner."

"A date."

Kael inched his head side to side. "I don't know about that. Does dinner have to be a date?"

I shrugged. "I think it's implied."

His lips corkscrewed as his eyes narrowed in contemplation. "Did we have a date last night?"

"No." My answer shot out without hesitation. "It was sex."

Satisfaction crawled up his face. "So we're on the

same page."

I nodded because I didn't know what the previous night had been.

Because I was new to the world of casual sex.

Because I'd spent my life raising a family.

Because I was forty-two and in over my head.

"So we agree that dinner can just be dinner. Dates are open to interpretation. And sex doesn't have to be a date or preceded by a meal."

In. So. Far. Over. My. Head ...

Kael prowled toward me. "Let's have sex then."

"Um ... no." My nervous laugh made an appearance.

"Why not?"

"Because my daughter is at home. And I said it was a one and done."

"Twice."

"You know what I mean." I backed away from the island as he closed in on me.

"Come on, Mrs. Smith ..." He hooked my waist with his arm before I hit the metal shelving unit with the herbs on it.

"Don't call me that." My breathless response added nothing real to my words.

My hands pressed to his chest as he dragged his nose along my neck, from my collarbone to my ear. "You say that, but I think you like the idea that we feel forbidden in your rule-abiding world."

"My daughter's home."

"It's not a date," he whispered in my ear. "I'm not taking you home."

Kael didn't just wake up my libido that had been asleep for years. He stripped it naked and flicked it with his tongue so hard I couldn't keep it in check with him in the same room.

My fingers curled into his apron, showing a little strength. I was older. Responsible. Mature.

We weren't having sex on a whim in a public place of business. "Not happening."

My body hated my mind's level of maturity. It was the only part of me that said no to Kael. My nipples, my heavy breaths, my flushed skin, my salivating mouth, and the trickle of arousal between my legs *all* screamed, "YES!"

He bit my lower lip and tugged it before sucking it into his mouth for a few seconds and releasing it. "Just the tip?"

I didn't want to grin, but it happened anyway. My head drew to the side as I tucked my chin to hide it. "Stop it ..." I choked on a stifled laugh. "It had just ..." I wriggled out of his hold on me and distanced us with a good five feet.

"It had been a while for you." His voice dipped into that Mr. Nice Guy tone. A touch of sexy and a whole lot of compassion.

"Yes."

"It's hard to stay in control when you've denied those basic needs for so long."

"Yes."

"Well ... then you had a good excuse for temporarily losing your mind. What was mine?" A little vulnerability leaked through his smile.

It held its own kind of sexy. It made me feel equally wanted. A handsome and ridiculously sexy man—twelve years my junior—*wanting* me in such a physical way.

"Does it have to make sense?"

Kael eased his head side to side.

"Does anyone have to know?"

Another subtle head shake.

"Does it have to mean anything?"

He didn't respond, but the confident expression he held answered my question. Kael didn't need a wife or a girlfriend. He didn't need someone to keep him warm in bed. And he seemed perfectly content with that life.

I needed ...

That was just it. I didn't know what I needed. But after a night with Kael, needing nothing beyond the now—the present moment—felt really good.

Liberating.

Gratifying.

Limitless.

It magnified just how suffocated and trapped I'd felt the last few years of my marriage.

"I'm going to need more than the tip. So I hope you planned for the unexpected."

"It's sort of my motto." His mouth quirked into a knowing grin.

My fingers unbuttoned my wool coat as he took purposeful steps toward me. I shrugged it onto the floor. His hands claimed my face first. I let myself melt into him, the warmth of his touch, the mint from the candy mixing in our long kiss.

The kiss.

I'd forgotten how amazing it felt to be kissed. To crave the taste of that person.

Our clothes dropped to the floor one piece at a time. My bare butt landed on the island, and he pushed into me as my limbs wrapped around him. We fucked. And it was glorious.

The profanity looping through my thoughts lost its taboo status. It wasn't a word that made me recoil as it had for years. It was just a word—the best word to define our indulgent sexual act. I wasn't searching for love or an emotional connection. *That* truth felt more sinful than the f-word circulating in my head.

I felt so many things as his mouth sucked my skin, as his hands caressed me intimately, as he moved inside of me.

Undeserving.

That was it. While I allowed myself into a bubble of pleasure, I felt a looming reality awaiting because I felt *undeserving* of stealing something so carnal, so private, so instinctual all for myself.

A drug that I didn't truly need. It just felt so. Damn. Good.

If we were nothing more than souls in mortal bodies, why did taking such pleasure have to be filled with rules and tainted in shame?

Why couldn't we let our brains and hearts love, but let our bodies *feel* the tangible things in life that made our hearts race, our skin tingle, and our muscles grip and pulse in immeasurable rapture?

Really?

Why the *fuck* not?

"I..." my lips brushed along his shoulder while he rocked into me, large hands keeping my ass from sliding off the edge of the granite "...hate how good this feels." My ankles tightened around his waist as I chased that orgasm he'd been flirting with forever.

Forcing my hands around his neck to unclasp, he guided them behind my back and restrained them with one hand. My shoulders reared back in response, and he ducked his head to suck in my nipple.

"ARG!" I jerked as he bit it like a piranha. Total sadist.

But he rebounded with his free hand, sliding it between our joined bodies. My muscles spasmed, gripping him in tiny little pulses.

Blurred vision.

A sensual narcotic racing through my veins.

The pinnacle of physical pleasure.

It occurred to me that I might go to Hell, but I'd go there infinitely satisfied with my earthly experiences.

Kael freed my arms and stabbed his fingers into my hair, crashing his mouth to mine as he stilled with his release and a low moan I felt deep in my own chest. "There's..." he panted, breaking our kiss and resting his cheek against mine while his fingers kept a firm claim to my hair "...nothing about you that's not perfection."

I chuckled, unlocking my legs from his waist as my left calf started to get a cramp. "That's the orgasm talking."

He pulled out of me slowly, resting his hands on my thighs. "Your legs are trembling."

Rubbing my swollen lips together for a few breaths, I rested my hands on his. "Can't imagine why."

He leaned in and grinned before brushing his lips over mine. "You taste better than that peppermint bark. And it's pretty fucking awesome." Those addictive lips made a lazy trip down my neck to my breasts, showing his tender side with them.

I loved the feeling of him savoring me. I loved

watching his eyes show appreciation of my gently used body. Kael made me feel beautiful and ageless with just his eyes.

Sometimes I swear Craig didn't even look at me. *Really* look at me.

Without feeling rushed, we pieced ourselves back together, stealing flirty glances. I had a secret. One I never had to share. For as long as we mutually wanted it, we could do exactly what we'd just done and walk away without any sort of accountability.

Sex.

Just sex.

"What's going on in that pretty head of yours?" Kael stole me from my thoughts as he disinfected the island, which made me grin.

I slipped on my wool coat and buttoned it. Had I been honest, I would have told him my brain escaped to the order of getting dressed ... or, really, undressed. Halfway through our marriage, Craig started to undress in a weird order before he'd get into the shower. I'd walk into the bathroom to see him testing the water temperature, wearing nothing but a T-shirt—occasionally socks too. It was quite possibly the unsexiest thing ever. A man child. A two-hundred-pound toddler who ran off before his mom could get his diaper and pants back on him. Bare ass and saggy balls exposed just below the hem of his shirt.

So. Weird.

It always made me cringe.

But I didn't tell Kael that. I came up with something less weird, but still kind of funny. "It's an indescribable feeling to have a sex toy that nobody knows about."

He barked out a laugh. "Sex toy, huh?" After tossing the rag into a bin and returning the spray to the shelf above the sink, he grabbed my coat lapels and kissed me again.

All the kisses.

Each one as good as the first and as addictive as the last.

"I'll add that to my resumé."

"You really should. Snow removal. Valet. And sex toy. You could run for mayor with that stellar skill set. Seriously. Run for mayor. Close up shop and get your name in the race."

"Close up shop? After I perfected my peppermint bark? Are you crazy?" He bopped the tip of my nose with his finger.

"Can't blame a girl for trying." I frowned.

"True." He turned and retrieved his coat from the hook by the storage room door. "But I can walk said girl to her vehicle since it's dark outside."

"I think the worst crime to have ever happened in Epperly was some graffiti at the new skate park."

"See ... that's what I love about this town. It's so pure and innocent." He led the way to the front door, unlocked it, and held it open for me.

I stepped past him. "Innocent? Sure. Except for that Elsie Smith. I hear she's a little promiscuous."

He laughed, locking the door behind us. "If I'm the only guy you're having sex with, then I'm not sure that counts as promiscuous."

We walked toward my Tahoe. No hand-holding. No linking arms. Nothing that would look suspicious to the few people still milling around the square.

"Well, what if you're not the only guy I'm having sex with?" Of course he was. But I needed to keep checking in on our situation. It really was too good to be true.

Oh the irony ...

So many young women looked for guys who would commit and be faithful. Give them that coveted monogamy. I was once that young woman.

Not anymore.

I wanted the opposite of everything I had with Craig. It wasn't that I wanted to erase a single minute of our lives together (save for the last day I saw him). I simply wanted a part of my life to truly be mine.

My needs.

My desires.

My secret.

He kicked the heel of my boot with the toe of his, a subtle gesture that no one else saw. "Then I'd better keep up on my STD testing and not ever oblige you with my naked *tip* again. Epperly may be a small town, but STDs don't care about population size."

I liked that he was the cautious one. Since really ... he would be the one spreading the hypothetical STDs. Twenty-two years in a monogamous marriage left me with a lot, but never an STD.

When we arrived at my SUV, I turned toward him before opening my door. We kept a safe distance of several feet, hands in our pockets.

"You really don't care, do you?"

His forehead wrinkled. "Care about what? I care about a lot, so you'll have to be more specific."

"You don't care if tomorrow night I have sex with some other guy. It's not cheating. You won't be upset."

The tension on his face remained idle for a bit, as if he had to contemplate what I said—or maybe how to respond. It felt weird. Had I read him all wrong?

Before I could clarify or rephrase anything, he relaxed his expression and lifted a single shoulder. "Your life, Elsie. Not mine."

My life.

A huge grin spread along my face. I had no intentions of having sex with some other guy ... at least ... not the following night. But the reality that I had a life of my own again felt so freeing.

"Great." I turned and opened the driver's side door. "Oh ..." I twisted to look back at him. "It goes both ways. In case you were worried. If you and Tillie have sex. That's fine. None of my business. Just make sure you're upfront with her. She's been through a lot. I'm not sure she'd be okay with a sex toy."

Kael's thick eyebrows eased up his forehead. "Okay ... um ... thanks for the heads-up. If it gets brought up, I'll let her know the situation."

"But don't tell her it's me. Remember ... this is our secret."

His chin lifted for a brief pause, inspecting me with a peculiar look before dropping into a sharp nod. "Got it. I should maybe have NDAs with my women, huh?"

Women? Was he serious?

I shook my head and closed my eyes for a second.

None of my business. None of my business. None of my business.

"Uh ... yeah. Sure." I hustled to get into my vehicle and shut the door, offering a quick glance and even quicker smile before shoving my Tahoe into reverse.

CHAPTER twelve

I'm not sure why he married me when my opinion means less than that of a complete stranger.

SEVERAL DAYS LATER, I put a huge *SALE* sign in the store window. That doubled my customers from the previous day, but it didn't do much to affect profits since I actually had to put stuff on sale—stuff I wouldn't normally mark down until Black Friday or the week after Christmas.

The day after that, I had a sign for complementary hot cider and pumpkin chocolate chip muffins. That brought in more customers, but sales only budged a little. A lot of token purchases were made, five-dollar-or-less items. And everyone had to pay with a freaking credit card. By the time I factored in the processing fee, I basically lost money for the day.

"He's running me out of business, and there's nothing I can do." I confessed my frustration to Amie on our early morning walk with Meadow.

"Then you need to let the shop go or else you need to play dirty."

"Play dirty?"

She had no idea I'd been playing *very* dirty with him. I came so close to telling her on multiple occasions, but I liked my secret too much. It was the first time in ... *forever* ... that I had something one hundred percent for myself.

"Start a rumor. Run him out of town."

I shot her the hairy eyeball. "Such as?"

"Maybe say you heard so-and-so got something like salmonella or some sort of parasite from one of his products. Rat droppings in his kitchen. Changing expiration dates on his packaging. So many possibilities. Or go after his shiny reputation. Say he said or did something inappropriate to you."

That wasn't entirely wrong. But I asked for it —literally.

"Not his character. It wouldn't be believable. Everyone has him on an unreachable pedestal."

"Then knock him down one inch at a time. The rat droppings will put an end to his cooking classes. A parasite issue or salmonella will kill sales on all edible items. So that leaves him with a handful of non-edible items, and I just don't think he has enough of those things to keep him in business on those sales alone."

I didn't want to run him out of business or out of town. I just wanted him to sell completely different products or be the fitness studio I'd originally hoped for. Why was that too much to ask?

"God ... I heard his peppermint bark will double your ass size and dimple your thighs." Amie blew out an exasperated breath.

"Well, it is really good."

"Oh? When did you try it?"

"Uh ... the other night. Rach caught me just after I closed the store. She practically dragged me over there to try it."

"And was the hot guy there?"

"What hot guy?" I kept my attention forward and my face straight.

"As if you don't know. The hot guy who wants into your old lady panties."

I giggled. "He does not." He definitely did. "And yes, he was there. No big deal. I can be civil with him, even if I want to put him out of business."

AND JUST LIKE THAT ...

I donned my big girl pants (and old lady panties) and headed off to work.

Everything had samples that day.

Every flavor of sausage roll.

Every tub of cheese.

Every tin of popcorn.

Jellies.

Chocolates.

Candies.

Everything.

I played the holiday music extra loud. Wore a bigger smile. Exuded a brighter attitude. And I sold stuff.

I pulled customers off the street. Asked them about their day. Complimented little details like earrings, nail polish, handbags, and the sure winner—*Wow! You're looking good. It's so nice to see you. Thanks for coming in today.*

Kael sold products because he brought something new to Epperly, but it wasn't olive oil and flavored vinegar. He brought his larger-than-life, genuinely kind personality.

I used to have that too. Then my marriage fell apart without anyone knowing. The passion for my husband died. And at the time, part of me died too.

After his fatal accident, I wanted out of Epperly. I *needed* to escape, but I couldn't. So my heart wasn't in it.

Until ... Kael Hendricks.

He became my escape. And a stolen hour or two with him made it easier to breathe again. Smile more. Engage with friends and customers. And maybe ... keep the family business alive.

By the time I arrived at the church that evening for our grief meeting, I felt ready to conquer the world.

"How is everyone's week going?" Rhonda asked as we quieted our chatter to begin the meeting.

Some "goods" and "okays" followed. I threw out a "great." Tillie Cunningham also tossed out a "great." Hers was louder, grabbing everyone's attention.

"Well..." Rhonda laughed "...looks like Tillie is going first."

"I had a date." Her face beamed as her posture straightened. "And I know everyone has been telling me to get back on the horse, but it's been hard. It's funny how we don't listen to those closest to us. That used to frustrate me about my husband. I wondered why he married me when my opinion meant less than that of a complete stranger. Yet ... I was talking to a customer at work a few weeks ago, and she suggested I do it. Make a date. I know ... I know ... all of you have been telling me this for months, and then one day a stranger suggests it and boom! It sinks in. I felt instant remorse for all the years I let that same trait in my husband irritate me."

"Your date was with Kael! That's right. Tell us all about it." Bethanne reached over and patted Tillie's leg.

The voice of reason told me to stay calm. Neutral. Unaffected.

"Okay. Yes. Well, I made him dinner. My white bean chili. He loved it. We talked about so many things, and it felt easy. I didn't expect for it to feel so easy. But he has this calmness to him. It's so inviting. Not once did I feel the need to unload my grief, which made me realize that maybe I'm no longer carrying around as much of it anymore. And the more we talked about our pastimes, places we've traveled, places we'd like to go ... this connection started to build. I know it's only been one date, but I have a good feeling about us."

Us.

Her declaration of them as a couple completely squashed that voice of reason. I'd had a good day. I was strong and confident. But I wasn't immune to all emotion—including that nagging jealousy.

"That is fantastic. Praise be to God," Rhonda said. "You should invite him to church this Sunday."

Tillie nodded. "I think I will. He's not religious—well, anymore—but he's such a good man. I can see him finding his way back and accepting Jesus Christ as his Savior. But once saved, always saved. So maybe he just needs a good church family—a little nudge."

Satan lived inside of me. In a tiny room down the hall from the sanctuary doors, I sat idle with Satan lassoing my soul. Evil words formulated in my head. I couldn't stop them from having a voice, even if I didn't let that voice out to the group.

Kael wasn't going to fall in line and confess his sins. He wasn't going to accept Jesus Christ as his Savior. He wasn't going to be re-baptized in the church and put a ring on Tillie's finger. He wasn't going to re-virginize himself and wait for intimacy until their wedding night. And it wasn't fair of Tillie to push him in that direction—to take advantage of his kindness.

And it wasn't okay for her to ... STEAL MY SEX TOY!

My hand flew to my mouth, trapping my laughter.

Laughing. At. Myself.

I couldn't believe my mind went there.

These women were my friends. We'd been with each other through so much grief. We didn't do anything but lift each other up and encourage each other to find life after loss. Tillie deserved *only* the best. She was in her early thirties, closer to Kael's age. Of course, he would find her appealing. She was genuinely kind, like him.

I used to be kind. I wasn't sure what happened.

"Sorry." I cleared my throat and dropped my hand. "Sneezed."

Rhonda relaxed her frown and nodded slowly. "Bless you."

"Thanks."

"How about you, Elsie?" Rhonda tilted her head to the side. "Anything appropriate you'd like to share today?"

Appropriate? Well played, Rhonda.

As if I would've ever had anything inappropriate to share. "I've been focusing on the store and trying to give it and our customers the love and attention that Craig used to do. It's brought some peace and sense of true accomplishment to my life."

"Oh!" Tillie perked up. "Kael had the nicest things to say about you and your store, Elsie. He said you have so much experience to offer since this is his first time in the retail business. He lost his mother last year. He said you remind him of her. It's really sweet."

His mother.

I reminded him of his mother. That was ... cringeworthy. It took the "Mrs. Smith" reference to a whole new level.

"Sweet." My eyes widened as I bit my lips together. "Yeah, that's ... definitely sweet."

"When did you start drinking *beer*?" Amie asked.

Glancing at my watch, I shrugged. "Ten minutes ago."

She rolled her eyes. "I mean ... you've never been a beer drinker. Honestly, I think you drink wine on my deck just to appease me."

I invited her for a drink at Welch's Pub in the town square. I hadn't been there in years. Craig hung out there a lot, as did most of the guys in Epperly. Beer and big screens to watch sports.

We were tucked toward the back at a round, high-top table. The loud chatter in the packed bar along with the country music flowing from the old jukebox made it a little hard to hear, but I wasn't in the mood to talk.

I just wanted to drink.

"Tillie Cunningham had a fabulous date with Kael.

They really hit it off." I sipped the foam off the top of my tap beer.

"Okay. And that's why you're drinking?"

My gaze remained affixed to the football game on one of the screens just over Amie's shoulder. "She said he talked about me. He said I remind him of his mother, who passed last year."

She took a sip of her red wine. "Well, if he liked his mother, then that's a high compliment."

Cupping my hands around the large beer mug, I nodded slowly. "Yup. That would be a great compliment had he not fucked me twice at my house and once at his store."

Amie spat out her wine.

I grimaced, glancing down at the red stains splattered on my white sweater.

"Oh my gosh! I'm sorry ..." She snatched her tiny cocktail napkin and leaned forward, blotting my sweater. "I just ... you ... oh my god ..." Her hands paused as her eyes shifted, our gazes locking. "You slept with him?"

Plucking the napkin from her hand, I shook my head and dipped the flimsy paper in my water glass. "We didn't sleep together. We fucked. And yes ... I now use the word 'fuck.' I drink beer and have meaningless sex. Started my New Year's resolutions a little early."

A slow grin worked its way up Amie's face as her saucer eyes remained unblinking. "Well ... welcome to the dark side. I ... I don't know what to say."

I didn't want to smile or laugh; I just wanted to drink beer and forget about my adventures in sinful freedom. But my stupid grin betrayed me. "Just say I'm justified in feeling a little—*a lot* weirded out by his reference to his mom."

"Frankly, I'm not sure what needs to be addressed first. The fact that you actually listened to me and had sex —*fucked* him." She smirked. "Or that I'm just now hearing about it. Or that he's ... dating Tillie? Sorry to break it to you, but I think the mother reference is at the bottom of the list. And at the very top is you *have* to tell me everything. Was it planned? Spontaneous? Did you jump him? Did he seduce you? When did you have it in his store? Was the store open? Was it in a storage room or bathroom? Seriously, Elsie! I need to know!"

Somewhere during her rant and endless line of questions, I spaced off—glassy-eyed and thinking only about one thing. "Do you think it's an age reference? I mean ... there's no way his mother had him when she was twelve. I'm not actually old enough to be his mom. And if it's not an age reference, do you think it's an appearance thing? I do have some gray hair showing that I thought was hidden."

When my gaze shifted to Amie's, she blinked at me with expressionless eyes and a neutral parting of her ruddy lips. "How was it? If you don't give me this, I'm breaking up with you. Tell me it was mind-blowing. Tell me he's a tireless, multiple-orgasms machine. Just ... tell me."

I grinned just before taking another swig of my beer. "It's a drug. And until tonight, it was this secret we had. Like it wasn't real except when we were together. He's ..."

"That good?"

Biting my bottom lip, I nodded.

"I hate you."

I giggled. "Don't. It went from uncomplicated, meaningless sex to Tillie Cunningham wooing him with her cooking, younger body, and an invitation to church so he can find God again." I frowned. "If he finds God, we'll be over."

Amie's brow furrowed. "You do realize ... you go to the same church. You believe in the same God."

I rubbed my hands down my face. "I don't know what I believe anymore. I know this feels like a midlife crisis. I was just hoping I could ..." I shook my head and dropped my hands from my face. "I don't know. I have this moment in my life that makes no sense but brings me such unfathomable pleasure. Like sowing my wild oats in my forties before succumbing to all the not-so-glamorous parts of aging that are just around the corner. And later I would ..."

"Say a hundred Hail Marys?"

I smirked. "My religion doesn't say Hail Marys."

Amie blew out a slow breath. "Tillie Cunningham ..."

"Yep. Epperly's sweetheart. If I weren't straight, *I'd* date her."

Amie snorted. "Amen to that."

"So ..." I shrugged one shoulder. "I walk away. It was just sex."

"Good sex." Amie simpered behind the rim of her wine glass.

"So good." Just as I swapped out my beer mug for my water glass, a group of guys filed into the bar. "Shit."

"You weren't kidding about the profanities. What?" Amie turned to follow my gaze, which led straight to the second guy in a line headed toward a recently emptied table. "Ooo la la!"

"Shut up." I positioned myself to hide behind her body so Kael wouldn't see me.

"New hot guy in town likes to hang with the guys, drink beer, and watch football. Sounds like Craig two-point-oh."

"Minus the beer gut."

"I'll have to take your word on that. I haven't seen his naked torso ... yet. But from the sounds of things, he gets around. Maybe I should reserve something for December so I can see firsthand what all the fuss is about."

"Not funny. Besides ... he'll be engaged to Tillie by then. Maybe. He's not a believer in monogamy. But people change."

"Jesus will change him."

I rolled my eyes. "That would be something."

"Well ..." She emptied the rest of her wine down her throat and hopped off her stool. "I have some patient treatment plans to go over before tomorrow. Do you need a ride home?"

I stared at my beer that was basically full, minus some foam off the top. "I think I'm good."

"Love you." She maneuvered around the table as I hopped off my stool and gave me a big hug. "I'm proud of your midlife crisis. If meaningless sex with a hot, thirty-year-old is a midlife crisis, then I need to get home and start planning mine. I'm six months older than you. I should have had him first."

I followed her to the door. It wasn't a midlife crisis. I hated that term. "Well, you can have him if you want to fight Tillie for him."

Amie shamelessly ogled him, welcoming his glance

in our direction. I tried to, again, hide behind her, but he saw me.

"Uh ... I don't think that smile on his face is for Tillie or me. Bye, Elsie." She took a sharp left to the door before I could squeeze past two crowded tables.

Kael scooted out of his chair, saying something to the other three guys at the table before making his way to me. I offered an awkward wave and stiff smile and shot out the door. When I glanced around the square, Amie was nowhere in sight.

"Not cool," I muttered to myself as the bar door opened behind me.

"Mrs. Smith."

I turned, jerking each side of my jacket together before zipping it. "Your mom, huh? I remind you of your mom. That's pretty messed up, Kael, considering the things we've done."

He tucked his hands into his back pockets and shuffled a few feet to the side as another group of men stuffed themselves into the bar. "You've talked with Tillie."

"She's in my grief recovery group at church. We had a meeting tonight. Yes, I know about your budding relationship. All of the things you have in common. I know she's going to invite you to our church this Sunday with the hopes of saving your soul."

"Saving my soul, huh? Sounds intense."

After zipping my stubborn jacket, I slipped on my mittens. "I'm serious, Kael. If you don't watch your step with Tillie, I won't have to put you out of business; the residents of Epperly will run you out of town for breaking Tillie's fragile little heart. Everybody loves her. I realize you think everybody loves you but take that times ten and you'll get a glimpse of the affection people have toward Tillie."

"Hey, I'm not arguing with you there. She's amazing."

It was hard to be angry with the truth. I didn't have an issue with Tillie being amazing. I had an issue with Kael saying it to me after what we had done together.

"She is. I'm sure the two of you will be very happy together. See you Sunday at church."

"Whoa ... whoa ... whoa ..." As I started to escape in the opposite direction, he grabbed my arm. "You know where I stand with marriage and happily-ever-afters."

"I do. But clearly Tillie doesn't. And you're young. You're allowed to change your views, especially if a game-changer comes along."

"And you're my game-changer?"

"No. Aren't you listening to me? Tillie, you idiot. Tillie is your game-changer."

"Is this jealousy?" He smirked.

"Ugh! No! I'm not jealous. I don't want to marry you. I don't want your babies. I don't want to invite you to my church."

"I told you ... I've had a vasectomy. No babies."

I frowned. "That wasn't my point."

"Then what is your point? Because I'm not getting it."

"Don't hurt Tillie. That's my point."

Lines formed along his forehead. "I wasn't planning on it. What is this really about?"

I deflated. "Look ... ten years ago, if someone would have asked me if I could see myself having no-strings-attached sex—no commitment, no love, no pressure for anything more—I would have laughed in their face. The idea would have seemed absurd. But now that it's happening to me, I don't know the rules. And maybe there are no rules. But I think I need some rules, at least for myself. Some moral boundaries. I don't ..." I closed my eyes and shook my head. "I don't care if you..." I glanced around to see if anyone was close by who could hear us "...have sex with Tillie. That's not my business. And while I don't want you to tell her you've done it with me, I *do* need you to be honest enough to let her know you have no intentions of being monogamous with her. Unless ..."

My nose wrinkled as I caught myself rambling and putting words into his mouth like I knew his intentions with me, Tillie, or any other woman in Epperly.

"Unless?" He took a step closer to me.

"Unless you are planning on being with her," I murmured. "Which is fine, and again ... none of my business." My gaze worked its way up to his. "You can't hurt me."

That was a lie, but I liked how strong I felt saying it.

"But Tillie isn't looking for casual sex. So don't hurt my friend."

"I want to touch you right now."

Swallowing hard, I surveyed the area again. The intensity of his eyes on me, the heat from his proximity, and the suggestiveness in his voice did euphoric things to my body.

"Are you wet, Elsie?"

I blinked and turned my head to the side.

"I bet you are."

That! That was what I wanted in my secret little world. Dirty talk. The high stakes of sneaking around. A man reading my body like he could feel my skin and the desire between my legs without even touching me.

But then ... Tillie Cunningham had to make him dinner.

"Follow me to my place."

I shook my head, keeping my gaze averted. "You just got here. Your friends are waiting for you inside."

"They'll understand."

My head snapped up, eyes squinted. "Understand?"

"Getting laid is better than beer, especially when your team isn't playing tonight."

"Kael! They saw you follow me out the door. If you tell them you're leaving too ..." I took a step back and offered a stiff smile as a couple passed us to enter the bar. "It will start rumors."

"That's what I love about small towns. All the rumors and gossip. It's why everyone thinks I'm going to church Sunday and courting Tillie Cunningham."

"Rumors are awful. And I don't want to be the newest one floating around. I have a daughter still in school here. And Tillie was speaking from her firsthand experience with you. I heard her. It wasn't a rumor."

"Well, she read into the situation."

"You were too nice to her!"

Kael's eyebrows jumped up his forehead. "Is that a thing? Is that even possible?"

My mittened hands covered my face as I chuckled. "I don't know. I ... I just need to go home and get back into quilting instead of other stuff."

"And I'm the other stuff?"

My hands slid from my face. "Yes. You're other stuff

for sure. Night." I turned and wandered toward the parking lot down the street.

"Am I better than quilting?" he hollered.

I laughed and kept walking. There was no way I was answering him.

CHAPTER thirteen

I married an old man, but he's only thirty-seven. Why must he take such small, short steps? He's average height. It's just not normal or manly.

"I WANT to talk about your virginity." The pot (me) sat across from the kettle (Bella) at the kitchen table.

"Why?" She smirked with her head angled toward her cereal bowl. "It's gone and I can't get it back."

I picked at my bowl of fruit. "I thought we could be friends and discuss your first time. If you used protection. If it was or is serious."

"Friends?" She raised her head. "Like how I'd talk to my friends from school?"

Tapping my fork on the side of the bowl, I nodded. "You're an adult. I'm an adult. Let's have an adult conversation about sex."

"Fine." Her lips pulled into pure evil, and I regretted starting the conversation before she had the chance to open her mouth again. "Did Dad go down on you often? Did you like it?"

My daughter made me blush. When did I lose my footing as the grownup in the house?

"See." She scooted her chair away from the table. "You don't want to talk about sex with me like we're *friends*. And I honestly don't want you to answer that question anyway." Her nose wrinkled before she turned and shuffled her bare feet to the kitchen sink.

"So ..." I cleared my throat. "You like oral sex?"

"Mom ... please ... just don't."

"Have you had more than one partner?"

"Right there." She turned toward me, resting her hand behind her on the edge of the counter. "My friends wouldn't ask that. At least, not in that way."

"In what way?"

"Like a doctor. How many sexual 'partners' have you had? Seriously, Mom. Just ... no."

"Then how many guys have you slept with? Made love to? Screwed? *Done it* with?"

"Mom!" She closed her eyes and covered her face while laughing. "Stop." She giggled.

I made a slow approach toward her and set my bowl on the counter before stealing a hug. "Fine. We don't have to discuss it if you don't want to. But I want you to know there is nothing you can't talk to me about. I'm still your fiercest protector, but I want you to feel like we can discuss intimacy. My mom never discussed it with me, and it led to a lot of shame." I pulled back, holding her at arm's length as I grinned. "It led to your two oldest brothers."

"They weren't planned?" Her mouth hung open with surprise.

"No. They weren't planned because your dad and I

didn't plan on having sex. We were raised to believe it was wrong to have sex before marriage. But we were young and in love. We were passionate and *unprepared*."

"I haven't had unprotected sex."

"Good."

She shifted her gaze to my hands holding her arms. "So ... are we done?"

"Yep." I released her and retreated two steps, maintaining my cheerful smile as if I didn't just get shot down in my attempt at bonding with my only daughter.

AFTER SLIPPING into my jogging pants and sweatshirt, Meadow and I waited outside for Amie. Ten minutes later, I pulled my phone out of my pocket to call her only to find a missed message from her.

> Amie: Sorry, client emergency. Have to cancel this morning.

Dropping my phone back into my hoodie pocket, I ventured down the driveway, turning north instead of my usual route going south. The air bathed my skin in its fall crispness, and snow still blanketed most of the ground, making my walk a little tricky in icy spots. Taking the first right, I trekked up the gradual hill toward the dead end where the Davidsons lived. Their daughter, Amber, was two years older than Bella, but they had become close friends through youth group at church.

My pace slowed as I recognized the pickup truck parked just off to the side of their driveway, where they kept their fishing boat during the summer. To my knowledge, Randall and Anna were in Arizona. They owned a place not too far from where my parents lived. Bella hadn't mentioned Amber being home from college for Thanksgiving break, but it was possible.

Still, it didn't explain why Kael's truck was parked there. The front door opened, and I shuffled to the side, yanking on Meadow's leash and hiding behind a tree. He stepped outside, toolbox in hand. Amber followed him with a blanket wrapped around her body and boots on her feet. Kael hoisted his toolbox into the back of the truck and turned toward her.

She stepped closer to him as if personal space meant nothing to her generation. Her lips moved, speaking words I couldn't hear. Then she smiled, gazing up at him. He returned a smile and nodded several times.

They were standing too close for comfort—not how one would stand next to a guy who did something like hang a picture or fix a leaky faucet.

Amber took another step into him, leaving no more steps to take, forcing his back to rest against the driver's door to his truck. He slid his hands into the pockets of his jacket. Amber spoke again. Kael lifted his gaze and glanced around. When he returned it to her, she lifted onto her toes and kissed him.

"What ... the ... fuck?"

He didn't seem to move. I couldn't tell if he kissed her back. It was too quick. He sure didn't push her away or turn his head. I was in too deep. Really ... I *really* did not want a boyfriend or a relationship. Just the sex.

Amber had to be ... twenty, maybe close to twenty-one. He was thirty. I was forty-two. Overthinking the age gap didn't work in my favor. That didn't stop the anger from brewing. I wasn't sure if my anger stemmed from him allowing her to kiss him. After all, we weren't anything. He could've had sex with a different woman every night.

Maybe that was it. Maybe I was upset that he was having more sex than me. Nothing stopped me from finding other guys to have sex with.

Okay. That wasn't true. Epperly had a population slightly under twelve hundred. And I knew just about everyone, and everyone knew me. It was basically like fishing in your own fish tank for dinner. Sure, there were single men in town, but once I took out the ones I would never have sex with, the ones that would never keep their mouth shut about it, and the ones I felt confident weren't carrying an STD—it left me with two, maybe three options including Kael Hendricks.

Brian Hosier was an attorney in town. He divorced five years earlier. Craig hired him for things like our will and rental contract advice. He was in his late forties with a mostly full head of hair and jogged every day.

Mike Holmes, a fifty-something banker who lost his wife to breast cancer nearly a decade earlier, squeezed into the final spot. However, Mike had a gait issue. I remember overhearing Melinda, his wife, talking about him to a friend at the cafe. She said, "I married an old man, but he's only thirty-seven. Why must he take such small, short steps? He's average height. It's just not normal or manly."

Maybe he had a really big dick and walking too fast sent it swinging like a wrecking ball. That unlikely, but not entirely impossible, scenario was the reason I added him to the list.

Mentally tucking away my short list, I edged around the tree to stay out of sight as Kael drove toward the main road.

"Meadow ..." I frowned as she squatted to poop just as the front door shut behind Amber. I reached into my pocket for a poop bag, but there wasn't one. "Ugh!" I grimaced at the pile she left. Seeing only Kael's taillights as he turned the corner, I kicked snow over the pile of shit and hightailed it toward the main street, deeming my walk to be over. When I turned the corner to head back home, Kael's brake lights greeted me from the side of the road.

"Good morning, Mrs. Smith," he sang with a cheerful tone while rolling down his window.

I continued walking toward home. "For some it is."

"What were you doing? Spying on me?"

"I don't know what you're talking about."

His truck tailed me down the street. "I saw you in my rearview mirror, hiding behind a tree when I left the Davidsons'."

"Congratulations on your twenty-twenty vision, and I wasn't spying." I sped up my pace as if I could outrun his truck.

"Then what were you doing?"

"Making a list of eligible men in town to fuck."

He chuckled. "Am I on that list?"

"I can't remember. It's a long list in alphabetical order. A lot with H's too. I'll let you know."

A horn honked, going in the opposite direction. I waved at Bella and so did Kael.

"You left a pile of dog shit on the Davidsons' property. I'm pretty sure that's frowned upon."

I shot daggers at him and sped up my pace to a jog. "You're frowned upon," I mumbled. When I reached the house, I kept pace right to the front door, even when I heard his truck pull into my driveway.

Door shut.

Shoes off.

Jacket off.

I marched straight up the stairs to shower.

"Elsie, is that about the kiss?" he asked ... coming into my house uninvited.

"Jeez ... come on in," I quipped as I turned at the top of the stairs to face him.

"Thanks. I just did." He unlaced his boots.

"You're not staying." I eyed him through tiny slits.

He glanced up from his hunched position. "Why? Because Amber kissed me?"

"No. God! You're so full of yourself. I have to shower and get to work."

"Your store doesn't open for two hours." He stood straight and glanced at his watch.

"You have to leave." I crossed my arms over my chest.

He prowled toward me, one step at a time. "Why? Because you're upset that Amber kissed me?"

"No." I rolled my eyes in exasperation.

"So ... let's take that shower."

"No." My feet moved backward to keep a safe distance between us.

"Take off your clothes." He deposited his coat on the banister and shrugged off his long-sleeved tee.

I told my eyes they weren't allowed to leave his face, but they ignored my request and drifted to his fantastic chest and abs as his hands worked the button and zipper of his jeans.

"If you're not upset about Amber testing the waters with me, then take your clothes off. Otherwise, I won't believe you."

"Cocky bastard." I ran out of steps to take, missing the doorway and bumping into the wall.

He ate my comment and returned a satisfied grin. When he ducked to kiss me, I turned my head. He made a second attempt, and I whipped my head in the other direction. Once he paused long enough to show a slight level of agitation in his narrowed eyes, I showed my hand.

Gah!

Why did I show my hand? I should have crossed his name off my sex list and moved on. Nope. I made a mom move by licking my fingers and wiping off his mouth—the mouth Amber had kissed.

His lips curled into a smile beneath my scrubbing motions. When I finished, he rubbed them together. "Do you want to urinate on me too?"

"Shut up." I laced my fingers behind his neck and pulled him to me.

Our hands turned into frantic claws ripping off clothes as our feet tangled and stumbled, navigating to the bathroom.

I had sex with him to prove I wasn't bothered by Amber—totally normal forty-two-year-old behavior.

"I think I like you spying on me." Kael ran a hand through his wet hair, towel loosely clinging to his waist.

"I wasn't spying on you." I buttoned my pink and white flannel shirt and tucked the front into my skinny jeans. "I was taking a walk."

"Down a dead-end road?" He let the towel drop to the floor.

My gaze shifted to his exposed cock like it compelled me to do it. When I forced a sharp correction and found his eyes overflowing with confidence from my wandering gaze, I escaped into the bathroom to dry my hair. "It's a nice wooded area. I've walked up and down that drive many times. It's not unusual to spot deer or foxes around their property." I turned on my hairdryer before he could quiz me anymore on my walking route.

By the time I finished drying my hair and applying a little makeup, he was nowhere in sight. I peeked out the window overlooking the front yard. No truck in my driveway.

Kael Hendricks was everything I thought I wanted in my so-called midlife crisis.

Sexy.

Kind.

Unattached.

Then why did I struggle so much with having exactly what I thought I wanted?

CHAPTER fourteen

I lived in the gray, answering all questions with "whatever, maybe, and doesn't matter." She said I never uttered the words yes or no. I fear I passed that gene to my son.

Round three of major snowfall hit Thanksgiving morning. It was an insane snow year—records breaking every week. I gave thanks that my three boys made it to Epperly the night before with their girlfriends. It was the first holiday that any of my children had invited a significant other, and then all three boys did it the same year.

Eight of us total, yet I felt completely alone Thanksgiving morning while making the gluttonous meal for the day as my boys slept in with their girlfriends and Bella cut potatoes with her headphones on.

"I'm so happy to have my kids here today," I said to see if Bella could hear me.

She couldn't.

I shook my head and chuckled to myself. "I can't believe all this snow and it's not even December."

Nothing.

"I'm having meaningless sex with Kael Hendricks. I hope you find a man who can give you multiple orgasms."

Nothing.

Then, as if I brought it to being with just the mention of his name, I heard something out front. Kael's truck turned into our driveway, blade down removing the snow. I watched from far enough back that I didn't think he'd be able to see me if he glanced at the window. It looked like he had someone in the truck with him. I couldn't make out details; they had hats on, and snow still swirled in the air.

"Wow!"

I jumped at Bella's voice.

"How nice of him to clear our driveway. Doesn't he know all the boys are home today?"

I shrugged. "How would he?"

"True. I should take him some coffee to say thank you."

"We don't have coffee."

Bella retreated to the kitchen. "We do. Linc brought some because he knew you wouldn't have any."

"I'm sure he's already had coffee." I followed her. "Besides, by the time you get it brewed, he'll be gone."

As soon as she started the coffee maker, she turned and grinned. "I'll run out and tell him to come in for a cup of coffee."

"It's Thanksgiving. I'm sure he's busy and wants to get home to his family."

She chuckled, brushing past me to the front door, where she shoved her feet into her boots and donned her coat over her T-shirt and pajama pants. "What family?

Amber said he doesn't have family in Epperly, and his mom died."

"When did you talk to Amber?"

"Few days ago. Apparently Kael fixed a frozen pipe at their house. Then he kissed her. I think he was at her house last night too."

It had been a week since I'd seen or talked to him. It was the day he left after shower sex without a goodbye. The day I used my saliva to wipe Amber's kiss from his lips.

The front door closed behind Bella before I had a chance to say or ask anything else. A few minutes later, the door opened, and she emerged with Kael and an older gentleman behind him.

I slapped a smile on my face, for the older gentleman. My gaze did its best to not make eye contact with Kael.

"I hope we're not intruding," Kael said.

"You're not. I'll check the coffee. Make yourselves at home." Bella played my role, said the things I should have said.

"Happy Thanksgiving, Mrs. Smith."

Mrs. Smith ...

Asshole.

"Happy Thanksgiving. Who's your friend?"

"This is my dad, Dan."

"Nice to meet you, Mrs. Smith." Dan pulled off his glove and held out his hand.

"Elsie. Please." I shook his hand. "It's a pleasure. You really didn't have to clear my driveway. I have three boys home today."

"We have nothing better to do." Dan grinned.

"Well, come in." I stepped aside and nodded toward the kitchen.

Kael took his dad's jacket and hung it on the coat-tree next to his. Both men left their stocking caps on. Dan headed to the kitchen first.

"After you, Mrs. Smith." Kael smirked.

I glared at him for a few seconds before following Dan. My body stiffened with a tiny jerk when Kael's hand slid under the back of my sweater, teasing my lower back with his cold fingertips.

Without turning around, I reached behind me and yanked it away.

"God ... you're feisty," he whispered.

"Cream? Sugar?" Bella set two mugs of coffee on the kitchen table and then grabbed herself a cup of coffee as well.

I returned to my food prep.

"Are you in college, young lady?" Dan asked Bella.

"No. Senior in high school. I'm hoping to get accepted to a college next year in a place a little warmer. SoCal ... Texas ... Florida."

Dan and Kael laughed.

"Where did you go to college?" Bella asked Kael.

"I didn't."

"Why not?"

With my back to the kitchen table, I continued stuffing the turkey and grinned at my daughter's question, as if college was a forgone conclusion for every person. Some people made millions of dollars with no college degree. Some people started college and got pregnant with twins only to spend twenty-two years being a full-time mom.

Kael laughed a little. "I had no clue what I wanted to be when I grew up. Still don't." That made Dan laugh too.

"So I traveled like a nomad. Odd jobs. Hiked across Europe. Slept on any sofa someone was willing to offer me. Made wine and olive oil in Tuscany and learned to captain a sailboat on the Mediterranean."

"That's so cool. So then ... why are you in Epperly?"

I snorted a laugh and glanced over my shoulder. Kael snagged my gaze for a few seconds with that Captain America grin of his. Bella's sour voice, when she said Epperly, made it impossible to imagine she'd stay in such a small, Midwest town her whole life.

Like I did. Barefoot and pregnant.

"I was born in Epperly," Kael replied.

That grabbed my full attention as I washed my hands and turned toward the kitchen table while drying them with the towel. There was so much you didn't learn about someone when all you did was have sex with them. I learned about Kael through other people.

"You were?" Bella's incredulity leaked through every response.

His dad chuckled. "Yes. My wife went into labor while we were on our way home from visiting my parents. Things progressed quickly on our four-hour drive, and Kael was born in the car with the help of a nice police officer while we waited for the paramedics. We spent two nights at the hospital here and then drove home."

"And that made you want to start a business in Epperly? Two nights in a hospital?" I asked, letting my own curiosity have its voice in the safe company of my daughter and Kael's dad.

Kael shrugged. "Sure. Why not?" He grinned before

sipping his coffee. That grin ... it said he knew what I looked like naked.

"The kid has always run on pure instinct." Dan and Kael exchanged knowing glances at his father's comment.

"I'm in the moment." Kael set his coffee on the table, shifting his gaze to me again for a brief second.

"I love that. I mean ... we're only guaranteed this moment, right?"

Kael nodded once at Bella. "That's how I figure it."

"It's why he won't settle down and pass on the family name."

"How long were you married before you lost your wife?" I asked Dan.

"Forty-one years. Three months. Five days." Dan didn't have to think. Not for one second. He knew because he cherished those forty-one years, three months, and five days.

I knew my stats with Craig too, but not because I cherished every single day—I kept track like a prisoner awaiting parole. "Is Kael your only child?"

Again ... I knew nothing about the man I'd been screwing as the best part of my so-called midlife crisis. Not that I really believed in that, but what was the point of enduring the maturing transition of the forties if I couldn't use all the excuses: midlife crisis, hormones, emotional burnout from raising a family? In my twenties, I used the "young and stupid" label to death. Basically, anything that wasn't quite right about my kids was because I was such a young mother figuring stuff out on a day-to-day basis.

Now the thirties ... that was where responsibility set in. Thirty was too old to not know better and too young to blame stuff on age. The forties were basically a redo of the twenties, but with more respect and more money.

"I'm an only child. They couldn't risk a sibling not living up to me."

"Sure, Son, keep telling yourself that." Dan shook his head. "We wanted more kids, but God didn't bless us with any more. I was good with it. My wife ... not so much. She hated my apparent lack of emotion. I lived in the gray, answering all questions with 'whatever, maybe, and doesn't matter.' She said I never uttered the words 'yes' or 'no.' Something about commitment issues. I fear I've passed that gene to my son."

Kael shook his head and smirked.

Dan continued, "Are you an only child, Bella?"

"Pfft ... I wish."

"Nice, Bella," I said before opening the bottom oven and sliding the turkey into it. "I have three boys. Twins, Chase and Linc, then two years later I had Finn, and just over a year after I had Finn, Bella decided to join us."

After I shut the oven door, the chandelier above the kitchen table started to sway a bit as a thumping sounded above it. Everyone glanced up at the light and then around the room. Earthquakes in the Midwest weren't impossible, but they also didn't involve a high-pitched "yes!"

The thumping sped up.

The chandelier swayed even more.

And I died of complete embarrassment when Kael and Dan tried to hide their amusement behind their coffee mugs. Bella covered her mouth, eyes wide and aimed at me.

"This is the first time my boys have invited girlfriends

for a holiday. And clearly the last." I offered everyone a tight grin for lack of knowing what else to say. But I couldn't ignore it.

"I'm uh ..." Bella stood. "Just going to run upstairs and tell my brothers it's time to help make the meal."

Maintaining my tight grin, I gave her a sharp nod.

"We should get going." Kael stood as well when Bella ran up the stairs.

"Mind if I use your restroom before we head out?" Dan asked.

"Not at all. It's just down the hall on the right." I pointed in that direction.

When the door clicked shut, I eyed Kael as he moseyed toward me. "Stop."

He halted, eyebrows lifted in question. "Something wrong?"

"You slept with my daughter's friend last night. That's crossing my comfort zone."

Kael's head tilted to the side, eyes narrowing. "I did? Huh ... wonder when she snuck into my house. And I'm surprised she didn't wake my dad. He's a light sleeper. Did we have sex? Was it good? She must have slipped out before breakfast, which would have been hard to do since I was up at four this morning to start plowing snow."

"Bella said that Amber said—"

"Oh ... my favorite Epperly rumor mill. Wow! It doesn't even take a break for Thanksgiving? Bella said that Amber said that Kimberly said that Mandy said that Tom told Dick and Harry that he overheard Mo and Curly talking about what's his name, who dated what's her name last year before you know who showed up and spoiled the whole thing with a grudge over you know what."

My lips quivered to disguise my reaction to what he said because it was funny *and* accurate.

Kael glanced right, looking for signs of anyone coming downstairs or out of the bathroom before leaning closer to me. My backside hit the counter, and he rested his hands on the granite, caging me with his body. My heart sounded the alarm, pounding out of control—frantic that we were going to get caught.

"Elsie ... if the whole town thinks I'm fucking every other woman *but* you, then our little secret is safe. Right?"

I couldn't ask the question I wasn't supposed to care about—was he fucking other women besides me? But I *wanted* to ask the question that I couldn't stop thinking about—WAS HE FUCKING OTHER WOMEN BESIDES ME?

"I just don't want you leading other women on. I've known Amber and her family since she was born."

After a few slow blinks, a tiny smile bent his lips. "Am I leading you on?"

"No." My head jerked backward. "It's just sex."

"But these other women, who you're so concerned about, can't have meaningless sex with the new, hot guy in town?"

"You are *so* not the new hot guy in town."

He was.

Kael left a trail of scorched panties in his wake just from his smile. I didn't have to engage in personal conversation with the other women of Epperly to know that I wasn't the only one having inappropriate dreams about Kael Hendricks. But I couldn't deny having a tiny shred of hope in my gut that I was the only one having sex with him.

Again, it was hard to explain. I didn't ... really ... I *didn't* want a boyfriend or the rumors and responsibilities that came with one. I just wanted to get my fill of the new, hot guy in town before he dipped his penis into every other hussy in Epperly.

Every other ...

Yep, I thought of myself as a hussy at that moment. After all, I did have a mental list of other available Epperly men I could have screwed. Even if the list comprised of only two other men besides Kael, it was still a list.

"You should run to the store later to pick up something you forgot."

"What?" I squinted at him. "I didn't forget anything. And the store is closed today."

"The convenience store on the corner is open."

Confusion kept a strong hold on my face.

"My dad will take a nap in about two hours. And you'll need to run and grab some milk." He stood straight.

"I don't need milk."

After glancing down the hallway and up the stairs, he opened my fridge, grabbed the milk, and dumped. It. Down. The. Drain.

My mouth hung agape, eyes frozen open.

The bathroom door down the hallway creaked, and Kael brushed past me. "Don't worry, I'll need milk too, in about two hours. I'll pay for yours as well."

Dan peeked his head back into the kitchen just as

Kael started toward the front door. "Tell that lovely daughter of yours 'thanks' for the coffee."

It took a few seconds to peel the shock off my face and conjure an expression that resembled kindness. I wasn't sure I hit the mark, but Dan seemed fine with my attempt. "Happy Thanksgiving," I managed.

CHAPTER fifteen

A fart is not a mating call.

My crew of four kids, three girlfriends, and a wound-up dog all made it to the kitchen an hour later. I couldn't look Linc's girlfriend in the eye, but it didn't stop me from shooting daggers at my son. I taught him better than that. Maybe I never said the actual words "don't pound your girlfriend and make her scream when other people are in the house," but I had to believe that one of my many speeches over the years implied such etiquette.

"Where's the milk?" Finn asked, inspecting the contents of the fridge.

"Oh ... uh ... we're out. I need to go get some."

"There was a full carton of it earlier." Bella felt the need to complicate things with her astute observations.

"I used it up."

"On what?"

Oh, Bella ... Bella ... Bella ...

"The stuffing."

"I didn't know there was milk in stuffing."

I gave her a tight smile as I set a pitcher of orange juice on the table for the boys and their girlfriends. "Well, you've never made stuffing before."

"My mom doesn't use milk in stuffing, but I suppose there are different recipes that call for different things," Chelsea, Linc's vocal little minx, piped in.

"But a whole carton?" Bella probed as she washed cranberries for me.

"No. I used the milk in the potatoes too." I really should have said potatoes to begin with.

"Emma's lactose intolerant, so make sure you let her know everything you added milk to," Chase mumbled while focused on his phone.

"I'll go get milk," Finn said.

"No!" I took a slow breath as my reaction drew everyone's attention. "I mean. Don't be silly. You have a friend here. Just relax."

"I can run and get it."

I frowned at Bella even though she didn't see me while facing the sink. She had done enough by inviting Kael and Dan inside earlier for coffee ... which led to the milk shortage.

"I'll go get it. I could use some fresh air after spending all morning prepping food."

"I'll go start the Tahoe to let it warm up for you." See ... I did teach Linc some manners.

"I'm not leaving right now." I glanced at the clock on the microwave. "I'll leave in about forty-five minutes."

Linc gave me a suspicious eye squint.

I cleared my throat and headed toward the stairs. "I have a few things to do first. That's all." Before anyone could question my peculiar behavior, I hustled up the stairs to find sanctuary in my bedroom.

AN HOUR LATER, I pulled into the convenience store parking lot just as Kael exited the building with a shit-eating grin, sexy swagger, and two cartons of milk. He deposited the milk into the back of his truck, climbed into the driver's seat, and pulled out of the parking lot.

"Where are you going?" I mumbled, following him despite my better judgment whispering in my ear, begging me to get my own milk and go home to my kids. But after walking in on Gwen scolding Chase for farting —using the words *a fart is not a mating call*—I felt my outing could be extended a smidge. It seemed unlikely that the cellphone-obsessed generation would be keeping track of the time.

A mile outside of Epperly, Kael pulled down a gravel road, and I had to put my Tahoe in four-wheel drive to follow him. It stopped at a dead end on the outskirts of a wooded area and the creek the kids used to hike along and play in when they were younger. He hopped out of his truck, holding a bag in one hand. With his other hand, he opened my door.

"My lady ..." He held out his free hand.

I rolled my eyes. "Where are we going?"

"You'll see."

I took his hand and jumped down into the snow. He shut my door then opened the door behind the driver's seat.

My laughter filled the crisp air around us with no

place to go but across dormant fields and through the naked limbs of trees lining the creek.

"My lady ..." He grinned, and I climbed into the back of the Tahoe.

"What's in the bag?" I scooted over to make room for him.

"Treats." He shut the door.

We sat on opposite sides in the back of my Tahoe with grins on our faces. It was odd and kind of amazing for no explainable reason.

"So ..." he angled his body toward mine a bit "...do you come here often?"

I snickered. "Um ... not as much as I used to when the kids were young. Of course, we'd bring the snowmobiles and drive them in that field over there." I pointed out Kael's window. "And in the summer the kids loved playing in the creek just beyond these trees. How about you? Do you come here often?"

Kael pinched his bottom lip, but it didn't erase his grin. "This morning, my dad showed me this road. It's where they pulled off for her to give birth to me. I think I knew even then ... that one day I'd come back to this spot with someone special."

I blew on my hands. "You are so full of it."

"Sometimes." He smirked.

"Your parents ... that's a lot of years of happily-ever-after. I'm having trouble figuring out your philosophy on life."

"That's good. I'd hate to be boring ... or worse ... predictable. Where's the fun in that?"

"True. But I feel a little guilty that everyone else seems to know you better than I do. Tillie knew about your mom dying and probably a hundred other things I don't know about you. Bella asked you some good questions this morning that revealed a part of you I knew nothing about. Yet ... I'm the one ..."

"Relentlessly screwing me every chance you get?"

"Crude." I narrowed my eyes.

"But true. I don't mind, Elsie. I haven't had this much fun with a woman in ... well ... maybe forever."

"You mean to tell me you haven't had meaningless sex like this before? I find that hard to believe, Mr. I Can Sail A Boat Off The Coast Of Italy."

"You like that?"

I rolled my eyes. "Do you care?"

"Yes. Impressing you is challenging and rather entertaining."

"I've lived in Epperly my whole life. That sets the bar pretty low."

"I disagree, but to answer your question, my 'fun' with you is more than sex. It's simply you. One minute you're feisty and stubborn as hell. The next minute you're all Mama Bear. I blink again and you're threatening to take me down as your competition, and then yes ... there's you letting go of all your inhibitions, and it's pretty fucking spectacular. I think I'm getting a different version of you than your husband had. I have nothing to base that on; it's just a feeling. It's like watching a toddler take their first steps. I feel like you're learning to live in the moment. And you're excited and scared. You're unsure of yourself. You worry about losing your footing, yet you can't stop because you *have* to know where it might take you."

I started to respond, but no words came out. We gazed

at each other for a few seconds as he waited to see if he was right about me.

"Interesting assessment," I said, almost whispering.

Was I that transparent?

"How do you feel?"

I narrowed my eyes. "Huh?"

"When my mom died, my dad said he could either live or live without her. So are you living or living without your husband?"

I nodded slowly.

"It makes no sense, right?"

I shook my head. Kael had no idea. "No. It makes perfect sense."

"Yeah?"

I nodded again.

"What does that mean to you?"

Taking a deep breath, I released it slowly. "Am I Craig's widow or am I Elsie?"

"What's the difference between the two?" He thought he had me. He didn't. My age gave me more wrinkles and gray hair, but it also gave me more life experience.

"One lives idle as an anchor, a living tombstone telling stories from the past. The other lives freely. Taking flight. Leaving everything behind."

A map of concern spread in shallow lines along his forehead. "Yes."

Before he could ask his question again, I answered it. "I feel like the bird." I nodded to the sack. "Now ... what treat did you bring?"

He gave me a few more thoughtful blinks before tearing his gaze from mine, pulling out a container, and opening it. "Caramel apple bread. Here."

I hesitated for a second when he broke off a piece and brought it to my mouth.

"I know for a fact you can open wider than that."

And just like that ... he made my cheeks fill with heat. Stealing my sage moment and turning me into a blushing young girl again. I took the bite. "Mmm ... that's really good. You made it?"

"I mixed ingredients and baked it. I sell this at my shop. It's one of my most popular items at the moment."

I spat it out, splattering it all over the headrest of the front passenger's seat. "Yuck! It's awful."

His lips parted, tongue idle, gaze ping-ponging between me and the caramel apple bread mess. "How old are you?" He narrowed his eyes as if it were a genuine question.

I wiped my mouth. "Old enough to know better than to give my competitor's products any sort of endorsement."

"Oh ..." He rubbed his lips together for a few seconds as he grabbed a big chunk of the bread. "You're going to endorse my products whether you like it or not."

"No—"

Before I could get my head turned away from him, he grabbed the back of it with one hand while his other hand shoved the bread into my mouth and all over my face.

"Stop!" I giggled and squirmed, but his mouth silenced me, his tongue shoving more bread into it. I fought him for three more seconds, at the most, before surrendering to the sweet bread, his demanding lips, and his exploring hands snaking under my sweater.

New low ... spending part of my Thanksgiving Day on

an abandoned road with my sex toy in the backseat of my Tahoe while my family waited cluelessly at home for me to return with a carton of milk. I felt certain not a single one of them would imagine me with a thirty-year-old man shoving my bra up to knead my breasts and pinch my nipples—driving me insane. I wanted his mouth where his hands were and his hands to get rid of all the barriers that stood between his naked body and mine.

We wriggled and maneuvered in the tight space, tossing jackets and shirts into the back of the Tahoe, scooching and twisting to get out of our jeans. Before I could rid myself of my panties, he shoved the crotch of them to the side and slid two fingers into me.

"Jesus ..." I closed my eyes while he teased my nipples with his teeth and tongue. He reached along the side of the seat and lowered the back of it, reclining my body right along with it. I was cramped and bent like a pretzel, but when he lifted my body a few inches farther, so his tongue could join his fingers between my legs, the pull of muscles straining disappeared. I turned into a contortionist willing to break bones, tear ligaments, or rip muscles just to feel his hot mouth on me.

One hand pressed to the window to brace myself and my other hand claimed his hair, keeping him there for as long as possible. Labored breaths passed my parted lips, my heavy gaze locked to his as he fingered me with one hand and gripped my inner thigh with his other hand. Every time his tongue flicked my clit, my vision blurred.

I swallowed repeatedly as everything inside of me dissolved. Kael hummed his pleasure, sometimes letting his eyes drift shut for a few seconds.

He didn't stop to tell me how I tasted. I *really* didn't

want to know that. I hated when Craig felt the need to describe that like a pussy connoisseur. Or my favorite ... "Elle, do you know how good you taste?" I'm sure some women loved that but not me. And the answer was always a silent "No. I haven't been down there tasting myself recently. Less talk. More tongue. Thank you very much."

Nor did I want Kael to ruin the moment by saying the words "eating me out." That phrase wasn't sexy, and it grossed me out. Overthinking oral sex, in general, grossed me out. All I wanted was for him to just ... do it. Put his mouth in places where I was too afraid to ask him with actual words. Sex wasn't an interview.

No questions. I hated questions. It wasn't sexy, and it came across as a lack of confidence. If I needed something more—something different—I would've spoken up or used nonverbal cues to get what I wanted ... what I needed.

It was why I used one hand to hold Kael's head between my legs. It was a nonverbal "FOR THE LOVE OF GOD. DON'T STOP!"

However, the most magical part about Kael's ability to read my nonverbal cues was he knew the second I loosened my grip on his hair, it was time for him to put on a condom and get inside of me. I wanted to let it build again together instead of mentally twiddling my thumbs for him to finish because he made me orgasm too quickly.

Making a woman orgasm quickly didn't deserve a special award. Driving her crazy over and over again until she begged for it ... *that* deserved a trophy or merit badge of some sort.

And ... he deserved the championship trophy if he could do it without narrating the whole damn situation aloud.

Kael grabbed his jeans and fished out a condom. Taking a seat next to the opposite door, he rolled it on as I shifted my body and straddled him. Our mouths crashed together, moans filling the silence. And we fucked in the middle of nowhere like animals who had no control over our actions—fed only by desire and lack of accountability to anyone else in that moment.

He made me feel like a horny teenager.

He made me feel drugged without a reason to ever be sober again.

He just made me *feel*.

And when it ended, everything lingered. The amorous glances persisted as we worked to piece ourselves back together in the cramped space. It wasn't a "what did we just do" vibe. It was a "life is fucking good" vibe. I was unsure how, after years of marriage, children, and church every Sunday, I managed to let go of the guilt and allow my body to enjoy the most pleasurable things in life.

But it happened. And it was magical.

"I need to get home."

Kael nodded and started to open the back door. I grabbed his arm. When he glanced back at me, I pressed my hand to his cheek and pecked at his lips—soft and featherlight as I smiled. He smiled too.

"I like kissing you," I murmured before kissing him slowly. It had been too long since I felt that kind of intimacy—that high from a kiss.

"I like kissing you too." He leaned in to steal back my

lips as I started to pull away.

There was a unique intimacy to a kiss, in some ways, more than sex. He took his time, letting his kiss move to my cheek and along my jaw before returning to my mouth. I liked the tenderness in his hands as they caressed my face and hair the way I caressed his. It was a mix of every sense—taste, touch, the whisper of lips moving together, the pine and mint of his scent, the tiny glimpses of his face so close to mine as my eyes fluttered open.

Nothing beat the perfect kiss.

I kissed Craig like that. At one time in our life, he gave me that high.

Maybe Kael was right. Maybe humans weren't made to be together forever. Maybe *'til death do us part* was a punishment more than a promise.

Instead of pulling completely apart, our foreheads rested together for a few seconds as we just ... lived in the moment. That one second followed by several more. We shared a few breaths and existed as something undefinable in silence. I thought of Snow Patrol's "Chasing Cars." Being with someone for a moment in time while just forgetting the rest of the world.

Just a moment.

Just a few breaths.

Just *being*.

The moment ended as all moments did. When I climbed out, he licked his thumb and wiped my face.

My nose wrinkled.

"Sorry. But you had food on your face because you insisted on acting like a child about a loaf of bread. Are you sure you're forty-two?"

Before his thumb left my cheek, I turned my head and bit it playfully. "I'm ageless around you. Stupid. Immature. And ... free."

"Thank god for that. I'm not sure I could afford you if you weren't free."

"Funny guy. Haha."

"Tell me..." he brushed my hair away from my face "... how will you react if anyone finds out about us? I think I need to prepare myself for that version of you."

"Now you're scaring me. Who's going to find out? Did you say something to someone?"

"That right there." He held up a finger between our faces. "That's what I'm talking about. That panic you get at the thought of someone finding out. We're doing *nothing* wrong. Well ... except in the minds of your Bible people."

"My Bible people?" I laughed. "You mean in the eyes of God?"

"No. I mean in the eyes of your Bible people."

"You think God is okay with what we're doing, but my church family would not be?"

He smirked.

"You're an atheist. Why am I even having this conversation with you?" I rolled my eyes then covered my face. "Ugh ... I'm having sex out of wedlock *with* an atheist."

"I'm not an atheist. And we're not committing adultery, so that gets you some counter points with the big guy. Right?"

No. Yes. I didn't know.

I was raised to believe you shouldn't sin. Period. It wasn't a scale that just had to have a balance of good deeds and sins. I had dirty sex on Thanksgiving in the back of my Tahoe on a dead-end road, but I also volunteered at a homeless shelter and donated to the food bank ... so all was good?

That wasn't how it worked.

Dropping my chin, I grimaced from the truth suffocating my conscience. "If anyone found out, I would feel ashamed."

Kael slipped his ungloved hands into the pockets of his jacket, his disappointment evident by that tiny gesture to physically distance himself from me. "Ashamed of me. That's great to hear."

"Not of you. Of myself for ..."

"For what? Being a grown-ass adult with physical desires? Are we spreading disease and adding to the overpopulation of the world? Are we breaking up marriages? Are we cheating on other people? What exactly do you have to be ashamed about?"

"Because I was married for twenty-two years. I've had four children. I'm not opposed to monogamy."

"Aaannnd ... what is your point? No one said you have to be opposed to monogamy or children. Sometimes humans mate for life and it works out just fine, whether we're really wired to do so or not. It's not your fault that your husband died. Had he not died, you would be happily married. Blissfully monogamous. A loyal superstar like a bat, wolf, or beaver."

Happily married.

Blissfully monogamous.

There was just so much he didn't know.

"Bat, wolf, or beaver?" I glanced up at him with one eye squinted.

"Yes. Three to five percent of approximately 5,000

species of mammals practice lifelong monogamy. Bats, beavers, and wolves are part of that three to five percent. And geese ... mustn't forget the geese—the ultimate example of a monogamous animal. Even if their mate is killed, they will not mate again."

Kael didn't simply choose on a whim to not get married, have children, and live a life free from the confines of monogamy. He'd researched it. Maybe to make himself feel better about not conforming.

"And humans?" My head canted to the side.

"I think we strive for lifelong sexual and social monogamy because of societal structure more than it being part of our natural state."

After a few seconds of searching for a proper response, I said the only thing that I knew for certain to be true in my life. And the only way to deliver it was with a frown. "Welp, clearly I'm not a goose."

Kael's head rocked back as he laughed. "No. You're not a goose. Not anymore. Maybe a duck. They're seasonally monogamous."

On another eye roll, I turned, opened the driver's door, and climbed inside.

Kael leaned inside and kissed me slowly. "Happy Thanksgiving."

I smiled and rubbed my lips together while fastening my seat belt. "You too. Are you making a fancy dinner with all the trimmings?"

He shook his head and chuckled. "No. Not for two people. I bought a rotisserie chicken at the store yesterday to make soup."

"Chicken noodle?" My nose wrinkled.

"Yep."

"On Thanksgiving?"

Another chuckle. "Yes. On Thanksgiving."

"That's …" I gazed out at the woods. "Sad. That's sad, Kael."

"Sad would be popcorn and a turkey roll from *Smith's*."

My head whipped to the side. "Asshole."

"Duck." He smirked.

My phone chimed with a text, and I glanced at the screen.

> Bella: You OK? It's been over an hour.

"Shoot. It's Bella wondering where I'm at."

He narrowed his eyes at the screen. "Tell her the truth."

"You idiot. I'm not telling her the truth."

"She didn't ask for your location. She asked if you're okay. Say, 'yes,' and tell her you're on your way home."

"And when I get home?"

"Tell her it's the holidays, and holidays are filled with surprises."

I grunted a laugh. "And later when she wonders about the surprise?"

"Oh, Mrs. Smith. I'm afraid you think your kids are more interested in your daily activities than what they really are. She's eighteen not eight. By the time you get home, she will have forgotten that she was even worried about you for a brief moment."

I texted her saying I was on my way home, but I shook my head while doing it. "My husband died in a car accident on a snowy night in December. Her concern is not that fleeting."

"I'm sorry."

After starting my Tahoe, I glanced at him and found a smile that didn't scream *"I killed my husband, and the least I could do is be a goose. But I'm not a goose. I'm a fucking duck!"*

"It's life." I lifted a shoulder.

"I don't mean for this to sound like anything but a sincere compliment. But you moving on enough to allow yourself..." his eyes shifted to the backseat for a quick second "...*this*. It says a lot about your strength to persevere."

Yes. I was amazing. A true saint. The world's best wife and mother. I deserved some sort of award. "That's kind of you to say. And maybe a little biased since you've been the recipient of my *strength and perseverance*."

"It's not a bad gig."

"Thirty. Single. Living life on the fly. Having sex with whomever whenever it suits you. Yeah ... not a bad gig. Now go make soup for your dad." I reached for the door handle, forcing him to take a step backward.

"Better bring your A-game tomorrow. I have some killer Black Friday specials going on." He smirked.

"Santa Claus comes to *Smith's* on Black Friday. Photographer. Free candy. Prize drawings. If I were you, I'd take the day off, so you and your staff don't get bored."

"Game on." He winked and shut my door.

As I put my Tahoe into reverse, he knocked on my window.

"Yes?" I rolled down the window.

"Milk, Mrs. Smith. Don't forget you left for milk." He strode to his truck to get my milk.

That was close …

CHAPTER sixteen

When he turned the bedroom light on at five in the morning, an hour before I had to wake up, I felt like he was silently asking for a divorce. It was a 'lightbulb' moment for me.

"DEAR HEAVENLY FATHER, we thank you for this time we have together and the food you've provided to nourish our bodies. As we approach the anniversary of Craig going home to be with you, may you continue to comfort our hearts. Amen." I opened my eyes and shared a genuine smile with my kids and the three additional young women around the oval dining room table.

Bella wanted to set a place for Craig and light a candle in his memory. So we did.

"Can I make a toast before we begin?" Finn asked, pushing out of his chair and lifting his glass of sparkling cider.

"Sure," I nodded.

He cleared his throat and took a deep breath. "To Mom ..."

I died.

My mind imagined a toast to Craig or an unexpected wedding proposal to his girlfriend. I never expected to hear my name come out of his mouth.

"Thank you for filling his shoes. There hasn't been a single second since he died that I've felt even a tiny bit less loved. And while I miss him beyond words, I'm so proud of the way you've kept him alive in this house, at the store, and with your love."

All the tears flowed freely, not only from my eyes but from everyone else at the table.

"To Mom," my other three children chimed in.

Finn ... he knew. He had always known. I *never* expected that from him. I think part of me imagined him holding an eternal grudge over the fight ... the request for a divorce. He questioned my right to fifty-percent of things. My, how my young boy had matured in a year. I hated to think how much of it was forced upon him from his father's death.

"How's business so far?" Linc asked as we started eating.

"It's okay."

"Just okay?" He raised a brow.

"There's competition. A cool food specialty store that's like something you'd see in a bigger city. It's called *What Did You Expect?*" Bella seemed a little too excited about the store that was trying to put *Smith's* out of business.

"That doesn't sound good."

"Thank you." I nodded at Chase. "It's not good. Epperly isn't big enough for two specialty stores."

"But Kael is *so* nice." Bella continued to play devil's advocate.

"Kael?" Chase frowned.

"Yes. He's the owner. He was actually here this morning. You would have met him had you not been sleeping in *forever*. He cleared the driveway. And he does all kinds of nice stuff for people. I'm pretty sure he and Amber are a thing." Bella and her rumors.

I hoped they were rumors.

"Are you sure about that?" I asked as casually as I could while focusing on my green bean casserole, stabbing at it with a little more force than was necessary.

"Amber seems to think so."

"How old is this dude?" Linc asked.

"Thirty," my expert daughter answered right away.

"And Amber is what ... nineteen?" Linc continued.

"She's twenty."

"Ten years. Wow. He's preying on the young ones."

Bella rolled her eyes. "Ten years is no big deal. They're both adults."

I liked the new direction of the conversation, even if it was about Kael and Amber. On the odd and awful chance that anyone found out about my new pastime, knowing how my kids—and maybe most of Epperly as a whole— would react was a good thing. Sort of.

"So you would date him? I mean ... if ten is okay, is twelve? Fifteen?" Linc asked Bella.

"Stop. You're being stupid." Bella shook her head. "But yeah ... I'd date him in a heartbeat if I thought Mom wouldn't have a heart attack." She shot me a smirk.

I mirrored her smirk, but mine was more from nausea, not any sort of orneriness. Kael and my daughter.

No. That didn't sit well with me.

He was in the middle—Bella twelve years younger and me twelve years older.

"So, Haven ... you're thinking med school?" I asked Chase's girlfriend.

I had to get the picture of Kael and Bella out of my head.

Kael and Amber.

Kael and anyone else.

Monogamy was ingrained deeply into my personality. It was how I was raised. It wasn't teaching an "old dog new tricks." It was rewiring my brain.

BLACK FRIDAY.

Smith's biggest sales day of the year.

Until everything went sideways.

Santa had an early case of the flu. The photographer's uncle died, and she had to cancel. And when I opened the boxes of candy canes, they were broken, missing some of the wrappers, and littered with mice droppings.

"It's fine. We've got this," Bella tried to reassure me.

To give our employees a long weekend, the kids helped at the store, as they had done for years before Craig died. Customers loved stopping by to catch up with our children. But I feared my children—as wonderful as they were—would not be enough to attract the usual crowd.

Santa guaranteed parents coming with their young kids. And that led to purchases.

"Where's Santa?" A young child burst with excitement as customers poured into the shop the second Linc unlocked the front door and turned on the neon *Open* sign.

"He's ..." Sick? I couldn't say sick. Did Santa get sick? Would it have scared young kids to think of him getting sick? If he could be sick on Black Friday, then he could be sick on Christmas Eve. "Running a little late. I think he stopped for hot chocolate."

Linc's eyes widened as he stood behind the young girl and her mom.

I grabbed Bella's arm. "You need to get on your phone and check with your friends. *Someone* has to own a Santa Claus costume in this town."

She snorted a laugh. "Yeah. I doubt it."

"Call Marilyn Hubert and ask her if we can borrow Leonard's costume."

"Why? Are you going to dress up?"

I gave her a tight grin as customers milled around closer to the register. "If need be, yes."

No. I would not be Santa. Leonard was easily two hundred and fifty pounds, and maybe six feet two inches. I was just over five-three and a buck twenty-five in weight.

"Whatever." Bella escaped into the back room while I fielded all questions about Santa and the missing candy canes.

"He's coming." I held firm to that promise. "And instead of candy canes this year, we have chocolate."

"We do?" Finn mumbled behind me.

"Yes." I grabbed the basket of individually wrapped truffles at the end of the counter. They were a dollar a piece. Fifty cents my cost.

"You're giving those out?" the mom asked.

"Of course." I smiled.

"Cha-ching," Finn said behind me.

The little girl grabbed three.

"Just one, sweetie," her mom said.

"But I used to get three candy canes for Christmas past, Christmas present, and Christmas future."

Way to go, Craig.

"Of course you get three truffles." I smiled.

"Cha-ching. Cha-ching. Cha-ching." Finn was just asking to be put in timeout.

I moved my hand behind my back and flipped him the bird.

After the girl and her mom moved on to look around the shop, I turned toward him.

His jaw hung open.

I didn't swear. And I didn't give people the bird. At least ... that was the mom he used to know. Things changed.

All things *fuck* took over my life. I used the word. I signed it with my middle finger. And I did it with Kael Hendricks.

I liked fuck.

For a moment, I considered getting a T-shirt that said as much or maybe a bracelet or necklace with *fuck* engraved someplace. The one around my neck at that moment said WWJD. I would keep that one for Sundays and grief recovery meetings.

"Did you seriously just give me the middle finger?" Finn whispered.

"I don't know what you're talking about." Pressing my lips together, I blinked innocently several times.

His mouth curled into a grin. "Who are you?"

I was the woman who let a man go down on her at the end of a gravel road on Thanksgiving.

"I'm your mom. Now go see if Bella's having any luck with the Santa situation."

The cha-chings started to add up, especially when customers came into the store, realized Santa wasn't there, grabbed *three fucking truffles,* and left without a purchase.

"No luck." Bella frowned, tossing her phone onto the counter like it was her phone's fault that we couldn't get the Santa costume.

"You just couldn't reach them?"

"No. I reached them. But they already loaned it out to someone else."

"Who?"

She shrugged.

"Santa's across the street!" hollered one of the customers, pointing to the window.

I craned my neck to see. "Son of a bitch."

"Mom!" Bella gasped.

My language startled another one of my children.

"Him." I glared out the window to the entrance of *What Did You Expect?* with a growing line ... There was Santa and a woman dressed up as an elf taking photos.

Kael Fucking Hendricks and one of his employees emerged through the entrance of his store with trays of hot drinks and what looked like some sort of goodies—probably that caramel apple bread or peppermint bark. They handed it out to everyone waiting in line.

In line for Santa.

In line for photos.

In line to buy newer, hipper specialty foods.

We were over.

Not that we were really anything more than wild animals who liked to screw, but *that* was over.

He could have Tillie, Izzy, Amber or anyone else in Epperly. Okay, not Bella. But literally *anyone* else. I didn't care.

I couldn't let him fuck me *and* my business. Not anymore.

"What are you going to do?"

"Not me. You."

"Me?" Bella squinted at me.

"No." I exhaled. "It can't be you. That would be too suspicious."

"What would?"

"Amie. I need to call Amie." I grabbed my phone and headed toward the back room. "Watch the register."

Amie answered on the second ring. "I heard." I didn't have to see her to imagine the cringe on her face.

Small town. Of course she'd heard that Santa was not at *Smith's* this year, but instead an imposter across the town square.

"Cindy told me. But you can't be mad. You're sleeping with the guy."

"We have never 'slept' together, and we never will. It's sex—*was* sex. Whatever it was or wasn't is now officially over. So I can definitely be mad that the one day ... the *one* day I had to keep *Smith's* afloat for the year has been ambushed by *him*."

"It's not his fault Leonard got the flu."

"It's his fault that he stole the costume! How did he even know to ask Leonard for it? I just found out this morning that Leonard is sick."

"Oh ... didn't you know? Kael is Leonard's neighbor. You know how chatty and kind Marilyn can be. I'm sure she offered it to Kael the second she knew Leonard wouldn't be able to be your Santa."

"She should have offered it to me!"

"Agreed. But I'm sure she figured you wouldn't be able to pull off Santa quite as well as Kael."

"I would have found someone else. And Kael isn't even the one wearing the costume. He's too busy serving hot beverages and delectable goodies to his customers. He's fucking me on every level, and I'm done. I need you to activate Plan B."

"Plan B?" Amie chuckled.

"Yes. I need someone to get sick from something in his store."

"You said that wasn't your game."

I sighed. "Yes. When I thought we could survive the loss in profits leading up to Black Friday and the final sprint until Christmas. When I thought the novelty would quickly wear off, and his overpriced oil and vinegar would be too trendy for this town. When I thought Santa Fucking Claus would be at *my* store today."

"Whoa ... nice holiday language."

Closing my eyes, I rubbed my temples. "Yesterday, Finn gave a toast. He went on and on about how proud he was of me, and part of the reason is because I've kept the store going. I've kept our family going. I've stayed in the same house. I've taken care of his grandparents. And he knows ... he knows the truth about the argument that happened before Craig died. So it meant *that* much more. It's not like Chase or Linc saying the same thing because they don't know. Which kills me that they don't know, but it would equally kill me if they did know. But Finn knows. And he still said it. I can't be responsible for his father's death *and,* only a year later, be responsible for the family business closing its doors while I let our competition *literally* screw me in every way possible."

"Well ... okay ... wow. In *every* way possible? Does that mean—"

"You know what I mean."

Amie sniggered. "No. I don't completely know what you mean. I think further explanation is needed. But we'll sort out those details later. For now, I'm your person. I will get sick and save Christmas for *Smith's*."

"Don't sound so dramatic. You don't actually have to get sick."

"To sell it ... I do. I have to get sick."

In spite of my brewing anger at the situation, I chuckled. "You can make yourself get sick?"

"Yes. I have some emetic herbs. Harmless, but they will cause vomiting. I'll head to his store, browse around, sample a little bit of everything and ... boom! I'll get sick. In his store. It's genius really. It won't be a minor rumor that I got sick from something at his store. There will be the visual for everyone there. Cameras. Social media. He'll be out of business by the end of the week."

Her plan cinched the already tight knot in my stomach. "I don't know ..."

"Elsie! You can't say that. If you weren't letting him screw you in very naughty ways, would you be thinking twice about this plan?"

Yes. I would have had many second thoughts about

her plan. I wasn't vindictive by nature. I wasn't out to destroy anyone.

I was …

Desperate.

Scared.

Drowning.

"We never had this conversation." I ended the call and hugged my phone to my chest as I closed my eyes. Being mean made me feel physically ill. I felt it after I completely unloaded on Craig the day he died.

"Two," Linc opened the door to the back room. "We have two customers. Old people, of course, because everyone under sixty is across the street visiting Santa and buying products that don't have a gazillion preservatives."

My jaw relaxed to say something. Something about bad luck, bad timing, and Karma. Then his words caught up to me. "You think our store is outdated?"

"Don't you? And don't lie. We know you don't eat anything from here. Even when products get close to expiring, you give them to neighbors, but Dad ate them. Sometimes, he'd live off beef sticks, spreadable cheddar, and popcorn for weeks because he refused to let things go to waste."

I nodded slowly. "So would Grandma and Papa Smith."

"And so would most of Epperly. But even before Dad died, things weren't doing quite as well. Not with online shopping. So it's not simply a product issue, and you know it."

We weren't giving the residents of Epperly a reason to get out of their recliners and go to an actual brick and mortar store. Except for that time of year when people wanted pictures with Santa.

Or cooking classes.

Or sexy new guys with killer smiles.

Or a shit ton of free samples of stuff they'd never tried before.

"So what's the solution?"

Linc shrugged. "Depends. Do you want to keep the store?"

No.

"I'm not sure. I feel like I should."

"Why? For Grandma and Papa? For Dad?"

"Maybe," I whispered.

"You don't need the money. I mean ... Dad had really good life insurance. Great investments. The house is paid off. You could get a job if you wanted to do something else for some extra money. You could move to Arizona. Bella graduates in the spring. What's keeping you in Epperly?"

"Your grandparents." Craig's closest sibling was a twelve-hour drive from Epperly.

"Should they really be your responsibility?"

Again ... another emotional dilemma. Not only was I not raised to be mean and vindictive, I was raised to care for those who needed help. It was part of my upbringing at home as well as in church.

"They have two other children."

I shook my head. "They'll put them in a home, just like your dad wanted to do."

"So?"

"So?" I choked on my disbelief. "They're still okay, Linc. They have their home and some dignity left. They don't need help bathing. They don't need adult diapers. They can cook some of their own meals. They just need a little help with the more physical tasks. Are you going to throw me into a nursing home the second I start to get arthritis? Bad knees? Pain in a hip? Is that what's around the corner for me? I brought you into this world, fed you, changed your diapers, taught you how to speak, kissed your wounds, made sure you had everything you needed, but when I need my lawn mowed or snow shoveled ... you're going to put me in a home?"

"Mom, if I'm not living in Epperly ... if none of your children are living in Epperly ... then what are we supposed to do? Move here to mow your lawn?"

"I don't know, Linc. Maybe move me closer to you so you can help me out."

"So we ... draw straws to see who gets to take care of Mom?"

Oh. My. Gosh.

He said that. And I know he didn't mean it to sound so harsh, like such an inconceivable burden ... like the opposite of winning the lottery. But it did. It sounded pretty awful.

"No. I would never want to burden any of you. I will happily retire to a ten-by-ten room, shit myself all day, stare out a window and contemplate where the heck I went wrong in raising my kids."

"Not cool, Mom." Linc shook his head. "And you're forty-two. Why are you even talking about something that won't be an issue for many years? And how do you know you won't find someone and decide to remarry?"

"I don't want to remarry."

"You're just saying that because Dad hasn't been gone

that long. You can't predict the future. Unexpected things happen."

I had so much to say about that, but it wasn't something I wanted to share with my young adult child who had his whole life ahead of him.

Views changed.

Needs changed.

Happiness shifted into new directions.

I wasn't afraid of growing old and being lonely. I was afraid of following an expected protocol, making decisions based on societal expectations.

Crap ...

I was making Kael's case.

"You're right. I don't know what the future holds."

"Promise me you'll talk to Mel and Jeremy. Maybe they'd be willing to move Grandma and Papa closer to them."

I knew Craig's siblings wouldn't be on board with that. Mel just made partner at a law firm in Miami. And Jeremy's marriage was on the rocks because he cheated on his wife a few months after Craig's death. He was kind enough to actually blame it on Craig—the stress of it. In a roundabout way, I was to blame for Jeremy's infidelity.

"Okay," I said through a fake smile. "I'll talk to them."

"Thank you." He sighed. "I'm taking off. I think you can handle the holiday rush on your own."

"Yeah ... shit!" I grimaced. "Shoot ... you know what I mean." I scrambled past him. "Stay here. I have to run a quick errand."

"Where are you going?"

I ran out the door, no jacket, no regard for Bella calling my name as well.

"Sorry. Excuse me. Sorry. Pardon me." I zigzagged my way through the Black Friday crowd congesting the square while shooting off a text to Amie: **Abort!**

Grabby hands kept me from getting there in a timely manner, like Pam from my grief group, stopping me by snagging my sleeve.

"Hey. I thought of you and our group the other night when my son woke me up at three in the morning by turning on the light in my bedroom."

"Um ... okay. Can't wait to hear all about it at group." I pulled out of her grip.

"Ben used to do that. When he turned the bedroom light on at five in the morning, an hour before I had to wake up. I felt like he was silently asking for a divorce. It was a 'lightbulb' moment for me. And now his son does it and will someday drive his wife crazy. I hope he can at least put away his clean clothes. I would wash Ben's clothes and put them on his side of the bed. He'd move them to the floor, where they'd stay for weeks until the dog made a nest of them, and they had to be washed again." She laughed.

I kept my forward motion but shot her a smile over my shoulder. "I'm sure you miss that now." Yay for me! I said the right thing. I reminded her to focus on the important things in life. Her inconsiderate bastard of a husband was dead. No need to keep dwelling on the past even if it had become the theme of our group.

"Ho. Ho. Ho ... young lady." Santa grabbed my arm as I budged in line, fighting my way to the entrance of *What Did You Expect?* Why did everyone feel the need to grab me?

Whipping my head back in his direction, I jerked my arm away. "I need to ..." My eyes narrowed. "Dan?"

Kael's father in *the* Santa suit winked at me. "Shh ... it's Santa."

After a few seconds of hesitation, I nodded slowly. "I uh ... need to get inside."

"Kael wants me to spend the afternoon at your store. So I'll see you in a few hours. Get ready for the crowd to shift to your place."

Why? Why did that anger me even more? Since when did kindness irritate me so much? Oh yeah ... since Kael Hendricks tipped my world on its side.

"Amie ..." I whispered, turning and bulldozing anyone who tried to block me from getting into the store. But just as I reached the door, customers poured out of it like opened flood gates.

"Yuck."

"Eww ..."

"Gross."

The herd of customers exiting the store forced me to step aside.

"Poor, Amie."

"I know."

"You think it's really botulism?"

"I don't know. That's what she mumbled while she was doubled over."

The passing chatter and incessant whispers filled the space as everyone scattered, even the lineup of children waiting to see Santa, dispersed in all directions. As soon as I found a tiny gap, I slipped into the store. And there she was, on her knees, close to the checkout counter.

Rachel wiped Amie's sweaty forehead with a damp

towel then handed her a glass of water while Kael and one of his other employees cleaned the vomit-covered floor.

"I sh-should ... have shopped at *Smith's* ..." Amie's shaky voice sent out a final declaration to the handful of remaining customers gathered around the crime scene.

Abandoned baskets of products littered the aisles like carnage.

"I'm very sorry, Amie," Kael said as he shoved soiled paper towels into a trash bag before standing and clocking me with a look I knew I'd never forget. "Your friend is on her knees in misery. Why are you just standing there, Mrs. Smith?"

I tore my gaze from him before he saw right through me. Then I rushed to Amie's side. Rachel wrinkled her nose and bit her bottom lip. Apparently Kael was the only one who wasn't truly sympathetic.

"Let's go." I, too, wrinkled my nose from the sour vomit smell as I helped Amie to her feet.

She hugged her midsection, blond hair matted to her sweaty face. "I'm so sorry, Elsie. I ... I should have known better than to try something that wasn't from your store. I deserve this. I'm such a traitor."

"Over-selling," I gritted through my teeth next to her ear.

Amie wanted to be an actress before she settled on her career as a chiropractor. And there was nothing I could have said or done to stop her from finishing the scene in her once-in-a-lifetime role. All I could do was cower under the eyes of everyone around us.

"What did I expect?" she belted out.

I wanted to die.

"Not this! Save yourselves!" We hobbled arm-in-arm to the door.

"Um ... Amie?"

We glanced around at Kael, holding up a phone. Amie's phone. He studied the screen, lips twisted as he brought it to her. "Oh ... wow. You must be pregnant, huh?"

"What?" Amie said.

Kael held up the phone so we could see her screen and my message. "My ... my ... Mrs. Smith. How ungodly of you to recommend your friend get an abortion." He added his own dramatic flair. He had his own way of turning heads and starting a terrible rumor.

She snatched it from his hand.

He smirked. "I would never tell a woman what to do with her body, but you really should consider adoption."

Amie inspected the screen, and then she shifted her gaze to me, maintaining a firm wrinkle of confusion along her forehead. I gave her a dead stare, trying to hide any sort of tell. But Kael knew. Even if no one else understood, he didn't miss the true meaning. Amid the new round of chatter bleeding out of his store into the square, the most viral gossip ever, we hung our heads in shame and wormed our way to my store and the long line of customers we'd just inherited because I was an asshole.

Craig would have been friends with Kael. I had no doubt about that. He would have sat next to him at the sports bar, drinking beer and placing bets on sports and business. My husband was competitive to a fault. He would have fought dirty, but not that dirty. All in good fun and friendly competition. He would have exploited all our longtime customers who were in their eighties and nineties and given credit to *Smith's* sausages and popcorn for their longevity.

He wouldn't have done what Amie and I did. Even my competitive husband had boundaries.

If Jeremy could blame Craig's death for his affair, I could blame Craig's death for my temporary lapse in sanity and moral judgment.

Right?

CHAPTER seventeen

He'd come into the house while I'd be in the middle of a TV show—stand directly between me and the TV— to tell me about a carburetor he was working on in the garage or why it took him so long to replace the brakes on the neighbor's vehicle.

FINN AND CHASE made sure Amie and her car got home safely since she was still feeling the effects of whatever herb she took to make her vomit. Bella, Linc, and I scurried around the shop the rest of the afternoon, dealing with the onslaught of customers. It ended up being one of our best Black Fridays (sales wise) ever.

"Coming?" Bella asked as I shut off the lights and grabbed my purse. "You go ahead. I have a few errands to run."

"Checking in on Amie?"

I nodded.

"That's terrible. And so bad for Kael. I mean ... clearly I feel for Amie, but I kind of feel bad for him too. What if it wasn't his fault? You know? What if it was the manufacturer's fault? There could end up being a recall on whatever made her sick, but in the meantime, nobody will go back to Kael's store. That's sad."

"Yes. It is. I'm sure he'll rebound. He's young and charismatic. Everyone loves him."

"Except you."

As I opened the door and stuck my key in the outside lock, I frowned at her. "What do you mean?"

She gave me a head tilt as if my question was ridiculous. "I see the way you look at him. And you're so tense and standoffish around him. You don't like him—either because he's *Smith's* competition or because you're jealous of his store *and* the fact that everyone does love him. It's not like you, but I see it. You can't stand him. And I don't really get it. You're a lot like him. I mean ... I'd think you'd like the products at his store. And you've always been someone to go out of your way to help other people."

"You're right. It's not like me. But you're also wrong ... I'm not jealous of him."

"Good. Because Amber is having a get-together at her house tonight, and he'll be there. I'm going, and I just don't want you to be pissed off if I don't act all douchey toward him." She stepped outside.

I pulled the door shut and turned the lock. "You know for a fact that he's going?"

"That's what she said."

Turning toward her, I deposited my keys into my purse and hiked it up onto my shoulder. "Have fun. No need to be *douchey* on my account."

Bella smirked before leaning in to kiss my cheek. "Sorry. That was a little douchey of me to say that.

Thanks. I will have fun. Tell Amie I hope she feels better soon."

"Will do." I waited for her to disappear around the corner at the end of the square before I headed to *What Did You Expect?* It was closed, but I could see the light on by the register.

I rapped my gloved hand on the door several times. Kael glanced up from the computer screen. He waited a few seconds with an unreadable expression before sliding off the stool and taking his sweet time to open the door.

"We're closed." He blinked at me with eyes void of that usual sparkle of life.

"I know. I thought we could talk before you go to *Amber's*."

"Why does her name sound so sour coming off your tongue?" He didn't open the door any wider or step aside as if he had any intention of inviting me in for that *chitchat*.

"Sorry. She's young enough to be my daughter, so the fact that we've been intimate makes it a little hard to swallow the idea of you and her together."

He shrugged and it was filled with an air of cockiness or lack of giving a shit about what I thought. "Well, she's not young enough to be my daughter, and she's a consenting adult so ..."

"Kael ..." I deflated. "I'm sorry."

He pulled his phone out of his pocket and tapped the screen. Then he held the face of it to me. It showed a green light and a microphone icon. "Sorry for what, Mrs. Smith?"

I remained silent, staring at the screen.

"Are you sorry for sending your best friend over to fake food poisoning at my store?"

I didn't react.

"Are you sorry for fucking me behind everyone's back because you were too ashamed to have something for yourself?"

I flinched.

"Or are you sorry that I don't need a church or even a God for that matter to be kind to other people? To do the right thing? Is that it? Are you feeling sorry that you've been preached to your whole life—WWJD—yet you *failed* miserably when things got tough? Or are you sorry that playing the grieving widow no longer gets you sympathy sales for your outdated shit?"

Tears filled my eyes as I continued to focus only on his phone screen.

"Go home, Elsie." He returned his phone to his back pocket. "I'm willing to clear your driveway, repair a leaky faucet, change a flat tire, or fuck you to Sunday, but I'm not willing to help carry your emotional baggage."

I didn't like to think about the twelve-year age gap between us when we were having sex. But I definitely didn't like to think about it as he so expertly schooled me on being a good person and doing the right thing.

Before I could formulate a response, a new plea ... he shut and locked the door on me. And I deserved it.

"Hey, Elsie. Did you have a good Thanksgiving?" Myra, Amie's mom, hugged me as soon as she opened Amie's front door.

"I did. Thank you."

"Amie's in the living room. She was feeling a little under the weather, so I brought her some of my homemade broth."

Dragging my guilty self into the living room, I affixed the proper, regretful grimace onto my face. It wasn't hard—I really did feel awful for Amie ... and Kael ... and my devil-lassoed-soul.

"Don't." She forced a groggy smile from her recliner, blanket over her legs, cup of soup in her hands. "You're not allowed to look so dang distraught."

I glanced over my shoulder.

"She's in the kitchen and a little hard of hearing. I didn't tell her the truth."

"Amie ..." I sat on the edge of her blue crushed velvet sofa. "I'm so sorry."

"Elsie—"

"Let me finish." I shook my head. "I know you're going to say that you offered to do it for me. That it was even your idea originally. But that doesn't matter. I mean ..." I frowned. "It does matter. It just shows what an incredible friend you are to me. Honestly, I'm not sure I'd purposefully make myself vomit and embarrass myself publicly just to help you get a leg up on the competition."

She chuckled before taking a sip of her broth. "So in the Thelma and Louise scenario, you'd bail at the last second and let me go off the cliff by myself?"

I nodded, pursing my lips to hide my grin.

"Bitch."

"I know." I shrugged.

"But did you have a great afternoon of sales?"

Another nod.

"Then it was worth it."

"No. That's just it. It wasn't worth it. My evil spawns have just put me through the wringer the past two days. First there was Bella's inviting Kael and his dad in for coffee yesterday morning two seconds after telling me that Kael and Amber are a thing. That got me all worked up. Then a milk run turned into sex in the back of my Tahoe by the creek. Finn's epic Thanksgiving toast. Mice droppings on my candy canes. Sick Santa. Stolen Santa. Linc suggesting I close the store and move to Arizona. The vomiting fiasco. It's all too much!" I threw my hands up in the air.

With her mug of broth at her mouth, she paused, unblinking, lips parted. "Sex in the back of your Tahoe?"

On a long exhale, my shameful gaze dropped to the floor as I nodded.

"On Thanksgiving?"

Nod.

"While all of your kids were at home?"

Nod.

"You're my idol."

"Nooo!" I covered my face. "It was so bad."

"Oh ... did you not ... did he not ..."

Flopping backward, I rested my head on the cushion and kept my face covered. "God ... no. I mean we did ... I did ... he did. And it was just ... Gah! So good. And unexpected. Raw. Primal. *Hot*. But wrong. I think. I don't know." I dropped my hands from my face but kept my gaze on her ceiling because there was no way I could look at her. "The windows were fogged up. The whole vehicle was bouncing. I was loud. He was unrelenting. He did things to me that ... I just can't even put into words how it made me feel."

Amie gulped so hard I could hear it. "W-well try. *Please* try to put it into words. I attempted suicide today for you. The least you could do is throw me a bone. Was it anal? Please say yes. My church-going BFF getting it up the backside in the back of her Tahoe on Thanksgiving gives me an odd sense of pride."

"No." I giggled, closing my eyes and rolling my head side to side. "Oral. Not anal. Then just ..."

"Just?"

"Regular."

"Regular?" She chuckled.

I snapped my head up, letting her see all the shades of my embarrassment. "Stop. You know what I mean. The ... *front*."

"The *front* ..." She nodded slowly. "You really should offer to sub for health class at the high school. Instead of anal and vaginal, you'd call it front and back. And *doing it* in the front or back door should involve a *fitted, single-fingered latex glove* over the male's *thingy*. Does that all sound about right, Mrs. Smith?"

More giggles ensued. And although I was hurting inside, the tiny break for laughter kept me from completely drowning. Amie always knew what I needed. "I don't know what I'm doing. And if he didn't run a competing business, I swear I wouldn't care. I'd just go with the moment and sort out the consequences later. And I crossed a line. *I* crossed it. Not you."

"But you asked me to abort, and I didn't see your message. Not that it would have mattered. The food was coming up, but I might have known to not blame it on him."

"Yeah. And he knows. I don't know if he'll tell anyone, but he knows."

Amie shrugged. "Then I'll tell everyone it was a mistake. That come to find out ... it was something I ate right before going to his store. He gets his customers back. You go out of business and move to Arizona. And everyone lives happily ever after. Except me. I'll miss your ass if you leave Epperly. And Craig's parents will too. *Not* that we are a reason for you to stay. Maybe Mr. Humpty Dumpty is worthy of sticking around for."

"Sex toy." I smirked. "I call him my sex toy. Well, not anymore. As we speak, he's at Amber's house for a little get-together. I think we know how this night will end. Besides ... he's not too happy with me."

"Ugh ... he's going for the younger body. Don't fret. You're nothing to balk at."

Pressing my lips together, I widened my eyes. "That's ... an interesting compliment."

She simpered. "It's age appropriate. Middle age is the death of excellence. Our highest hopes are mediocre. It's when 'good enough' is the high bar. 'Nothing to balk at' and 'not the ugliest, not the flabbiest' ... they're all age appropriate. Definite compliments. So if a guy has sex with you, and he says, 'It wasn't the worst,' I think you have to accept that as a compliment. Just the fact that a thirty-year-old guy, that looks like *him,* wants to put his dick inside of you and move it around is really a huge accomplishment. I'm quite envious."

"Move it around?" I snickered. "I think you'd be a fantastic sub for sex-ed too. Man puts thingy in woman's front hole, moves it around, and voila! Baby nine months later."

"Who's having a baby?" Myra traipsed into the living room, bringing me a cup of tea.

"Thank you." I wrapped my hands around the hot mug and inhaled the cinnamon and plum aroma as she eased onto the opposite end of the sofa.

"Nobody's having a baby. We were just talking about men and women. About getting older. About relationships," Amie said.

"When your dad died, everyone said I should remarry. Remember?"

Amie nodded at her mom.

Myra released a heavy exhale. "But I didn't want to train another man. I was done having children. You were grown and gone. The house was quiet, but not awkwardly quiet. Your father used to come into the house while I'd be in the middle of a TV show—stand directly between me and the TV— to tell me about a carburetor he was working on in the garage or why it took him so long to replace the brakes on the neighbor's vehicle. He'd also do it if I was in the middle of a good book. But ... if I had nothing preoccupying me, like during dinner or around bedtime, he had nothing to say. So many times I felt like he was just stealing all the good oxygen in the room."

I grinned at Myra's honesty while Amie coughed a laugh. "Wow, Mom. Stealing all the good oxygen? That's harsh."

Myra lifted a single shoulder. "The truth usually is. That's why most people lie so much. The world was built on truth, but it runs on lies. Over time, we bend the lies to make them true, to make ourselves feel less guilty about our honest feelings. I loved your dad, but I also hated him for making it so hard to love him some days. Does that make sense?"

"Yes." My reply shot out without a second's warning. And that was when I knew ... I saw it in Myra's eyes. The silent acknowledgment, the hint of sympathy.

Six.

Six people knew.

Amie had told her mom the truth about me and Craig. I wasn't mad. I was envious of Amie living so close to her mom—of them being so close. I didn't have a bad relationship with my mom, but it wasn't a best-friend kind of relationship.

"What do I do?" I changed the subject, giving my attention to Amie again.

"About Kael?"

I nodded.

If she told everyone it was her mistake ... the food poisoning was from something else she ate and Kael shared a different—more accurate—truth, it could have tarnished her reputation in Epperly. If I told the truth, it still would have made her look bad for agreeing to do it for me.

"Sleep on it. We'll talk tomorrow." Amie shot me a reassuring smile.

"What if he's at that little get-together telling everyone the truth?"

She shook her head. "I doubt it."

"Why?"

"Because he's a nice guy." Her nose wrinkled, finishing her thought without saying the words. *And we screwed him over today.*

Just after two in the morning, the doorbell rang, startling me and sending my heart into its usual who-died arrhythmia. Tying the sash to my robe, I hurried down the stairs and opened the door.

"I believe she belongs to you," Kael said as he stood in front of me with a passed-out Bella cradled in his arms. She had vomit down the front of her shirt.

I never imagined the day would come that seeing my underaged daughter drunk and having to be carried to the door would be a huge relief, but as I eyed the rise and fall of her soiled chest, I felt nothing but gratitude.

"Um ..." I stepped closer as I was going to take her from him.

"What are you doing?" He frowned at the notion. "Move."

I stepped aside and followed him up the stairs. He laid her in her bed and headed right back downstairs without giving me a second glance. I kissed Bella's forehead. "Be right back."

She barely mumbled.

"Wait!" I called after Kael as he opened the front door to leave. He turned and tucked his hands into the pockets of his jacket as his truck idled in the driveway behind him.

"Thank you. She's not usually one to drink. Must have been some party."

"She seemed to be having a good time."

"Was she with anyone ..." I hugged my arms to my waist. "A guy?"

"I wasn't there to chaperone or take notes for anyone's

parents. You'll have to ask her about that." He turned and headed toward his truck.

"Did you provide the alcohol?"

He didn't answer.

I shoved my feet into someone's snow boots, probably one of the boys' from the extra four inches in the toe, and clomped after Kael. "Did you hear me?"

He whipped around just as he opened his door. "No, Mrs. Smith. I did not provide the alcohol. Why? Were you going to report me to the police if I had been the one to provide it?"

He made me feel old. And used. And ... just awful. And yet, I deserved all of it and then some.

Still ... it didn't make it hurt any less.

"No." I couldn't force my gaze up to meet his dull eyes. It stuck to his chest, suppressed by so much shame. "I ..."

The truth.

I started to tell him the truth. I was a breath away from letting him be number seven. But he didn't want to help carry my baggage. And that was a shitload of baggage.

"You what?"

"I really appreciate you bringing her home. And Amie is going to make sure everyone in Epperly knows that she didn't get sick from anything at your store."

"And you're going to let everyone in Epperly know that you put her up to it?"

I tried so hard to force my gaze up a few more inches, but I couldn't. "Yes," I whispered.

"If you wanted me out of Epperly, why didn't you just ask me to leave?"

There it was. That was all it took for me to meet his gaze. "If I asked you to leave, you would leave?"

"Yes." His affirmative answer held a lot more confidence than mine.

He was the better human ... times a million.

Atheist. Gigolo. Best human.

"Why?"

"Because I don't ever want to be a burden on anyone."

Internally, I grinned. Had he decided to have a family, he would have insisted his children put him in a home to not be a burden on them.

Not me. Nope.

I liked to guilt my children way in advance.

"Did you and Amb—" I shifted my gaze to the side.

"Finish."

I shook my head.

"Did Amber and I ... what? Have sex? Kiss? What are you digging around for?"

"Nothing."

"Does that bother you? The idea of me with *her*? Or does the idea of me with *anyone else* bother you?"

"I have to check on Bella." I started to turn, but he grabbed my waist.

"I don't expect a forty-two-year-old woman who was married for twenty-two years and who has four children to be good at casual sex. But I do expect someone with your level of *maturity* to know how to use your words. Say what you mean. And don't be so fucking ashamed of it. Just say it. You can't lose what you don't have."

Him.

I didn't have him.

Nobody had him.

"It's *her*. Her age and my daughter's age." That was half true. But half-truths were all I had to offer at the moment. The full truth had too much baggage. "I don't care whose bed you crawl into. And for the record, I don't *want* you. I've raised enough men in my life, and I'm fucking exhausted." My words seemed to bring that sparkle back into his eyes.

"I'm not screwing your daughter's friend. Are we good?"

"Well ... I don't know. After today's unfortunate events ... *are* we good?"

He had every right to hate me.

"My dad is heading home at eight tomorrow morning. Be at my place by nine. I like my coffee black." He grabbed the tie to my robe with one hand while his other hand snaked between my legs, shoving my panties aside, and ripped a gasp from my chest as he filled me with his fingers.

"Y-you can't..." I gulped as my body stiffened "... just do this."

He forced every hair on my body to stand erect, and with the slightest movement of his fingers, he made it impossible to tell him no. "And yet ... here I am doing it. My hands are a little cold from giving you so much of my time tonight. I needed to warm up." His thumb applied a little pressure in a circular motion. "And you are *so* fucking warm, Mrs. Smith. See you at nine."

Just as quickly as he violated me, he hopped into his truck and backed out of my driveway, leaving me a mess in oversized boots with a vomit-covered teenager waiting inside for me.

I was living the dream ...

CHAPTER eighteen

My husband scratches his junk then sniffs his fingers. I don't think he knows I see him, but I do, and it's a total turnoff.

"Are you mad?" Bella mumbled as I helped her out of her clothes and into the shower.

"Did you try to drive home?"

She shook her head as her groggy eyes fought to stay open while the sour stench of her vomit—intensified by the steam from the shower—turned my stomach. Vomit odor twice in one day. Lucky me.

"Then I'm not mad. It's okay to be young and curious. It's the stupid part I'm not okay with. If someone has to drive you home and carry you to bed, I'm okay with that. I just need …" I choked on my words for a few seconds. "I just need to know you're always coming home." My lips pressed to her head for a few seconds before I helped her into the shower.

Bella vomited two more times before falling into a restful sleep around three in the morning. I never fell asleep.

I stared at the ceiling, feeling every inch of empty bed beside me. The sheets felt colder.

The air heavier.

The silence more deafening.

The void Craig left started to feel like a black hole.

And there I existed on the edge of it. The guilt said I needed to fall into it, attempting to fill it. The little voice in my head—the same one that gave me the courage to ask him for a divorce—it said I needed to walk away from everything that pulled me toward that infinite life of despair. Break away from the shackles of that guilt.

"Give me grace," I whispered to ... someone.

God?

Craig?

My children?

My church friends?

Where was the light? I had never felt so lost. Was that freedom? Did I need the very boundaries I tried so hard to tear down?

Some of my friends said that when they became empty nesters, they had to get reacquainted with their spouses again. And they'd hoped they still loved that person they fell in love with before parenthood took center stage.

I didn't make it that far.

I didn't want that second first date with Craig Smith.

I wanted out.

He wasn't the one I needed to get to know again. It was me. I let myself get so completely lost in everyone else. And I wouldn't have changed one single thing about that life. I didn't regret those twenty-two years.

However, I knew I'd resent each new day that I pretended to still be in love with him.

"Do you hate me?" I said in a thick voice as a tear slid down the side of my face. "I wouldn't blame you if you did. I ... I just didn't know how to say it, how to explain it. Then it just ..." A few more tears followed the first one. "It just came out all at once. Like my..." I pressed a hand to my chest, curling my fingers into my skin "...heart exploded. The truth needed to be set free. *I* needed to be set free. I needed to stop hating myself for feeling the way I did. We were too real to ever live a lie."

I sniffled and shook with silent sobs as I fought to finish. "I wanted to let you go." Those words burned my throat as the faint outline of the idle ceiling fan blurred on the other side of my tears. "But n-not like th-that."

THE BOYS ASSURED me they'd get Bella fed and hydrated the second she awoke. I said I needed to check on Amie.

I lied.

Myra had that covered.

"Just sex," I said as soon as Kael answered his door, looking unfairly sexy in low hanging black sweatpants and no shirt.

Hair wet and messy from a recent shower.

Pine and cedar scent swirled around him along with a nuttiness from the coffee cup I handed him.

He grinned. "Just sex."

I stepped inside and took off my boots while simultaneously shrugging off my wool coat, letting it drop to the floor.

His walls might have had crazy bright paint on them. The floor might have been all hard surface with scattered area rugs. The ceilings might have been vaulted with rustic fixtures hanging from long chains. And there was a possibility he had a Christmas tree in a sitting area off to my right.

I wasn't entirely sure because I took no more than a passing glance as I made my way into his arms the second he sipped his coffee and set it on a small credenza to his right.

My hands pressed to his bearded face as our lips moved together—that indescribable kiss. When he pulled back to appreciate my eagerness, my brows drew together. "I might cry. Promise me you won't stop, and you'll ignore it."

He mirrored my furrowed-brow expression.

I lifted onto my toes and brushed my lips over his as the tears filled my eyes. "Just promise," I whispered.

After a few seconds, he blinked. "I promise I won't stop." He lifted me until my legs encircled his waist, and he carried me down the wide hall to his bedroom. As he laid me on his bed, his mouth covered mine, his tongue making deep strokes while I dug my fingers into the thick muscles along his back.

Resting his body weight on one forearm, he took his opposite hand and wiped the tears from my left cheek.

I turned my head to break our kiss. "Don't."

"I'm not stopping." He kissed the wet trail of tears along my other cheek. "But there's nothing about you I can ignore."

Taking his face in my hands, I made him look at me. I didn't know what I was searching for or what I wanted to say until the words came out on their own. "Make me feel ..." I whispered.

He kissed along my collarbone to the hollow of my neck. "Feel what?"

"Just ..." I closed my eyes, raking my hands through his hair and down his back. "*Feel ...*"

He made me feel wanted.

He made me feel sexy.

He made me feel alive.

But mostly ... he made me feel a little found.

After I played with my sex toy—the term I needed to remember to keep things in perspective because I had love and commitment ingrained in my sappy little forty-two-year-old heart—I hid in the corner of his bedroom with my back to him while I dressed.

"The uh ... baggage comment. I wasn't trying to be insensitive. The prospect of going out of business had me a little salty."

I glanced over my shoulder as I buttoned my gray, fitted pants.

He tucked in his red tee. "I'm just saying that if you need me to carry like ... one bag, or just hold it for a minute, I can do that."

Pausing for a moment, I nodded. "You want to know why I was crying."

"I'm saying you can tell me—if you want. I can listen. Probably can't solve a damn thing. But I'm not a total asshole. So ..."

"Thank you." I found a tiny but genuine smile. "I'm good for now."

"Cool. So ..." He rubbed his sexy lips together and prowled toward me. "About our working relationship ..."

I anticipated his hands finding my waist or maybe sliding around my neck to gently guide my head and my gaze to him.

Nope.

He clasped his hands behind his back and drew in a long breath. A *really* long breath. Then he held it for an impossibly long time.

After a few seconds, I realized my breathing was on pause as well.

"Business is business. Right? I mean ... that's why you allowed your friend to put on such a pathetic and cringeworthy display at my store. Correct?"

Where was he going? I blinked a few times, biting the inside of my cheek. "I made a poor decision in the moment—fueled by anger and frustration. I tried to stop her, but it was too late."

"Anger? Why were you angry?"

I brushed past him toward the bedroom door. "Don't act so innocent. You stole my Santa."

"My dad?"

I turned halfway down the hallway, Kael just feet behind me. "The costume." My eyes narrowed.

"My sick neighbor offered me the costume. Honestly, I said no at first because I knew he was supposed to be at your shop. But then we thought it would be a win-win to have him wear it and split the day between our two businesses. Your afternoon seemed to be better than my morning."

"You should have told me! Why would you not call or drop in quickly to tell me the plan?"

His hesitation and the ghost of something ornery or deviant that crossed his face gave away his true intention.

"You were trying to get a reaction out of me. You wanted me to be upset so you could make me eat crow when your dad came to my store *after* allowing me to think the worst of you. You were just asking for me to behave badly."

He played me.

He played me, and he did it while looking like the victim and then the hero.

His mouth twisted. "I toyed with you—a tiny bit. But you crossed a serious line to the dark side."

"*Toyed* with me?" I jabbed my finger into his chest, revenge constricting my pupils. "*You* are the sex toy, not me."

Toy. I meant to say toy. Only toy. I was the cat. He was the crippled mouse. I was the puppeteer. He was the puppet.

No sex. Why did my mouth let my brain win?

He lit up like the town square Christmas tree. "Damn ... I think I love being your sex toy. I like your face red and your hands balled at your sides. Is that wrong?"

"Yes. It's wrong and sadistic. Not a sex toy. You're a pet toy." I turned and stomped to the front door, plucking my jacket off the floor while stabbing my feet into my boots.

"No. You said sex toy. I have good hearing. I heard you perfectly." Complete delight and an arrogant tone of victory carried his words.

"You're a guy. You heard what you wanted to hear. And all things translate to sex for you. It's not your fault that you're genetically wired to think about sex all day long." I reached for the door handle.

He grabbed me, spinning my body around, my back hitting the door. The Kael Hendricks eye sparkle was back and on steroids. "You think of me as your *sex toy*. You've said it before."

I deflated, angling my gaze to the side. "*Not* in the way you think."

"I think you're using me for sex. I think you're using me like a human dildo. I think you get a high knowing that other women in your little town of Epperly are throwing themselves at me, but I'm only into you—in the most literal sense. I think you like the secrecy. The simplicity. The sinfulness."

He waited.

I kept a straight face.

He waited some more.

His body towered over mine, keeping me in my spot and plastered to the door until I gave him something back—acknowledgment. Nourishment for his male ego.

"Fine." I shrugged, giving him a fleeting glance. "It is in the way you think. Now, move so I can get to work."

There wasn't another step for him to take, yet he found one, sucking all the air from my personal space. "Are you sure you're done playing with me? I think we both have a few extra minutes to spare."

"Careful. I'd hate for my shiny new toy to lose its luster."

"Mrs. Smith ... I'm not losing my shine in your eyes anytime soon. And you fucking know it."

I burned in his presence, and *he* knew it. He pounced on every opportunity to reveal my weakness—him. Kael Hendricks was my weakness. The only thing that annoyed me about him was his incessant need to wear clothes and do things that didn't involve giving me an orgasm. That and his natural flirtatious nature that drove all the women crazy.

"By the way..." he stepped back to give me a breath or maybe exhale the one I'd been holding "...I made a marketing decision after the vomit incident. I felt it was necessary to recoup a few customers. It was before you told me that Amie planned on making things right. So I just want to make sure we're good. That's what I was getting ready to tell you earlier when I mentioned our working relationship. Business being business."

I tipped my chin up and cleared my throat. "Of course ... business is business."

"Great." Without touching me with any other part of his body, he leaned down and kissed the corner of my mouth. I felt his lips bend into a smile.

I didn't trust that smile.

"Have a great day at work," he whispered, giving me a faint chill along my neck and down my spine.

SLOW DAY.

I wasn't sure what my competitor's marketing decision was or if it affected my slow sales day.

Until ...

Grief recovery group.

"Rhonda just called. She's running a few minutes late. We can pray and start without her. Or ..." Kelly, shrugged nonchalantly. "We can real talk."

"Real talk?" Deb asked.

"She wants to talk about the things our husbands did that we don't miss." Bethanne winked at Kelly. "Right?"

"We can just wait for Rhonda." I smiled. What had I done to our little *church* group? Only one of us needed to go straight to Hell.

Me, of course.

Yet everyone else seemed to have a guilty conscience too. Real emotions weren't supposed to feel so wrong. My husband drove me crazy and died. I didn't physically wrap my hands around his neck and strangle him—even if I thought about it in that weird, uncontrollable part of my brain. Everyone had dirty, awful, shameful, unimaginable thoughts float through their heads on those rare occasions.

"It's ... freeing." Kelly shared a sheepish grin. "I can't fully explain it. Missing him is the part that comes naturally. It's the part that everyone understands—everyone expects. It's easy to miss all the good times. *But* it's hard to live with the regret over the parts that weren't great. I miss a million things about him ... does that make it okay to not miss a dozen things that I literally started to hate about him? A million to twelve. That's not terrible. Right?"

Silence settled over our group for a few minutes, letting Kelly's words hang in the air—a familiar cloud I knew all too well.

"A tiny rock in your shoe on a ten-mile walk. It's so freaking tiny compared to your foot. The size of a grain of salt. And the view is amazing. You love that pine scent filling the cool air. You know the soft trickle of the nearby stream is the most relaxing sound ever."

"Blue sky." Kelly took over, and I smiled at her. "Soft breeze. Archways and canopies of trees. A wonderland. *But* ... you can't enjoy any of it because the tiniest little thing is irritating you. It's hijacked your mind. And no matter how hard you try to ignore it, you just can't let that tiny thing go. It slowly steals your enjoyment ... your happiness. And if you don't get rid of it, you know it will ruin the hike, and you'll regret not doing something to remedy the situation."

"*But ...*" Bethanne spoke up. "It's not just you on the walk. It's a group of people."

Pam nodded slowly as she picked up the story. "And you don't want to disrupt the pace. You don't want to ask them to stop for you."

Kelly wiped a tear. "You don't want to complain. You don't want to be difficult."

"So you go with the flow," I said, not knowing when the mood of the room shifted, but it did. And everyone shared the same moment ... the same thoughts without really saying much at all. "Until you can't take it. And you say something."

"And you realize you should have just stayed quiet because when they see the rock ... it looks so tiny. And you look ridiculous for making a big deal out of nothing," Bethanne finished the scenario.

Or you empty your other shoe filled with more tiny rocks. Then ... you let them know the rocks are their fault. They leave ... and never return.

Fucking tiny rock ...

"My husband scratched his junk then sniffed his fingers. I don't think he knew I saw him, but I did, and it was a total turnoff." Bonnie wrinkled her nose—so did everyone else. "I mean ... it was his junk, not mine. It wasn't the end of the world. It was just a gross thing he did. I suppose it was no different than someone smelling their armpits to see if they have BO. Right? I suppose he just couldn't bend his nose down that far."

A few of us snorted suppressed laughs as Bonnie smirked.

"Rick would gag on his toothbrush ... Every. Single. Time."

"Toby had a few teeth knocked out from playing hockey, and he wore a removable denture or bridge thing in public. But at home, he took it out because it was uncomfortable. And I totally understood. You should be able to just relax at home. But ... here's the awful, embarrassing *but* ... I hated looking at him with missing teeth. So I didn't. He'd talk and I'd look at anything but his face. Quick glances to make eye contact, but I couldn't look at his mouth. Terrible. Right?"

A collective head shake moved like a wave around the room. Maybe it was terrible, but we *all* had our "buts," so it felt hypocritical to judge—it felt unchristian to admit it aloud.

WWJD? He would've looked at Toby's gnarly smile and seen past it to his beautiful soul. But Jesus walked on water, so I always found the WWJD bar to be a bit high for the average modern-day sinner.

The "I loved my husband *but*" statements rolled off the tongues of all the sinners/widows that night.

"Eating with his mouth open."

"Removing his dirty underwear and tossing them on the bed right before getting into bed."

"Always talking politics."

"Scoping out women—not so slyly."

"Assuming I would cater to him like his mom—laundry, cooking, cleaning, picking up after him."

"Butchering all the songs on the radio by singing to them without knowing the words."

"Never walking the recyclables to the garage, just leaving them on the counter like they would grow legs and leave on their own."

"Tea bags on the edge of our clean sink."

"Long fingernails."

And then ... the original scratch-and-sniff comment took second place as Rhonda arrived late. And she'd heard the next comment all too clearly.

"He wanted to go down on me when it was that time of the month."

Silence.

So much deafening silence.

Rhonda cleared her throat, clutching it at the same time, eyes like saucers. "Wh-what are we talking about, ladies?" She stressed the *ladies* as if to remind us that we were in fact expected to act like ladies.

Not whores.

At least, I felt like that was what Rhonda's tone of voice insinuated. The whore part might have just been my guilty conscience. Abby letting Ryan go down on her during her period didn't make her a whore. It made her ... lucky? I was actually quite horny during my period, especially toward the end. But I didn't have sex during it. Craig never even suggested it. And oral sex during that special time of the month? No way. But I didn't like meat that wasn't charred. Ryan probably liked his steak rare.

Abby, with her back to Rhonda, cringed. We all cringed, even if outwardly we tried to act like Mom didn't just walk in on us talking about some bloody good sex.

"Abby was just remembering how Ryan would go

down to the pharmacy during her menstrual cycle to get sanitary napkins and chocolate. What a total sweetheart, huh?" Bethanne for the save.

I wasn't sure if Rhonda bought it, but there was no way she was going to question it and risk the actual topic going any further.

"That is sweet." Rhonda eyed me. ME!

What did I do? Oh, right ... I turned our church-based group into a confessional of all the things that drove people crazy about their significant other, instead of the gathering of gratitude and prayer that it was meant to be.

My bad.

Rhonda took a seat and cleared her throat—still eyeing me like the troublemaker. "I was sad to see your competitor using your product labels to promote his products. I know it's smart marketing, but in such a small town, it felt like a low blow. I'm sure it was a desperate attempt to recover from the business he lost on Black Friday after Dr. Jennings blamed him for her illness that turned out to be something else. It's all very unfortunate." She took way too much pride in telling me that.

Of course, I had no idea what she was talking about.

"Oh ..." She read my mind. "You didn't know?"

"Know what?" I played it extra cool.

"That Kael posted your products' ingredients next to the ingredients in his products on his shelves along with a list of things that have been shown or suspected to cause heart disease, hypertension, obesity, and cancer. It was a little jarring to see how much fat, salt, and preservatives, that I can't even pronounce, are in your products." She chuckled. "I'm sure that's what gives them such a sinful taste but seeing it like that made me think twice about consuming them. Especially since my doctor just put me on cholesterol medication."

Business is business ...

Biting my lips together, I nodded slowly.

Well played.

CHAPTER nineteen

"But-uh ... so anyway ... yeah." My husband used space holders in conversations. He talked in fragments, ending his incomplete thoughts with "you know ..." I didn't know— nobody knew. Everyone else nodded politely as if they did know because Craig was a nice guy. Nice guys didn't need to speak in full sentences.

MONDAY MORNING, I knocked on the door to *What Did You Expect?* thirty minutes before it was supposed to open for the day. Kael grinned as he approached the entrance.

"Nice surprise," he said after unlocking the door. "But..." he glanced over his shoulder "...one of my employees just arrived. We could probably do it quickly in the bathroom if you're not too loud."

"You've put me out of business. Happy?"

A deep line formed between his eyebrows. "What?" He retreated a step and opened the door wider to let me inside. "Can you get things set up in the kitchen for tonight's class?" he asked his employee. "I need a minute with Mrs. Smith."

The woman nodded and closed the door to the kitchen behind her. She could see us but hearing us would have been a little more difficult, especially since he had jolly holiday music playing fairly loudly through the speakers.

I perused up one aisle and down another while he shadowed me. The labels Rhonda mentioned were no longer on the shelves, but I'd since heard from several other sources that they were there all day the Saturday after Black Friday.

It didn't matter.

"How did I put you out of business?"

"By coming to Epperly." I shrugged, keeping my distance and my back to him while pretending to be interested in all the unique items on his displays.

"Does Epperly not support a free market? You have more than one bank and grocery store."

Two.

We had two banks and two grocery stores. A third bank or a third grocery store would not have survived. Well, the new one might have, but one of the other ones would have had to close its doors. Banks and grocery stores were essential businesses. Specialty food stores were not. One was enough, and outside of the holiday season, one specialty food store was too much.

"I didn't say you did anything wrong. It's a free market. You had every right to start up a business here. But it doesn't change the facts."

"Which are?"

I stopped at the end of an aisle and turned toward him, crossing my arms over my chest. "I'm closing the doors to *Smith's* for good at the end of the year."

"Because of me?"

I nodded.

"Elsie ..."

"Don't apologize. Don't give me the business is business speech. I don't want to hear it. I'm not even mad."

I was a little mad. At whom? I wasn't sure.

Myself?

Craig?

Kael?

Customers?

I felt numb. Maybe it was the anniversary of Craig's death approaching. In so many ways, I felt just as lost and trapped as I did a year earlier. Another tiny rock in my shoe that I couldn't ignore any longer. It made me angry, irritated, and a little reckless.

"I don't know what to say."

I shook my head. "There's nothing to say. You should be proud. Victorious. You'll do well. Everyone loves you and your store the way they loved my husband and his family's store for so many years. And if you stick around long enough, some young asshole with a fresh idea will move into town and force you to close your doors. Think of it as the circle of life in the business world."

"Young asshole. Is that what I am to you?"

"To Mrs. Smith, shop owner. Yes. You are. To me, Elsie ... you're my sex toy." *That* felt victorious.

That look on his face. After years of watching men put women in their place—in Epperly that meant barefoot, pregnant, and rubbing a pot roast—it felt slightly gratifying to be the one doing the objectifying.

I expected the same grin as the first time he heard me call him a sex toy. No such luck.

"Well ..." He glanced toward the kitchen, but not as if anything in that direction had his focus—more like he just didn't want to look at me. "I'm truly sorry for Mrs. Smith. My intention was never to run anyone out of business. As for Elsie, I'm happy I can scratch her itch and entertain her needs." He sounded anything but happy.

That victorious gratification began to burn out like a fire without oxygen. "It's what you wanted too. Right?"

He grunted a laugh and faked the worst smile ever as he nodded slowly, bringing his attention back to me. "For you to scratch an itch?"

"Yeah," I whispered.

Four kids and twenty-two years of marriage made me a good reader of people. Except Kael. I couldn't read him. Or maybe I could, but I was too afraid to see something that either wasn't really there ... or worse ... that was there.

"Sure."

Terrible answer. I hated sure. It meant anything but sure. The only word more aggravating than "sure" was "whatever." Two of the most dismissive words in the English language. I was at a loss for words, but I refused to fill the space or say something as awful as "sure" or "whatever" just to appease the person in front of me.

"Don't say that."

His lower teeth scraped his upper lip a few times. "Say what?"

"Sure. Don't say 'sure' and don't say 'whatever.' Say nothing or say everything. I can't handle vagueness. I can't handle you communicating ... or lack thereof ... like my husband. Don't fill space with but-uh. Don't say 'you know' because you're too lazy or impatient to finish your thoughts. I *don't* know."

He glanced at his watch. "I'm going to go with saying nothing then because I don't have time to say everything. And if I'm being honest, I don't know what everything is right now. So if you don't like vague, then it has to be nothing. And I hope I've completed my sentences well enough so you *do* know what I mean."

"You can't be mad because *I'm* going out of business. I'm sorry. That's just not allowed. So if I've offended some delicate part of your ego because I've managed to separate what you've done to me professionally from what you've done to me personally, then maybe you need to start practicing what you preach a little better."

"What I preach?" Kael rested his hands on his hips and leaned forward a few inches. "What does that mean?"

"It means … you can't give me that look like you're not okay with being someone's sex toy when you don't want anything more from a relationship than sex."

"I never said that."

"You did!" My voice boomed, eliciting a quick glance from his employee in the kitchen.

"No. I didn't."

"You don't believe in monogamy."

"No." He shook his head. "I never said that."

"You totally said that."

"I said I wasn't sure if humans are meant to mate for life."

"Same thing." I crossed my arms over my chest.

"Not the same thing. I never said humans can't be monogamous or that some don't have a natural desire to be monogamous. But monogamy doesn't mean mating for life. It simply means one partner at a time—for however long. And maybe that's eternity, but that should be a choice not a contract."

My lips parted in preparation of saying something, but that something never came.

"I have to open my store."

When I didn't move, not one blink, he reached forward and hooked my index finger with his. It made that malfunctioning organ behind my ribs ache. "I don't expect anything, and I don't think you do either. But I also don't want to be with anyone else right now. So call it monogamy or just good old infatuation with one person, but that's where I'm at right now."

I stared at our hooked fingers. "For how long? How long will you only want to be with me?"

"How should I know?"

Because my heart likes to know these things before making an investment.

I shrugged. "I don't know."

"Expectations are a prelude to failure." He released my finger.

My gaze lifted to meet his. "What are we without expectations? Lost?"

"Free."

"How would you feel if you found out I was having a ..." I cleared my throat as Bella glanced up from her plate on our first night alone again since the boys left after Thanksgiving.

"A what?" She paused her fork near her lips.

I hadn't touched my food. Kael was the only person who knew I was planning on closing the store after Christmas. Why I chose to tell him first ... I had no idea.

"What if I said I've been *intimate* with someone for the past month? How would you feel?"

She squinted at me, mouth agape. "Skeptical. Uh ... I'd ask who? There's like ... one *maybe* two eligible men in this town who are worth looking at."

"Who?"

Bella shook her head slowly and shrugged. "Mike Holmes and Brian Hosier."

Pathetic. Epperly was so dang small. It didn't take her more than two seconds to name two of the three eligible bachelors in Epperly.

"Is this hypothetical? Or did you have sex with our banker or Dad's attorney? Or are you thinking of dating one of them? What's going on?"

"I'm not having sex with or dating Mike or Brian. My question was how would you feel? Regardless of who it hypothetically is or would be."

Her gaze dropped to her plate as she used her fork to pick at her eggs. "I mean ... it would feel a little weird. It's always been Dad. But I'm not naive. I know you're too young to never think about getting married again."

"Whoa. No. I'm not talking marriage, Bella."

Her head shot up. "You're not?"

I laced my fingers behind my neck and looked up at the ceiling on a long inhale. "What if I wanted ..."

"Sex?" Bella laughed as if it were a ridiculous thought.

Releasing my neck, I leveled my head, eyeing her without blinking. "Would that be so crazy?"

Her head jerked back a fraction, eyebrows knitted while her eyes shifted side to side for a few seconds. "Kinda. I mean. You just want to live with someone? You don't want to get remarried?"

I raised her so well in the eyes of the church—except for a few minor slips like losing her virginity before marriage and underage drinking. Even if she didn't follow the rules, she knew them. She knew them well enough to hold me accountable to them.

"I don't want to live with anyone at the moment except you." I blew out a long breath. Beating around the bush was getting me nowhere. "What if I had sex with someone just because I wanted to have sex?"

Lord help me. I never imagined those words coming out of my mouth directed at my eighteen-year-old daughter as if I needed permission to have sex. She sure didn't ask me for permission before she had it.

"Then I'd say you're going to Hell." Bella smirked.

It nearly brought me to tears because I felt this shift between us. Yes, she was and would always be my little girl. But in that moment, she became my friend, a young woman who I could confide in to at least a small degree.

"I hope not because that would mean you're going too."

"So ..." She rolled her lips between her teeth. "Are you having sex with someone?" The transparency of her expression sent waves of guilt through me. She wanted the answer to be no.

"You look pained, Bella. Is it because the idea of me having sex makes you cringe? Or is it the idea of me having sex with someone who's not your dad?"

"Both. Brian is Jaime's uncle. And Mike helps coach

the football team. So when people find out, it's just going to be a little weird because we go to church and you're not married. I know it's not like you're having an affair—" Her eyes widened. "Oh my gosh! Please tell me it's Brian or Mike. Please don't tell me you're having sex with a married man."

I flinched. "No! Of course not."

She blew out a long sigh. "Okay. Just promise me that if you go public with this, you give me a heads-up so I can figure out what to tell my friends. And can you just tell me now, is it Brian or Mike?"

It's Kael. And he makes me feel twenty again. And he's also the Devil for running Smith's out of business.

I didn't tell the kids I was closing up shop after the holidays. Dealing with the anniversary of Craig's death while trying to muster holiday cheer seemed like enough to think about without the doom and gloom of the family business closing.

"It's not—"

Bella held up her finger as she brought her phone to her ear. "Hey, Erin ... yeah. I'm planning on it. Cool. Seriously? That's totally sweet. Meet you there around six." She ended the call.

"Holiday Fest?"

Bella nodded. "*What Did You Expect?* is doing face paintings for ten dollars, and all the money goes to Toys for Tots. That's so cool, huh?"

I nodded. "Very cool."

"I might do it. Kael's one of the people doing the painting. It's for a good cause, and I can think of worse things than having him look into my eyes while being just inches from my face." She waggled her eyebrows. It was so not her. It was her dad. Craig waggled his eyebrows all the time.

"Please don't forget you're a senior in high school."

"So." She put her plate in the dishwasher. "I won't be much longer. And let's be honest. Guys my age are stupid and immature."

"Maybe." I stood behind her waiting to put my plate and coffee mug in the dishwasher too. "But thirty isn't just a little older."

Such a hypocrite. We were the same difference in age from Kael's thirty.

"Besides, I thought you said he's interested in Amber."

She turned, shuffling a few steps to the side to fill a glass with water. "She said they've messed around, but it's not serious."

My breakfast knocked at the door to my throat, begging to be expelled from my stomach as it roiled thinking about Amber and Kael "messing around." Whatever that meant.

The tiny upside, and it was minuscule compared to Amber and Kael, was Bella forgetting that she wanted to know who I was having, or thinking of having, sex with. But I felt certain it would only be temporary.

CHAPTER twenty

He made me feel stupid. He dismissed me. I gave him too much of myself, including my dignity.

EPPERLY'S biggest annual event was Holiday Fest. Everyone gathered in the square to shop, eat, listen to live music, ice skate in the rink they constructed just for December every year, and if there was snow on the ground, there was a snowman contest judged by the local business owners. Possibly my most important decision that year.

Kidding.

We saw a slight uptick in customers simply because *everyone* in Epperly gathered in the square. I even sold some of our subpar-will-give-you-cancer-and-hypertension shit that was a staple at *Smith's*.

"You seem oddly happy." Amie filled her cup with the free hot chocolate I had for the customers and sprinkled a spoonful of mini marshmallows onto it.

I remained perched on the stool behind the counter,

gazing out the window at the packed town square—a snow globe.

No wind.

Light snow.

Temperature hovering around thirty.

"It's a great night." I shrugged.

She glanced around the shop and chuckled before whispering, "No one is buying much."

I shrugged again. "Don't care."

"If you're trying to stay in business, you should care. You cared enough a week ago to let me get really sick and blame it on your competition." Her voice remained at a whisper.

"I'm closing the store on the thirty-first," I confessed in a monotone voice that wasn't loud enough for anyone else to hear, but definitely above a whisper. When I shifted my attention to Amie, she gave me a sad smile. She wasn't shocked. We'd talked about it too much.

"I'm proud of you."

I grunted. "Thanks. I'm not sure it's a decision that deserves that kind of recognition. Craig's parents won't be proud of me."

"So what happens after that?"

"Nothing. I go back to my lonely housewife—house-widow—life until Bella graduates and goes off to college. Then I ..."

"Don't."

I shifted my gaze to her again. "Don't what?"

Amie grinned. "Don't fill in that blank yet. Just let it happen when the time comes. I realize everyone will be asking you what's next, the way we're trained to ask seniors in high school what their plans are after they graduate. You don't have to have a five-year plan. You don't have to have a five-week plan. Just go with the flow. Do it for those of us who didn't lose a husband with good life insurance and smart investments. Do it for those of us who follow tiny home Instagram accounts and dream of escaping all men in favor of living in a community of women."

A smile crept up my face. Tiny homes. I couldn't see my claustrophobic friend living in a tiny home. "Good investments and life insurance. Lucky me. I bet if he could have a voice from his grave, he'd ask to revise his will to cut me out of it. And rightfully so."

"No." Amie shook her head. "Not rightfully so. You supported his business, raised his four children, and helped take care of his parents. That shit's worth something."

I gave a tight smile to a customer who drifted closer to the checkout just in time to hear "that shit's worth something."

Amie's gaze followed mine, and she offered a smile too.

"Listening to a man brag about unloading the dishwasher or the incessant need to announce every single thing he did in a day. That *stuff* is worth something. Give him a bone! Men are dogs ... they just are. They need constant praise and rewards. Women are pack mules—we work without praise for long days, recover quickly, and wake up the next day plodding right along again. No treats. No pats on the head. No belly rubs."

I loved my best friend. Retiring to a tiny home

community of women with her would have been an honor.

Bella and her friends burst through the front door with their faces painted. Bella looked like an elf with an adorable pink nose. Two of her friends were painted in reindeer faces, and the third friend was the Grinch.

"Wow! How cute!" Amie gushed.

"Right?" Bella grinned. "Kael is so talented. And it only took him ten minutes to do it. I paid twenty dollars instead of ten since it's for a good cause. And he smelled like mint and pine. I think I was drooling."

"Oh my god! I know!" Her friends all chimed in with their dreamy gaga gazes.

"You should get your face painted." Amie nodded toward the door. "Maybe get a pat on the head or let someone rub your belly ..." she mumbled with a smirk on her face.

"Can't. I have a shop to run."

"Mom! Go. We'll watch things. Do frosty. It will blend well with your gray hair."

My jaw dropped. I did not have gray hair. That anyone could see. I colored it.

"Ouch." Amie laughed.

I continued to shake my head as Bella tried to nudge me off my stool. "You girls go have fun. This *old gray lady* will stay here."

"I was kidding. Just go. All the other store owners are getting their faces painted too. Kael has a few of his employees painting as well, but they aren't as good. So make sure you get in his line." Bella gave me a final nudge while Amie eyed me with a shit-eating grin on her face.

There was no way I was getting in his line. I grabbed my coat and purse and dragged my reluctant ass out the door. All the shops would be closing in another hour so the snowman competition could be judged while the band played until midnight for the slew of ice skaters.

"Great night."

I glanced behind me as I wormed my way into Kael's store. "Hi. Yeah. It couldn't be more perfect," I replied to Mike Holmes, the banker, one of the two eligible men in Epperly. Three ... but not according to my daughter.

"How's business?"

Dead.

"Good. 'Tis the season to be grateful for every customer." As I pulled off my mittens and slipped them into my pockets, Kael glanced up from the table covered in a palate of paints, brush in his hand, white paint smudge on his nose and smeared along his beard.

He gave me two seconds, maybe three. Without so much as a smile, he returned his focus to the young girl on the stool next to him getting her face painted.

"Well, I'm definitely stopping by tomorrow to grab all my favorites from your store. One-stop Christmas shopping," Mike continued the small talk, saying all the right things.

"That sounds great. I'm not placing another order this year, so early shopping is a good idea."

"I bet you're running pretty ragged ... you know ... kids, work, Craig's parents. I don't know how you do it."

Apparently, I'm a pack mule.

The lines moved forward, and I veered into the shorter line that wasn't Kael's. "Yeah. It's been a crazy year, but I'm doing fine. The kids are doing well. And I can't do much about Craig's parents' situation, but every day I can help them stay in their home is a good day. How are your parents? I heard your dad had heart surgery a few weeks ago."

"He did. But he's recovering really well."

I nodded. "That's good."

"Yeah." Mike had a look. It was different and yet familiar. Before I could place the familiarity, he spoke again with a nervous demeanor. "Say ... how would you feel about getting a drink sometime? Or if you don't drink, we could share some nachos at the bar and grill."

A date.

Almost a year after Craig's death ... a guy asked me out on a date. I wondered how long he'd been thinking about it. Or maybe he just asked it on the fly out of nowhere. I actually liked that scenario better.

"Um ..." I thought of the rumors. Drinks or nachos at the bar and grill was different than screwing Kael in private. I was ready for sex, but was I ready for a small town to plan my next wedding? That was what would've happened.

Marry Mike or move to a different zip code.

"Maybe. Let me think on it until you come by the shop tomorrow."

He chuckled. "That's fine. No pressure. I honestly wasn't sure if I should ask or what the appropriate time to wait should be."

My nose wrinkled. "It's not that. It's..." I lowered my voice "...small-town gossip."

"Ah ..." He nodded. "Gotcha. Well, you can always

have dinner with me at my house if privacy is what you need. Just..." he held up his hands and smiled "... throwing that out there. Again, *no* pressure."

"Thanks."

"Do you need to get back to your store, Mrs. Smith?"

I pivoted toward Kael's slightly gravelly voice as he cleaned his brushes. "My daughter is watching the store. It's fine."

He jerked his head toward the empty stool next to him. "I'm sure she wants to do something besides watch the store. I'll squeeze you in now so you can get back. I don't think anyone would care." He winked at the next person in line.

Tillie.

Tillie was next in his line. She gave him a flirty grin and shook her head. "Elsie can go next. That's fine."

"No. Really." I pointed to the other employee whose line I was in. "I can wait."

"Get over here." Kael patted the stool with his hand.

I gulped and started sweating in all the embarrassing places. My body cheered at the opportunity to be closer to him. My head wasn't as excited. Wearing a sheepish grin for cutting in line, I weaved my way through the congestion to his stool, climbed onto it, and slipped off my jacket.

He took my jacket and purse and set it on the floor behind the table before smiling at me. He wasn't allowed to "mess around" with Amber then give me that smile.

He just ... wasn't.

"What do you want me to do to you, Elsie?" His suggestive smile twitched.

"Doesn't matter." I averted my gaze over his shoulder to Tillie drooling over him with so much adoration in her eyes.

She gave me a smile—the isn't-my-future-husband-awesome smile.

"Something wrong?" he murmured, dipping a brush in blue paint.

"Nope."

"For someone who doesn't like vague, you sure know how to dish it out." He kept his voice low and his face close to mine, putting us in a little bubble where no one else could hear us over the Christmas music and chattering customers.

"If your 'good old infatuation' with me is over, then I expect to hear it from you, not from my daughter."

He continued to paint my face, gaze on the brush, but his forehead wrinkled. "Not following."

"She said you were 'messing around' with Amber," I whispered. "And that's fine. This isn't love. I just *cannot* be with you like that if you're messing around with a girl my daughter's age. I'm sorry. I don't have the mental capacity for that right now." I shot Tillie a tiny smile as she leaned in to hear us. My smile made her back up again.

"The Epperly rumor mill." He grunted a tiny laugh. "Do I really have to comment on it?" His gaze made a sudden shift to mine. It was a challenge.

What was I supposed to say? That I didn't trust him? Say nothing and risk being the most gullible person in the town? It wasn't fair of him to ask me that.

"I cleared their driveway the other morning." He ripped his attention from mine, and it felt like a Band-Aid ripping away ... leaving something raw.

I needed an answer, and he needed me to trust him. It sucked that we needed different things in that moment. But with twelve years between us, I wasn't sure we would ever need the same thing at the same time unless it was an orgasm.

"When I got out to shovel the walk to their front door, she stepped outside and threw a snowball at me. I threw one back at her. So if that's messing around ... then I'm guilty."

Amber lied. She intentionally led her friends to believe she had done something sexual with Kael. I was disappointed in her the way a mother would be disappointed in their child.

Kael seemed to be disappointed with me, but not like a parent frustrated with a child's immaturity—more like a scorned lover.

"You're shaking," Kael whispered inches from my face as his brush slid across my forehead. "You need to hold still."

I swallowed hard. "Sorry."

A tiny grin pulled at his lips. He rested his left hand on my leg to still my bouncing knee. I felt it a little higher than my thigh. "Did you do something different with your hair?" He made small talk like Mike, but Mike didn't draw my nipples into pointy weapons with just his voice.

Kael always surprised me. He sucked at holding grudges. He sucked at being anything but nice. Even his evil moments faded quickly into something irresistible. Of course Tillie looked at him like he hung the moon—he probably did.

"I washed it." I smirked.

Kael chuckled and released my leg to change brushes, dipping the smaller brush in white paint.

Did the whole store see us? Did they see my red cheeks, erect nipples, and tiny, panting breaths rushing past my lips? I felt completely exposed, like he was seducing me in front of the whole town. I felt his anger and disappointment, but I also felt the chemistry between us, slowly building like it always did.

"I love your cheekbones ... they're perfection." His brush ghosted over my cheek.

"Stop," I whispered with a shaky voice.

"I will not," he whispered—his words only for me as his minty breath infiltrated my nose, so close to my face. "I love this tiny dimple that comes out when you smile."

"Kael ..." My heart hammered in my chest. "Please stop."

"And I love your lips."

I knew no one could hear him, and that made the words even more intimate.

His brush traced my lips, and I couldn't breathe. The heat on my skin burned to the point of pain. I needed out of there, but I couldn't leave. And he took his time as if he knew I needed out—as if he was making a point.

As if ... he was punishing me.

So I closed my eyes and thought about my dead husband and all the responsibility that came with his death. I thought about foods I hated and chores that sat on my long to-do list. I thought about anything but Kael using the word love over and over again.

I wasn't his to love in any way.

Not my cheekbones.

Not my dimple.

Not my lips.

And certainly not my heart, even if I felt the stroke of his brush hit me there like a hunter's dagger laying claim to it. There was nothing worse than giving something away to someone who didn't appreciate it or even want it. Kael didn't believe in love. He couldn't be a good steward of anyone's heart.

Minutes, hours, days later ... it felt like *forever* ... he stepped back. "Done. That will be ten bucks, my snow queen."

I blinked open my eyes.

"Oh my gosh ..."

"How beautiful ..."

"Oh! I want that!"

"It's like Elsa from Frozen!"

Eager customers ooo'd and aww'd while gawking at me. I returned a nervous smile as I climbed off the stool. Kael helped me into my jacket and handed me my purse.

My shaky hand reached into my purse and pulled out a twenty.

"I'll get you change."

I rolled my eyes. "Just ... keep it. Donate it. Whatever."

He smiled, slipping it into a jar filled with money. "Well, thank you, Mrs. Smith. That's very generous." He magically slipped back into Kael Hendricks, nice guy and fellow shop owner.

Before I could even get out of the tiny space behind his art table, Tillie threw her arms around Kael. "Good to see you. I've missed you. We really need to do dinner again."

Everyone grinned and pointed with delight at my face as I made my way out of the store. When I sneaked one last peek back at Kael, his gaze was already on me. He winked.

I couldn't hide my instant reaction—a knowing smile that felt like our little secret.

By the time I wormed my way back to the store, stopping every two seconds for compliments on my face, it was time to close up for the rest of the night's activities.

"Oh my gosh! Mom!" Bella's mouth fell open. "Not fair! Your face!"

I grabbed my phone out of my pocket and brought up the camera to have a look at what everyone was fussing about. "Dang ..." I whispered at the beautiful shades of blue swirled along my face and outlining my lips. But it was the intricate detail to all the snowflakes that gave a wow factor.

I liked it a lot.

Too much.

I liked *him* a lot.

Too much.

"Did you ask for that?" Bella snapped several photos of my face with her phone.

"Nope. I just said he could do whatever he wanted with my face."

I wanted him to grab it with both hands and kiss me until I forgot how to breathe, until my knees gave out, until the rest of the world faded into nothingness.

But the stunning face painting was a nice second choice.

"For real? Well, we are totally jealous." Bella frowned and her friends nodded with similar envy on their young, pouty faces.

"I'm going to use the restroom and lock up so I can

take my place at the judges' table. Are you girls going to make a snowman?"

"Of course. Laters, Mom."

As soon as I used the restroom and locked up shop, Kelly practically jumped me. "Elsie!"

I whipped around.

"Whoa ... I mean ... Elsa." She smiled, eyes wide. "Your face painting is a freaking masterpiece."

"Yeah. He did a good job. I wasn't expecting it."

"Well, listen ... I just wanted to catch you before the judging started."

"Okay." I pulled my white stocking cap onto my head and slipped on my mittens. "You caught me. What's up?"

We walked toward the center of the square.

"I'm selling my house and moving out of Epperly."

With surprise pulling at my painted face, I gave her a side glance. "You are, huh?"

"Yes." She returned a confident nod. "You ... your generosity and bravery for opening up to the group about the real stuff ... well, it's changed me. I felt like leaving here, the place where we met, married, and wanted to start a family—*and* the place where he's buried—would feel like I was running away and forgetting about him. I worried so much about what everyone would think. But you showed me that my feelings are important too. And I shouldn't be afraid or ashamed of them. You've been a huge role model."

Ugh ... not a role model at all.

"Kelly ... I'm not worthy. Really. But thank you. I'm happy for you. Leaving Epperly is just living your life. You can't change the past no matter how long you stay here. And beneath the headstone in that cemetery is just a body. It's not him. You carry him with you in spirit. And he would want you to be happy."

As we approached the table where the other shop owners were gathering to judge the snowman competition, I turned and hugged her. "Love you, lady. You've got this."

"Thank you, Elsie ... Elsa." She winked.

As soon as I turned toward the group getting settled in their chairs, Penelope, the owner of *Spoons*, gave me a conspiratorial grin. "So ... what's up with Kael Hendricks only giving *you* the Elsa face painting?"

My eyes shifted side to side. "Uh ... I know nothing about it."

"Well, apparently you left and the last few people in line asked for the same thing, and he said it was an exclusive Elsa for Elsie. What makes you so special in his young eyes?" She really punctuated the *young*.

I shrugged, tightening the scarf around my neck. "I think he feels bad for stealing my business this year."

"Oh ... wow. Has it been bad?" Concern kidnapped her playful banter.

"No. Well, of course competition will steal some business. I'm just kidding. I don't know why he was being weird about the face painting. He's kind of a goof like that."

"He really is." Penelope sipped her hot drink and shifted her attention to the snowman-making contestants fighting for fresh snow to roll into balls while playfully lobbing a few at each other.

"Where's Kael?" Grant, the art gallery owner asked, leaning forward to see everyone seated at the long table.

"He finished painting faces. Last I heard, he was

helping the Albertsons. Their oldest is sick, so they were struggling to keep up with getting trees strapped to vehicles," someone else offered.

The Albertsons owned the only tree farm within twenty miles of Epperly. Holiday Fest was their biggest night for selling trees, but they did heavily rely on their oldest son to help get trees secured to roofs—especially since Tobin Albertson had a kidney transplant just four months earlier.

"Of course he's helping the Albertsons. Last night he helped me clean the kitchen at my cafe when he saw my light was still on. One of my employees had to leave early. He's a saint if there ever was one." Penelope sighed. She had a husband and two young girls, but it didn't stop her from swooning over Kael and his generosity. "I heard he's removed snow from your driveway on more than one occasion." She nudged my arm.

I nodded slowly. "Yes. He did. It was very kind of him."

"I bet Bella has eyes for him. I know *all* the girls do. But rumor has it, he and Tillie have really hit it off."

Stupid. *Fucking*. Rumors.

The head judge took the small stage, where the band played beneath a canopy with heaters, and announced that the competitors had to stop working on their snowmen. We judges were given sheets of paper to vote for our top three. Of course, I voted for Bella's which she built with her friends. Nepotism was alive and well in Epperly.

They ended up taking third place, but no one seemed to care. The prizes were large gift baskets of products donated by the business owners in the square—including some cancer causing shit from *Smith's*.

The band resumed its holiday greatest hits as the crowd navigated toward the skating rink and to the cash bar that also served hot drinks for the kids. I milled around the area, pretending that I wasn't looking for Kael, but I was. And when I found him helping tie the last tree to the Buckman's Subaru in the parking lot at the end of the square, I just stopped and stared at him.

He didn't see me yet. He was too busy laughing and chatting with the Albertsons as they used brooms and shovels to remove the bulk of the pine needles littering the area, disposing of them in the big dumpster behind *Spoons*. After it slammed shut, Kael walked toward the square with Mr. and Mrs. Albertson.

I remained in the shadows under the awning to Raine's Insurance Agency on the corner by the parking lot. As if he sensed me, Kael glanced in my direction. He said something to the Albertsons, and they continued toward the square as he trekked my way in his brown boots, jeans, jacket, and beanie.

"Spying on me, Mrs. Smith?" He grinned as he approached me.

My words caught in my throat, making it hard to breathe. Maybe I was broken. What if my heart didn't know how to do anything but love?

"I need you to stop."

"Stop what?" He backed me into the door.

My gaze shot around us, searching for anyone seeing his close proximity to me, but it was dark. We were hidden to anyone not looking hard to see if two figures were tucked under the awning away from the street lights.

"Stop being nice."

"To you?" The corner of his mouth curled into a sly grin.

"To everyone."

The toe of his boot hit the toe of mine, and it nearly made me fall to pieces. I had no idea how fragile my heart was until he shook it with a look, with a touch, with a simple kiss. He made it weak. He made me weak.

"You want me to stop being nice to *everyone*? That's an interesting request. Can I ask why?"

Blinking back the tears, I cleared my throat and let my gaze attach to the crowd at the skating rink beyond his left shoulder. "It's not fair to be all the things ... and then ... just ..." My quivering lips pressed together.

"What is *all the things*?"

I didn't move. I couldn't. Not an inch. Not a breath.

It wasn't just my heart—my entire existence seemed to be on the verge of crumbling.

"Elsie, look at me." His finger lifted my chin.

My eyes closed—but not before a few tears broke free, sliding down my painted face. He didn't want to carry my baggage.

I didn't want to have baggage, and I didn't think I did.

Until ... Kael said those words. I had *so* much baggage, and it was tangled around my heart, constricting my chest, making it so hard to breathe.

"Say nothing or say everything." He fed my words back to me.

I blinked open my eyes. Again, like the day at his house, he wiped away my tears.

"Nothing," I whispered.

His brow wrinkled. "Why nothing?"

"Because I'm not ready to say goodbye. And everything would be too ... final."

"Why?" He kept prodding.

"Because I let you touch me too deeply. And it's made me *feel* ... *w*hich is what I wanted. It's what I needed. I wanted to feel alive not ..."

"Not what?"

"Nothing."

"Say it."

My head inched side to side. "Nothing. I choose to say nothing."

Kael took a few steps backward. "Now what?"

I shrugged. "We go back to your place and have sex. I go home. You sleep three hours, wake up, and do good things for people. Wash. Rinse. Repeat."

His expression seemed to harden for a few seconds as he drew in a deep breath, held it, and blew it out his nose in a harsh sigh. "Why go to my place? You have a back room to your store. Don't you have a backdoor entrance as well?"

He sounded different. Colder.

I didn't like it.

I also didn't want to say everything. I chose nothing. I made my bed—the bed where I wanted him to fuck me. And that was what he was offering me.

Nothing more.

Nothing less.

Just our no-strings-attached status quo.

I returned a barely detectable nod and reached into my handbag for the keys to my store. Kael followed my lead, keeping a short distance between us. No one was in the parking lot, so we easily slipped into the small, dark, storage room to *Smith's*. As soon as the door closed behind us, I reached for the light switch.

Kael grabbed my wrist to stop me. I couldn't see anything. There wasn't a window or even a sliver of light from under the door. When I started to turn toward him, he grabbed my waist from behind, shoving me forward until my hands landed on a pile of boxes against the wall. With his chest to my back and my hands splayed onto the boxes, he ripped my scarf off, sucking and biting at my neck while his hands roughly unbuttoned my jeans.

The second he unzipped them, he curled his fingers around the waist and yanked them down my legs, taking my panties with them. The cold air arrested my skin, but the ripple of goose bumps didn't last long. They didn't stand a chance against his lips and hot tongue mapping a trail up my legs.

I couldn't see one damn thing, but I felt him ... his mouth and his fingers between my legs. My hands slid forward, gripping the edge of the box, my fingernails scratching the cardboard.

I didn't think sex with Kael could feel more carnal than it did on Thanksgiving in the back of my Tahoe. I was wrong.

He wasn't looking into my eyes. I wasn't facing him. There was nothing personal or intimate about what we were doing. It was nothing but fucking.

No kissing.

No flirty glances.

No clinging to each other.

The moment felt as dark as the room.

But I couldn't stop.

Like every time before that night, Kael knew what I wanted even if it wasn't what I needed.

He willingly became my addiction—the needle, the narcotic.

He fed it.

He jumped off every cliff with me.

He was my highest high ... and my lowest low.

No condom.

No questions.

No objections.

I sucked in a sharp breath when he entered me—one hand clenching my hip, one hand gripping my shoulder as he pounded into me.

Why?

Why didn't it feel more wrong?

Why didn't I feel used?

Everything in that moment was a metaphor for my life. Eyes wide open but blinded by the dark. Seduced by anything that felt like the opposite of the twenty-two years with Craig. Reveling in taking risks and equally as intoxicated by the idea of eschewing the moral code ingrained into my conscience.

It wasn't a midlife crisis—it was a catastrophe on every level of my being. What initially felt like a quest for independence—a rebirth of my individuality—turned into the demise of my heart, the tarnishing of my soul. I didn't lose myself from being married to Craig for twenty-two years; I lost myself when he died because he took such a huge piece of me with him.

I let him define me.

That woman I used to be didn't need to be found. I needed to be redefined.

But ... not by a man.

Craig made me feel stupid. He dismissed me. I gave him too much of myself, including my dignity.

Kael could give me an orgasm that made me temporarily lose all coherent thoughts—and he did.

He could make me desire sinful things—and he did.

He could add cracks to my already frail heart—and he did.

But he couldn't define me. I didn't *need* him.

I wouldn't be his success or failure.

I wouldn't be his crutch.

And I definitely wouldn't be a forgone conclusion.

Never again.

The second I could open my eyes without them rolling back in my head ... which was right as he eased out of me, I pulled up my panties and jeans. "Thanks."

He chuckled. I couldn't see him, but I heard his zipper and labored breathing. "You're welcome."

"I'm going to see if Bella needs anything before I head home. So ... are you decent?" Blindly feeling around with my hands, I found the doorknob.

"As decent as I'll ever be."

I opened the back door and glanced over my shoulder, getting my first glimpse of Kael since we did ... *that*. Pieced back together as if nothing happened, he straightened his beanie and followed me out the door. Again, he remained a good six feet behind me as we made our way to the square. When we turned the corner and rejoined the crowd, I peeked behind me one last time, but he had already headed left, and I was heading right.

Kael made no quick peek over his shoulder.

Not a second glance ... probably not a second thought.

There was a reason I put my heart in a jar and stored it on the highest shelf—he couldn't be trusted with it.

Neither could I.

If given the chance, I would have handed him the fucking jar.

CHAPTER twenty-one

Reading my mind and reading between the lines were not the same things. One required an emotional connection, the other required consciousness.

Two weeks later ...

IN YOUR FORTIES, two weeks passed in a blink—unless you were missing someone. With the clock ticking down to the anniversary of Craig's death, I was missing him, my boys, even Bella since I seemed to only catch her for a few minutes in the mornings before she headed out the door. Amie put in extra hours at her clinic to prepare for a little time off over Christmas and New Year's. Meadow was my companion, a good companion.

Alone I could handle. After raising four children ... and a husband ... alone time nurtured my soul. If I could make it to January, I'd be in alone time heaven. It wasn't that I wouldn't feel extra grief, guilt, and sadness every year as the anniversary of Craig's death approached, but the first year felt the most raw.

Kael?

Well, I hadn't seen him since Holiday Fest. I wasn't necessarily avoiding him, but I also wasn't going out of my way to run into him. And clearly he was going about his days in the same manner.

However, with the first snow in two weeks, his truck pulled into my driveway a few minutes after Bella left for school. There wasn't a lot of snow, but he still made his three swipes just as I was heading out the door to take Meadow for her walk.

He stopped before backing all the way out of the driveway. I smiled, or at least tried, as I approached the door to his truck and released Meadow's leash so she could sniff and do her morning business.

My heart tripped over itself as he hopped out of the driver's seat in his usual jeans, boots, coat, and beanie. His beard looked shorter like he'd recently trimmed it, and that smile of his made it hard to find a deep breath.

I'd missed him too.

"Good morning." He blew on his hands and rubbed them together.

I tucked a few stray hairs under my red stocking cap and let my smile have its way—all the way to my ears. "Morning. Thanks for this. I could have easily shoveled it."

He didn't respond right away, but after a few seconds, he nodded. "Yeah, but it was a good excuse to see you." His words wrapped around me like my favorite sweater.

"I feel bad that you felt like you needed an excuse to see me."

Instead of putting his hands on me, he shoved them

into the pockets of his jacket. "I figured if you *needed* anything, you would have contacted me."

Sex. If I needed sex.

When my gaze slipped from his, he cleared his throat. "And I know it's getting close to the anniversary of your husband's death. I thought you could use some space—time with your family."

Finding his eyes again, I chuckled. "Thank you. I don't have my family with me yet. Occasionally, I pass Bella in the hall or kitchen. My boys won't be here for a few days, along with my parents. It's just been me and Meadow."

Kael nodded once. "I haven't heard any rumors about your store closing. I've seen a few sale signs in the windows, but no chatter about it closing. Did you change your mind?"

"No. I'm going to announce it after Christmas and hopefully clear as much out as possible before the first." I shrugged. "The rest I'll donate. Whatever ... right?"

A slight cringe formed along Kael's forehead. "Elsie ..."

"I don't want it. The store. I never did. So don't give me that look. Maybe you were the perfect excuse."

The tension on his face didn't seem to ease up any. "So what's next?"

"I don't know. I might make a quilt. I've started several over the past year. The walls could use a new coat of paint." That melted a little tension from his face. "When Bella leaves for college, I'll sell the house. It holds a million memories, but I only feel the bad ones. And that sucks. Craig's ... everywhere."

"And that's bad?"

Meadow heeled next to me as if to say, "Let's go, Mom!" I smiled at her. "Yeah, that's bad. Anyway … thanks again for clearing my driveway."

"Of course."

"I'd better get this girl walked so she doesn't destroy the house while I'm at work."

"Want some company?"

I blinked at him a few times. Yes. I wanted company. I wanted *his* company. But I couldn't ignore the rumors that a simple walk would start.

"Um …"

"Let them talk." He smirked.

I bit my lower lip and wrinkled my nose.

"Fine." He closed his door and his boots scuffed down the driveway to the sidewalk. "I'm taking a walk. If we take the same route … so what?"

I giggled. "Your truck is parked in my driveway."

"Let them talk," he hollered as he continued down the sidewalk.

Rolling my eyes, I guided Meadow to follow his tracks. We trailed behind him for several blocks as he whistled "Jingle Bells" followed by "I Saw Mommy Kissing Santa Claus." An unavoidable grin spread across my face. I had the normal appearance of walking my dog.

The yoga pants.

Sporty boots.

A dog.

Kael looked like his vehicle broke down, and he was walking to get help—whistling a tune.

Meadow veered off to the side to poop. I thought she did it at home—apparently I was distracted by Kael. I didn't tell him to stop or wait. After all, we weren't walking together. As she pinched off an enormous turd, I reached into the pocket of my jacket to get a poop bag.

"Not again …" I deflated.

"Is there a problem?" Kael turned around but kept walking backward, keeping us distanced.

"I don't have a poop bag." I glanced up to see a guy in his front window, sipping his coffee as my dog took a shit in his yard. There would be no kicking snow over the pile of steaming poop and running.

"Shit happens. Let's go."

I covered my mouth, so the homeowner didn't see me talking. "He's looking at me. I have to pick it up."

"With what?" Kael laughed.

My nose wrinkled. "Meadow … why didn't you do this in our yard?" I grumbled, bending down to scoop up a large pile of snow beneath the poop. Then I turned and headed back home, carrying the poop on the clump of snow like a stranded polar bear on a melting piece of ice. Time was of the essence with the sun peeking out, expediting the melting of the snow along with the heat of her turd.

"I can't believe what I'm seeing." Kael taunted me as he jogged to catch up. "Just drop it."

My pace doubled. "I can't just drop it. It's frowned upon. Someone will see me."

"You weren't worried about anyone seeing you leave shit behind the day you were spying on me and Amber."

"I wasn't spying on you. I was hiding from you."

"Same thing."

"No. It's not."

"You were behind a tree … watching us. A classic case of spying."

"Spying implies I followed you. Which ... I did not."

"Then why hide behind the tree? Why not just keep walking your dog and give us a wave?"

The snow was melting ... too quickly.

"This is a stupid conversation." I started jogging.

"You wiping Amber's kiss off my lips ... so fucking sexy."

I rolled my eyes, but he couldn't see it. "Stop gloating."

"Did you go on a date with the banker?"

"If I did ... are you going to wipe his kiss off my lips?"

"Wow ... you kissed him?"

"Do you care?"

"Not really."

I turned and threw the turd at him. He ducked, avoiding the collision by inches.

"WOW! You threw that at me? What did I do?"

I glanced behind him at the poop. We were in front of my house, so it landed in my easement. "I'm not emotionally dead like you. I care. Sorry ... I just do."

"I don't think I'm emotionally dead."

"You are. You just said you didn't care."

He rested his hands on his hips. "Because I thought that's what you wanted me to say."

I shook my head. "No. That's bullshit. I think you want me to be with other people, so you don't have to worry about me emotionally clinging to you ... so you don't have to *carry my baggage*."

Kael winced, and I turned, taking my emotionally-out-of-control self into the house before I said anything else, before I showed him all of my baggage.

Depositing my coat, mittens, and scarf onto the floor

like I didn't give a shit— and I didn't—I kicked off my boots as the door opened behind me. I closed my eyes. "Go. Save yourself."

He sighed. "The baggage statement. That came out wrong. I didn't mean it the way it sounded."

"You did. And that's fine." I shuffled my socked feet into the kitchen.

Moments later, I felt him at the threshold to the kitchen, eyes on me, but I kept my gaze out the kitchen window, hugging my arms to my waist.

"And I chose nothing," I said, feeling every ounce of defeat from the previous year. "I chose to not ask you to carry one single bag of mine. I wanted the sex. I got the sex. And it was good. But I can't stop. I can't see the line. And maybe some of us just aren't wired to see that line."

"I don't understand."

"You're too good!" I whipped around to face him. "This whole fucking town can't stop talking about you, and it's driving me crazy."

"Um ... okay. I didn't ask for anyone to talk about me. I think it's just a small town, and everyone talks about everything."

"Well, you don't have to give them *so* much to talk about. You don't have to shovel snow and rake leaves. You don't have to be Mr. Handyman one day and drive old ladies to visit their daughters the next day. All the changing tires, loading Christmas trees, clearing windshields, and warming up cars ... it's insane. And it's not fair!" My voice escalated to an outright yell, and he was only ten feet away.

He glowered. "You're mad because I'm nice?"

I shook my head a half dozen times. "Not nice. You're

lovable." The word lovable had never sounded so angry ... so negative.

"What's wrong with being lovable?"

After retrieving an apple from the produce drawer in the fridge, I turned toward him again, taking a big bite, hoping it would keep my mind and my emotions from spewing out of control. "I don w-ah of oo," I mumbled over my huge bite of apple.

He tugged several times on his earlobe while scrunching his face. "Sorry. I didn't catch any of that."

I chewed ... and chewed. Once I swallowed, my gaze fell to the floor. "I don't want to love you."

"Then don't."

Pinching the bridge of my nose and closing my eyes, I eased my head side to side. "Your world is so black and white. If I could control my feelings that easily, I'd still be married." I forced myself to look at him. "Instead, he's dead and I'm here. I said I wanted you to make me feel ... feel alive. *Not* in love."

Don't cry ... don't cry ...

I continued, "So you need to turn around and walk away because I can't stop. And I hate feeling so out of control. I hate not being able to love the right man but falling so hard for the wrong one. And I get it ... this is Karma. I deserve this. But you don't. So ... please walk away."

Stiffening, I gripped my apple tighter as he took slow steps toward me. "Go ..." I whispered.

"Give it to me."

"Give what?" I couldn't look at him. He would make me cry, and I wasn't just on the verge of tears; I was on the verge of crumbling to the ground.

"Your baggage."

I shook my head, staring at his jean-clad legs.

He eased the apple from my hand and set it on the counter.

"No ..." I croaked past the lump in my throat as unshed tears blurred my vision.

"Yes ..." he whispered, standing so close to me without making physical contact.

"Nothing ... *we* chose nothing."

His index finger hooked mine. "Well, that was the wrong choice."

"What's the right choice?" I whispered.

"Everything."

"You don't want my *everything*."

"Maybe I do."

My gaze inched up his body to his face. As soon as I found his eyes, I blinked. Tears raced down my cheeks. He didn't move. We stood facing each other with two fingers clasped.

"You're so good ... but I'm not. I'm selfish. I'm cruel. I'm a killer."

His forehead tensed.

I closed my eyes hoping to stop the tears, but they wouldn't quit. "I couldn't ignore all the little things about him that angered me ... annoyed me. I let it build. I suppressed it. And over time, it turned into something so toxic I could barely breathe." Blinking my eyes open, I let them focus on his chest. "He was just eating breakfast. And he said something he'd said a million times before. But I just ... *couldn't*. Not that day ... not ever again."

I sniffled while hiccupping on a shaky breath. "And something inside of me just snapped. Like an avalanche ...

it was unstoppable. One ugly comment led to another. Just ... two people who had loved each other for what felt like a lifetime ... slinging mud, ripping open old wounds, and slashing new ones. And he thought it was just me having a moment. A breakdown. He ..." I choked for a few seconds, covering my mouth with my hand while I silently sobbed.

Kael tightened his grip on my finger, but that was it. He gave me space.

"H-he had n-no idea ..." Squeezing my eyes closed, more tears made their way free. "I w-wanted out. I n-needed out." Forcing my eyes open, I met his gaze and swallowed the choking emotions. "I said I wanted a divorce." I bit my quivering lip for a few seconds. "And he left. That was the last time I saw him."

"Elsie ..." he whispered.

I lifted and dropped one shoulder. "Only two of my children know. Amie knows ... I think her mom might know. That's it. So to most everyone, my story is tragic and that of a grieving widow. It is tragic. I am a widow. But my grief is complicated—my *baggage* is heavier than most people imagine."

Kael kept an unreadable expression on his face. What could he say? There wasn't anything to say. Yes, I knew I didn't actually kill Craig. I knew it was an accident. But sometimes the heart held onto the guilt until it left a permanent stain. I would *always* feel responsible for Craig's death no matter what my brain could rationalize.

"Go be thirty, Kael. Be the wanderer you were born to be. You are kind beyond words. You carry a lot of baggage for people, but you also know how to let it go before it breaks your back. I don't regret my life's path. Don't ever regret yours. And don't let someone take you down a road you don't want to explore. I'm sure you've left an unintentional trail of broken hearts because it's impossible to not love you."

"You love me?"

I released his finger and brushed past him. "Does it matter?"

"I think it matters to you."

Laughing in the most painful way, I planted myself on the opposite side of the kitchen as far away from him as possible. "Once. I think we should have had sex once and moved on. That's as casual as I can be. That was my lesson to learn. I let Craig go because I knew he loved me in a way I couldn't reciprocate any longer. And unrequited love is awful—for both people."

"Jesus ..." he whispered, resting his hands on his hips while glancing up at the ceiling. "You think I'm incapable of love. You think my not wanting a wife and children means I don't want love ... or that I don't know how to love."

I shook my head. "I don't know what you feel. And maybe that's because I can't imagine what my life would have been like without marriage and children. I just know that when Craig died, part of me died. And the only thing that kept me together was the comfort of my children. Love, in my life, has been defined by everything you don't want. So ... I don't know how you feel. If you don't have family, what *do* you have?"

"I have the people in my life. And maybe it's not the same people now as it was ten years ago. And ten years from now, it might not be the same people as now. I've met many people on my travels. And in those moments, they were my friends ... they were my family."

"Women ... you've had relationships. You've been monogamous?"

"Yes."

"And how did that end?"

"Mostly good. Sometimes bad."

"Because they wanted you to commit to more?"

His face twisted and he shook his head. "Because one side or the other was no longer feeling satisfied with the relationship. So it was time to move on. And I suppose in a perfect world people would fall in and out of love at the same time, but it's not a perfect world."

"Have you ever lived with a woman?"

He nodded. "Once. We were roommates?"

"Not intimate?"

"We had sex. Then it ended."

"Because you had sex?"

"Because we were roommates."

I frowned.

"For the record ... I haven't lived very long with anyone, male or female. I like my space. It keeps me grounded and happy. And therefore, I have more energy and desire to spend my time helping others because I'm not sitting around being pissed off at a million tiny little things someone does that drives me insane."

Ouch.

I flinched.

"You asked. I'm giving you total honesty. I think kids are great. I was really good at being one. I just don't want the responsibility, and I don't think this world needs to add to its population at the moment when we haven't figured out how to take care of all the humans who are already here."

"You don't want to commit to eighteen years with another human to raise a child? Or you're saving the Earth?"

"Maybe a bit of both."

Really ... he deserved all the credit for his honesty, even if it was blunt and a bit harsh for my love-marriage-baby soul. I let his words sink in for a few seconds—maybe a few minutes—while he showed patience and stayed.

Why was he staying? I told him to leave. I let him go. I begged him to leave.

"Have you ever had your heart broken?"

"Yes."

Not the answered I expected. Yet it gave me ... hope. It made me feel not so alone. Captain America wasn't invincible after all.

"Are you thinking about your mom? Was that the one time you've had your heart broken? When she died?"

A soft smile crept up his face. Adoration. It looked good on him. I think I got that same look whenever anyone talked to me about my kids.

"Yes. She broke my heart when she died. But she wasn't the first. I know what unrequited love feels like. And it's awful. But it's life. No regrets."

I glanced at the clock on the microwave. "I'm late. I need to get to my shop. Don't you have work too?"

"Rachel is opening it this morning. But yeah, I need to go shower and head that way."

I closed my eyes and pressed my fingers to them, internally cringing at how puffy they felt from my crying.

"Well..." I attempted a weak laugh to lighten the mood "...thanks for listening. Clearly, I needed to have a good cry today." Sensing his approach, I kept my eyes closed and my hands at my face.

"I'm actually a great listener. I just never have great advice." He pulled my hands away from my face. "I can plow snow. My handyman skills are pretty good. All manual labor is a strong suit of mine. I'm not terrible at sex." He smirked. "I just don't have all the answers to life. On a good day, I have the answers to *my* life. So I live in the timespan of moments because I like the now. I can deal with now."

"Youth ..." I smiled. "In my next life, I want to be you, Kael Hendricks."

"That's kind of you to say. But let's hope that's a long ways off." He pressed his lips to my forehead and left them there for several slow breaths. "I did something over the past two weeks that isn't common for me." He turned, heading toward my front door.

"Well ..." I followed him. "Where are you going?"

"To take a shower." He shoved his feet into his boots and squatted down to tie them.

"You can't say something so cryptic and then just ... leave. What did you do?"

He stood and zipped his jacket. "I missed you."

And then ... he disappeared out the door.

There wasn't a shelf high enough to keep my heart. Not an ocean deep enough. Kael wasn't human. If he wanted my heart ... he would find it. He would take it. And I would just wait for him to give it back ... holding my breath ... focusing on the *now*.

CHAPTER
twenty-two

I don't miss you because you're no longer in my life ... I miss you because you're no longer in this life.

THAT AFTERNOON, Ruddy's Roses delivered a bouquet of flowers to the store. I looked at Kandi as she marked down more products per my request. She shrugged.

"They're for you, Elsie." Cynthia, the driver for Ruddy's, smiled at me as she set them on the counter.

"Wow ... okay. Thanks." I waited until Cynthia left before grabbing the card.

"I bet they're from one of your kids ... since it's close to the anniversary of ..."

Craig's death.

Kandi didn't say it. She didn't have to.

If that were the case, then they'd be from Finn.

That smile is a good look on you.

"So ... who are they from?" Kandi charged the checkout counter.

"I don't know. There's no name on the card."

She plucked it from my grasp. "Aw ... that's so sweet." After staring at it for a few seconds, her gaze lifted to mine. "Kinda weird coming from one of your kids, especially with no signature. Do you have a secret admirer?" Her voice crescendoed.

I rolled my eyes. "And who would that be?"

"I don't know. That's why he would be a secret. Or it could be Dr. Jennings. I can see her sending you flowers this time of year. You know ... with the anniversary of ..." Kandi's nose wrinkled.

"Craig's death. You can say it, Kandi. I won't fall to pieces. And yeah, you're right. It's probably from Amie." I grabbed my jacket. "Going for soup. Can I bring you back anything?"

"I'm good. Thanks."

I nodded and headed down the way to *Spoons*. The line wasn't as busy since it was after one o'clock, but there were still five people ahead of me.

"Elsie ..."

I grinned at Kael's voice behind me, but I didn't turn around. *Elsie* out of his mouth touched me differently than his usual, playful *Mrs. Smith*. Maybe after my confession, he realized I didn't want to be Mrs. Smith.

We didn't exchange anymore words or glances as the line inched forward. After I ordered my soup, I moved off to the side to wait for it. A minute or so later, Kael joined me. He made a point of brushing his knuckles against mine as he turned to face the to-go counter.

It lit me on fire. I didn't miss his smirk as I unzipped my jacket and loosened my scarf.

Again, he brushed the back of his hand against mine.

"Stop," I whispered.

"I don't want to stop," he whispered back.

Then as if Karma had hopped on her high horse for the day, Tillie Cunningham waltzed through the door. I prayed for my order to be called as soon as possible, but that didn't happen. She spotted us and beamed in response. There was very little wiggle room in the corner, so my attempts to distance myself from Kael were futile.

"Hey ... just the man I was looking for." Tillie slipped off her gloves. "Hi, Elsie."

I gave her a stiff smile with raised eyebrows as I clasped my hands in front of me—far away from Kael's wandering hand.

"Hey, Till ... what's up?" Mr. Nice Guy didn't stumble for a second. It wasn't how he acted ... it was simply his natural character.

"I have pot roast in the Crock-Pot and a pie ready to go in the oven. How do you feel about dinner with me tonight?"

"Kael ..." They called his name before mine.

I ordered before him. What was going on?

"That's a great offer. I love pot roast. But ... Elsie already invited me to dinner tonight."

What the fuck!?

Tillie shifted her eyes to me holding nothing but total confusion in her glare like she didn't hear him correctly. I could relate. It had to be a bad dream. He did not just call me out like that.

"You did?" Tillie narrowed her eyes.

"Excuse me, ladies. My order is ready." Kael escaped the crowded corner to grab his order at the counter while my jaw unhinged, eyes unblinking.

"Elsie, are you having a dinner party or something?" Tillie tried to make sense of why Kael would be having dinner with me.

My gaze lifted past her shoulder to Kael weaving his way out of the cafe toward the door. He threw me under the bus.

Why?

I didn't want to lie to Tillie, but he left me with no choice, and that pissed me off that he would do that to me.

"Elsie? Did you hear me?" Tillie prodded.

Bringing my attention back to her, I started to search for my voice. "Uh ..." Out of the corner of my eye, I saw Kael stop just before the door. When my attention shifted back to him, he turned, lips twisted in a contemplative expression.

Regret.

He regretted saying what he did. I started to blow out a sigh of relief as he made his way back toward us. He was going to make things right again with Tillie, so I didn't have to lie to her.

Tillie redirected her attention to him as well.

Then he did what no one in my life had ever done before ... he exposed me. *All* of me. His right hand slid along my cheek, fingers threading in my hair as he brought his lips to my opposite cheek, depositing a soft but deeply intimate kiss near my ear before whispering, "I love you, so deal with it."

Tillie's lips parted as her face lost all color. I didn't have issues with color. My face felt as red as the tomato bisque soup in the bag waiting for me at the counter.

"Order for Elsie," they called.

Kael didn't give Tillie one single glance before vanishing out the door after lighting my fragile world on fire.

Tillie turned and shouldered past a few people as she stumbled out of the cafe. It wasn't until I grabbed my bag that I realized a lot of eyes were on me.

Fucking small towns.

They saw everything. It was only a matter of time before everyone knew.

Bella ...

She was still at school, her last day before the start of Christmas break.

Livid.

I was so livid.

Let them talk.

After throwing me to the wolves, I was in total agreement. It was time to let them talk.

"How was—" Kandi started to talk the second I returned to the store.

"I have an errand to run." I tossed the store keys on the counter. "Can you close up?"

"Um ... I've never closed up before."

"There's always a first." I grabbed the flowers, leaving my soup behind and stormed out the door, across the square, and right into *What Did You Expect?*

I can say with certainty that Kael's employees, including Rachel, and the aisles filled with customers didn't expect me and my outrage.

Crash!

I pitched the glass vase of flowers at the register, aiming for his fancy display of bottles behind it.

Bull's-eye.

The flying vase missed Kael by inches as he stood toward the corner behind his employees at the register, eating his soup, shoulder against a beam, one ankle crossed over the other.

The store fell silent as shocked expressions ping-ponged between me, the broken glass, and Kael.

"Deal with *that*." I turned and pushed through the doorway out into the frigid air. It didn't affect me, not with an inferno of anger racing through my veins.

In spite of the speech I gave Kelly about our loved one's bodies being just that ... bodies, I found myself driving to the cemetery to visit Craig's body—or at least the ground above it and his headstone. I was good with anything symbolic at that moment.

"Hey." I dropped to my knees in the snow, not caring if my jeans got wet or if I wouldn't be able to stand after kneeling for too long. "It's me, your terrible wife. Ex-wife. Widow ..." I sighed and closed my eyes for a few seconds before opening them again and staring at his name engraved on the granite with "Beloved father and husband" beneath it.

Husband.

"I don't know what I am right now. Not a good business owner. I'm closing the doors in less than two weeks. Not a good mom. Bella is about to find out I've been having sex with someone twelve years younger than me. Yeah ... I went younger. You would have too. And I'm about to be shunned from the church because I stole Tillie Cunningham's love interest. I still don't think it's a midlife crisis. I think I might just be a terrible human being. When Bella graduates, I'm going to leave Epperly. You can truly rest in peace."

On another long sigh, I twisted around and fell back in the snow, so my body was on his grave, gaze aimed at the sky. I moved my arms and legs in and out, making a snow angel.

"Want to know the hardest ... coldest ... rawest truth? I don't miss you because you're no longer in my life ... I miss you because you're no longer in *this* life."

Admitting that aloud, if only to a partly cloudy sky and a cemetery filled with embalmed bodies, made me feel a little better. At the core of all the truths and real talk I had with the grief group, or even with Amie, the hardest thing was acknowledging *how* I missed Craig. Had we been given the chance to divorce, I knew I would have seen him occasionally because we shared four kids together. Without kids, I could have moved halfway around the world and lived the rest of my life without him, and I didn't know if my heart would have ever truly missed him.

That hurt the most. That numbing reality that I would have been okay without him for ... the rest of my life. It was the jagged knife that cut so deeply it punctured my soul. In some ways, it made me question if I had a soul.

Why was falling out of love a flaw?

Still ... I *did* miss him being alive. I grieved his absence in our children's lives. It pained me beyond words to know that he wouldn't walk Bella down the aisle if she got married.

"Stirring up trouble today, huh?"

I grinned at the words of my friend.

Amie plopped down next to me, leaning back as well to make her own snow angel.

"Thought you had a job."

"I do. I have several jobs actually. But news quickly spread that the job I needed to attend to the most right now is being your friend."

"Fucking small-town gossip."

Amie laughed. "It's the worst."

"I don't know what I'm going to say to Bella."

"May I suggest the truth? At this point, I think it's your best bet."

"What if I don't know the truth?"

"Well, you know something. Tell her what you know. Then tell her what you don't know. Show her that we never stop changing. Show her that life never stops giving us opportunities to build character and be humbled by unexpected circumstances. She'll love you more for not having all the answers. Humans gravitate toward imperfection. Like comfort food."

"You want me to be her macaroni and cheese?"

"Yep."

I chuckled. "I love you."

She reached over and rested her hand on mine, giving it a tiny squeeze. "You should."

"I loved him too." I blinked and let several tears fall for Craig.

"I know you did. Everyone knew. You have four beautiful souls living on this earth because of that love. I've never told you to forgive yourself because there's nothing to forgive. It's okay to fall in love. And it's just as okay to fall out of love."

CHAPTER twenty-three

I'm not a goose. I am a duck. And I'm okay with it.

"Hi." Perched on the bottom stair, I smiled at Bella the second she opened the front door.

She paused, eyeing me with an unreadable expression. Then she shut the door and pulled off her boots. "Did you have sex with him?" When she glanced up at me, unzipping her coat, her face wrinkled into pain or maybe it was disgust.

"Yes."

She blew out a breath as if I'd punched her in the gut. "Oh my god, Mom. He's young enough to be ..."

I lifted an eyebrow.

"Twelve. He's twelve years younger than you. That's just ..."

"He's twelve years older than you. And at Thanksgiving, you seemed to think that was an acceptable age difference."

"So you decided to sleep with him because of me?

You decided to what? Steal him before I could graduate and have him?"

"You're going to college. He's not. I don't think you were going to have a summer fling with him."

"It ..." She shook her head over and over again, stomping past the stairs, straight to the kitchen. "It's not about me. It's about Amber and Tillie. Oh my god, Mom ... he kissed you right in front of her. How could you do that to her?" Bella jerked open the fridge door and grabbed a carton of yogurt.

"I had sex with him before he had dinner with Tillie."

"Stop!" She grimaced, peeling open the yogurt. "Stop saying you had sex with him."

"Okay ... so let's revisit the conversation we had awhile back. You were okay with me having sex with Mike or Brian as long as I gave you a heads-up. But you're not okay with Kael? Is it because I didn't give you proper notice or because he's twelve years younger than me?"

She shoveled the yogurt into her mouth, stress eating like I used to do. "It's everything. It's that he's no longer the hot new guy with the cool store. He's now the weird new guy screwing my mom."

"Screwing me makes him weird?"

"Stop! Don't say that." She flinched like my words jolted her.

"Say what?" I laughed.

"Screwing."

"It was your word, not mine."

Fucked. I liked the word fuck. However, I had a strong vibe that Bella didn't want to hear me say that either.

"So what do you want me to do?"

"I ... I don't know. Tell me it's over. Tell me it was a

mistake. Tell me he's going to be with Tillie or Amber. Tell me the rest of my senior year won't be about you and your *young* boyfriend. Can you do that? Can you let something not be about your *needs* for a few more months while I finish school and get the hell out of here? I realize that's hard for you. After all, you couldn't hold your tongue last year just long enough to get through the holidays before asking Dad for a divorce."

It was my turn to flinch. That hurt. Even if I deserved it. It still hurt.

Bella sighed, dropping her spoon in the sink and the yogurt carton into the trash. Then she rested her hands on the edge of the counter and hung her head. "I'm sorry," she whispered. "I didn't mean it."

"It's okay if you did."

"No." She turned, eyes red, regret bending her lips downward. "It's not okay. And I *didn't* mean it. I'm just ..."

"Yes," I whispered.

She lifted her gaze to meet mine. "Yes what?"

"Yes. I can stop letting things be about my needs. I never intended for my needs to overshadow yours, and it breaks my heart to know that's what has happened. I'm ... truly sorry, Bella."

She forced a partial smile. It was sad. It was painful. I closed the distance between us and pressed my hands to her cheeks.

"It was just sex, right?" she asked. "You don't *love* him. Right?"

I smiled. "I love *you*. And I love your brothers. And in spite of how things ended, I loved your dad. He was, for so many years, the love of my life. We did great things together." I kissed her forehead so she would know without a doubt that *she* was one of those great things. "But sometimes we change, and sometimes the passion dies. This goes against everything I was raised to believe. But I'm not sure if humans are meant to mate for life."

She pulled back and released a tiny giggle. "Mate for life?"

I shrugged. "The divorce rate isn't exactly low. And it's higher for people who get married when they're young. Maybe it's because they are young, or maybe it's just *a lot* of time to spend with one person. I married your dad when I was twenty. And we stayed married for twenty-two years. Most of them were really good years. We weren't a failure. Not in my eyes. And you're proof of that. So are your brothers."

She didn't respond right away, but I waited for her to tell me what she needed. I focused on my world—my truest love.

"Was it just once? Like a drunk mistake?"

"Kael?" I asked for clarification. I knew what she meant, but I needed to buy a few extra seconds to respond.

Tell her the truth.

Amie's words jumped to the front of my mind. I avoided answering the love question because I really didn't know how to answer it. Or maybe I did, I just couldn't put my heart through verbally acknowledging it.

"It was more than once. And we were sober."

"Mom ..." Her face soured again. "Whose idea was it?"

I rolled my eyes on a slight chuckle. "It was mutual."

"Was it here? God ... tell me it wasn't here."

"Bella," I stroked her hair. "This is clearly distressing to you. And it shouldn't be. It's over."

Okay, my heart definitely felt that. I had to take a hard swallow to let that truth slide past said heart.

"So ..." I continued. "There's no need to talk about it. If I recall correctly, you don't like talking about sex with me."

She nodded a half dozen times. "You're right. I don't want to know. Like ... ever. And I'm never going into his store again."

"Good call."

Curling her hair behind her ears, she headed toward the stairs. "Mom?"

"Yeah?"

She drummed her fingernails on the railing a few times with a sheepish grin on her lips. "Maybe just one sex question."

I braced for it and cleared my throat. "Anything."

"At your age, is it still..." she scraped her teeth along her top lip several times "...good?"

Restraining my full grin, I replied softly, "Yes."

Rubbing her lips together, she nodded some more. "Okay." After climbing two more steps, she stopped. "One more. Then I'll be done. Promise."

I slid my fingers in the back pockets of my jeans. "Ask away."

"Do you think you'll fall in love again? The kind of love you felt for Dad when you first fell in love with him?"

That girl ... she knew how to wring all the emotions from me. "That would be amazing, wouldn't it?"

"You deserve it. I mean ... not until I'm out of Epperly, but someday you should open your heart to fall in love again."

I smiled. "Thanks. Your blessing means a lot."

Her grin doubled and she finished making her way up the stairs without asking any more questions.

Bella didn't stay for dinner, so I ate alone and focused on how awesome it was to be alone. I had a lot of alone time on my calendar. In fact, I had a good five months until she graduated. Five months of sitting at home with Meadow, quilting, reading, taking walks, and not thinking about my physical needs.

I could do it.

I pretty much did it for the last few years of my marriage.

After dinner, I took Meadow for a walk in the dark because I didn't care to be seen out and about in the light of day. Not yet.

Maybe it was by chance or maybe it was subconsciously intentional, but I found myself standing in front of Kael's house all decorated in holiday lights. Making a quick glance around for peering eyes, I hurried up his walk and knocked on his front door.

A few seconds later, he opened it, making a quick inspection of Meadow before eyeing me with a curled lip expression.

"What's the damage?"

His eyes narrowed a fraction.

"At your store. I broke a lot of bottles behind your register. What do I owe you?"

He nodded slowly. "Is that why you're here? To write me a check?"

"No. I don't have my checkbook. I was just in the area,

and I thought I'd stop by and ask so I can get you a check tomorrow."

"Do you want to come inside?"

"Why? Do you have to add up the total?"

"No. I just don't think that's why you're here. So I assume you want to come inside."

"I don't. We're over. This isn't a booty call."

"I didn't figure." He nodded toward Meadow. "Booty calls don't usually involve dogs. And why exactly are we over?" He cocked his head to the side.

"Because you had to make a big display, and now the whole town knows."

"Fuck the town."

"I can't. My daughter is in high school. And she deserves better than her mom fucking the new guy or the whole town for that matter. My selfishness took her dad away almost a year ago. I'm not going to make the rest of her senior year a miserable experience because everyone's talking about her mom screwing a guy who is twelve years younger than me and twelve years older than my daughter."

A line of concern formed along the bridge of his nose. "That sucks. I'm sorry. It's..." he nodded behind him "... okay for you to step inside. It's cold. And to my knowledge, no one is spying on my house."

I looked around and stepped inside, against my better judgment. But if I were being honest, all of my judgment by that point was bad.

"Lie down, Meadow." I dropped her leash and pointed to the entry rug. She obeyed as I removed my boots.

"Hot chocolate? Tea? Cider? Wine? Beer?" Kael rolled out the welcome wagon as I removed my jacket.

"I'm good." I walked around and took notice of all the things I missed the day I was there for sex and only sex.

A fire burned in his fireplace, a Christmas tree twinkled with little white lights in the corner of his living room, modern furnishings dotted the open spaces, and black and white photos accented his bright blue walls.

"I visited Tillie."

My head snapped to the side, gaze ripping away from the photo of him and his parents. "You did?"

"I did." He took a seat on his sofa, resting one ankle on his opposing knee.

"And?"

"And she's good. Disappointed. But good."

"Disappointed in me or you?"

"Both."

I frowned.

"Disappointed that I don't want to go to church with her, date her, and eventually get married. I think it helped when she realized that it's not *her*. But that's also when she realized that you must know this already, so she just came out and asked me if we'd had sex."

My shoulders slumped. "And what did you say?"

He shrugged one shoulder. "What do you think I said?"

I pinched the bridge of my nose. "I'm the town whore."

"No. That's not what I said."

I dropped my hand from my face and tried to grin, but I failed. "That's not what I meant. I'm saying it as a fact, not that I think you told her that."

"She deduced that on her own, especially after I told her about licking your pussy in the back of your Tahoe on Thanksgiving."

Nausea roiled in my stomach. For a few seconds, I honestly didn't know if he was joking or not, probably because I was stunned by his crass and very blunt recollection of that event.

"Joke. That was a joke. Elsie. Take a breath." He chuckled.

I took a breath, but it did little to make me feel better. "Well ... it would appear I'm done going to church here. Or leaving the house for that matter. Maybe Bella will do my grocery shopping."

"Would it help if I left?"

"What do you mean?"

He rested both feet on the ground, leaned forward, and planted his elbows on his knees, hands folded in front of him. "What if I closed my store and just ... moved on? I wasn't going to stay here forever anyway. We both know that. If I left now, maybe the rumors and gossip would die down quicker. You could leave your house, and Bella could finish her senior year in peace."

"You just opened your store. You renovated it. Surely you have a business loan for all of that."

He nodded. "I do. But I'd find work in some other place and pay it off eventually."

"No. You stay. It's five months until she graduates. I'll sell my house. We'll go stay with my parents in Arizona this summer. And after Bella starts school in the fall, I'll figure out what to do from there."

"Arizona in the summer. Sounds miserable."

"Bella loves the heat. Me? Not as much. But I won't melt."

He stared at his folded hands. "You should do what you need to do. But for the record, I will miss you."

"Until you won't. You're not a goose or a wolf or a beaver. You're a duck. I'm a duck. We'll find other people to fu—"

"Don't." Kael shook his head. "I would never guess you're forty-two, but if you finish that sentence to make it rhyme, I will buy you denture cream and a girdle."

"Fuck." I giggled, shuffling my fuzzy-socked feet to him.

He unclasped his hands and pulled me between his legs. My hands rested on his shoulders and his rested on the back of my thighs. When he dropped his forehead against my belly, I threaded my fingers through his hair.

"I love you, Elsie. And I'm not saying it to change your mind about anything. I'm saying it because I think you need to hear it. And I'm saying it because I hate that we were together so many times and you thought I was incapable of love. So ..." He lifted his head and gazed up into my eyes. "I love you. I regret nothing. And I will miss you."

"You're no goose."

Kael chuckled. "I'm not a goose. I'm a duck. And I'm okay with it. I'm just saying right *now,* and maybe for many more nows to come, this duck loves you."

"And this duck loves you too. But ... I love my daughter more. I love her like a goose would. And she needs me to be boring and practice sexual abstinence until she graduates and moves away from Epperly."

"I understand."

Taking a few steps back, I continued inspecting his place. "For a wanderer ... a nomad ... you don't hesitate to really make a home. I mean ... your walls are painted a blue that I'd bet wasn't the color on them when you moved in. And all the photos on the wall—it feels homey, and that doesn't fit the thirty-year-old guy who doesn't like commitment."

"I disagree." He leaned back and laced his fingers behind his head. "It fits the guy who lives in the now. For now, I'm here. And now is all I have. So paint the walls, hang photos, get a few house plants, and a welcome mat —anything less is just waiting for something better."

I liked his eyes on me even if I never understood why ...

So I asked, "Why me?" Adjusting one of the ornaments on his tree, I kept my focus away from his expression. It was a hard question to ask. And maybe it sounded insecure, but that wasn't it. I didn't love him because he was thirty and looked like Captain America. That would have been attraction. *That* would have made it easy to have a one-night stand.

"Why Epperly? Why blue paint? Why grilled cheese for dinner? It's just a feeling. A lingering feeling. Some feelings are fleeting. Some stay with you, demanding you pay attention. They are unforgettable. It was sex ..."

"Until it wasn't ..." I whispered, turning toward him.

"Until it wasn't ..." He nodded. "It's the way you blush and divert your gaze when I say something nice about you. Then, in the next moment, you're threatening to 'take me down.' It's jumping into a freezing lake then hopping into a hot tub. It's this invigorating feeling. It's awakening. And honestly, it feels good to let myself love you, knowing you expect nothing because you've already had everything. And you don't really *need* me."

Kael saw the version of myself that I wanted to be long before I got there.

"What makes you think I don't need you?"

"You're here."

I didn't respond. I couldn't.

He stood and made his way to me, my heart beating faster and harder with each step. I shivered when he gently brushed the palm of his hand over my cheek. "You're here to say goodbye."

Tears burned my eyes. "Yes."

The pad of his thumb caught the first tear. "It was a moment ... at *Spoons* when I turned around and exposed us to all of Epperly ... it was a moment. A feeling. I had to jump. I needed to know what it felt like to love you in front of the world. I needed to let us shine, if only for a few seconds before everything collapsed around us."

I rested my hand over his, leaning into his touch. "How did it feel?"

He smiled. "You tell me."

"It felt ... freeing. It felt ... real."

Kael kissed me, confirming that it was real, reminding me that life was nothing but a moment, and no one was guaranteed more than one. We were real, even if we weren't forever.

It took a long time to let go. Some moments deserved extra seconds ... a few more breaths.

When I took a step back, he kept his hand on my face. I slowly took another step away from him, his touch fading away. "Thank you."

"For?" His eyes narrowed.

"Not letting me sit around and die an old goose."

His grin reached for his ears. "I'm sure I'll see you around."

"Maybe." I shrugged, turning to get my coat, boots, and dog. When I reached for the doorknob, my aching chest drew in a deep breath.

Wait for me ... I so desperately wanted to say it, but I didn't.

"Merry Christmas, Kael."

CHAPTER twenty-four

Sometimes amazing things come to an end. It doesn't mean you wish they'd never happened. If I had it to do all over again ... I would have married the same man. I would have chosen the same path. We were real; we just weren't forever.

A COLLECTIVE LOOK of shock hit me when I arrived for my last grief meeting at the church. Stopping at the entrance to let everyone get a good look at Epperly's number one sinner, I pulled my lips into a tight smile.

"Elsie," Rhonda said, lifting her chin, looking down her nose at me.

"Hi." My gaze went to Tillie, but she quickly averted hers.

"Here's a seat by me." Kelly pointed to the empty chair between her and Bethanne.

"Thanks." I walked across the room—the walk of shame—and took a seat.

No one said anything, in spite of me being fifteen minutes late. Surely they'd been talking before I arrived. Probably about me.

"Listen ..." I swallowed my fear and embarrassment. "This is my last time with the group for reasons I'm sure all of you are well aware of. I'm taking a break from church too. I do a fantastic job of judging myself. I am and always will be my hardest critic. Tomorrow is the anniversary of Craig's death. And it brings a special kind of pain that no one in this room knows about. Until now ..."

I risked a quick glance up from my folded hands in my lap. "The tiny rock in the shoe. The little things that I didn't love about Craig. The little annoying things that crawled under my skin and ate at my soul ... they ended my marriage. But they didn't ruin it. I have four beautiful children, a heart filled with love, and a mind packed with memories of a long and successful marriage. Sometimes amazing things come to an end. It doesn't mean you wish they'd never happened. If I had it to do all over again ... I would have married the same man. I would have chosen the same path. We were real; we just weren't forever."

Two men ... I loved two men that way. Time didn't matter. Love didn't keep track of time. It lived in the moment.

Confusion spread across every single face in the room.

"There are probably many labels for what happened to me. A midlife crisis. Maybe I lost my way spiritually and emotionally. Maybe I just hit this emotional wall that I couldn't get past without letting something—someone go. A fall from grace. A breaking point. Maybe it was as simplistic as being human ... truly human. But I snapped. The day Craig died, I let all those tiny rocks push me over the edge. I just ... felt like I was crawling out of my skin—completely losing myself to a toxic relationship.

"We fought. Words were exchanged that were driven by anger and pain. Resentment. Exhaustion. Discontentment. It all boiled over. And I asked him for a divorce. He left. And he never came home."

Kelly handed me a tissue. It was only then that I realized I was crying.

"Thank you." I blotted my eyes. "I wanted out, but not like that. It was supposed to be my loss ... not my children's loss. I've spent the last year figuring out who I am without Craig. And it's not a shop owner. And when Bella leaves for college next fall, I'm going to feel a little less like a mom. I didn't set out to have a relationship with Kael. If I'm honest, it was sex. Yes ... out of wedlock, sinful sex. And it made me feel so many things. Each one in and of itself doesn't matter. It was the simple fact that he made me *feel*. He made me question things I've never allowed myself to question because I was raised to *not* question. I was raised to read the Bible, go to church, and follow the rules obediently. And I did ... for many years."

Kelly rested her hand on one leg as Bethanne rested a hand on my other leg. It pulled more tears from my eyes, and their kindness made my heart bleed a little more.

"So I need to step back and find my way, allow myself to really see things and not blindly follow. Because ... it didn't feel wrong. Being with a man who wasn't my husband ... it didn't feel wrong. And I don't know if I'll ever want to have a husband again, but I want companionship. I want intimacy. As immature and elementary as it sounds ... I *do* wonder why something that feels good on so many levels has so many rules. If it's consensual ... why is it wrong?"

"Well, the Bible says—"

I held my hand up to stop Rhonda's interruption. "It was a rhetorical question. I know what the Bible says. I've read every single word in it. And I can interpret it to support whatever makes me feel good about my life. I mean ... that's why there are so many different takes and beliefs about God. Right? No one can prove there is a God. It's faith. So I'm going to have a little faith that God gave me a brain to think, a heart to feel, and a conscience to do the right thing in a world where we don't always know what that is. We are told to love one another. We are told to not judge. So I hope you can WWJD that when I walk out that door."

I stood. "I miss him ... Craig. The world was a better place with him in it. And I could have shared a million things I loved dearly about him. I could have convinced myself and everyone else that he was perfect and he was everything. But that would have been a lie. He wasn't perfect, and he was a lot of things, but not everything. And to heal, I needed to let go of the things I didn't like about him. And you—willingly or maybe not so willingly—let me do that. So ... thank you for letting me be a part of your lives—your successes, your failures, your grief, and your realest moments. You are loved by me—unconditionally. I will always show you grace. I will always be a friend if you need one."

A few of the other women shed tears with me as well. Not Rhonda. And not Tillie. That was okay. As mixed up as my emotions and feelings about life were in the moment, I knew one thing for sure—no two people shared the same journey. I wasn't necessarily in a better place, just a different one.

When I arrived home with groceries for Christmas with my kids, everyone's car was parked in the driveway or on the street—just my kids and my parents, who Bella picked up from the airport two hours south of Epperly.

"Hey, Mom." Linc hugged me as soon as I climbed out of my Tahoe.

"My baby." I hugged him back and all six feet five inches of him lifted me off the ground. "Have you been here long? I went to my meeting at church before the grocery store. I didn't expect to see anyone arrive until later tonight."

"We wanted to surprise you." He set me back on my feet. "Bella just got home with Grandma and Grandpa, and Finn went to get Grandma and Papa Smith."

"I didn't plan on dinner for everyone."

"And ..." Linc opened the back of the Tahoe to help unload groceries. "Chase ordered pizza, and it will be here in thirty minutes." He leaned over and kissed my cheek before carrying grocery bags into the house.

My family left me speechless. They had no way of knowing the full extent of my emotionally rattled state. Yet they were there for me.

"There's our girl." Dad hugged me the second I removed my boots as Bella took the sacks of groceries from my hands.

"Hey, Dad. Good to see you. How was your flight?"

"Smooth as could be."

"Hi, Mom." I went straight from my dad's arms to my mom's arms.

"Baby girl." She kissed the side of my head. "How ya doing, honey?"

"Good. I'm good." I pulled back and smiled. I *was* doing good. In spite of the shit show called my life the previous months, I felt oddly at peace with my uncertain future.

No plans. And that was okay.

No Kael. And while that didn't feel as okay, it was life in the now.

He taught me that.

"Are you sure?" She pressed her hand to my cheek.

"Of course." My face contorted in a little confusion at her sudden concern. It wasn't like she'd recently called me to check in.

"Well, we're here now and everything's going to be okay."

I wasn't sure what that meant, but I didn't have time to ask because Finn came through the front door with Craig's parents.

A good ole Griswold family Christmas.

We ate pizza, and the boys shared with their grandparents how college and jobs were going. Bella remained uncharacteristically quiet. More than that, she wouldn't hold eye contact with me for more than a few seconds.

"Can I say something before we leave the table. I didn't expect everyone to be here tonight, but it actually feels like the right time to make this announcement."

Everyone eyed me suspiciously.

Too suspiciously.

What was going on?

"After much thought and careful consideration, I have decided to close the store at the end of the year." Just like that ... a hundred pounds lifted from my shoulders.

Linc reached over and covered my hand with his. "We know. Well, we didn't know for sure that you were planning on it and had set an actual date. But we were going to suggest it."

"Uh ... *we*?" I gave him a narrow-eyed inspection before sweeping my gaze around the table. So many sad and pained faces.

"It's kinda why we're all here tonight." Chase eyed Bella briefly before returning his focus to me.

I laughed nervously. "What do you mean? You arranged everyone to be here to suggest I close the store?"

"Not just the store." Finn took his turn speaking. "This is more like an intervention."

Bella ... she kept her gaze on her plate with a half-eaten piece of pizza on it.

"An intervention?" My eyes widened. "For ... what?"

"Sweetie," Mom gave me that motherly, overly sympathetic look, "we know."

"Know what?"

Bella squirmed, but she still wouldn't look at me.

"We know about your *young* boyfriend. And the breakdown you had at the young man's store. We know you've been showing signs of mental distress at your grief group. Unwarranted anger. And..." she shot Craig's parents a quick glance "...we know you asked Craig for a divorce right before he was in the car accident."

Oh.

My.

God.

A *fucking* intervention? It had to be a joke. I did nothing wrong. I wasn't crazy. I wasn't losing it. I was *honest*. I was human.

I immediately gauged Linc's and Chase's reaction. Were they mad I never told them the truth? And Craig's parents ... *that* news and the news of me closing their store.

But nobody looked mad or disappointed, just painfully sympathetic. Except Bella ... she bled shame with her complete avoidance of me.

She was the rat.

And I wasn't mad at her. I was really confused because I was good. I did all the things I needed to do.

Closing the store.

Breaking up with Kael.

Confessing to my grief recovery group.

And I was going to come clean to Linc and Chase right after Christmas.

I. Was. Good.

What in the hell happened?

I thought Bella and I were good.

"I see ..."

I didn't actually. It was all a blur, mass confusion running rampant in my head.

"So ..." I drew in a long breath. "What exactly are you intervening? Because I'm not in my group anymore. Tonight was my last night. I'm not with the *younger* man anymore. I already said I was closing the store. What's left for me to do?"

"We want you to come to Arizona with us so that we can take care of you. Just until you recover." Mom glanced at my dad as he wrapped his arm around her shoulder.

"Take care of me? Recover?" I couldn't hide my reaction. Just totally aghast. "You can't be serious." I *was* planning on moving to Arizona after Bella graduated, just temporarily—and not for anyone to take care of me because I needed to recover from anything.

"It's just that your actions have been a little reckless. And not everyone experiences grief at the same rate. And given the fact that you were unhappy in your marriage before Craig died, well ... all the more reason for your timeline of grieving to be off or delayed. When we're grieving, we're not always ourselves." Mom eyed the kids as if to let them know she had things under control ... she would make me see why I needed an intervention. And my kids seemed comforted by her doing that. Finally, a solid mother figure taking charge.

I waited for it all to sink in because it was really hard to swallow. Had I been that bad? "I was honest with the women at church, and in return ... they felt safe to be honest too. And I never wanted to take over the store. So ... I don't see what I've done wrong."

Craig's poor parents. I wasn't sure how much they were following everything or how much my family had disclosed to them before dragging them into such a mess. They didn't need to know about me and Craig, not like that. And if they didn't know about the store before Finn brought them to the house, then it was a really shitty way to break the news to them in the context of me asking their son for a divorce. It was all too much.

"And the young man you've been seeing?" Mom continued, as moms did—poking, prodding, interrogating.

"He's thirty, not thirteen. And we ..." The "we were only having sex" defense didn't feel appropriate, but it was the best defense that didn't make it look like I was trying to replace Craig with a much younger man—or infatuated with him in a way that would seem desperate and truly edging the midlife crisis explanation. I sighed. "I'm not moving to Arizona. Not now, anyway. And if or when I do, it won't be for anyone to keep an eye on me or help me through any sort of grieving."

"Mom ..." Bella broke her silence. "I'll be fine. I can stay at the house until it sells and then stay with a friend until graduation."

The little shit. I mean ... I wasn't trying to be mean or let angry thoughts take over my mind, but she was the instigator. I thought we were good. Why didn't she talk to me more about everything—about Kael—if she was really that bothered by it? I told her I would end things with him, and I did.

I laughed, making brief eye contact with every single person at the table so they would know there was nothing wrong with me. "I'm not leaving my senior in high school home alone and then off to live with someone else."

"Mom..." Linc gave me the most pathetically sad smile "...do this for us. If you love all of us, you'll take care of you."

"I am taking care of me!" My anger built because I didn't like the looks they were giving me. "I've been going to a grief group for months, and I've finally started sharing my feelings. I'm so fucking sorry if they're not the feelings you want me to have. But they are mine!"

Shock.

They all looked shocked.

"And yes ... I've started using the word 'fuck.' And I like it. I like to say it, and I like to do it with Kael Hendricks. I like to do it in the back of my Tahoe, at his store, at my store, in the shower, and on the sofa." I pointed to the living room. "So yeah ... next time you go to sit on the sofa, just know that I *fucked* Kael on the sofa and the floor too. That's me taking care of *me*. So I don't need to go to Arizona for therapy. I need to do what I want when I want for one goddamn time in my life. I've raised four kids, helped run a family business, gone to church every Sunday, and been the *only* person standing between Ron and Mary and a retirement home. So if you *really* care about me the way you claim to, then you'll back the *fuck* off!"

A note about crazy ... most people weren't truly crazy until someone tried to make them feel crazy. And in the midst of making the case against being crazy ... crazy sometimes happened.

Silence.

Not a breath.

Not a blink.

I wasn't sure anyone at the table still had a pulse.

It wasn't something I could take back. I'd gone too far —just a smidge.

Ever so slowly, I stood, resting my fingertips on the table while releasing a long, slow breath. "I'm not lost. I'm not having a midlife crisis. What I just said was a reaction from feeling attacked and cornered. I apologize for my offensive language and oversharing. I have bit my tongue with every single one of you at one point or another over the years. I have witnessed you making decisions that I wouldn't make. I've rolled my eyes and sometimes cringed. But I've done my very best to let you find your way. Let you be you. Life is incredibly hard all by itself. High expectations and stern judgments only serve to bring people down and make them feel bad about themselves. Your actions are between you and your God. I won't tell you what to think, who to love, or what you should or shouldn't do with your body. If you want to get biblical ... then here's the deal. You have one thing to do. Love. That's it. It's that simple. You don't have to police me or anyone else. The *one* lesson that mattered the most to me while raising you kids was for you to know that being kind humans and showing love to everyone is the greatest purpose—maybe the only true purpose—you have in this life."

No one offered anything in return. And that hurt.

These were my people.

My parents loved me. I knew that without a doubt.

My kids loved me. I felt it to my bones.

And Craig's parents used to love me. At that moment, I didn't know how they felt because I was closing their store, I wanted to divorce their son before he died, and I gave really explicit details about *fucking* a man who wasn't their son.

Yeah ... they hated me.

Were Linc and Chase upset that I never told them about the fight before Craig died? I didn't know anything because it *all* got thrown in my face at one time. And I broke under the pressure.

"I'll be upstairs if anyone needs me. Thanks for dinner and the nice surprise." My teeth clenched as my mouth pulled into a tight and ridiculously insincere smile.

CHAPTER twenty-five

He seemed good with the 'til death do us part promise, but he slipped on the 'love, honor, and cherish.'

"Elsie ..." Mary eased open my bedroom door as I worked on a quilt in the corner by the window.

Glancing over my shoulder, I searched for a sign to gauge her devastation or heartbreak over the pain that my nosey kids and I had offered over the dinner table. "Hey, Mary."

She made her way to me. "That's lovely." Her head nodded to my half-finished quilt.

"Thanks."

"Craig visited us ..." She stood behind me and gathered my hair, gently stroking it and combing it with her fingers.

I tipped my chin forward.

"After you two argued, he visited us."

Pain tugged at my heart and wrinkled my face.

Mary continued to play with my hair. It felt so kind,

but I couldn't figure out why she would show me such kindness if she knew more than I thought.

"Craig said you wanted a divorce."

Tears filled my eyes with a pain I hadn't felt since I first found out about his accident. I couldn't imagine being in her shoes. If I had a daughter-in-law who asked my son for a divorce and he later died in an accident, I'm not sure I would have been able to look her in the eye ever again, let alone go an entire year without saying something.

And I know I wouldn't have been kind ... stroking her hair after hearing her say such vulgar things about her intimacy with a man who wasn't my son—in front of my grandkids.

God ... I had so much going through my head—excuses, explanations, lies, truths—but it all jumbled together, and it felt too disrespectful to utter a single word. Really ... what could I have said?

How was I supposed to tell Mary that I'd fallen out of love with her son? She thought the world of him, as mothers do. How could I have ever made her see things the way I saw them?

"I should have left Ron twenty years ago, too."

Wait. What?

I didn't hear her correctly. There was *no* way I heard her correctly.

Gentle hands played with my hair. "There was this window of opportunity. Kids were moved out and focused on their own lives. Grandchildren were young enough that we wouldn't have had to explain anything to them. I still had my teaching certificate and might have been able to get a job to support myself. My parents were still alive to help if I'd needed them. But ... I couldn't do it. I wasn't brave enough to do it."

"Why?" I whispered. "Why did you want to leave him?"

"Because he took me for granted. And he took our wedding vows for granted. He seemed good with the *'til death do us part* promise, but he slipped on the *love, honor, and cherish*. I raised the kids and supported the business in ways no one ever saw. I cooked, cleaned, and made sure I was bathed and smelling good for him every night. *Every night,* Elsie. I have it on good authority that your generation doesn't have to have sex *every night*. I did."

I tried to restrain my smile, but it was hard. I couldn't believe Mary was talking about her sex life with me. Honestly, Mary was the type of woman who had the Virgin Mary feel to her. The idea of her having sex three times to get pregnant seemed like three times too many or just three times too unlikely. There were other women at the church who gave off the same vibe. Like Rhonda. I couldn't imagine them having sex unless it was clinical like getting pregnant with a turkey baster—legs in stirrups, head wrenched to the side, eyes pinched shut.

"You didn't feel loved, honored, and cherished?"

"No." She took several steps backward and sat on the edge of the bed as I turned on my vanity stool to face her. "*You* know why ... 'Wives, submit to your husbands as to the Lord. For the husband is the head of the wife as Christ is the head of the church.' I felt like he expected me to be submissive. So many of my fellow sisters in the church were happy to be submissive ... let their husbands have the role of head in the marriage and they the helper. Some even felt like it was a privilege ... an esteemed position. 'Wives should submit to their husbands in everything.'" She gave me a tight smile as if to say *what do you think about that*?

"Ron expected you to be submissive?" I was surprised by that because I never saw that side of their marriage.

"Don't look so shocked. It was also my job to play the role of the happy wife and mother so that no one would ever think to question my discontentment. Small town. Big religion. I couldn't just leave Ron. I would have had to leave Epperly. But at the time, my parents were alive, and they needed my help. Sound familiar?"

I recoiled.

"Don't think I haven't seen it ... haven't seen *you* doing everything in your power to keep us in our home. Don't think that I don't understand that our kids would have put us in a home in a heartbeat had it not been for you."

Tears stung my eyes.

"Let us go, Elsie. You've been a good wife and mother, and you've been good to Ron and me so much more than our own kids have been. But it's time for you to move on. And while I'm heartbroken that I've lost a child, I don't blame you. Not one bit. It was in fact an accident. And it could have happened just as easily had he run out to get a loaf of bread."

I didn't believe that. His mind was not in the right place to be driving. And if he was angry, he was probably speeding. I knew from experience that Craig got heavy footed when he was worked up about something.

"Stop."

I glanced up from my thoughts to meet her gaze.

She shook her head. "I know where your mind is going, and I just want you to stop. Stop feeling responsible. Stop carrying the guilt. Stop looking back. Do something for yourself ... do it for *me*." She grinned. "Let me live vicariously through you. There's still so much life for you to live, sweetie. Take your second act."

"I loved him," I whispered because I needed so badly for her to know that. I did love Craig with my whole heart for so long.

"I know, Elsie. And I loved Ron. I still love him. Sometimes love isn't enough. Sometimes freedom is greater than love. Or maybe it's the ultimate love. I don't know."

"But my kids and my parents think I'm losing it. I half expect to be hauled away in a straitjacket for a psychiatric evaluation and heavily medicated for the next few years."

Mary belly laughed. "I don't think so. They're just concerned. You've given them submissive Elsie for too many years. It's going to take them awhile to get to know free Elsie. Give them time. Show them that your love for them hasn't changed."

I scooted off the stool and knelt in front of her, hugging her waist like a child. "Thank you, Mary."

She again stroked my hair. Part of me felt like it should have been my mom comforting me and encouraging me like that, but the fact that it was Mary made it more impactful, and it gave me true closure to my marriage—the life and loss of Craig.

FINN DROVE Ron and Mary home while Chase and Linc took Meadow for a walk. Since my parents were staying at my house for two weeks, avoiding them seemed pretty unlikely. So after a long bath, I slipped into my favorite flannel lounge pants and shirt and feigned some bravery and confidence before making my way downstairs.

Bella glanced up from the floor, muting the television as I stood at the threshold to the living room. My parents sat in opposite recliners which was weird for them. They were usually the snuggly couple.

The sofa.

No one wanted to sit on the sex infested sofa.

So ... I did. I liked the sofa a lot.

"Elsie ..." Mom gave me a sympathetic smile.

"Listen," I cut her off. "I lost it. And I'm truly sorry for that. There really is no good excuse. I felt backed into a corner, ganged up on, and attacked. Still ... it's no excuse for saying the things I said. Even if it was all true." I glanced up to see Linc, Chase, and Meadow at the arched entrance. "Sit down. You need to hear this too."

They took seats on the floor next to Bella. Meadow jumped up on the sofa with me, the only one who didn't care that I'd had sex on it with Kael.

"We're all adults. It's not the most comfortable thing in the world talking about my sex life with my kids and my parents. But here we are ... talking about it. You don't have to approve of what I've done, but it doesn't make it wrong. I did nothing wrong, except maybe in God's eyes. But that's between me and God. I'm sorry if this has caused any of you pain and embarrassment." My attention landed solely on Bella. "It was never my intention.

"But ... I'm not going to let you treat me like there is something wrong with me. I married the man I loved. I raised a beautiful family with him. And then I no longer wanted to be married to him—not because I regretted anything. But because I changed over the years, and I wanted something else in my life—even if I didn't know what that was."

"A younger man?" Bella mumbled.

"No. Not a younger man. This isn't a lost and found story. I wasn't, and I'm still not looking for someone. Not looking for anyone to replace your dad. I am whole without a man in my life. It's hard to explain." I rubbed my temples. "This sounds awful, and it's not the best explanation, but it's the easiest. It's like when Bella wanted peanut butter and jelly every single day. It was your favorite. You loved it so much that you couldn't imagine there ever coming a day that you didn't want ... *need* a peanut butter and jelly sandwich. Until ..."

"I hated it," she whispered.

I nodded. "Yeah. I'll never forget the day you just couldn't eat one more sandwich. I asked what had happened. I thought maybe someone at school had made fun of you for taking the same thing for lunch every day, but you said you didn't know. All you knew was that you didn't want another sandwich, and even the smell of it turned your stomach."

"Dad was your PBJ?" Linc lifted an eyebrow.

I chuckled. "Yes and no. The point is something changed. Something shifted. And I didn't want to be married to him any longer. I didn't want to be married to anyone. I wanted to go a different direction in my life. I'd raised you kids, and I wanted *me* to matter again. I didn't regret the past ... I don't know how many times I can say that to you or what I can do to make you understand that. But I knew if I didn't say something or do something that I would start to regret each new day. It wasn't supposed to end in a big fight."

I wiped a stray tear as Bella blinked out a few tears as well. "We were fused together in so many ways. I should have known separating wouldn't be easy, and it wouldn't come without pain. Twenty-two years of marriage doesn't end without feeling a little torn ... a little broken."

"But the accident—" Bella sobbed, and it made more hot tears run down my face.

"It was just that ..." Linc hugged her. "An accident."

Kindness packed the hardest punch. Always. But especially when you didn't feel completely deserving of it.

"This young man ..." Mom spoke up. "Do you love him, Elsie?"

I wiped my face. "He's not my happiness."

CHAPTER twenty-six

You're the best kind of want.
You're the worst kind of need.

OVER THE NEXT FEW DAYS, I managed to convince my family that I wasn't losing it.

We visited Craig's grave and flipped through family photos in old albums and more recent digital photos. We laughed and cried watching video footage from family vacations, birthday parties, and the many Christmases we spent together as a family.

We weren't a failure. We were a book. A beautiful love story that ended more tragically than it should have. One chapter ... we had one bad chapter. If I'd had it to write over again, that was the only chapter I would've edited.

One day.

I would have changed one day of our marriage. The last day.

That was not a failure. It was one day.

One. Fucking. Day.

Twenty-two years of marriage deserved a better

ending than the smell of bacon and an ill-executed proposition for sex. At the very least, it deserved a well-thought-out letter or a private dinner with a rehearsed speech.

"The Christmas Eve crowd is a mile long out the door at *What Did You Expect?*" Bella sulked as she glared out the window while two measly customers milled around our store.

"It's because they're running thirty-percent off today," Gabriella, one of my two customers said. "I'm headed there next to get vinegar for my mom. I just thought I'd browse around here for a bit and stay warm until the line dies down a bit over there."

Bella closed the distance between us and lowered her voice. "Mom, you cannot let him do that."

"Do what? Run a sale?" I chuckled, determined to not let anything ruin our Christmas.

"This place used to be filled to capacity the day before Christmas—everyone grabbing last-minute gifts. Now look at us ... we have two customers, and they're *both* probably sucking up all our heat while they wait for the line across the square to go down."

"Bella, we're closing the store in a week. Does it really matter?"

"Yes." Pain filled her eyes.

"Why?" I tilted my head and gave her my most sympathetic expression.

"I don't know ... it just does." She rubbed her eyes before any tears could escape.

"Is this about your dad? The store? Or is this about *him*? Are you still mad about us? It's over. We're not—"

"I'm mad because you let him take advantage of you.

Had his store been the one going out of business, he would have been upset. And he wouldn't have been interested in you that way. He played you, Mom. And I hate it."

"Bella—"

"No," she continued to whisper-yell at me. "He's sitting over there gloating. You can't see it, but I guarantee he's really proud of himself for winning."

"It's not a game."

"To *him,* it's a game. You're just too trusting to see it."

I could let the store go.

I could let Kael go.

But I couldn't watch my daughter grapple with her emotions like that—thinking I didn't do more to fight, even if it was a losing battle.

"Then we do something."

"Yeah?" She grabbed a tissue from behind the counter and fixed her smeared eye makeup in her phone's camera screen.

"Yeah. It won't change the outcome of the game, but we throw the Hail Mary anyway."

"What do you have in mind?"

My lips twisted. "Do we still have some cans of spray paint in the back?"

Bella shrugged. "Maybe."

We did.

We had several cans of red paint.

Perfect.

I slipped on my jacket and headed out front, shaking a spray can while Bella stayed inside with our two, fake customers.

S A L E

EVERYTHING
F R E E!

Bella's jaw dropped when I walked back into the store. "Are you serious?" Her smile grew.

"It's on the window now. That paint doesn't come off easily."

Gabriella and the other heat-seeking customer squinted to read the lettering backward and through the front displays. "Are you serious?" Gabriella said, eyes wide and focused on me.

"Serious. No hoarding. Whatever you can carry out in one trip with your two hands. Go tell your friends."

It happened in a matter of minutes, but it felt like seconds. The line across the street ran like a heard of buffalo toward *Smith's Specialties*.

No price checking.

No swiping credit cards.

No standing in line ... except to get into the store.

It was looting, but legal and less destructive.

Women were shoving stuff into their purses and pockets before walking out the door completely loaded down with free goods.

A few longtime customers and generous souls at least took a few moments to ask if we were going out of business and thanked us for our many years of service to the community.

I glanced at my phone and the text from Kael. "Stay here, Bella. Make sure no brawls break out."

She giggled at the sheer level of greediness in our town. Epperly wasn't a town filled with struggling people, but it didn't stop the embarrassing chaos of the free-for-all from erupting. "I've got this."

Escaping to the back room, I unlocked the door to the outside and Kael sitting on an overturned crate, sipping something from an insulated mug.

"Don't you have a store to run?" I zipped my jacket and closed the door behind me, leaning against it with my hands in my pockets.

He took another sip from his mug. "No customers at the moment."

"Bummer. I know how that feels. Are you upset?" I dared him to be upset or even the slightest bit aggravated about my massive sale.

"Do I look upset?"

"I don't know your looks well enough to say for sure. I mean … no. You don't appear all that upset."

"Did you do this to upset me?"

I shook my head.

"Well, there you have it. No harm, no foul."

"I did it for Bella. She wanted to get back at you."

Kael nodded slowly. "And she's mad at me why?"

"She thinks you played me."

"Played you? I'm pretty sure you broke up with me."

"Well, we weren't together, so there wasn't an official break up."

"We were having sex, and that stopped."

"You miss the sex?" I raised an eyebrow. He had a much longer list … a much deeper pool of candidates in Epperly than I did. Even if he didn't want to marry Tillie, I felt certain Amber would have made herself available to him. Hell … I think Amie would have volunteered.

"Damn right."

I laughed.

"You don't?" he asked just before taking another sip of his drink.

"Yeah. I miss the sex."

"I miss the conversation." He smirked.

"The conversation? We didn't talk. We had sex."

"Not true. We talked about life. We talked about relationships and religion. We could probably even talk about politics. I have some interesting views on it as well."

"I'm sure you do." I couldn't hide my grin. Life felt right ... in place with Kael. I couldn't explain it. Just a feeling. *That* was the feeling he so expertly gave me.

I fell backward, barely catching myself before falling onto my ass when the door opened behind me.

"Mom ... what are you—" Bella helped me regain my balance as her gaze bounced from me to Kael sitting on the crate. "Oh, hey, Mr. Hendricks. How's your day-before-Christmas sale going? We're killing it. Our whole inventory is nearly gone."

"Bella ..." I rolled my eyes.

Kael bit his lips together to contain his amusement with my melodramatic daughter.

"I'm sure you're pissed off at my mom, but you should know it was my idea. She might be blinded by all of..." she waved her hand in front of him, gesturing to his body "...that. But I'm not. Your nice guy act doesn't fool me."

"Bella ..."

She turned toward me. "Why are you giving him the time of day?"

I shook my head. "I'm not giving him anything. Now, what did you need when you came out here?"

She huffed. "Amie is inside looking for you."

"Okay. Tell her I'll be right in."

"I'll wait." Bella crossed her arms over her chest.

God ... I loved that girl. With her fire, she would rule the world. She was everything I knew I could be but didn't have the courage to actually be.

Kael stood. "I'll let you get back to your customers. I was planning on closing early today anyway. Now I can surprise my employees with an even earlier start to their holiday. Merry Christmas to you and all of your family."

"Come on, Mom." She tugged at my arm.

"Bella." I peeled my arm from her hold. "Give us a minute."

She sighed. "One minute. I'll be right on the other side of this door, waiting, so if he tries anything ..." She scowled at Kael.

Again, his lips worked to suppress his amusement. As did mine.

As soon as the door shut, we stared at each other in silence, both of us knowing Bella's ear was glued to the other side. I glanced around the parking lot, but nobody was in sight. Pulling my phone from my pocket, I texted Kael.

> Me: Kiss me.

He read my message on his watch and grinned, chin tipped downward staring at it.

Everyone deserved a Christmas wish. That was mine.

The second he glanced up at me, he took two steps and slid his hands along my face, cupping it as his mouth covered mine. It warmed me from the tip of my cold nose to my tingly numb toes. It made my heart race as my brain gave me a nice dopamine buzz. I imagined the Kael effect was stronger than ecstasy, the high of endorphins racing through my body.

It wasn't love. It was attraction.

Love was the feeling I knew I'd have when he was no longer touching me.

Love was the ache in my chest when I thought he would never kiss me again.

Love was missing his smile.

Love was craving the sound of his voice.

My fingers claimed the front of his jacket to steady myself. When his lips released mine, he didn't let go of my face.

He lingered.

That was the story of Kael Hendricks. Everything about him lingered.

His intoxicating scent.

His paralyzing touch.

The life in his eyes burning brightly.

Then there was something that I couldn't quite name, couldn't exactly put my finger on. It was that undefinable thing that lingered the most. And it wasn't that I wanted Kael the way young Elsie Stapleton wanted Craig Smith.

I didn't want him.

And I didn't *not* want him.

I didn't know what to do with him because I didn't know the new rules for my life. There was some defining left to do.

He opened his eyes and brushed his nose against mine. I parted my lips to speak.

"Shh ..." he whispered, a reminder that Bella was a breath away, ear to door.

I love you.
I don't know what that means in my life anymore.
You're the best kind of want.
You're the worst kind of need.

When he took a step back, I wondered if he could read my mind. His smile said yes—such a sublime picture before me. He tipped his chin and retrieved his phone, again ... no words were exchanged. As he turned and sauntered away, my phone vibrated.

> Kael: Merry Christmas <3

CHAPTER twenty-seven

When we failed to acknowledge individuality and honor autonomy, our very existence lost meaning

I MADE a timeline of my life.

Let's say I lived to be a hundred. Why the heck not?

Add three years of dating to our twenty-two-year marriage, and that meant I spent twenty-five percent of my life with Craig Smith, raising four kids. The previous seventeen years, or seventeen percent, of my life was spent being a kid and going to school. That left fifty-eight percent (or fifty-eight years) of my life unaccounted for.

The "second act" Mary referenced.

When we failed to acknowledge individuality and honor autonomy, our very existence lost meaning. I learned to recognize the difference between chapters and the entire book.

I shared chapters with many people who came and went from my life—Craig included. However, the book was my story and my story alone.

"Don't let anyone else write your story." I smiled at

Bella's final words to her graduating class as she stood at the podium atop the stage in the auditorium.

My words ... she repeated the words I said during a toast I gave the day we officially closed the door to *Smith's Specialties*. It was bittersweet. The end to many chapters of my book, of my kids' books, Craig's, and his parents'.

I spent the rest of winter and most of spring quilting, painting, and helping get Mary's and Ron's things sold so they could move to assisted living. Then I sent Bella off to Arizona to stay with my parents until she moved to her dorm in College Station, Texas. Our house hadn't sold, so I stayed in Epperly.

I hadn't spoken to Kael since Christmas Eve. He plowed my driveway the rest of the winter. Occasionally, he gave me a two-fingered steering wheel wave if he passed me on my morning walks with Amie and Meadow.

For the most part, I stayed at home. I honored Bella's request to not make anything about *my* needs while she finished her senior year. What I didn't do for my kids ...

Then two weeks after she moved to Arizona, I ventured out. Really ventured out. I passed by the space that used to be *Smith's Specialties*. Nothing had opened yet, but they finally posted a *Coming Soon* sign—a fitness studio. I laughed out loud.

"Of course ... now it opens."

Continuing down the sidewalk, I popped into *Spoons*. I hadn't been there since the day Kael outed us to all of Epperly in front of Tillie. To my surprise, most everyone kept to themselves, offering friendly smiles as I waited in line.

Finding a table by the window, I enjoyed my cup of

soup and garden salad, watching residents mill around the square in the early June heat. After I finished my lunch, I continued making my way around the rest of the town square, ending at *What Did You Expect?*

Nerves sent my breathing a little off-kilter as I opened the door. What would it be like to see him up close? Would he look at me the same way? So many thoughts raced through my mind.

A new face greeted me from behind the counter. "Welcome. Let me know if I can help you with anything." She smiled.

I nodded. "Thanks."

The place wasn't as crowded as I'd remembered it being, but it was the middle of a Tuesday in June. I recognized a few faces, friendly ones that gave me quick smiles and returned to their shopping. I grabbed a basket and started piling stuff into it.

I'd been secretly dying to start my own collection of specialty vinegars and oils, but I couldn't do it with Kael as my competition. Over two hundred dollars later, I swiped my credit card and mustered the courage to ask my burning question. "Is Kael in today?"

"No. He's been gone for weeks. Camping in Utah with friends."

I nodded. "Sounds fun."

"Yeah. He's not here that often. Rachel manages most everything. Kael likes to travel ... a lot."

I smiled. "Yeah, I've heard that. Are you new to Epperly?"

"I am." She handed me my receipt. "I met Kael years ago when he traveled to Toronto."

"Ah, you're Canadian?"

"Yes. Can't you tell from the accent?" She laughed, curling her blond hair behind one ear as she showed off her perfect teeth and youthful complexion. "He offered me a job and has been letting me stay with him until I figure out where I want to be. I'm at a weird crossroad in my life." She shrugged.

A beautiful *young* girl was staying with him. Nope ... that didn't bother me at all.

"Well, thanks. Have a good one." I grabbed my bag and pushed through the door. "Oh ... excuse me." I ran right into someone.

"Hi."

When I glanced up, squinting against the sun, I realized it wasn't just someone. It was Kael with a thicker beard and even longer hair. Tanned nose and cheeks. White smile. And that familiar sparkle in his eyes.

"Hi." I finally returned his greeting after staring at him in disbelief for several moments.

He nodded to the bag in my hand. "Looks like you bought one of everything."

I glanced down at the bag and shrugged. "Just supporting local businesses."

As a couple squeezed by us to get into the store, Kael took a step back so I could get out the door and out of their way. We met going into winter, so it was strange seeing him in cargo shorts, a well-fitted tee, and sneakers instead of boots.

"You look good. I like your shorter hair."

I reached for my chin-length hair and smiled. He still managed to make me blush just from his proximity ... from the grin on his face and mischief in his eyes. "Thanks. I needed a change."

"Change is good." His hands went straight for his back pockets, his usual stance. It pulled back his shoulders, made him appear a little taller, and definitely fit the Captain America persona.

"Your employee ... friend ... roommate ... uh ..." My nose scrunched as I fumbled my words. "She said you were in Utah."

"I was. Just got back this morning. We drove through the night. I'm in need of a nap." He yawned. "But I wanted to check on things here first."

It took me a few seconds to realize he'd stopped talking. I found myself enamored with the simplicity of his presence before me. I knew I'd missed him, but I wasn't aware of just how much until he stood a few feet from me. "Well, I won't keep you. I just ventured out beyond the grocery store and the bank for the first time in months. So ..."

"Finish your quilts?" He grinned.

Gah! I loved that grin.

"Three of them."

"Painting?"

I chuckled and nodded. "Every room. I've tidied up the landscaping and potted lots of plants. I didn't start my usual garden because I'd hoped the house would sell, but clearly nobody wants to move to Epperly. And who can blame them?"

"Bella leave for school?"

"Not yet. She's in Arizona for the summer with my parents. She'll move to Texas the first of August. I already have my airfare booked to help her get settled."

"And you?"

"And me ..." I grinned and sighed. "I'm just living in the moment." My smile intensified in response to his.

"What are you going to do when the house sells?"

"*If* it sells? I don't know. After Bella starts school this fall, I'm thinking of traveling. Maybe I'll learn to make olive oil in Italy or captain a boat on the Mediterranean."

Kael nodded. "All good plans."

"Actually, I'm leaning toward Peru."

"Peru?" He lifted his eyebrows.

"Yes. Machu Picchu. The Amazon."

"Sounds amazing."

"Over the years, our family vacations involved anywhere we could drive to. Four kids. Owning a retail store. It wasn't conducive to international travel."

"Well, now's your time. I'm happy for you."

"Thanks."

Why did it hurt to see him? Oh ... right. My heart never let go. "So ... you have a roommate. That's so not you."

He glanced through the window behind me. "Yeah. Claire's doing her own searching for a new direction. I needed some help at the shop, and she needed a place to live for a while. It's just good bartering."

I nodded slowly. "Well, I'll let you get inside to see her. I'm sure you missed her." My gaze didn't quite reach his face. "Maybe I'll see you around now that I'm venturing out. Get some sleep."

"I'll walk you to your vehicle." He reached for the bag in my hand.

"What? No. Don't be silly." I tried to pull away from his hand wrapped around the handles of the bag next to mine.

"I'm not being silly." He pulled the bag out of my grip and headed toward the parking lot like it was a forgone conclusion that I was parked there.

I was.

"You are being silly." I huffed, catching up to him.

"I'm not. I'm being greedy."

"Greedy?"

"Yeah." He shot me a quick sidelong glance. "Looking for any excuse to spend a few extra minutes with you."

There he went ... reaching for that jar on the highest shelf with my heart inside it.

"What about Claire?"

"Claire already spent time with you. It's my turn."

Smart ass ...

I couldn't hide my grin. "Kael ..."

He found my Tahoe with ease ... probably because he'd parked right next to me. As soon as he reached the driver's door, he turned. "Elsie."

In a silent standoff, we held our ground as if waiting for the other one to blink.

"Have you missed me?" He blinked first.

"Does it matter?" My head tilted to the side as I curled my shorter hair behind my ear.

"No." His eyes shifted, inspecting me from head to toe. "But *have* you missed me?"

The familiar thrill and anxiety of falling in love came rushing back. My mind raced with possibilities and fear. My heart fluttered as it tried to find its normal rhythm again. I don't remember falling out of love with Kael, yet there I was ... falling in love with him again. A disorganized euphoria of emotions made it impossible to speak.

"Are you really not going to answer me?"

I shrugged. "Do I really have to?"

"Are you seeing anyone?"

My lips twisted. "Does it matter?"

"No." He grinned, bending to the side to set my bag on the ground. "But *are* you seeing anyone?"

I giggled, shaking my head.

"Is that a no?"

"It's a 'you're crazy.'" I unlocked my doors and gave him a gentle nudge with my elbow, so he'd step aside. I grabbed the bag and opened the door. "It's been good seeing you." I told my heart to just chill out and play it cool for once.

"Who's mowing your lawn?" He blocked the door with his body after I climbed into my Tahoe.

I fastened my seat belt. "I mow it."

"Have you ever thought about paying someone else to do it?"

"No. Why?" I slipped on my sunglasses.

"Well, I'd be willing to make the same deal with you on your lawn as I did clearing snow from your driveway."

Pressing my finger to the top of my sunglasses, I slid them down to the tip of my nose, eyeing him over the frame. "Oh, yeah?" As hard as I tried to play it super cool, I felt the burning in my cheeks and the prickling along my skin as my breaths struggled to stay even.

He nodded slowly, that grin *killing* me as he reached for my face to remove the strands of hair blowing across my lips. "It's the Christian thing to do."

"Funny ... I've always thought of you as Satan."

"I can see that." He rested his hands on the edge of the roof. His T-shirt slid up and his shorts slid down, giving me a glimpse of his abs and the trail running south of them. "So ..."

Snapping my gaze up to his face, I swallowed hard. "Yeah ... so ... Friday works. You can mow my lawn Friday."

He tapped the roof three times and stepped back. "Friday."

I shut the door and held my breath until he was in my rearview mirror. Then I released a harsh breath. "Oh, Elsie ... you're in trouble."

Friday

MY HANDS SHOOK as I tried to thread my needle just after one o'clock. I'd woken up at six that morning, walked with Amie and Meadow, and showered for nearly twenty minutes—shaving, exfoliating, conditioning.

Lemon water.

Stared out the front window.

Read a few chapters of my book—near the front window.

Quilted by the front window.

Lunch on the front porch.

And back to more quilting.

Amie: Is he there yet?

Me: No. (crying emoji)

Amie: Lol. He'll be there.

Just as I typed the crying emoji four more times, he pulled into the driveway. Pursing my lips, I blew out quick shallow breaths followed by several deep ones as I angled myself away from the window so I could see him, but he couldn't see me.

"Jesus ..." My lips parted as he shrugged off his shirt, tucked it into the back of his worn jeans like a rag, and lifted his lawnmower out of the truck bed.

Over the next hour, I drooled. He mowed, trimmed, and edged my yard. After he loaded everything into the back of his truck, I adjusted my strapless sun dress, rubbed my glossed lips together, and stood idle at the door, waiting for him to knock or just barge in like he'd done so many times before.

"Breathe, Elsie," I whispered, closing my eyes.

They sprang to attention, wide and panicked the second I heard the rumble of his truck starting. I threw open the door as he backed out onto the street and put it in drive.

"Wait!" I ran down the driveway in my bare feet, toenails freshly painted red, as he headed down the street. "Kael!" I stopped in the middle of the street, releasing my flailing arms to my sides when I realized he didn't see me.

Then his brake lights illuminated. He pulled off to the side of the road.

My phone vibrated in my right hand.

Kael: Going to shower.

Me: Kiss me.

Kael: I'm sweaty.

> **Me:** Kiss me.

> **Kael:** Later.

> **Me:** Kiss me.

> **Kael:** Soon.

> **Me:** I'm living in the now. KISS ME!

Kael hopped out—shirt covering his tan torso again. He ran his arm across his sweaty forehead while walking a straight line down the middle of the street toward me. "Your dress is white."

"Kiss me."

"People could be watching," he continued making his way back to me.

Twenty feet.

Fifteen feet.

"Kiss me."

Ten feet.

"You're such a horny duck." He smirked.

Five feet.

"Kiss—"

He kissed me.

My face in his hands.

My feet lifted onto my toes.

My heart in the jar on the top shelf—crashing to the ground.

EPILOGUE

After two months of sex—so much sex—holding hands in the town square, flirting over lunch at *Spoons,* and ignoring the judgmental glances from some of Epperly's residents, it was time for me to leave for Texas to get Bella settled into her dorm.

I took my house off the market since it wasn't getting any lookers anyway. Kael and I agreed there was no reason to live together, even if we shared the same bed most of the time ... even if there was an extra toothbrush at his place and mine. Autonomy mattered to us. Space mattered. It not only mattered; it made our time together mean more.

After my boys moved, they'd come home to visit. And there was this shift. They weren't home to hole-up in their rooms or hide in the basement; they were home to visit me. We shared more meaningful conversations. Our time together was intentional, not just a convenience of shared space.

With Kael, we made the choice every day to be alone or be together. Our time together was always intentional, always meaningful.

"You should come with me to Peru next month," I said while packing my bag for Texas.

Kael rubbed Meadow's belly from their sprawled out positions on my bed. "Have you ever taken a trip all by yourself?"

"No. I got pregnant in college and raised four kids. I don't feel like I've been going to the bathroom by myself for that long. And honestly ... Meadow occasionally follows me in there to watch me do my business. I think she feels it's only fair."

He chuckled. "Then you definitely need to take a trip by yourself. It's an incredible experience. It's healing. It's a confidence booster. It's the opportunity to let something be only about you. You'll learn to trust yourself more—to rely on yourself. It will edge you out of your comfort zone. And you'll get to know yourself in a way you've probably never had the chance to do.

"I took my first solo trip out of the country when I was twenty-four. It changed me. I matured. I found a deeper meaning to my life and learned to create my own happiness. It forced me to make new friends and redefine the meaning of family ... and in some ways the meaning or purpose of my life."

I zipped my bag. "Either you are a true believer in this 'solo tripping' or you desperately want to get rid of me for a while."

He sat up and pulled me to stand between his legs. I rested my hands on his shoulders, knowing he meant every word—wondering if my marriage would have ended had Craig valued my emotional health and championed my independence so much. The problem with marriage and most of the vows people made to each other was there weren't the actions to back them up. It was like my kids apologizing all the time, but their actions didn't reflect those apologies.

My wedding vows with Craig should have been more specific:

I promise to encourage you to take trips by yourself, not burp before kissing you, and always use complete sentences that don't end in "ya know."

"Love, honor, and cherish" were just too broad.

"I'm not broken," Kael said.

"What do you mean?" I glided my hands up to his neck and teased the hair at his nape.

"I have as much capacity to love as any other human being. My choices don't reflect my abilities. I'm not bad at love or broken. My feelings aren't less intense or less sincere. It's *because* I love you that I want you to love yourself. People love to quote Richard Bach's 'If you love someone, set them free. If they come back, they're yours; if they don't, they never were.' But my philosophy is a little different. To me, the ultimate love is freedom. It's not releasing someone; it's respecting their right to never be caged in the first place, never *belonging* to anyone but yourself. When people so desperately *want out* of a marriage or relationship, that implies they feel imprisoned with a need to escape. I don't want to ever be anyone's prison.

"Stay or go. It should always be your choice, Elsie. It doesn't mean you can't have love or choose to be monogamous in your sexual ... endeavors." That irresistible smile overtook his whole face.

"Are you choosing to be monogamous in your sexual endeavors?" I trapped my lower lip between my teeth.

"Yes. You leave nothing of me for other women. And somehow you've managed to possess my thoughts even when we're not together."

Love was risky.

Life was risky.

But they were also exhilarating and meant to be experienced without the crippling fear of getting hurt. I had to risk it. I would embrace my choices and not hide them from my family or anyone else.

"My heart's still learning to deal with these new feelings ... new possibilities."

His eyes narrowed. "Such as?"

"What if we don't last?"

Kael nodded with careful consideration. "I get it because my heart can't stop thinking ... what if we do?"

The End

Christmas in Birdville

Chapter One

HENRY

THE AFINA HOUSE WAS MINE, until I lost it with a straight flush. Let me repeat ... a straight flush. My great grandfather built the Victorian farmhouse for his bride, Marian, in what is still one of Ohio's smallest river towns. Birdville has a population of just under seven hundred.

The firstborn male inherits the Afina house. After my dad died two years ago, my mom moved to Germany where she and my dad had planned on retiring in the same town where my great grandfather was born.

She moved out.

I moved back in.

Thankfully, I kept my trailer. It's like the universe knew I'd fuck things up.

We're not a wealthy family—we've just always owned the most coveted house in Birdville. We were a coal mining family before my grandfather became a plumber, like my father, and like me.

So while I sit in my pickup truck outside the Afina house, I can't help but think of my mom's announcement that she's coming to Birdville for Christmas.

That fucking straight flush.

Since I lost the family home just over six months ago, this will be my first time back inside it—as a hired plumber.

I knock on the door three times. It takes an eternity for someone to answer.

"You must be the plumber," a fifty-something woman says, blowing at her silver and blond bangs to expose her kind blue eyes.

I hold up my toolbox and give her a guilty shrug.

"It's the bathroom down the hall and to the right." She shows me a canning jar filled with what looks like the makings for cookies. "I have to finish putting these together. Let me know if you have any questions Mr. ..." Her gaze slides to my shirt and the name tag I'm not wearing.

I refrain from sharing my real name in case she makes the connection to it and the house she stole from me. Okay, it technically wasn't her, but the sting is still too real to give a shit. I glance at the jar in her hand and smile. "Mason. Mason Ball."

"Very well, Mr. Ball." She shoots me a courteous smile and sashays to the kitchen.

I'm pleasantly surprised. She seems normal.

After I lost the house, the loan shark put it up for auction. Serena Soro, a writer of some sort, purchased it and nearly everything in it. I'd never seen her until today, nor had anyone else to their knowledge. She has everything delivered to her house. Rumors have been flying around since the day the moving company pulled into the driveway and unloaded her belongings.

She's a recluse.

A vampire.

A witch.

A serial killer.

A child trafficker.

And a million other wildly crazy speculations.

Not gonna lie ... I stuck a few bulbs of garlic in my toolbox just in case.

After fixing the slow flushing toilet and the leaky faucet, I poke my head in the kitchen. It's all so familiar, even the sweet smell of sugar and vanilla bean wafting from the kitchen. My mom loves to bake.

Even the furniture is ... *was* mine. However, there are no Christmas decorations. Not so much as a string of tinsel or sprig of mistletoe. Our house used to be the biggest attraction in town over the holidays. Garland for days and enough indoor and outdoor lights to illuminate a whole galaxy.

"You're good to go," I say.

She glances over her shoulder, a bit of flour smudged along her cheek. "Thank you. Can you leave an invoice?"

"Sure." I take another glance around the kitchen. "Did you know this house has been here for generations?"

"Oh ..." She measures baking powder and deposits teaspoons of it into the long row of jars. "Are you originally from Birdville?"

"I am." I scribble out an invoice. "Do you like the house?"

She chuckles. "Sure. What's not to like? It's charming

with a beautiful view of the river. The woodwork is a work of art. Every room feels like a warm hug this time of year."

I no longer feel that warm embrace, but it does have a beautiful view. There's an attic room with a colossal window that makes one feel suspended over the water because the drop beneath it is so steep. Growing up, it was my favorite room. My sister thought there were ghosts up there. After she died, I believed *she* was the ghost in the room. I wonder if she's still up there, trying to figure out how in the hell I managed to lose the family home.

"Well, here you go." I place the invoice on the counter away from the lineup of jars. "Let me know if you have any issues. I think it should be fine now."

"Do you bake?" she asks.

"Sometimes," I say, hoping reheating pizza in the microwave counts.

She screws a lid on one of the jars and hands it to me with a wink. "For you, *Mason Ball*."

Embarrassment fills my cheeks. Women are too observant for their own good. I clear my throat and offer her a sheepish grin. "Thank you."

Chapter Two

"Henry, I saw your van at the Afina house this morning. What was she like?" My neighbor, Doyle, coughs from his old gray Chevy Malibu. Cigarette smoke billows out the one-inch crack of his window. Betty won't let him smoke in the trailer since he set the last one on fire, so he spends most of his days smoking in his car while on neighborhood watch. The only thing that needs watching is him—so he doesn't set anything else on fire.

"Uh ... she was fine," I say, glancing up from my mail.

Doyle coughs up part of a lung. I expect a red *splat* against the window. Thankfully, there isn't one. "Was she a hottie?" He waggles his bushy, white eyebrows before pinching his lips around his cigarette.

"I'd say she's in her fifties, so I'm going to decline making any comment on her level of hotness."

"Fifties, huh? She got a good pair of legs on her? I'm a leg guy. But you know this because you've seen my Betty."

"Indeed." I smile. "I've seen your Betty. There's something about her. I can't quite put my finger on it, but it's special for sure."

"Fingers to yourself, Henry." He holds up his cigarette while wiggling his other fingers. "These digits will be the only ones to touch Betty's *specialness* you speak of." He winks at me. "If you know what I mean."

I taste a little bile. "Good talk, Doyle ... good talk." With a quick wave, I retreat into my trailer, peel open a can of wild caught salmon, and spread half of it on two slices of bread with some mayo and sweet relish.

My phone screen lights up with a text from my mom. It's the middle of the night in Germany. What's so urgent?

> Mom: The garland's in the attic. Use ribbons to tie it to the railing. Wire will scratch the wood.

"I don't know if it's still in the attic," I mumble my reply. I'm on the fence about telling her the truth via text message or waiting until the last possible minute when I see her in person.

No garland.

No railing.

No house.

The Penneys might save me on this one. They have to. Five years ago, they had a house fire across the street from our house. Lost everything except human lives. Mom repeated, "It's just stuff, Elizabeth," to Mrs. Penney on so many occasions I lost count.

Just a house.

Just furniture.

Just materialistic things that don't matter in the bigger picture.

With Christmas upon us, I have to believe my mother will heed her own sentiments and stay focused on that bigger picture when she discovers the Afina house and all of its belongings are no longer in the family.

Here's the bigger picture: I haven't gambled, not once, since I lost everything.

Baby steps.

Chapter Three

A BONE-RATTLING gust of wind shakes my trailer in the middle of the night like an earthquake. In fact, when I wake to silence, I'm certain that's what happened because there's no wind. I lumber from my bed to get a drink of water and see if anything was damaged. While I tip back a glass of water, my vision snags on headlights pointed at the back of my trailer in such close proximity it seems unlikely they're not on my property.

"What the hell," I mumble to myself.

Squinting to see if anyone's in the vehicle, I grab my jacket and swing open the door.

A white BMW is parked in my yard. Parked is a generous word. Crashed is more like it. The hood is bent from taking out my mailbox which is on its side beneath my bedroom window.

I knock on the driver's window. "Yo! What have you done? You're in my yard! Are you alive?" I frown when the hunched body resting against the deployed airbag doesn't move. "Are you okay? Need me to call an ambulance?" I ease open her door.

A woman lifts her head with long dark hair stuck to her face. She blinks several times. "Where am I?"

"You're in my front yard. It's a ... no parking zone. I'm calling for help."

"No! No. No. Please no." She pounds her fists into the deployed airbag and searches for the seat belt. "No police. No reporters. No one." Her fingers peel the hair away from her face before she squeezes her body out of the car like the first stick of gum in a pack.

"You've done some damage to my property." I nod to my mailbox on the ground.

She flinches when a gust of wind barges past me right into her car. "I'll pay for it."

"I'm sure you will, but I want it in writing, which means we need to call the police and make an official report."

"Cash. I'll give you cash." She rubs her forehead with her palm. "Wait ... crap ... my wallet is at my house. Listen, help me get my car back to my house, and I'll pay you double the damage and a little extra to keep this between us." Her tired, brown eyes catch the glow of my porch light while she tucks her black hair behind her ears.

She's rather ... pretty.

And it's the middle of the night.

She's shaky.

And she just mowed down my mailbox with her fancy car.

Yet ... she's still mesmerizing for some reason.

"Why do you need help getting your car home? You

can see over the airbag, and the dent in your hood isn't too bad. It should run just fine."

Her nose wrinkles while she hugs herself. "I-I'm feeling a little woozy. I think it's best if I'm done driving for the night."

"It's after two in the morning, and you want me to what? Drive you home because after nearly hitting my house and killing me *you* feel a bit woozy?"

She's broke. She stole this car, and she's broke. What other reason would there be for her to be out at this time? Drugs? Maybe.

Her pouty lips dip into a frown. "It's the holidays. Where's your spirit of giving?"

I cough a laugh. "Spirit of giving? That's just perfect. It's always the person with the short straw getting lectured on things like the *spirit of giving*."

She blinks slowly several times. "You have beautiful eyes. Did you know that?"

Pfft ...

Is she trying to flatter me? Does she think batting her eyelashes at me and complimenting my eyes is all that's needed to remedy the situation? Is this supposed to get my dick hard?

It's hard, but it's more of a middle-of-the-night confusion, maybe even an angry kind of erection.

"Where do you live?" I ask.

"Five minutes from here."

"Fine." I fake a grumble, but I'd be lying if I said I'm not curious about her situation. And her. But mainly her situation.

Minutes later, she's murmuring directions to her house.

I nod with each one. "What were you doing in the trailer park at two in the morning?"

"Research." She stares out her window.

"Researching what?"

"The area."

"Why?"

"Do you always ask so many questions?" She pins me with a look that would make a lesser man shudder. A lesser man with average eyes, not beautiful, blue eyes like mine. Yeah, yeah … I fell for her compliment.

"When I'm driving strangers home in the middle of the night, I feel entitled with my line of questions. I'm Henry, by the way."

She nods several times. "I'm aware."

"Did I tell you my name earlier?" I squint at the road, trying to recall when I told her my name.

"Go right here. Then left."

I turn right and then left.

"Last one on the right," she says.

I let up on the gas, the tires slowing to a stop before I reach the driveway.

"What are you doing?" she asks.

I stare at the Afina house. "You live here?"

"I do."

"I was here yesterday. I met the owner. She wasn't you."

Her head whips in my direction. "You were here yesterday? You're the plumber?"

"Um … yeah. Why?"

"I …" She squints for a few seconds. "I had no idea."

I laugh. "Why would you?"

Okay, this chick is not playing with a full deck of cards.

She shakes her head. "Lola ... uh ... you met Lola. She's my assistant. I'm Serena."

"You're the writer?" I pull into the driveway.

"I am."

"I don't know if anyone in this town has seen you ... until now."

"I don't go out much." She steps out of the car.

I follow her to the front door, zipping my jacket against the nippy air.

"Cash work?" She heads down the hallway. Just before taking a right into the office, she glances over her shoulder and eyes me. I think she has a tiny grin stealing her lips, but it's hard to see in the dim light.

Do I amuse her? Is she flirting with me again?

I tear my gaze from hers and glance around more than I did yesterday. My mom is going to kill me for losing everything. Unless ...

"I have a better idea," I mumble.

She returns with an envelope. "Will two thousand cover your mailbox and your time driving me home?"

It's a fifty-dollar mailbox. I charge seventy an hour as a plumber. Two thousand is more than generous. Or at least it would be if I didn't need something else from her. "Listen, Serena ... can I call you Serena?"

"It's my name. Go for it."

"What are your holiday plans?"

Her eyes narrow in distrust. "Well ... my plans are to pretend it's not the holidays."

"Great. So you don't have family coming into town? No big parties? Nothing like that?"

Her head eases side to side.

"I don't want your money. I want to stay here for the holidays with my mom who will be arriving in a few days."

Serena blinks for a good five seconds. "This isn't a bed and breakfast."

"I don't need it to be a bed and breakfast. I just need it to be ..." I pop my lips a few times and adjust my shoulders into the most confident posture I can manage.

"To be what?" Her head cants.

"Mine. I need it to be mine just for the holidays. Until December twenty-seventh to be exact."

"You need what to be yours?" Her eyes narrow even more.

"This house."

Another long series of blinks. I'm not sure if she's in shock or deep thought.

"Why?" she asks.

"This house is called the Afina house. It has been since it was built three generations ago by my great grandfather Hermann Bechtel. I inherited it two years ago after my father died and my mother moved to Germany."

Serena doesn't respond for several long moments. She's too busy chewing on the inside of her cheek, lips twisted. "So why'd you sell it?"

I bob my head side to side. "That's complicated. I didn't have a choice, but my mom doesn't know. And if I don't have to tell her before Christmas, I'll choose that option."

"What's my role? If I'm not the owner, how will you explain me to your mom?"

Holy Christmas miracle ... is she really considering this? Just like that?

I honestly hadn't gotten that far, but now I need a solid plan. "You could stay at my place. A house swap for the holidays. No need for you and my mom to meet."

Her brows draw together for a beat before she covers her mouth and snorts. "House swap? *This* for your trailer?"

"What's wrong with my trailer? Aside from the fact that it no longer has a standing mailbox?" I cross my arms.

Her nose scrunches. Then it relaxes as she sighs. "I'll stay upstairs in the attic."

"For two weeks?"

She nods. "There's a mini fridge."

"If my mom sees you—"

"She won't."

This is too good to be true. I best not press my luck, so I nod.

"Why'd you lose the house?"

I narrow my eyes. "Why'd you run into my mailbox?"

"I have narcolepsy."

"What?"

"It's a neurological disorder where—"

"I know what it is. I just wasn't expecting that to be your reason." I roll my eyes. But if I'm honest, I don't really know a lot about narcolepsy, probably just a generic idea that it has something to do with not being able to stay awake.

"I'm more dangerous during the day. Sadly, I'm less likely to fall asleep at night. Except tonight." She frowns. "That was unexpected."

I chuckle. "Tell me about it."

"Why'd you lose your great grandfather's house?"

I glance at my phone. "It's a quarter after two in the morning. Can we finish this conversation another time?"

Serena nods several times, curling her hair behind one ear.

I still don't get why she's going along with this so easily. Not that I'm complaining.

"Where are you going?" she asks.

I open the door. "Home."

"How will you get there?"

"Legs. I've got a working pair. See you Monday. That's when my mom arrives. I'll bring groceries, clothes, and some photos to put back on the mantel. And we'll have to decorate for Christmas before I pick her up from the airport. Are the decorations still in the attic?"

Her head inches side to side.

"Where are they?" I ask.

"I uh ... gave them away."

"For Frosty the fucking snowman's sake ... did you get rid of *all* the decorations? Not having this place decorated for the holidays is nearly as bad as no longer owning it. How am I supposed to explain this to my mom?"

She shrugs. "Not my problem. It's my house. And I don't decorate for Christmas. I had to get rid of some shit. Why would I keep it?"

"Shit? It's not shit. Do you have any idea how many dollars in outdoor lights you gave away?"

"No." She lifts one shoulder.

"Sorry, writer woman, you must be rich. Lucky you. But I'm not, and now I have to buy a crap ton of lights to replace the ones you gave away." I shut the door behind me.

"Hey!" she yells when I reach the sidewalk. "You can't be mad at me for that. Are you out of your mind?"

I keep trekking my way toward home. "You ran into my mailbox and stole my house. I can do whatever I want."

Chapter Four

SERENA

"Hi." I open the front door to my ... guest? No. That's not right. Roomie? No. He's not a roomie.

Tennant? Nope. Not unless he's paying rent.

"Are ... you going to invite me in?" Henry asks.

"Of course. I was just trying to figure out how I would explain you if I had to."

Henry stares at me with his duffle bag slung over a shoulder. "To your assistant?"

I shake my head. "She went home for the holidays. I mean ... just to anyone."

He pulls off his beanie to reveal his dark head of matted hair. But those eyes ... their blue perfection makes up for everything else that's a little unkempt. "I'm a thirty-one-year-old male. Six-two. A Pisces. I'm freakishly good at badminton and pickleball. Single, but not desperate. And I might have a walnut allergy because when I eat them my tongue feels like it's been attacked by razor blades." He shrugs. "You could start there if you have to *explain* me."

I step aside and press my lips together for a beat before murmuring, "Not exactly what I meant."

Henry stomps his brown work boots on the mat before stepping inside. "I'll put my stuff away. If you want to help out, you can get the lights out of the back of my van and take them out of their packaging."

"I don't want to help you do that." I follow him to my bedroom, where he shoves clothes into drawers and onto hangers next to my clothes. "Do you know if there are hidden areas in this house? A secret door? A space beneath floorboards. Anything like that?"

Henry exits the closet, tossing his duffle bag on the floor and kicking it under my bed.

"Why do you ask?"

"Because I'm looking for something."

"If it's in a hidden spot that you know nothing about, then it's safe to say it's not yours."

I lift my chin. "Everything in this house is mine."

He smirks. "I'm in this house."

Don't grin. Don't grin!

I grin.

Henry's amusement vanishes. "You scare me."

"Why?" My accidental amusement sags into a frown.

"Because you're too okay with this."

"Okay with what? Owning you?"

He scoffs. "You don't own me."

"I own your *family* house. Your mom doesn't know you lost it. And you're living with me for the next two weeks. I think I pretty much own you."

"I'm going to buy this house back from you. It's only a matter of time." He jogs down the stairs.

I shove my feet into my boots and snag my coat from the hook before following him to his van. "You are not buying back this house. It's not for sale. It will never be for sale again as long as I'm alive."

Henry chuckles, throwing open his van's side door. "So how's this going to go down? You're leaving me the house in your will? Or I'm going to have to..." he peeks back at me, and his gaze ping-pongs in both directions before a toothy grin steals his face while he makes a throat cutting gesture at his neck "...to you."

I frown. "The latter."

He lifts his eyebrows. "Really? I'm going to have to ..." Again, he makes the throat cutting gesture.

"Stop." I giggle.

"See. You're laughing." With a load of lights in his arms, he struts to the front porch, dropping them unceremoniously on the top step. "That means you know how nonsensical it is for you to want to die in this house or die because of this house. This is a family heirloom to me."

"Yet you lost it or let it go. How exactly did that happen?"

"I'm just saying *if* my mom finds out you're in the attic, I'm going to need an explanation for you."

"That was a terrible subject change." I laugh, following him back to the van. The next thing I know, my arms are weighed down with lights. "I'm not helping you." I dump the lights on the top step next to the rest of them. "I have work to do."

"Writing?" he asks on his way to the garage.

I feel like a little dog chasing him, always two steps behind.

"We need to stick to discussing the things that matter," he continues. "How I lost this house is not important. The woman in the attic is very important. You could sneeze too loudly, and my mom will hear you." Retrieving the ladder from the wall where it's been since I bought the fully-furnished house, Henry takes it outside and props it up against the house.

"I'm now 'the woman in the attic?' Gosh ... just seconds ago I thought I was the homeowner."

With a little headshake, Henry grins. "Welcome to my world."

"I'm going inside. Enjoy decorating this house for the last time."

"Thanks for your help, Siri."

"Serena," I grumble a breath before closing the front door.

Chapter Five

HENRY

Sexy Siri is a tough one. Her lack of generosity makes it hard to think of her as sexy, but I'm willing to overlook her lack of help in the spirit of Christmas—and maybe a little because she accepted my offer. A fifty-dollar mailbox and no police report in exchange for two weeks at Hotel Afina.

I'm very suspicious of her lack of resistance to the idea, but I don't have time to figure her out. I have to figure out how I'm going to tell my mom that I've let her and the entire Bechtel family down. I fumbled the legacy ball. I'm a disgrace.

"Darling!" Mom hugs me, her thick red cardigan falling off her shoulders while her purse and carry-on bag hang from her arms.

"Hi, Mom." I squeeze her tightly. It's been too long since we've been together. Even if she'll likely disown me after Christmas, I'm not going to let it ruin our reunion.

"It's so good to be home again." She sighs while handing me her bag. "Have you visited your father and sister?" she asks as if they're in a house cuddled up next to the fireplace instead of six feet under dead grass and an inch of snow from last week.

"I have not. I thought we'd go together." Or not at all. I'm not a fan of visiting graves. That's not where I feel close to the deceased. Dad's ghost sits next to me in my work van, and Emily hangs out in the attic.

"Lovely idea." She chatters the whole way to the house and waltzes toward the front door, leaving me to carry her belongings. "Where's the wreath?" She halts several feet from the front door.

"It broke. Last year. I was going to find a new one but …"

"You knew it was impossible since I made it." Mom glances over her shoulder while opening the door. She gives me a smile and wink.

"Yup." I had no idea she made it, but my feigned-innocent smile lies.

"Oh … where's the garland on the stairs? And the mistletoe over the door? Henry …" She peeks her head into the living room. "Where's the Christmas tree?"

"I thought we'd pick one out together." I rest my hands on her shoulders.

There's a clunking sound that comes from upstairs. I cough to see if it muffles the noise. "What's that?" She straightens, eyes narrowed.

No such luck.

"What's what?"

"That sound."

I shrug. Again, there's a *clunk*.

"Someone's upstairs," she says, heading toward the stairs. "Who's here?"

"Mom, wait ..."

"Did your Aunt Jan make the trip from Nebraska?"

"Mom—" I chase after her with her bags in my arms.

"OH!" Mom jumps at the top of the stairs.

Sexy Siri, wrapped in a towel, hair wet, eyes wide, slowly opens her mouth into an "O" or maybe an "oops."

"Oh my goodness! You have a girlfriend?"

Serena says, "No" at the same time as I say, "Yes."

Shit!

Mom's eyes widen, red lips parted, and she releases a tiny gasp. It *is* gasp worthy. That, I won't argue. I've never had a girlfriend. I've had dates. Hookups. And a slew of awkward, sexual-tension filled situations with customers. Sadly, married women. But no girlfriend.

And definitely not a girlfriend who's half-naked and denying that she's my girlfriend.

Mom covers her mouth with a cupped hand, and she's getting ... *dammit!* She's getting all teary-eyed. I'm going to dash every single hope and dream she's ever had for me.

No house.

No real girlfriend.

Merry-fucking-your-son-is-a-loser Christmas.

"Finally!" She quickly wipes the corners of her eyes.

Serena (yes, I know her name) stiffens, tightening the sash of her white robe as my mom hugs her, ignoring Serena's adamant "no" answer to the girlfriend question.

"I think I've waited my whole life to meet you," Mom squeaks with choked emotion.

Nobody waits their whole life for anything. The

female genetic code comes with an extra chromosome of drama—sheer ridiculousness.

Serena's eyes look like they might pop out of her head from the tight hug and total ambush.

"Honey..." I wet my lips and clear my throat "...buns ... uh ... surprise! My mom is here for Christmas."

Mom holds her at arm's length. "You're so beautiful. I always knew my boy would find a beautiful woman. *Finally!* I'm getting grand babies."

Oh no ... fuck me. Did she really say that?

Serena doesn't blink. Not once. Her gaze darts between Mom and me. A silent plea for an explanation.

"Sorry. Where are my manners? Mom, this is Serena. Serena, this is my mom, Martha." I pray for points from Serena for saying her name correctly.

"Serena. What a beautiful name. I can't believe Henry's kept you a secret."

Serena's brows scrunch together when she shifts her attention to me.

"Well, we're good at keeping secrets. Aren't we, doll face?" I wink at her.

She's going to kill me. My balls have already started their retreat to safety.

"So ... good." Serena finally manages two words.

"Well, get dressed." Mom kisses her cheek. "I'll change out of my travel clothes and start dinner." Mom heads toward Emily's old bedroom while Serena murders me with one look.

The bad kind of murder that involves slow torture.

"Give me a sec," I manage to say past the tight grip of death around my neck. I've never seen someone go so long without blinking. She's going to need some eyedrops. This house is rather dry in the winter.

By the time I deposit my mom's belongings in Emily's room, Serena is gone. The creaky stairs don't allow me to sneak up on her, which makes her condition quite shocking.

She's naked.

This is worth repeating. She's. Naked.

Granted, her back is to me.

Granted, she's in the process of stepping into a pair of polka dot underwear.

Granted, I should have asked if it was okay to come up here.

But ... she had to have heard me.

"Why the look, *boyfriend*?" Serena shakes me from my thoughts.

I tear my gaze away from her body and focus on her eyes. "It's not like I was planning on this. You knew I went to get my mom from the airport. Why the hell did you wait until the last minute to take a shower? A noisy shower at that. Jeez ... could you have been any louder? What was I supposed to tell my mom?"

"It was the shampoo bottle. Then my conditioner. And I fell asleep after you left, so when I woke, I didn't have much time. But I needed a shower."

She's speaking, but I'm too focused on her tits, taking a quick mental picture of them before she pulls a fluffy pink sweater over her wet head.

"Shower," I mumble. "Got it." While she steps into a pair of light blue jeans, I mosey toward the antique desk in front of the window. My attention shifts from the overcast December day to her desk littered with pens, highlighters, a keyboard, and an open notebook. "What is this?"

"It's nothing. And it's personal. And mine. So please give it back." Serena reaches for the notebook when I snag it from her desk.

I turn in a slow circle, using my height and wingspan to keep her from taking it. She's like a dog jumping for a toy being dangled just out of her reach. "Hermann Bechtel? Why is my great grandfather's name in your notebook?"

She nabs it, but it's too late to erase what I've seen. "Because ..." She hugs the notebook while I inspect her, void of all trust. She's a slippery creature. I thought I was the one in control ... taking advantage of her mistake. Am I wrong?

"He built this house for my great grandmother, *Afina*."

"Your ..." My thoughts trip over themselves. "Are you a cousin or something? I hope not. I've had a few inappropriate thoughts that I would never have about a cousin. I don't get it. My great grandmother's name was Marian not Afina. What are you talking about?"

"Don't worry your pretty little head about it." She closes the notebook and shoves it into the middle desk drawer.

"What's your play?"

She crosses her arms. "My play?"

"Yeah. You've been entirely too agreeable about all of this. You're asking about hidden spots in the house. My great grandfather's name is in your notebook. You've been relentlessly flirting with me. You're obviously confused about the history of this house. I've seen you naked, which makes me think we might have sex. But now I think we might be related, so my mind is thoroughly fucked at the moment." My thoughts don't come out in order. I must have hit the shuffle button on my brain before I spoke.

Filter off.

Play shuffle.

Serena scoffs. "We're not having sex, Henry." She blushes and averts her gaze when she says it. "Your family has spent generations memorializing a house and the man who built it when it's all been nothing but a glimpse of a tragic love story." Her dark eyes meet mine again, but the blush remains. "Why do you think it's called the Afina house?"

I blink several times. My dick has entered the conversation making it hard (pun a little intended) for me to focus on anything but her pink cheeks and the way she keeps wetting her lips. "The house is blue. Afina is blue in Romanian."

"Albastru is blue."

"How do you know?"

She rolls her eyes. "I have family from Romania."

"So you're asking me to believe that this house was named after your great grandmother who was not my great grandmother?"

"I'm not asking you to believe anything. I'm just stating facts."

"Henry? Can you help me with dinner?" Mom calls from the main level.

"Yeah. Just a sec." My lips twist, eyes narrowed at Serena.

"You can't look at me like that. That's not how a boyfriend looks at his girlfriend." She winks and blows me a kiss before turning and plopping into her chair. "Shoo ..." Her wrist flicks over her shoulder. "I have work to do."

"If you say anything to my mom about your ridiculous theory—"

"It's not ridiculous. It's the truth. But don't worry, I'm not going to ruin anyone's Christmas. You're going to do that all on your own."

"Because I said you're my girlfriend?"

She twists, glancing at me over her shoulder. "The house, Henry. She's going to be crushed that you lost the precious family home." Her full lips twitch into a tiny grin. "But I'm flattered that you think she'll be sad when she finds out I'm not your girlfriend." On a shrug, she returns her attention to the computer. "I *am* quite the catch."

I grunt and head toward the stairs. "I bet you fall asleep during sex. You and your narco ... whatever. I'd hardly call that quite the catch."

Chapter Six

SERENA

AFTER CAREFUL CONSIDERATION, I've decided I can be Henry's girlfriend for two weeks if it gets me full access to his mom who probably knows a lot more about his great grandfather than he does. I bet she knows every crook and cranny of this house as well.

"How do you feel about oyster stew?" Martha asks, her hands busily chopping an onion.

"I feel like your son didn't mention my shellfish allergy." I smile.

Henry shifts his gaze after retrieving a pot from the hanging rack above the stove. His lips part to speak, but he says nothing.

"Oh dear ..." Martha frowns at him.

"However, I'm usually fine with oysters, clams, and scallops." I wink at Henry whose blank expression morphs into a tiny scowl.

"Thank goodness. This recipe was passed down from Henry's great grandma Bechtel."

"So she made it in this very kitchen?" I ask before opening the fridge to see how well he stocked it.

Very well.

It's at maximum capacity.

"She did indeed. This house is incredibly special to our family. Maybe ..." Martha glances over at me with a sheepish grin. "Maybe one day you and Henry will have a son and the tradition will continue."

"Mom—" Henry's face flushes as he adds a shot of Coke to his glass of whiskey.

I shut the fridge door. "What if we have girls?" I'm a writer. I can play this imaginary game.

"Well, I suppose times are changing. Should you have all girls, I think your firstborn girl should have this house. Don't you?" Martha looks to her son for approval.

Henry eyes me for a second.

"Henry, what exactly was wrong with all the things I left you?" she asks while rifling through the drawers. "I don't recognize a single thing in this kitchen. You could have at least put your new items in the same spot. It's what makes most sense."

He smirks, focused on his drink while swirling it. It's a jab at me, but Martha doesn't know it. *Yet.*

"Ask Serena. She's the one who insisted we get new stuff. And she organized everything."

"In that case, it's fine." Martha smiles at me. "Henry's never had a girlfriend. You can do anything you want to the house if you stay with my Henry."

He coughs, slowly shaking his head. "Thanks, Mom."

"How did you two meet?" She slides the chopped onions into the soup pot.

"I was signing books at a bookstore in Cincinnati, and Henry was in my line." I lean against the edge of the counter and cross my arms.

"Really? What do you write?"

"Literary biographies. I love history, studying the human condition, and finding common threads among us. There's nothing better than being transported to another time in another person's shoes who has lived a life rich in experiences, conflict, scandal, and even a little peril. I'm a sucker for tragedy and love."

"I can't wait to check out your books. And when did you start reading, Henry?"

He gulps the rest of his whisky and Coke and wipes his mouth with the back of his hand. "I was looking for a gift for my neighbor, and I saw Serena. She gave me the come-hither look, so I jumped in her line. She can't get enough of my eyes and my pretty little head."

Martha laughs. "Now that sounds more realistic. You do have beautiful eyes, just like your father's. All the Bechtel men have had beautiful blue eyes."

"Tell me more about the Bechtel men." I rest my hands on the edge of the counter.

"Well, I'm sure Henry told you his great grandfather built this house. It's called the Afina—" Martha starts to give me details.

"Why is it called the Afina house?" I interrupt.

Henry frowns at my question while refilling his glass.

I stare at the bottle before making eye contact with him again.

"Sorry, would you like a glass, *darling*?"

I slowly shake my head.

"Henry's great grandfather, Hermann, named it after the love of his life."

My heart constricts while my skin tingles with goose bumps. *She knows!*

"A Siamese cat named Afina. She died suddenly. Hermann found her dead the morning after his first night in the house. Can you imagine?" Martha slowly shakes her head.

"A cat?" I say, barely a whisper.

"Yes." Martha nods.

It's not that simple.

A cat?

A CAT?!

It's a flat-out lie. And weird. Absurd is more like it. Nobody in the whole Bechtel clan knows the meaning behind the name of this house they cherish—or now covet—so much.

Chapter Seven

HENRY

I can't focus on work.

Merry cluster-fuck Christmas to me.

Serena is unpredictable and therefore untrustworthy. Worry strangles me every second I'm not home—well, at her house. Will she go off on her conspiracy theory about Afina to my mom? Will she let it slip that we are not in a real relationship? As is, we have to fake going to bed together every night. When my mom shuts her bedroom door, Serena goes to the attic to write. And I think—I hope—she spends most of the day, while I'm gone, falling asleep in the middle of taking notes in her secret little notebook.

"What are you working on now?" I slow my movements when I hear Mom's voice coming from the kitchen as I untie my work boots.

"I'm telling the story of a woman from a century ago who died of influenza eighteen months after she met the love of her life. She was a dressmaker in Cincinnati. They met when he came into her shop to order a dress for his mother. It was love at first sight. He built a house for her much like—"

Oh shit ...

I fake a cough so they hear me while I tear off my coat and hat.

"Is that you, Henry?"

"It is." I poke my head around the corner. Cutout cookies, piping bags of frosting, and holiday sprinkles cover every inch of counter space. Cinnamon and vanilla fill the air along with Christmas music from my grandpa's old turntable in the adjacent sitting room.

"How was your day, honey?" Mom smiles.

Serena smiles too, but it's not comforting like Mom's.

"Fine." I wash my hands.

"There's a powder room sink for your hands, Henry," Mom scolds. "I taught you better than that."

She did. But I can't leave them alone for a second. Had I stopped to fix Mrs. Andrew's clogged drain today instead of tomorrow, the atmosphere would be much different. Seconds count.

Ignoring Mom's reprimand, I reach for a decorated cookie.

"No. Take one of those," Mom says. "Serena decorated them. Eat her cookie. It will make her feel good after an afternoon of hard work in the kitchen."

Serena's cheeks bloom deep red. She's thinking about me eating her cookie. She's thinking it will make her feel good.

I'd do my best.

My gaze shifts from blushing Serena to my mom. It's

the only way to keep my dick in check. "Mmm ..." I take a bite of the cookie. "Serena's cookie is good. Sweet. Moist." I lick my lips and glance down at the sprinkles that drop to the floor. "And a little messy."

Serena bites her lips together and focuses on the piping bag in her hands and the snowman she's tracing in white.

"Kitten, you look a little tired. Have you had a nap today?"

Serena's gaze shoots to mine, nose wrinkled. She's not a fan of "kitten" or maybe pussies in general.

Oh well.

"Serena has narcolepsy. I don't know if she's mentioned it," I say to Mom.

"Oh dear. I didn't know that. Honestly, I don't know a lot about it. Is that a sleeping disorder?"

"No worries." Serena shoots me a stiff smile. "Your son doesn't know much about it either. And I'm good. I want to help finish these cookies and clean up. Besides, your mom and I were in the middle of a conversation."

"Oh, no, dear ... we'll talk later. And I'll have this cleaned up in no time. You go rest. I insist."

"No. I couldn't possibly—"

I slide my arms around Serena's waist, pressing my chest to her back. She stiffens. I stiffen as well, just not in the same way. "Come on, my sweet little Christmas elf, let me take care of you." I rest my chin on her head, thinking about kissing it, but I'm not sure we're there yet, in our fake relationship.

Serena's breaths quicken.

"Martha ..." She attempts one last plea with my mom.

"Go. Really."

I smile at mom. *Thank you, Mother dearest.*

On a pitiful sigh, Serena surrenders, wiping her hands on a towel. "Thank you, Martha."

"No. Thank *you*, sweetie."

Oh joy ... they're using endearing terms too. Have they also planned the wedding? I wonder what Serena's planning on wearing for our wedding night? I'm partial to light pink and lace.

"I don't need a nap," Serena grits between her teeth while we ascend the stairs.

"Good. That means you'll stay awake while we chat, button nose."

"What are we chatting about, little chestnut?"

I grin.

"So glad you asked." I slip my hands into the pockets of my cargo pants when she turns toward me after reaching the attic. "I thought we had an understanding. You keep your made-up story to yourself."

She crosses her arms. "First, it's not made up. Second, she asked about my current project."

"Then you lie to her."

"Whoa ... no. Just because you're lying to your mom doesn't mean I have to."

I smirk. "So if you're not lying to my mom, then you think we're in a relationship." I take a step closer to her.

She swallows hard.

"I'll confess, since I've never been in a relationship, I can't speak from experience, but I have it on good authority that people in a relationship have sex. *Eat cookies.*"

Her lips part, and I can hear her breaths one right after the other. I have *no* idea where I'm going with this or what I'm doing. Just like I have no idea why I've been mesmerized by this woman since she plowed over my mailbox.

It's a joke. We're joking. Bantering. Pretending. Right? Yet she helps herself to a long glance at my mouth before slowly inching her gaze back to mine.

"I'm never selling this house," she says like it's the only thing she can say to sound confident.

"We'll see about that." I let my gaze slide along her body.

"You should uh ... go help your mom clean up the kitchen."

Scraping my teeth along my lower lip, *not* thinking about my mom, I murmur a slow "Uh-huh."

"You look like your great grandfather." Her unexpected comment brings my attention back to her face. "I've seen pictures of him."

I slowly shake my head, closing my eyes briefly. "What are you talking about? Is this about your fictional account of the history of this house?"

"No."

"Then where are the pictures you have of *my* great grandfather?"

"They burned in a house fire my mom had several years ago."

"Convenient."

Serena frowns. "I'd hardly call it convenient."

"It's convenient that you're trying to make claim to this house. And from what little I heard you tell my mom, I think you're trying to imply your great grandmother was the great love of my great grandfather's life."

"She was. And if I find the hidden spot where he

put letters from my great grandmother, Afina, and photos of them, then you'll see the true history of this house."

I chuckle. I can't help it. This is ... crazy. "And you're writing their story?"

Her head bounces into a noncommittal nod. "Well, I'm writing her story, and he's part of it. She was orphaned. Then homeless. She was a survivor and very brave."

"And she got influenza?"

Serena nods.

"And she died in this house?"

Another nod.

"If ... and it's a big if ... what you're saying is true, why do you think my great grandfather said Afina was a cat that died? Seems pretty insensitive to 'the love of his life' don't you think?"

She shrugs. "I think he loved your great grandmother. If he was the man my great grandmother described in her journal, if his letters to her were true, then he was a good man. The kind of man who would love someone enough to make her feel like his first love even if she wasn't. I don't think true love is rare; I think what's rare is the ability to truly love. I think good people recognize the abundance of love, the heart's ability to infinitely expand."

I nod several times. "Sure. I'll take your word for it."

She returns a shy smile. "Are you broken, Henry? Or have you not found your Afina? Are you still looking for the right person to crack open your heart and let your love flow freely?"

On a nervous laugh, I shake my head. "Is that what

you think this Afina person did for my great grandfather?"

"I do."

"And who have you loved? Who opened your heart?"

"Well, I think the story of Afina and Hermann opened my heart as a young girl. I've loved. I've been married."

I can't help my surprise. "Really?"

"Yes. I married my publicist. He died of a heart attack. He died on Christmas morning."

Oh fuck ... is she serious?

"Hence you not celebrating Christmas ..."

With a half smile, she shrugs.

"I'm an asshole."

"Only for losing the family home, but it worked out for me, so I'm not complaining."

"It's not that simple."

"It never is," she says.

I give her response some consideration. I give *her* some consideration. "Well, I thought we were going to have fake relationship sex, but I feel like your dead husband put a damper on the moment. No disrespect to him, of course."

She chuckles. "Well, that's kind of you to not disrespect my dead husband as if it's his fault you suck at relationships. Real or fake."

"Ouch. That's harsh."

"Am I wrong? Are you living a life that will be worthy of ink on paper?"

"Listen, Henry, if a woman doesn't make you think ... really think ... then keep moving. Find the one who takes your mind before your heart."

My dad's words echo from the past. He used to say my

mom was the smartest person he'd ever met. Wise beyond her years. He said he fell in love with her words before she bewitched him with the rest of her enchanting self.

I'm not sure I like Serena's Afina story, but I find myself thinking all kinds of things when I'm with her. And not just the things that make my dick stir—although, that happens a lot in her presence as well.

"I'm going to help my mom."

Chapter Eight

"I LIKE HER, Henry. You're a lucky man." Mom glances over at me when I grab a dishtowel and start drying the dishes.

"Yes, I've definitely outdone myself."

Just not in the way you think.

"She told me she lost her husband on Christmas."

"She did."

She opened up to my mom before she told me. That's not part of a fake relationship.

"She said it's been hard to get in the Christmas spirit since he died. She also said making cookies with me today was the first time she felt like maybe one day she'd feel something besides grief. I think you've been a godsend to her."

I bribed her to let me stay here. I'm not sure that counts as a "godsend."

With little to say in response, I finish helping mom with the dishes and head up to check on Serena. I can't stop myself from navigating toward her. It's a foreign feeling.

When I open the door to the attic, Serena's conked out on the blue velvet sofa, cuddled under a blanket.

I ease into her desk chair. Leaning back, I stare out the window, reminiscing about the days my sister Emily and I spent in this attic (when she wasn't scared of ghosts) pretending we were in a snow globe. Sometimes we'd snoop through boxes, hunting for presents. But mostly, we listened to Christmas music on my grandpa's old turntable and pieced together the train set that belonged to our dad.

With a smile on my face, I run my hand along Serena's antique desk. The screen lights up when I bump the mouse, filling most of it with lines and lines of words.

Words like "Afina." It's dotted all over the page.

Afina swiped her toe through the water, sending the cold droplets in Hermann's direction.

"Watch it, unless you're prepared to take a swim with me," he said, his voice guff.

Afina didn't miss the outline of a smile behind his thick beard. His legs swayed from the horizontal tree trunk dangling over the edge of the lazy Ohio River current. It was a rare moment to see Hermann with his brown trousers rolled up to his knees, shirt off, suspenders gathered at his waist.

"What are you doing?" Serena moves the mouse and the screen switches to an ocean with cliffs in the distance.

"I came to check on you."

"You mean snoop?"

I shake my head.

"What are you doing up here?" She yawns while pushing the desk chair. It rolls away from the desk just enough for her to wedge herself between her computer and me. Her arms cross, eyes narrowing. "I don't let anyone read my work until it's complete."

"Is it weird that I don't know anyone else with narcolepsy?" I cross my arms, mirroring her.

"It's like … one in two thousand people have it. You live in Birdville. Population: just under seven hundred. You do the math."

"So you sleep all day?"

"I nap as needed."

"And when you're not napping, you write stories about Afina and Hermann. Is it possible your great grandmother made everything up? Is it possible he asked Afina to make a dress for my great grandmother Marian, and Afina let her imagination run wild? Jealous of Marian and her life? Jealous of the house he built for her and not Afina? Is it possible that what's been passed down in your family is fictional?"

She snorts, and I try not to like her smile, but I do. I like everything about her. Or maybe I just like being in this attic again, sharing space with someone.

"It was love at first sight for Afina and Hermann."

"I don't believe in love at first sight," I say, staring out the window over her shoulder.

"No?"

I return my gaze to her, ready to shake my head, but I don't for some unexplainable reason. "Do you?"

Serena smiles. "I believe in chemistry. Feelings. Emotions. A look. A smile. Perfect words at the right moment."

Words …

She continues, "I don't think love is a culmination of

anything. I don't think it requires time. I think it's a moment. The right one. No explanation. It doesn't make sense. It's just a mystery as old as time. People have been trying to define and redefine it forever. And much like life itself, no one really knows how long it will last. I mean ... maybe forever. Maybe not. But who cares? *Now* is as good as it ever gets."

Words. She has damn good words. "When are you going to tell me why you were scared shitless at the idea of me calling the police the night you hit my mailbox?"

Serena eyes me for several seconds, an impeding frown just seconds from capturing her lips. "When are you going to tell me how you lost this house?"

I shake my head and chuckle. "Tit for tat?"

"Sure." Serena wets her lips.

I stare at them too long before clearing my throat and averting my gaze to the plush white rug on the floor. "I have a gambling problem. I mean ... I didn't, but when my sister got sick, I couldn't bear to watch my parents lose this house because of medical debt. I had a knack for winning. In hindsight, it was just dumb luck."

Her nose wrinkles while she bites her lower lip. I kinda like it for some reason.

"They thought I was doing side jobs," I continue. "But let's be honest; it would have taken a ton of side jobs, and not giving Uncle Sam his cut, for me to have made a dent in the bills for those experimental treatments. I think Dad always knew I was doing something a little shady. And Mom didn't blink or even take a moment to do any of the math. Every single one of us would have walked into a bank with a ski mask and a gun had we thought we could've gotten away with it.

There's really nothing you don't do for people you love."

Serena nods slowly, and a tiny flinch makes the muscles around her eyes twitch, but it's gone as quickly as it happens.

"Emily surged into remission. Or so we thought. All that fighting ... then boom! A fucking blood clot takes her. Just..." I pull in a long, shaky breath through my nose "...gone."

"I'm so sorry," Serena whispers.

I blow that same breath out my mouth. "I needed to feel like everything wasn't lost. The gambling became an escape from the grief. Money ... property ... just ... everything. It all felt so insignificant without Emily." It takes a few moments of silence, silence for Emily, before I can look at Serena.

She quickly wipes her eyes.

Was she crying?

"Then my dad died. And I gambled away that pain too. I kept going until I lost everything."

"And your mom never knew?" she whispers.

I shake my head. "Fate stepped in, and she moved to Germany before I lost the house. I think it would have destroyed her. Emily ... my dad ... then the house that had been in our family for generations."

Resting her hands on the side of the desk, Serena's gaze drops to her feet. "My husband died three years ago. He was my publicist. My lover. My best friend. He was the good morning kiss I miss more than anything. He was the warm embrace that lulled me into a peaceful slumber." Glancing up, she offers a sad smile. "He died on Christmas. It destroyed me. We buried him, and days later I brought in the New Year with a lot of alcohol. In fact, I spent the following year drowning in alcohol. I ran my husband's golf cart into the swimming pool. I was *so* intoxicated. My seventy-three-year-old neighbor saved my life."

"Numb is good," I whisper.

She shakes her head. "No. It's awful. What's the point of being here if we don't feel anything? I sobered up, and I let the pain in. Then I was diagnosed with narcolepsy which one doctor thought might have been triggered by my husband's death and the alcoholism that ensued. My publisher threatened to drop me after the golf cart incident. Then I wrecked my car, completely sober, because I fell asleep at the wheel at three in the afternoon. I hit a tree. There were some pictures of it that got out and rumors of me falling off the wagon. My blood test came back negative for alcohol, but my publisher was not in the mood to believe me. Without proof, they had to give me one more chance. So now, I have to stay out of trouble. They couldn't care less if I'm driving drunk or driving asleep."

"No police reports," I say.

"No police reports." She returns a sharp nod.

"I'm a dick. Staying here. Wrapping the whole damn house in decorations which must cause you more pain—"

Serena shakes her head. "I'm not triggered by the holidays. I'm just not in the mood for them. I don't know … it feels disrespectful to him to enjoy this time of year. Is that weird?"

"No. I mean … you're asking the guy who's pretending

this is still his house so he can lie to his mom. Oh ... and he's told her you're his girlfriend."

A beautiful, although hesitant, smile graces her face. "I'm sure there's worse things in the world than being your girlfriend."

It gives me a moment of pause. Is she ... flirting with me? Have I been right this whole time?

"So what do you do to escape the pain if you don't drink?"

She glances over her shoulder at the window and the picturesque view of the swirling snow above the river. "I write," she whispers before turning back toward me. "What do you do to escape the pain if you don't gamble?"

"Drink." I give her a sheepish grin and shrug a shoulder.

Her eyes widen for a second, lips parted, then she covers her mouth and snorts.

I smirk, scooting the chair closer to her. Why? I have no clue. It just feels necessary.

My invasion of her space sobers her humor rather quickly. She drops her head and clears her throat while squirming a bit in our now confined space. "Did you ever sit on Santa's lap at the mall?" she asks, scraping her teeth over her bottom lip. It's unexpected.

It's also sexy. Is she trying to be sexy? If so, it's working. Wetting her lips. Asking me ridiculous random questions. It's all working.

My socked feet slide next to hers. "Maybe. Have *you* ever sat on his lap?" I lift my gaze from our feet to her slow blinking eyes, her soft parted lips, and her long black hair pulled over one shoulder with a few strands falling in her face.

She eases her head side to side while pushing off the desk. I lift my hands, pausing a second before pressing them to the back of her legs, the thin material of her leggings soft against my calloused palms. I'm way out of my league. Lost in a forest without a compass. For once, I don't mind feeling lost.

It's been a shitty few years. Inches of snow barricade us in this house. And I can't help but touch my fake girlfriend.

"Is this how you would do it?" she asks, crawling onto my lap, hands sliding around my neck.

I return a nervous laugh. I'm not sure why since I was the brave one to make the first move. "I wouldn't choose this exact position, but I'm one hundred percent certain Santa would be fine with you sitting on his lap like this."

Serena grins, bending forward. Her lips brush my ear as she whispers, "Are you going to ask if I've been naughty or nice?"

I retract my earlier statement. If she did this to the old guy at the mall, she'd give him a heart attack. Granted, he'd die a happy man.

"I uh ... I think it would be nice if you just decided to be a little naughty ... with me." My hands mold to the curve of her ass while she presses her palms to my cheeks and kisses me. An inferno of lust heats my face; her hands might burn. It's hard to breathe. Suffocation has never felt so good.

Fuck, I hope I'm not the schmuck who has a heart attack.

Her tongue slides along mine, and she tastes sweet like cookies. I don't know if it's the massive amount of blood my dick is demanding, but for some reason I'm dizzy.

Lost.

Floating.

"My husband died three years ago ... My lover ... My best friend ... The good morning kiss I miss ... The warm embrace that lulled me into a peaceful slumber."

Her words replay on a loop in my head. My fingers ghost up her back on the inside of her sweater only to find she's not wearing a bra. This discovery sends another round of blood to my dick, making things really uncomfortable.

Standing on her knees, she discards her sweater, tossing it onto the floor. I lift my gaze to hers when she threads her fingers through my hair, her tits inches from my face. Keeping my gaze affixed to hers, I tease her nipple with my tongue.

And cup both breasts.

Squeeze them until her mouth falls open.

I'm dying here ...

Heavy breaths rush past her lips. Those dark eyes drift shut for a brief second before opening in a slow blink. A tiny, sharp inhale hisses through her teeth the second I switch to her other nipple. When her hips rock into my chest, I begin to unravel.

I lift her to the sofa where she fumbles with my pants. I stretch, tug, and peel her leggings down to her feet, and she kicks them off.

God ... where is her underwear?

It's as if she knew when she got dressed that I'd be ripping her clothes off, determined to put my dick inside of her.

I mumble a quick, "Condom?"

She strokes me a few times as both of our chins dip to

watch her. It's sexy and mesmerizing. No joke ... this might kill me. My arms flex while I hover above her, and my hips slowly rock into her touch. Her warm ... soft ... touch.

"I don't care," she says.

Is that really an answer? She doesn't care if I wear one? She doesn't care if she gets pregnant? An STD?

I mull this over for all of ten seconds before my brain makes this quick calculation: she's an adult who knows how babies are made and STDs are spread. She's educated. So "I don't care" must mean she's already handled the birth control, and she thinks I'm an unlikely candidate for passing around STDs. That's all I need to know before I let her hand guide my dick between her legs.

She's reckless and I'm daring. The alcoholic and the gambler. What could go wrong?

"Fuck that feels good," she says when I push into her.

Her vulgarity is hot. Really hot. My thoughts go a hundred different places all at once.

Does she want me to go slow? Is she feeling as needful as I am, wanting nothing more than for me to pound into her over and over? Is she good on the bottom? Would she rather be on top?

Her legs hug me to her while her lips peck at mine. Her rocking pelvis says fast.

I can do fast.

She digs her heel into my ass.

Hard.

I can do hard.

Her nails curl into my back, and I lose all control.

Unfettered need feels as good, maybe even better,

than any high I've felt from gambling. This is messy, clumsy sex. We're not out to impress each other; we're in it for the endgame. The glorious release.

We kiss.

We lick and bite.

We claw and grab, looking for any sort of leverage to go faster and harder.

Animals. Yep. We're completely animalistic.

"Oof!" I hit my head on the floor when we fall off the sofa.

Serena grins without pausing a second to see if I'm okay. She tosses a leg over and rides me hard.

The room fills with tiny grunts, heavy breaths, and the rhythmic slapping of skin. I roll us so Serena's beneath me.

As I move inside her, my face hovering just above hers, she grins. It's the "what are we doing?" grin. I return the same grin, but I also feel a tiny stab in my chest. It's something new. I want to slow my pace because this unfamiliar feeling is one I kinda like. One I don't want to end. One I feel the need to explore.

When that feeling starts to distract me from the task at hand, I kiss her lips, her neck, her breasts. I close my eyes and think back to the last time I felt this way.

That's easy ... never.

She arches her back and stills, gripping me with her hands and her legs. I come so fucking hard I can't hold my head up, so I drop it next to hers, my lips at her ear.

"Damn. Just ... damn." A slight shiver shakes me.

Her giggle spreads along my sweaty skin like she's touching me everywhere at once. "Damn indeed, Henry Bechtel."

I should move. Remove myself from her. Face that awkward moment of deflated passion. We can't cuddle. That requires something more than jacked-up hormones on a snowy day.

But ... Serena's fingers feather along my back, and her legs remain firmly wrapped around me. I feel the pulsing of her heart next to mine. And I wonder if I'm the first man she's been with since her husband died.

Should I say something?

It was just sex. I think.

My lack of relationship experience is really messing with me right now. There's a low probability that my next move will be the right one. I definitely wouldn't bet on myself right now.

"Thank you," she whispers.

You're welcome?

My pleasure?

Sure thing?

Anytime?

All terrible answers.

I lift my head, searching her eyes for the right one.

Nope. I don't have it.

I go for a tiny nod and a sincere smile, hoping less is more.

In the next breath, I step into my pants while Serena fishes her arms into her sweater.

"I'm uh..." I poke my head through my shirt "...I'm going to clear your driveway in case you need out. Then I'm going to help my mom with dinner. Then—"

Before I can list off the rest of my plans for the day, Serena lifts onto her toes and kisses me, ending with a smile before leaving my lips. "I'll see you at dinner. I need to write." She wraps the blanket from the sofa around her waist and disappears down the stairs.

I follow her, but I continue on to the main level when she disappears into the bathroom.

"Everything okay?" Mom asks while browning ground beef in a pan. The woman is always in the kitchen.

I run my hands through my hair and make sure my fly is zipped. "What do you mean?"

"I went upstairs to freshen up before making dinner and I..." she grins, redirecting her gaze to the pan "... heard something in the attic. Everything up there creaks with the slightest movement. I heard a lot of creaking."

Nope. We are not having this conversation. Not ever.

I grab a glass of water. "I'm going to clear the snow from the driveway."

"She's sweet, Henry. And she loves everything about this house. And she looks at you like you're her world. I think it's a sign." Mom continues to stir the meat. I nab another cookie from the cooling rack. Serena *should* love the house since she owns it. As for the way she looks at me? I have no clue.

Chapter Nine

SERENA

I AVOID Henry for days and days. I mean ... we pass each other in the hallway, but all I can do is give him a quick smile and chirp, "Lots of writing to do."

Carolers stop at the house every night, and every night Martha serves them hot drinks and the cookies we made. I think of Jack and the day he died, but in the next breath I think of Henry ... and Afina and Hermann. My grandma used to tell me her mom's love story with Hermann, and she always ended it with *"Maybe there's a young Hermann Bechtel out there who will build you a house and help you fill it with children."*

In the early morning hours of Christmas Eve day, while Henry and Martha are sill asleep, I search the main floor for the hidden spot—the letters and photos I know are in this house. It's only a matter of time before I find them. They hold the other side of the story I'm writing. I need my grandmother's words. The ones she wrote to Hermann.

When the drawn shades begin to glow from the first rays of the morning, I give up. My socked feet climb three steps.

I stop.

Then I retreat to the wider first step that's always creaked a little more. It's always had a little wiggle to it.

Creak. Creak. Creak.

It sings a different tune than the rest of the stairs.

My eyes dart around the foyer, looking for something to use on the stair. I search the kitchen, the bathroom, then the living room.

"Perfect," I whisper, plucking the matte black poker from the rack of fireplace tools in front of the hearth.

Wedging the pointed end under the loose stair, I lever it until the first plank of old wood lifts with a snap. Cringing, I stop and listen for any movement upstairs. Then I carefully pry it back some more, each inch releasing a tight whine. My hand fishes into the tiny gap, and I feel around, hoping something like a rat doesn't bite my finger. Just beyond the loose debris, like dirt and saw dust, I feel something softer.

I try to retrieve it, but I can't. The opening is not big enough. I know I've found the letters and photos. I just ... know. Adrenaline takes over. I no longer ease the wood planks from the bottom stair; I use the poker to rip them apart and retrieve the cloth covered bundle of history.

"Serena! What have you done?"

Glancing up at the stairs, I see Martha in her robe and slippers, shock distorting her beautiful features while she grabs the railing and navigates the stairs. "You've ruined that step. What are you doing?"

I stare at the splintered pieces of wood surrounding me, but my gaze quickly returns to the treasure on my lap. "I've been looking for this since the day I moved in here," I whisper, tugging at the twine around the cloth-wrapped package.

"What the hell is going on?" Henry's voice drifts from the top of the stairs.

I lift my head, eyeing both of their pained expressions. "I found it," I say with so much relief and an unavoidable smile.

"Found what?" Martha sidesteps my mess and bends to pick up the broken pieces of wood.

"Serena ..." Henry says my name slowly, just as slowly as he descends the stairs.

A small stack of black and white photos rests on top of the brittle, yellowed folded pieces of paper. His photos are different than the ones Afina had, but they tell the same story. They were in love.

"What is all that?" Martha asks.

Henry squats beside me, taking one of the photos. Hermann is hugging Afina from behind, kissing her cheek while she smiles. I bet it was a giggle.

"Afina wasn't a cat. Afina was the woman Great Grandfather Bechtel built this house for," he murmurs with a slightly defeated tone.

"That's not true," Martha says, clearly flustered.

"It's true." Henry stands and hands the photo to her while I open one of the letters, instantly recognizing the handwriting from Afina's journal.

"This is why I bought the house. To find these letters."

And just like that ... I let the truth slip.

"What are you talking about?" Martha asks.

I glance up at Henry from my cross-legged position on the floor.

He frowns. "I lost the house." Henry proceeds to tell his mom everything.

There are tears, not just from her. There're smeared along my cheeks as well.

Emily.

The expensive treatment.

Debt.

His father dying.

The addiction.

The pride and need to protect his mom.

"So ... you ... what? Just happened to start dating the woman who stole our house?" Martha's desperation bleeds with each word.

"She didn't steal it. And the opportunity to keep this from you for a little longer just sort of arose, and I took it because I felt so much shame and regret."

"Well, when you get married, the house will be back in the family. I mean ... you're going to marry her, right?"

My heart constricts as I stand, brushing off my legs; Martha's so desperate for this to be true—and it constricts because I'm emotionally invested in his answer. *Really* invested in it.

TRUTH? I think I fell a little in love with Henry before I ever met him. I'd built up this idea of a Hermann Bechtel heir in my head, and when we came face to face, he didn't disappoint.

Mesmerizing blue eyes.

A boyish smile.

An irresistible personality.

"I'm not marrying Serena. She's not my real girlfriend. This has all been a terribly cruel farce to save face."

I'm not his girlfriend. Okay. That's fair. Sex doesn't equal a relationship.

"You lost it *all*? Everything?" Martha says. Her words barely audible.

Henry nods.

Martha shakes her head, and her expression morphs into a harder one, anger … resentment. Hate? She aims it at me. "You can't have this house. I don't care what you think this Afina woman meant to Hermann. This was Marian's house. This is where she raised her children and her children raised their children and …" She swallows hard and clenches her jaw. "This is where I raised *my* children. My Emily died in th—" A sob rips from her chest. "T-this house. And my husband …"

"Shh …" Henry pulls her into his arms and strokes her hair.

I wipe a tear from my cheek. I feel her pain. But my family's life hasn't been without tragedy either. I have no words. I choke on every single one that tries to find life past my lips while watching Henry collect his and his mother's personal belongings and load them into his van. After Martha heads toward the driveway, Henry stands at the front door.

He can't even look me in the eye. "The night you hit my mailbox, were you *researching* me?"

"Yes," I whisper.

"For your fucking book?" His gaze finds mine. It's no longer soft and endearing. It's stony. Angry.

"No. I wanted to—"

"Save it. Just save it for someone who cares. Enjoy the house and your pile of letters and photos. You can go back to your life as a recluse."

The door clicks shut.

I wait … I ponder … for a full thirty seconds before running outside in my socked feet and no jacket. As Henry backs out of my driveway, I bang on the passenger window.

He stops.

Martha won't even look at me.

I open her door and slap the pile of letters and photos onto her lap. "*You* read them. *You* look at all the photos. I don't need them. I already know. I know Hermann was a good man who loved Afina. I know he built this house for her. And I know he moved on to love another woman and have a family with her. I know that generations of Bechtels have lived here. But now, it's my time. It's my time to live in this house … that he built for *my* great grandmother. This house is ready to tell a different story."

I slam the door shut and run into the house, freezing, and shaking right to my bones.

Chapter Ten

HENRY

"Hey," I say the next morning, emerging from the bathroom, showered and dressed, hair wet and in need of a trim, along with my scruffy face.

Mom gives me a sad smile. Last night she refused to take the bedroom. From the looks of the bags under her eyes, I don't think she did much sleeping last night. The photos and letters are scattered all over the sofa beside her.

She looks ... defeated.

I did this.

"Merry Christmas," she says with very little merriment to her greeting. "It's a beautiful love story."

I run my hands through my messy hair and take a seat in my recliner, resting my elbows on my knees. "I'm sorry I lied to you. I'm sorry I let things get so out of hand. I just wanted to save Emily. I just wanted to—"

"Don't." She shakes her head. "Don't do this, Henry.

I'm not angry. I'm grateful for everything you did. And I'm sad." She pulls in a shaky breath. "I'm sad that I didn't see it. What kind of mother doesn't see that her child is struggling? I was so focused on Emily that I just ..."

"I'm fine." I nod several times. "I'm fine. This trailer is all I need. We both know it's unlikely I'll ever need more than this."

She grunts a little laugh and shakes her head. "You had me fooled. Both of you. I thought I felt the chemistry between you. I thought I *heard* it." She rolls her eyes at herself. "I thought I saw something in the way you looked at her and the way she looked at you." She nods toward the scattered letters. "When I read these letters, I could hear Serena's voice. And I could imagine it was the two of you falling in love. The kind that takes you by surprise. Something undeniable. Do you know what I mean?"

I take a minute.

Mom laughs again before I can answer her. "Of course you don't. But I wish you did, Henry. I wish you could experience that indescribable feeling of love. That connection that just ... happens when you least expect it."

Okay, Dad ... I hear you.

I stand, slowly gathering the letters and photos.

When I set them on the counter and grab my jacket, Mom gives me a narrow-eyed gaze. "Where are you going?"

"I'm going to see if there are grandkids in your future."

It takes her a few seconds. Then she gets teary-eyed and presses her hand to her chest. "It was real," she whispers.

I pull on a beanie and grab the pile of letters and photos. Then I wink at her. "Frighteningly real."

On my way to the Afina house, I wonder how this works. I'd seen my dad do it on countless occasions.

Groveling.

What are the chances I nail it the first time?

I knock several times on the wreath-less door. Then it hits me.

It's not just Christmas. It's the anniversary of her husband's death. What am I thinking?

I turn to head back to the van. Then I turn and take several steps back toward the house. And again, I retreat toward the van. "Fuck!" I kick a pile of snow and nearly fall on my ass. In the process of keeping my balance, the letters and photos scatter all over the ground. "You're an idiot, Henry," I scold myself, dropping to my hands and knees to pick everything up. "Two weeks," I continue talking to myself. "You fell in love in two fucking weeks? How ridiculous. It's not love. It's just that your dick was caught off guard." I continue to gather the letters and photos, just ... mumbling away at myself. "But your dick isn't in your chest, and that's where you feel her. What's that supposed to mean? Have you thought about that?" My third-person conversation reaches an all-time low.

"It means you love me, Henry Bechtel."

I freeze, glancing up at the porch while easing my butt onto my heels.

Serena smiles. The snow-melting kind of smile.

"I shouldn't be here." I shake my head. "I'm an asshole. What I said ... it was terrible. And your husband died—"

"On Christmas." She walks down the porch steps in

her fluffy boots, leggings, and red sweater. "I had to let him go on Christmas." Her hand reaches toward me. "Take it."

I stare at her hand, then I take it, lumbering to my feet with most of the photos and letters clutched in my other hand.

Serena's dark hair falls behind her shoulders when she gazes up at me.

"What now?" I say.

She lifts onto her toes until her lips are a breath away from mine. "Now ... don't let go." Her lips bend into a grin as they touch mine.

The End

ACKNOWLEDGEMENTS

This book was incredibly hard to write because it exposed my fears and my doubts. It also healed me and reminded me to always be honest about my needs. Tim, I have to thank you first and foremost for marrying me twenty-two years ago and allowing me to bloom and morph, to chase my dreams, to keep my independence. You've been my Craig, but in so many ways you've also become my Kael. No one knows what the future holds, but I think we have a good chance at being geese. Love you, always.

Mom, thank you for being an example of change. Thank you for taking to me to church and then showing me that it's not a sin to question all the things I learned in that church. Despite what Dad might say, you have taught me to keep an open mind.

This book truly came to life when I asked my readers to share the things about their significant others that drives them crazy. Your response brought tears of laughter and sadness. I felt less alone in my own thoughts and sometimes a little more grateful for the man (men) in my house that drive me crazy. Thank you for your honesty. Thank you for trusting me to share your experiences through these characters so that every reader can feel like me ... a little less alone, and maybe a little more grateful.

I think the saying goes something like—behind every great man is a great woman. In my case, behind every great author is a magical unicorn assistant. Jenn Beach, you are my unicorn. And with five book releases this year, you deserve so much credit for my sanity and taking the wheel ninety percent of the time—including formatting and revamping old covers. THANK YOU!

I've had the same editor since I wrote my first cringeworthy manuscript. Max Dobson, thank your for being a mentor to this amateur writer who wanted nothing more than to share these crazy stories in my head. I can't imagine writing without you.

To the rest of my editing team, thank you for scouring through pages of words and making them shine. Monique, you will always be my Number One Bitch. ;) It's an honor to have you polish my manuscript with such a sharp eye. Kambra, Leslie, and Sian, thank you for being the first eyes to see *all* the hideous errors and for loving this story in a special way. And finally, thank you to Sherri, Amy, Bethany, and Shabby for always being so generous with your time to proofread for me. I'm one lucky girl to have you in my circle of awesomeness.

Nina! I found my person this year. In Nina Grinstead's words—PeRson. Thank you, Nina, for so wholeheartedly immersing yourself into my books, and patiently guiding me through new game plans and exciting opportunities. You are so much more than PR to me. Thank you for assembling an awesome team through Valentine PR to reach new audiences. Christine, Kelley, Brittany, Mary, and all the names I'm probably forgetting ... my sincerest gratitude for your hard work and kindness.

Thank you to my dear friends, Cleida and Jyl, for being my sounding boards and voices of encouragement. I miss our girl time and hope we can plan epic adventures in 2021.

Finally, a very special thank-you to my three boys, Logan, Carter, and Asher, for defining my life in the most permanent way. I have been and hope to be many things in this life, but by far my favorite is Mother.

ALSO BY Jewel E. Ann

Standalone Novels

Idle Bloom

Undeniably You

Naked Love

Only Trick

Perfectly Adequate

Look The Part

When Life Happened

A Place Without You

Jersey Six

Scarlet Stone

Not What I Expected

For Lucy

What Lovers Do

Before Us

If This Is Love

Right Guy, Wrong Word

The Fisherman Series

The Naked Fisherman

The Lost Fisherman

Jack & Jill Series

End of Day

Middle of Knight

Dawn of Forever

One (*standalone*)

Out of Love (*standalone*)

Because of Her (*standalone*)

Holding You Series

Holding You

Releasing Me

Transcend Series

Transcend

Epoch

Fortuity (*standalone*)

The Life Series

The Life That Mattered

The Life You Stole

Pieces of a Life

Memories of a Life

ABOUT THE AUTHOR

Jewel is a free-spirited romance junkie with a quirky sense of humor.

With 10 years of flossing lectures under her belt, she took early retirement from her dental hygiene career to stay home with her three awesome boys and manage the family business.

After her best friend of nearly 30 years suggested a few books from the Contemporary Romance genre, Jewel was hooked. Devouring two and three books a week but still craving more, she decided to practice sustainable reading, AKA writing.

When she's not donning her cape and saving the planet one tree at a time, she enjoys yoga with friends, good food with family, rock climbing with her kids, watching How I Met Your Mother reruns, and of course... heart-wrenching, tear-jerking, panty-scorching novels.

Receive a FREE book and stay informed of new releases, sales, and exclusive stories:
https://www.jeweleann.com/free-booksubscribe

Made in the USA
Monee, IL
06 November 2024

69529601R00236